94

DEADWOOD

PETE DEXTER

PENGUIN BOOKS

PENGUIN BOOKS
Published by the Penguin Group
Penguin Books USA Inc.,
375 Hudson Street, New York, New York 10014, U.S.A.
Penguin Books Ltd, 27 Wrights Lane,
London W8 5TZ, England
Penguin Books Australia Ltd, Ringwood,
Victoria, Australia
Penguin Books Canada Ltd, 10 Alcorn Avenue,
Toronto, Ontario, Canada MV4 3B2
Penguin Books (N.Z.) Ltd, 182–190 Wairau Road,
Auckland 10, New Zealand

Penguin Books Ltd, Registered Offices:
Harmondsworth, Middlesex, England

First published in the United States of America by Random House, Inc. 1986
Reprinted by arrangement with Random House, Inc.
Published in Select Penguin 1987
Reprinted 1987
Published in Penguin Books 1989

5 7 9 10 8 6 4

LIBRARY OF CONGRESS CATALOGING IN PUBLICATION DATA
Dexter, Pete, 1943–
Deadwood.
I. Title.
[PS3554.E95D4 1987] 813'.54   86-30422
ISBN 0 14 01.2729 1

Printed in the United States of America
Set in Janson

For
Dorothy and William Selz,
of Vermillion, South Dakota

I would like to take a moment here to thank Mrs. Marjorie Pontius, who runs the Carnegie Library in Deadwood. The town of Deadwood and I are both lucky she is there.

The large events and the settings of this novel—the fire that destroyed Deadwood, the assassinations of Bill Hickok and the China Doll, the weather, the life and travels of Charley Utter—are all real.

The characters, with the exception of Malcolm Nash, are also real, and were in Deadwood at the time these events occurred.

CONTENTS

PART ONE

BILL

1876

The boy shot Wild Bill's horse at dusk, while Bill was off in the bushes to relieve himself. It was lucky for everybody but the horse that it happened when it did, but not so lucky it had to be God's hand in it. It always took Bill a while in the bushes—it wasn't dusk when he'd gone in there—and things have to happen sometime.

The boy's name was Malcolm Nash. He was the younger brother of Charley Utter's wife, and had ridden with Charley and thirty-six mules up from their home in Empire, Colorado, first to Cheyenne, where they met Bill, and then east and north toward the Black Hills.

Charley always had a hard time saying no to his wife.

The boy tried to be helpful, but anything he couldn't break, he lost. The more Charley studied his awkward deportment, the more he wondered at the unreliable nature of human jizzom. The boy and Charley's wife didn't look like each other, even the coloring, and the boy hardly spoke. It was something Charley wouldn't have minded studying, the contrary results of spilled seed. The boy was a strong back, though, and he was polite. He addressed Bill as Mr. Hickok and called everybody else by the same names that Bill did, and he carried a broken-handled old Smith & Wesson in a sash around his waist, butt-first, the way Bill carried his Colts.

Charley had been against bringing the boy from the first suggestion. In his wife's eyes, that amounted to a confession of all the unsafe and unfaithful behavior he and Bill got into when he was away from home. It was peculiar, the way her feelings about Bill had changed. She'd spoken well of him before they were married, and once told Charley he was half famous just for being his friend. Of course, Bill had seen her compromised since.

The boy had no such reservations. Bill had made four visits to Colorado in the last ten years, to hunt bear or watch Charley get married or just get drunk, and Bill was always good to him, keeping the whores and whiskey out of his gunfight stories so he'd grow up right. Bill did not recognize the boy when they all met in Cheyenne, but said it was because Malcolm had become a man.

The boy would have worn carrots in his hat if Bill did.

They'd left Colorado late in the spring, Charley and Malcolm and the mules, and met Bill in Cheyenne, where he was organizing a wagon train. They got to his rooming house at seven o'clock in the morning, June 22. The lady superintendent reported Bill had already combed his hair and walked up the street to the Republican Hotel for cocktails, which she implied was his morning habit. "I expect he'll be back in half an hour, walk through the door carrying a full glass of whiskey, and finish his toilet," she said.

Charley wasn't surprised. It was the history of things that Bill would wear out his welcome.

Charley saw the lady was not going to invite them in to wait, and so he and the boy walked down the street too, and found Bill standing at the far end of the Republican Hotel bar, squinting into the light from the doorway as they came in, trying to decide if it was trouble.

Charley had been to Cheyenne in March, when Bill had married the famous circus performer Agnes Lake, and even getting married, Bill had been in a brighter mood than he was now.

"Did you know they held elections last week?" he said when he saw who it was.

Charley said, "Where?"

"Right here. Cheyenne." Bill was a good American but he never liked elections. It was like the railroads, an unrefutable sign that things were going to hell. "The new city officers have published a list of fifty men they charged with vagrancy," he said. "Put it up all over town, issued warrants for the arrests."

Charley waited. Bill pulled a piece of paper out of his sash and unfolded it on the bar. Charley bent over and looked. The boy stood still, watching everything they did. The list was alphabetical, and most of the names on it Charley recognized for thieves or killers of one sort or another. The twenty-seventh name was James Butler "Wild Bill" Hickok.

"Well," Charley said, "it's the price of fame."

"Look down there at the bottom," Bill said.

Charley's finger went to the bottom of the list and started up. The fifth name he touched was his own, only they'd misspelled it. Charles "Colorado Charley" Udder. Charley hated it when they spelled him like that.

"What kind of slander is this?" he said. "I am a respectable businessman from Empire, Colorado."

Bill picked the paper up off the bar, folded it, and put it back in his sash. "Nobody from the police department has been by to arrest me," he said. "I gave them a few days to make up their mind if they were going to."

That night at the hotel bar, Bill laid down the rules of his wagon train. He would take only seventy wagons to Deadwood, nobody who was sick, no firebugs, no whores. Seventy wagons was enough to be safe from any party of Indians, but more than that and you couldn't be safe from yourself. Bill didn't want any bad apples. The trip would take two weeks, and each man, woman, and child had to carry a firearm, and pay him fifty dollars.

None of this discouraged the assembly at the Republican bar, which applauded him. The Black Hills was the wildest and the richest place on earth, and no man into his cups would admit things were wild enough for him right there in the hotel. Wagons on the way to the Hills had already come through from California, where the gold had begun to peter out, and pilgrims were headed there from the other direction too. Ohio, Indiana, Illinois, Iowa—for three years the grasshoppers in the States had come in over the crops like black clouds, and when they left, they'd taken it all with them. Bill had seen that with his own eyes in Iowa after he'd taken Agnes Lake home to St. Louis to wait for him until he got back on his feet.

It wasn't the way Bill would have put it to Agnes Lake, but some time had passed since he'd had a pot to piss in. Charley couldn't see him telling her about that at all. There was a respect between Bill and Agnes that did not invite inspection of the parties.

Bill and Charley and Malcolm and the mules waited four days, until Bill was satisfied nobody was coming to arrest them, and then he set a time to leave. Daybreak, June 27.

By nine o'clock Bill saw none of the boys from the Republican were going to show up. What had shown up was a Jew that wanted to set up a hardware store, and two peddlers. Four wagons, if you counted Bill and Charley's. Bill collected fifty dollars from each of them, and they started east, Charley driving the wagon, Bill sitting on his horse, a handsome old gelding he'd named Peerless, drinking cocktails.

The boy rode one of the mules.

Anyone but Bill would have rethought it right there. He had it in his head there was something waiting for him in the Hills, though. Charley couldn't get him to say exactly what; he thought Bill might not know either.

They met another wagon train at Fort Laramie, five days out of Cheyenne. Twenty-eight wagons, most of them full of whores. Some Chinese, some American. The filthiest whores Charley had seen up to then, here is what the Americans had for names: Dirty Emma, Tit Bit, Smooth Bones, and Sizzling Kate. The Chinese had little feet. They couldn't walk more than a few steps and stayed close to their whore man.

Bill joined wagons. He didn't like it, but the Indians were a fact. Once the whores heard who it was, they came after Bill's person night and day. Bill never gave them a look, and in the end he went to one of their wagons and talked to a whore man named Al Swearingen, who was importing a fresh load of girls for his place in Deadwood, and they didn't come by again.

The boy went to the wagon with him, carrying that old Smith & Wesson in his sash, and came back with a new purpose in life. Charley didn't see what it hurt, and didn't stop the boy when he went back to the wagon later, after sunset. He went that night and the night after, and the night after that. That's where he was before he shot Bill's horse.

They'd stopped early in the afternoon, in sight of the Hills. On that day, in that light, the Hills were as black as the Devil's dreams. It looked to Charley like once you got inside you might lose the sun's light forever. Charley put it out of his head.

The boy tethered and fed the mules, washed his face, and headed over into the whores' wagons. Al Swearingen, the man that Bill had spoken to about his whores, came over a little later carrying a bottle and three glasses, and offered up a drink of whiskey to celebrate finding the Hills. He was pale-eyed and bearded, the kind that was planning ten days ahead every day of his life. Bill took the drink, Charley didn't. The whore man's fingers had been all over the insides of the glasses.

Bill drank half of what the whore man poured him and waited to see what it would do. The man said, "This is a historic day, pards," and threw his down. Bill looked at him. The man said, "I mean, finding the Hills."

Bill studied his glass. He put his finger in the whiskey and came out with a speck of a gnat and rolled it off his fingers. Charley said, "Did you think we were going to miss the Black Hills?" North to south, they ran a hundred miles.

"No," he said, "I certainly didn't mean nothin' like that." And Bill laid his eyes on him again, calm and cold, until he went away. That was the way Bill handled annoyances when he could. He never threatened a soul unless he meant it.

The whore man went back to his own wagon. It was bigger than the others and brand new. The boy had been inside it, and said it looked like the finest hotel. The boy had never been in a hotel room in his life. Charley saw them then, the boy and the whore man, climbing into the back with two of the girls.

"Malcolm's back with the whores," he said. Bill smiled and shook his head. He couldn't see that far himself.

"It's a sign of health, knowing what you want," Bill said.

"He's young," Charley said.

"That's another sign," Bill said. He was thirty-nine years old. One of the whores shrieked and came halfway out of the back of the wagon, and then something grabbed her from behind and pulled her back in. "What are we, a day out of the Hills?" Bill said.

"More," Charley said. The Hills had been in view since early that morning. It wasn't like coming into the Rockies, that seemed to grow out of the earth in front of your eyes. Until you were close, the Hills just seemed to get darker.

"What do they look like?" Bill said.

"Shit, Bill, you seen the Black Hills." Bill shook his head, stubborn. Charley said, "They look black."

Another whore went into the wagon, and then a couple others followed her. The wagon shook and rocked and somebody in there started to sing. A weak, whining voice that strangled itself on the up notes.

"Could you tell them I once killed a woman for singing like that?" Bill said.

Charley thought it over. "I can't tell something like that," he said.

"I won't make you a woman-killer." As he said that, the voice stopped cold, right in the middle of "Beautiful Dreamer." "Maybe the boy killed her for you," he said.

"He's been with us what, ten days, and we already made him an opera critic," Bill said.

Charley said, "Of course, maybe he stuck his peeder in her mouth."

Bill shrugged. "Then we made his peeder an opera critic." Bill stood up, still holding the whore man's glass. "You see that dog?" he said. The dog belonged to the whore man too. It was resentful and short-haired and never looked you in the eye, and it had a head the size of a cow's. It was walking through the wagon horses now, worrying them, about thirty steps away.

"I see it," Charley said, surprised that Bill did. Thirty steps was farther out than Bill's eyes usually went.

"A gentleman's wager?" Bill said.

They bet five dollars, and Bill turned his back to the animal, dropping the arm holding the glass, and then he spun, his arm half a second behind the rest of him, and when he let go of the glass it carried the distance like a line of piss, sparkling in the light, and hit that monster square in the head. The dog screamed. "Sounds like he saw a snake," Bill said.

Charley had never seen anybody throw like Bill. It was magic, the way things connected for him. Bill climbed into the wagon and came out with a bottle. He pulled the cork with his teeth and spit it onto the ground, signaling his intentions. It was a bottle without a future. He took a drink and handed it to Charley. Charley wiped off the lip and joined him. The whores were shrieking again.

They passed the bottle back and forth two or three times and then Bill stood up to go into the bushes. He walked around the wagon horses and up a little hill. There were some weeds there and trees, thick enough to afford privacy.

Whatever kind of blood disease Bill had, it had gotten worse since March. The morning Charley found him in the hotel bar, he'd asked how it was, and Bill told him he thought his piss had to cut a new bed through there every time he went. Charley didn't ask him about it again, there was such a thing as leaving some distance. He knew, though, that Bill was afraid he'd given a case of it to Agnes, and thinking he'd done that made him love her the more.

He'd been in the bushes half an hour when the whore man came scrambling out of the front end of the wagon. The boy came out the back end, half dressed and trailing whores, carrying that old Smith & Wesson in his right hand. One of the whores had a bottle, there wasn't a trace of color to what was inside. She was holding on to that with one hand and trying to hold on to him with the other. "It don't mean nothin'," she said to him. "Come back in the wagon, 'fore you get injured."

The boy got himself loose and headed toward the front of the wagon, with intentions to use the gun. Charley saw right away that he meant it. The whore man had run from his wagon and climbed into the back of another. It belonged to one of the paper-collars that had signed up in Cheyenne. There was a needle gun back there— the peddler had shown it to Bill at the first camp—and if the whore man found that, the boy was as good as dead.

Charley moved to slow things down. "Here now, Malcolm," he said, "get hold of yourself." And the boy turned, shooting before he could see who it was. Old Peerless was tied to Charley's wagon, and he never even flinched. He was like Bill in a fight. The ball went in right behind the shoulder. Peerless stood still for half a minute; the boy froze at the size of the mistake. Then the old horse turned his head back, like he was trying to see what it was changing things so fast, and then he dropped onto his knees and a tremor took over his hindquarters, and he wasn't looking back anymore, because he knew what it was by then.

He died in no time at all. The boy forgot the whore man, and in the time it took him to walk over, the horse had passed to the other side. Malcolm was still holding the broken-handled pistol, but he'd forgot it was there too. "Mr. Hickok's horse," he said.

Charley said, "Damn near Mr. Hickok's friend," although in truth the ball had been a long ways from finding him.

"He can kill me if he wants to," the boy said.

Charley said, "He doesn't need your permission for that." He saw the boy was having trouble holding on to his feelings.

"I'll leave the train," the boy said. "I'll tell him what I done, give him my mule, and set out on my own."

Charley went over to the wagon where Bill had left the open bottle. He took a drink and offered one to the boy. "The Indians would cut you up and leave you staked out to dry with your peeder in your mouth," he said. As it turned out, that was an unfortunate choice of warning.

It turned out, the boy had been in the back of the whore man's wagon, encumbered with the soft parts of several women, and felt a mouth on his member. It wasn't the first time, all of them liked to do him like that. But the whiskey had made him reckless, and with all the nipples and legs and hands to occupy him—the boy said he loved to kiss their hands; Charley said, "You don't have to tell everything"—he didn't notice who it was doing their business down there.

"It was a lot of giggling," he said, "and I had a head of steam. But when the seizure passed I looked down, and Mr. Al Swearingen had his mouth where it should of been one of the ladies."

Charley was twice glad he hadn't drunk from the whore man's glass. The boy told him the story while they were waiting for Bill to come out of the bushes. Malcolm was standing shoeless in his long johns, still holding the gun. The whore man hadn't come out of the peddler's wagon. Charley didn't like him in there with a Springfield needle gun, so he walked over and kicked the side.

"Come out of there, Mr. Swearingen," he said, "or I'll burn it." There was a gathering of whores watching now, even some of the Chinese. Charley never saw such hopeless faces. Something moved in the wagon, but nothing came out. A minute passed.

"You got that boy's gun away from him?" the whore man said.

"What I got is kerosene."

Another minute went by. "It ain't my wagon," the whore man said.

"Or mine," Charley said. "I'll give you one minute." The whore man came out the back, yellow-toothed and nervous, smoothing his hair. He hadn't cleaned the wetness from his beard yet. One of the whores giggled, but he shot her a look and it died.

"Where's the boy?" he said.

"Let it alone," Charley said.

"Tell that boy that him and me got unfinished business," he said. "He owes me for the girls. It ain't no free ride with Al Swearingen, tell him that."

Charley turned around for one more look at the whores, and then he went back to the boy. He was sitting cross-legged on the ground beside old Peerless. In the dark the horse seemed bigger. "Listen," Charley said, "there's no reason your sister's got to know about this."

"What I heard," the boy said after a bit, "was it ruins you for girls."

"Where'd you hear that?" Charley said.

The boy shrugged. "I heard once you been with a man you don't want a woman no more."

"You weren't exactly *with* him," Charley said.

"I been sittin' here, thinkin' of every girl I seen over there, and I don't want one of them," he said.

Charley said, "Shit, that's not your manhood talking, that's good taste."

Then the boy looked over at Peerless, like he'd just remembered he was there. "And now I went and shot Mr. Hickok's horse. In my whole life, things never gone so bad all at once like this."

Charley stood right over the boy, the old horse was still giving off heat. "You want me to explain to him what happened?" Charley said. Bill'd had that horse a while.

"No," the boy said, "I got to tell him myself." Charley started off, thinking he'd need some room to do it. "The trouble is," the boy said, "I don't know how it happened. Things just never went to hell before like that, all of a sudden."

Charley said, "You keep your eye out for Mr. Swearingen so it doesn't get worse."

The boy laughed. "He ain't even a man," he said.

"Malcolm," Charley said, "the first thing you learn will be the first thing you know, but listen to me on this. When they're bad, there's things that kind will do to you that nobody else could think up."

But the boy wasn't paying any more attention than the horse was, so Charley took a walk up the hill to catch a last look at the day. He met Bill coming out of the bushes, buttoning his trousers. Bill put his death eyes on him, cold and steady. "It's me," Charley said. Bill was stone blind at dusk.

"I heard the shot," he said. Charley saw him wipe a tear out of the corner of his eye. "You just get settled down to piss, and then somebody's shooting, and the piss ducks back inside and you got to start all over . . ."

"Maybe they got a physician in Deadwood Gulch," Charley said. "Or Belle Fourche. They got to have medicine in Belle Fourche." Bill smiled at that. Something had told him there was an issue to be settled in the Black Hills, maybe between him and God, and he couldn't see anything as inconsequential as a doctor getting in the middle of two such forces.

Besides, he'd been to doctors. In Cheyenne, and before that. He had a saddlebag full of pills and medications. "I hate to be in the bushes with my peeder out when the shooting starts," he said. A little later he said, "It's not as easy to forget there's people around as it used to be, you notice that? You can't just walk forty yards into the trees and feel like you got it all to yourself. Somebody is always grabbing a gun over a whore to remind you it ain't all yours, and who you got to share it with." He dropped a line of spit between his moccasins.

"You always liked it quiet, Bill," Charley said. "You spent a life in pursuit of quiet." Charley didn't talk that way except to get Bill off his pessimism and morbidity.

Bill reached out and grabbed the back of Charley's neck, and Charley kicked his feet out from under him, and they rassled on the ground until Bill got Charley's windpipe. Bill let him get him in some holds before he ended it, though—Charley knew he'd let him—so by the time Bill let go they were both good and stretched. They lay on their backs, breathing hard and wet. Bill was chuckling.

"What I was saying," he said, "I don't mind the noise, it's just getting to be a weaker class of people all the time that's making it."

"That's true," Charley said.

Bill said, "It's got too damn easy to make noise."

"Bill," Charley said after a while, "the boy shot old Peerless." Bill sat up in the dark, Charley stayed where he was. There was a warm place over Charley's eye where they'd cracked heads. He touched it and found a lump about the size of a spoon. "He got all excited in the wagon with the girls, and somehow the whore man ended up suckin' on his peeder."

"So he shot my horse?"

"He was shootin' at me, thought I was the whore man, and hit Peerless instead. Got him dead in the heart." Bill sighed and pulled his knees up to his chest and circled them with his arms. Charley's legs had been broken, and he always noticed the things other people could do with theirs.

"That was a consequential animal," Bill said. Charley sat up then and his nose started to bleed. He'd tried to butt Bill, but Bill had sensed it coming and got underneath him. "I had him a long time."

"Six, seven years," Charley said. "Since Kansas, at least. He was there at Abilene." It seemed like the time to mention Abilene, where Bill shot Mike Williams. Mike was the only man Bill ever killed by accident, to Charley's knowledge. He was a policeman—

they'd had an election and the winners hired their nephews as policemen, after Bill had made the place safe to be a policeman—and it was the luck of things that when Phil Coe came after Bill in the street, Mike Williams came around a corner and Bill shot him through the head, thinking it was one of Phil Coe's brothers. Then he shot Phil.

The newspaper wouldn't let it heal. It brought Mike Williams back from the dead every week, like a blood relative. The editor called him a *fine specimen of Kansas manhood*, and declared a "Crusade to Rid Abilene and the State of Kansas of Wild Bill and All His Ilk." Those were the exact words, because for a while after that Bill called him "Ilk."

It wasn't the newspaper that got Bill and Charley out of Kansas, though. It was a petition. It was left with the clerk at the hotel where they stayed, three hundred and sixteen signatures asking Bill to leave, not a word of gratitude for what he'd done. He sat down in the lobby with the petition in his lap, running his fingers through his hair. He read every name—there were six sheets of them—and when he finished a sheet, he'd hand it to Charley and he'd read it too.

It was the worst back-shooting Charley had ever seen; they even let the women sign. Bill shrugged and smiled, but some of the names hurt him. He thought he had friends in Kansas, and looking at the names he saw they were all afraid of him.

What ran Wild Bill out of Abilene was hurt feelings. This business with the horse might of hurt him too, it was hard to tell. "The heart?" he said.

"He never felt it," Charley said. "Never believed it if he did." Bill ran his fingers through his hair. There were leaves and twigs in it from the rassling. He stood up and slapped the same from his britches, and headed off down the hill for the wagons. Charley waited a minute and went down there too.

Al Swearingen had sent some of his whores out for firewood and built himself more fire than he needed. The Chinese had smaller fires. Most nights, the Chinamen let their girls out among the rest of the wagons, but with the shooting they kept them close and shouted at them in Chinese when one got too far away. Charley admired the excitement in their language.

They had their own manners, too. The first time Charley saw them eat, it was a day and a half before he could look at food again. Charley wasn't any paper-collar, and everybody west of Boston ate with their fingers. He'd sat down to feed with all kinds of human beings, including Indians, but he never saw anybody but the Chinese put their fingers *inside* their mouth, at least not three at a time up to the second knuckle.

On the other hand, if you lined up fifty Chinese to take a bath every day for a month, every day the same Chinaman would get the water first, the same Chinaman would go second, and so on right through to number fifty. They had a way to arrange everything, and an order to everything, and Charley expected that was a kind of manners too.

That's how their wagons always ended up in the same place. They drove in every night behind the Americans and then went off to themselves. The head Chinaman had the youngest girls, although in truth there wasn't much reason to pick one over another. From the point of looks, it was a dead heat. There was one, though, that the head Chinaman kept to himself.

She rode alone in the back of his wagon, and nobody ever got a look at her except at night, when he'd let her out. Just a few minutes. He stayed at her side and wouldn't let anybody close, so you might see her climbing in or out of the wagon, or you might see her hobbling along beside the Chinaman out beyond the light of the fire, face like a statue from Egypt, but you'd never get close enough to see what it looked like. Charley heard that Al Swearingen had tried to buy her, but the Chinaman wanted too much money.

When Charley got back to the wagon, Bill was sitting on old Peerless. He'd found a fresh bottle. The boy was five feet away, digging a grave. The ground was wet and heavy—it rained every day of the spring there, but it wasn't hell storms like the ones Charley had experienced in his previous visit to the Hills—and the boy was throwing mud over his shoulder at a pace that figured to kill him in three minutes.

"Sit down and watch this," Bill said, and he slapped a place next to him on old Peerless's belly.

Even in the dark, Charley could see that the horse had begun to swell. He sat down on the ground instead, then reclined to an elbow to stop the hurting. He didn't know how, but in the last few years the leg problems had crawled up into his hips. When he was settled Bill handed him the bottle, and when he'd taken a drink he called the boy off and asked if he wanted some too. The boy's labor had produced a trench nine feet long east and west, and he was digging off toward the south now.

He put the shovel down and took the bottle. He drank three swallows as fast as gravity let him, and gave it back. He couldn't last long at that speed either. "You plantin' a garden, Malcolm?" Charley said in a soft way.

The boy didn't answer. He just picked up the shovel and began throwing mud again. Bill took the bottle out of Charley's hands and had at it. "You never seen anybody bury a horse before?" Bill said.

The boy dug south for six feet, and then started west. He was breathing hard, and now and again Charley could hear it catch in his throat. There was a family resemblance about this. Back in Colorado, the boy's sister would sometimes cut firewood until her hands bled after Charley went into the mountains and got drunk.

For a while, Charley and Bill just sat still, watching. The boy came nine feet west, until he was even with the place he'd started, and then spaded his way back north to meet it.

"What kind of a missionary have you become?" Charley said.

He stopped digging again and took another drink. Charley could see they were going to need another bottle. "I intend to give him a proper burial before I leave here," the boy said. "I kilt him for no reason, and it's the least I can do to set it right."

Charley dropped off his elbow and lay on his back, and looked up at all the stars in the sky, trying to empty his mind. Against all efforts, he began to laugh.

The sound of that set something off in Bill too. As long as Charley had known him, however bad things got, Bill always found something to smile at, but there weren't five people in the world who ever heard him laugh like he did then. He laughed and rocked back and forth on old Peerless's belly until he fell off. The whole time the boy was still digging. If anything, the sound of it seemed to drive him harder. When he could talk again, Bill said, "And this is the easy part. Think of the box he's got to build."

The boy would not stop, though, except to drink. He got drunk and threw mud from one side of the hole into the other. Bill and Charley got drunk too, quieter now, and watched until the boy hit himself in the head with the shovel and stumbled down into the bed he'd dug for the horse. It might have been two feet deep by then. He landed on his back and lay still. Then he turned over and got his knees under him. He seemed to settle there, and then he just fell over and went to sleep.

That's where they found him in the morning, still asleep. Bill picked him up under the arms, so when he opened his eyes he was already standing up. There was blood on both of the boy's hands where blisters had broken and he'd worn through the skin underneath. So he was useless to work. He held on to Bill for a minute, finding his balance and looking around him, shocked, like raiders had come in the night, shot the horse, and torn up the earth.

"I got to finish it," the boy said.

"Leave the damn horse be," Bill said. He'd done all his laughing the night before. There were noises from the other wagons as the whores kicked each other awake. Some of the Chinese had kept their fires through the night and the smell of their food was everywhere. There wasn't a clean breath of air in two miles. Charley thought of fingers inside those mouths.

"You can have my mule," the boy said to Bill. "He ain't much . . ." The boy's mule was tied with some of the others. They were blowing to get started. One of the whores was screaming at her whore man over at the other end of camp. Bill didn't like any kind of emotion before his morning cocktail, and climbed up into the wagon and poured himself a drink into a glass. He sat up there, sipping it and chewing jerky, while the camp got itself ready to leave.

After a while he climbed down the other side, walked up the hill, and disappeared into the bushes. The boy hitched the wagon and threw Bill's saddle into the back. Charley washed and shaved and cleaned his teeth. He had a real mirror to shave in. The boy said, "You think Mr. Hickok might change his mind? I wisht he'd take my mule."

"Bill doesn't want to talk about transportation this morning," Charley said. By now old Peerless was swollen twice his regular size around the stomach, and the place where the boy's ball had gone into him was black with insects. Bill had had that horse a long time.

He came out of the bushes just as the sun broke the sky over the Black Hills. He'd combed his hair and tied it in a knot. He walked down the hill, right past the wagon. Charley thought he might not have seen them—you could never tell when Bill wasn't sure of himself, he didn't give anything away—but he passed Charley and the boy and went right to Al Swearingen's rig. The whore man sat on his cushions eating boiled eggs and watched him come.

"It's a beautiful day to enter the Hills," Swearingen said. "An omen for the future."

"You got somebody can handle horses?" Bill said.

The whore man smiled and swelled. "I got these girls trained to do everything I tell them," he said. "Completely obedient."

"Get one that can drive," Bill said, "and move your person inside the wagon." The whore man didn't blink. "Don't show me your face again," Bill said.

The whore man patted down his beard. Everybody in earshot stopped what they were doing to watch. "Al Swearingen drives his own wagon," the whore man said.

"Then Al Swearingen mistood his omen," Bill said.

The whore man looked at Bill half a minute, long enough to see what he needed to, and then called one of the whores from another wagon. Smooth Bones. From what Charley had seen, she was the best of the lot. She wasn't more than seventeen or eighteen, the same age as the boy, and if she'd had teeth in front she might of been pretty. Of course, if she'd had teeth in front they mightn't of named her Smooth Bones too. You could *what if* yourself right out of this world.

She sat on the cushion next to Swearingen and he gave her the reins. "Tell that boy it ain't settled," he said. And then he crawled into the back.

Bill sent the boy ahead to scout, mostly to get him out of his sight. Thirty-two wagons were safe from Indians. He climbed up next to Charley and said, "I ought to of finished it and got the whole episode out of my mind."

Bill could put things out of his mind, once they were dead. The boy moved a quarter of a mile out in front, and beyond him were the Hills. The wagons strung out in back of Charley and Bill, the wheels creaked and the mules blew and complained and once, just after they'd straightened into a line, Charley looked back and saw old Peerless lying in the dirt, next to a hole that was supposed to be his grave. It looked like God Himself had dropped him out of the sky, and he'd bounced once when he hit.

Let the Indians figure that out.

THEY CAME INTO DEADWOOD DOWNHILL, FROM THE SOUTH. THE gulch fell out of the mountains, long and narrow, following the Whitewood Creek, and where things widened enough for a town sign, that was Deadwood. It was noon, July 17. The place looked miles long and yards wide, half of it tents. The Whitewood joined a smaller creek—the Deadwood—at the south end and ran the length of the town. The mud was a foot deep, and every kind of waste in creation was thrown into the street to mix with it.

The mountains that defined the boundaries were spare of live trees. There were thousands of the dead, charred black trunks lying across each other on the ground.

"How's it look to you?" Bill said. He was handling the reins, sitting tall and handsome, nodding at voices when somebody called to him from the street. The word of who it was in the wagon got through town before Charley and Bill made a hundred yards.

"Like something out of the Bible," Charley said. They rode through, the mud sticking to the wheels and the mules until it broke off from its own weight. It took most of an hour to get the train down Main Street, stopping to shake hands and once to give an interview to a reporter from the *Black Hills Pioneer*. Although he enjoyed a taste for the printed word, Charley winced to hear there was already a paper in town.

They went farther north, and the population changed. Whores and roughs and gamblers stood in the doorways, holding drinks, shooting their guns into the air. It was a part of the city called the badlands, and it was as far as the whore wagons went. The place was shabby, but the ladies there looked better to Charley than the load they'd delivered. Some stood in the windows, as good as naked. "What part of the Bible?" Bill said, when they were alone again.

"Where God got angry," Charley said.

A hundred people suddenly came together in the street in front of them. Bill steadied the mules, and one of the men climbed halfway onto the wagon with them and shook Bill's hand. He was wearing a cheap leather coat, fringed, and two pistols.

"Captain Jack Crawford," the man said. Bill gave him his left hand. "On behalf of the city of Deadwood, Dakota Territory, I would like to welcome you and your party, and express the hope that you are here to settle and prosper. We can use men of your ilk here."

Ilk again.

"Thank you," Bill said.

The man seemed to notice Charley then, but couldn't bring himself to let go of Bill's hand. "Captain Jack Crawford," he said to Charley. "Scout, poet, and duly authorized captain of the Black Hills Minutemen. We can always use volunteers, lads, with the Indian situation."

"Charles Utter," Charley said. "Does this place have a bath-house?"

The question drew its share of comment from the crowd, which

Captain Jack pretended not to hear. He pointed back up the street and said it was five blocks on the left. "You passed it on the way in," he said. Then he looked around and said, "It's too bad there's not more who have asked the question." Before they could get him off the wagon, Captain Jack had told them where to graze the mules and where to find women, and that he had personally ridden with Custer and Buffalo Bill Cody.

They turned around and found a place to camp on the other side of the Whitewood Creek, between the badlands and the bathhouse, across the street from the Betwix-Stops Saloon, which was a canvas tent. The proprietor had turned two barrels upside down in the doorway and laid a piece of lumber across them, and was selling whiskey from the States at fifty cents a shot.

They left the wagon three yards from the creek and blocked the wheels with logs. The boy took the mules to the north end of town beyond the badlands, where the canyon widened and the ground was flat and grassy. Charley got his blankets from inside the wagon and threw them over the top to air out. Bill sat on a tree stump curling his hair around his finger.

"I've got a feeling about this camp," he said, "a premonition."

Charley stopped his chores. He had known those who made a career of black feelings, but Bill was never like that, and Charley took this seriously.

A month after the shooting in Abilene, for instance, a reporter appeared from Philadelphia—that was a class of paper-collars Charley would like to have studied, reporters—and told Bill how Bill had stood in the middle of the street, Phil Coe and four of his brothers shooting at him from every cowardly angle the area afforded, and that Bill had operated there, calm as an engine, picking them off one by one. The reporter said, "How do you sustain your courage in the face of death's odds?"

Bill never blinked. He said, "When you know in your heart the bullet hasn't been made with your name on it, there is no tremble in your hand at the weight of a Colt."

The reporter took it down word for word—Bill had to say it twice for him—and then he got drunk four nights straight and then he got on the stage east and went home to Philadelphia. Bill said later he was a good reporter, although he never straightened him out on how many Coes he killed that day—or how many policemen—but what he said about knowing the bullet hadn't been made yet for him, that was true. He'd told Charley much the same thing.

The change in him came with the blood disease, or with Agnes, or with losing his sight. Charley was not sure those were separate things.

"What kind of premonition?" he said.

"This is the last camp," Bill said.

"We could go somewhere else," Charley said. "We're not married to this place yet."

Bill shook his head. "There's something here for us," he said. He looked up and around, and Charley believed that in his own way Bill could see the hills around them clearer than he could. It had something to do with the way things connected for him. "You don't wind up in a place like this for no reason," Bill said.

BOONE MAY WAS LYING IN A BED ON THE SECOND FLOOR OF THE GEM Theater on top of Lurline Monti Verdi. He loved to say her name. He was finished now, but he liked to lie on top of her and watch her face when she panicked. After the passion left her, Lurline's thoughts always went to suffocation.

Boone May was oversize—he had a head on him a foot across—and he would lie on her until her breathing changed. Then she would push at his chest with those little white hands. "Boone, honey, I can't breathe . . ." And a couple of minutes later she would be pounding his head with her fists, screaming he was killing her. Boone loved the feel of those soft little fists against his head as much as the sound of her name. Nobody ever came to help.

Screaming didn't mean a thing at the Gem Theater, and even if it did, everybody knew when Boone was upstairs, and he was the last man on God's earth you wanted to walk in on during fornication.

He waited for her now, patiently. There was a chair beside the bed, where he'd left his clothes. All except his underwear, which he only removed under sheets. His pants were buckskin, and he'd hung them over the back. On top of that was a leather bag, drawn together at the top by a piece of rawhide. Frank Towles's head was inside it. There was a two-hundred-dollar reward for Frank, but the way things had got between Boone and Sheriff Bullock, he'd have to ride back to Cheyenne to collect. That's where Frank was wanted.

Boone May didn't know where it went wrong between him and Seth Bullock. The way it always worked, when road agents was identified, Bullock always sent him and W. H. Llewellyn out to bring them back. W.H. was Boone's partner. They hired out as messenger guards for payrolls and gold shipments together, and they both took it as a compliment that the sheriff always came to them to bring in the worst agents. The way the business worked, somebody always got shot, them or the agents. Boone May had begun to see that the sheriff didn't care who that was, and did not take that as such a compliment.

She began to push at him now, and he smiled. He had teeth the size of a dirt farmer's fingernails. Lurline Monti Verdi was a singer and a blackjack dealer, and she fucked more highwaymen than there was bullets to shoot them. She liked that risky feeling. The head would be a surprise.

"All right, Boone," she said. "Get off now . . ."

He lifted his legs up off the bed to put more of his weight on her chest. Her mouth was painted into a little heart, and he could see the tip of her tongue in there in the dark. She began to squirm, but each way she rolled he moved against it, not letting her move an inch.

Her teeth clenched and she bucked, but he stayed on top, watching her mouth. It wasn't the feel of her underneath him now, it was all in her face. And then she begged him. "Please, honey, I can't breathe. Really, this time . . ." And then one of the fists hit his ear.

"You're killing me." She said that over and over, banging him, turning red and then white, and he watched it until he was sure it was real, until she quit hitting him with her fists, until she couldn't scream. In the end, her eyes came wide open and fixed on him and waited to see if he was going to call it off or kill her.

Boone stared at her, feeling the warm, sweet places where her fists had hit his head. He put his hands against the mattress on either side of her and pushed up half a foot. She took that much air.

Boone looked down at her breasts, the scar across her stomach—Doc Howe had made a mess of that, sewed her up with fish line—the little tangle of hair down where her legs come together. Boone had hung a man last year in Hill City who married a whore and then killed her for all the men she'd had. They paid Boone fifteen dollars to do it. He set the killer on his horse under a pine tree and put a rope around his neck—for fifteen dollars you didn't get much in the way of trappings—but before he slapped the horse out from under him, he asked if he had any last words. The man looked him dead in the eye and said, "Boone May, you know why God put hair on a woman's pussy?"

Boone was taken back. "This here's your last words," he said.

The killer said, "To camouflage the hook," and went off into eternity.

Lurline put an arm over her breasts and turned halfway over. His arm stopped her. "One day you're going to kill me, ain't you?" she said. He leaned down and kissed her shoulder, then her neck.

"What do you think?" he said.

"I think you'll kill me," she said. He moved off her and lay down on his back, smiling. She sat up and looked the other way. Her back was smooth and pale, it looked like you could snap it between your fingers.

"Well," he said, "there's worst ways to go." He watched her back, and before long he saw her shoulders move forward, like she was coughing. In a minute she'd be laughing out loud, it was the same every time. He reached under the sheets and found his long underwear, and got himself decent. He didn't get out of bed, though.

"I brung you a surprise."

She turned around and smiled. "Where?" she said. Her eyes were wet in the corners. She wiped at them with the back of her hand, and then pulled down on her cheeks, like she was stretching them. "You never brung me nothing before," she said. He could see she didn't believe him.

There was something happening outside, they heard the noise. It sounded like a dogfight. Maybe Pink Buford had found somebody to fight his bulldog. She put on her shoes and walked to the window, and then stood there with her hands on the sill for a long time, buck-naked, watching it. Forgetting that he said he had something to give her.

Boone looked at the leather bag, then back at the window. He didn't like to be treated incidental. "Lurline?" he said. She didn't say nothing, didn't seem to hear him. It wasn't no dogfight, the excitement wasn't the right pace. "What is it, a wagon train?"

She turned back to him, smiling. "You ain't going to believe this," she said, real happy now. "It's Wild Bill down there. Wild Bill in Deadwood."

Boone got out of bed and went to the window. He looked out and saw half the population of the badlands standing in the street in front of a wagon, some from the proper end of town, too. While he was watching, Captain Jack Crawford climbed up onto the wagon and shook hands with the man holding the reins. He was sitting straight and serious, wide shoulders, dressed in expensive buckskin. The one with him was small, and dressed even fancier. Both of them had hair down to the shoulders.

"That ain't Wild Bill," he said, but he knew it was.

Lurline had left the window and was back sitting on the bed, dressing. She put on her undies and her garter belt and stockings, and then pulled her dress over her head. The more she put on, the less he liked her. "I brung you a surprise," he said again. He wished he'd stayed on top of her a little longer, help her remember him.

She slipped her feet back into her shoes—they were more like slippers, now that he noticed, you couldn't take two steps in the street but they'd get sucked up in the mud—and headed for the dresser. She had a bottle of toilet water there, along with smaller bottles of perfume. She splashed some into her hand and rubbed it all around her neck and then down the front of her dress.

"That little sissy with him probably got more shit on than you do," Boone said. She didn't seem to know he was in the room. She dropped on her knees and reached up under the dresser, came out with a bone-handled mirror, and fluffed at her hair with one hand while she held on to the looking glass with the other. From her expression, she wasn't satisfied with what was there.

She hid the mirror back under the dresser, taking her time with that, and headed toward the door. He stepped in front of her, and she stepped back, suddenly finding him there. Boone was faster than he looked, that was where a lot of characters was fatally fooled. And Boone May never gave you a chance to fool him back.

"You don't care what I brung you?" he said.

She looked at him without sparkle. "All right," she said, "what is it?" It wasn't the way it was supposed to be, with her crawling all over him, begging.

"Something from Cheyenne," he said. He saw an interest stir. Maybe she thought it was something to wear. Lurline spent every cent she made on clothes. She had four dresses that he knew of.

"Well?" she said.

"You got to find it," he said.

She shrugged, then looked over at the pile of clothes on the chair. "It's in there," she said. Boone smiled at her, and she walked over, the heels of her slippers making hoof noises across the pine floor, and picked up his pants. There was pockets in back, and she reached in and come out with Harry Pine's front tooth. Boone had broke it off while he was looking for gold teeth, and kept it for good luck. He meant to have a piece of jewelry made with it.

"What the hell?" she said.

"That ain't it," he said. "Put it back."

There was an oration in the street outside, then some clapping. She looked toward the window, forgetting what they were doing again. "I'm missing everything," she said.

"It ain't nothing special," he said. She picked up his coat and put her hand in the pockets. She dropped the coat on the bed, beside his pants, and touched the leather bag. He smiled at her.

She picked it up, interested in the weight. The bag was tied, and it took her a while to pick open the knot. "You ought not to chew your nails," he said.

She got the knot loose and separated the pieces of rawhide. He stood still and watched her face. She opened the top and looked inside. "What is it?" she said.

"Look and see," he said.

She reached in, stopped, and then pulled it out by the hair. She held it up in front of her, eye to eye. He thought she was going to scream. "Shit," she said, "it's just Frank Towles."

"It's his head," he said.

She put it back in the bag and dropped it on the bed. "You been everyplace in the Hills with that head," she said. And then she walked around him, smelling like flowers, and went out the door. Boone didn't stop her this time.

He heard her slippers on the stairs and closed the door. He took Frank Towles's head out of the bag for a look. It wasn't true that he'd been everyplace in the Hills with it. He'd only had it three days. He'd tried to sell it to W. H. Llewellyn for $150, and save himself the trip back to Cheyenne, and he might of offered it for sale at the Green Front. That was all. Not everyplace in the Hills. It was strange, now he thought about it, how something could be worth $200 one place and not another. A head only had one value. A thing was worth what it was worth.

He put the head back in the bag and tied it shut. Then he put on his pants and shirt and boots, and decided to move camp to Nuttall and Mann's Number 10 saloon, where the bartender— Harry Sam Young—was mixing the most expert gin and bitters in Deadwood. Pink gin was all Boone drunk, since he discovered it. It was Pink Buford's drink first, of course, he named himself after it. Besides owning the best dog in Deadwood, Pink might of been the best cardplayer too. He received visions at the card table. Boone admired Pink Buford for what he had, and wished there was a way to take it away from him.

He put his gun in his pants and started out of the room. Before he got to the door, though, he looked at her dresser. He got on the floor and felt underneath. She'd hid the mirror in back, on top of a board. He saw his face in it once as he brought it out, and again in one of the pieces, after he'd broke it on the headboard of the bed.

BILL AND CHARLEY HAD BEEN IN DEADWOOD FOUR HOURS WHEN THE Mex rode into town carrying the head of an Indian. He held it up, away from the giant pieces of slop that were coming off his horse's hoofs, yelling some kind of Mexican yell. He rode to the bottom of the badlands, and then back up into the respectable part of town, and then back into the badlands. It was the most excitement since the wagon train, and the miners and roughs followed him up and down the street—some of them making the same noise he was.

"What is it?" Bill said. He and Charley were standing at the tent across the creek from their wagon, trying some of the fifty-cent whiskey. The man who owned the tent had given them the first drinks free. He said it was an honor to own the spot where Wild Bill Hickok first set his feet on Deadwood soil. He said he might put up a sign to commemorate it.

"It looks like a Mexican on a stolen horse carrying somebody's head," Charley said.

"That's an Indian," said the man who owned the tent. He'd hung calico on the inside walls to brighten the mood. "There's a town reward, two hundred and fifty dollars for any Indian, dead or alive."

"That one's dead," Charley said. His humor sometimes grew an edge when he drank.

Bill shook his head. "I never heard anything like that. Paying Mexicans two hundred and fifty dollars to kill Indians."

The man who owned the tent poured them another shot. There had been twenty or thirty others there drinking with them, but they'd left now to follow the Mex. "It's the law," the man said. "It used to be twenty-five dollars, but it went up after what they done to Custer."

"Custer?" Bill said.

"Kilt him and everybody with him. Two, three hundred boys of the Seventh Cavalry up to the Little Big Horn in Montana." Bill shook his head. "June twenty-fifth," the man said. "You didn't hear that?"

"We been out of touch," Bill said.

"We're all out of touch," the man said. "The pony express—shit, you might as well just walk out here and deliver your messages in person. But Custer's a fact. Terrible mutilations, no survivors." He waited to build the suspense before he told Wild Bill what kind of mutilations, which had been the focus of conversation in town ever since the news arrived. "A polite way to put it," he said, "if Custer had survived, he wouldn't of had no eyes to see, and he'd of had to squat to piss."

As soon as the man said that he saw it hadn't set right with Bill. Maybe they were friends. He tried to soften it. "That being the case," he said, "he's better off dead."

Bill finished the shot and headed off in the direction of the Mex. "I didn't mean nothin'," the man said to Charley. "I was just explainin' the problem."

Charley watched Bill walk across the street, his chin up, not even looking at the mud, and then down the other side into the badlands. They were shooting guns down there now, and Charley wondered where the boy was. Lord, don't let the boy get shot. Charley Utter had lived thirty-seven years, most of it unworried and natural. He'd hunted and fished and run trap lines into all the tributaries of the Grand River. When they'd found gold in Colorado, he'd bought and sold claims. When the gold began to peter out, he ran supplies into the newer, more remote camps. He'd made more money than any miner he knew, and held on to most of it. He'd been shot twice in the legs by accident, hunting, but he'd never had to pull a gun on a living soul. As much as you can, he'd even gotten married on purpose.

It did not sit with him that now, in the space of a spring, he was dreaming at night of Bill's blindness, and doing everything for the boy but powdering his ass. It wasn't that they'd asked him, it was like a sickness he'd caught.

Two different sicknesses. He'd been to the edge of the canyon with Bill, and could predict him better than anybody alive. He was tied to Bill, who was like his own person. There was one side that got Bill women and money and included the stories people told about him, and there was another side he kept to himself. Except

Charley felt like he was keeping Bill's private side for him now. The public side was as wild as ever—a reputation always changed slower than a man—and more and more, Bill occupied himself in that. Charley imagined it was the blood disease, or going blind, but Bill sometimes seemed to lose track of the line between the stories and what was true.

The boy, on the other hand, was a problem connected to his wife, and when Charley worried about the boy, it was the purest self-interest. Charley's wife was named Matilda Nash. He'd married her on September 30, 1866, when she was fifteen years old. She was the cleanest human being Charley ever saw. She had readable eyes and pale, English-type skin, and she used to sit on the bearskin rug he'd given her father with her chin pressed against his knees and believe every lie he told her about the places he had been and the things he had done.

Her father was a baker from Bath, England. Charley had a picture of that place in his head. Her mother had died at the birth of Malcolm. Everything considered, she did the honorable thing. Tilly brought the boy up herself, mad at him every minute, complaining about him to anybody who would listen. And she would kill you if you agreed with her.

And after the boy and her father were asleep, she'd sit at Charley's feet—he didn't sit on the floor himself because of the ache in his legs—and listen to his stories. She seemed to understand everything he said, including the way it was between him and Bill. It never occurred to him that she was sitting there smiling, making lists of the things she was going to change.

Charley opened his pouch and watched the man who owned the tent pinch out enough gold dust to cover the cost of what they'd drunk. Whiskey was less than two dollars a gallon back in the States, and what the man took had bought maybe twice that. "The overhead doesn't hurt you much here, does it?" Charley said, looking around. He was always interested in how people made a living.

The man smiled and leaned closer. "I don't know nothing about that," he said, and Charley could see that was probably true. "You think I could still put up a sign?" he said. "I don't want to do nothin' to upset Wild Bill more than he is."

"He won't mind," Charley said, and started off.

The man said to tell Bill he was welcome to come by and look at the sign anytime he wanted. "And you too," he said.

Charley walked back down into the badlands and found Bill in the company of the Mex and Captain Jack at the bar of the Green Front Theater. There was a crowd of miners and gamblers and reprobates around them, a lot of drinking and backslapping. Somebody discharged his pistol into the floor, and the smell of the powder stunk worse than the miners.

A man stood in the doorway holding his hat upside down and asked Charley for a dollar. The hat was full of paper money. "It's a donation for the greaser," the man said. "On account of the Indian he killed." Charley put a dollar in the hat and moved toward the bar.

Bill was standing next to the Mex, both of them facing Captain Jack Crawford. Charley noticed the Mex was missing half an ear. The gun went off again—Charley saw the smoke this time, it floated up into the ceiling like a departed soul—and then the place went quiet. Captain Jack cleared his throat and opened a copy of the *Black Hills Pioneer*, and began to read out loud. "A Missive to Buffalo Bill Cody," he said, "from Another Old Indian Scout, Captain Jack Crawford. By Captain Jack Crawford."

It took Charley a little while to realize it was a poem.

> *"Did I hear the news from Custer?*
> *Well, I reckon I did, old pard.*
> *It came like a streak o' lightning,*
> *And you bet, it hit me hard.*
> *I ain't no hand to blubber,*
> *And the briny ain't run for years,*
> *But chalk me down for a lubber,*
> *If I didn't shed regular tears."*

Charley pried his way through the assembly and got to Bill, who didn't see him. He and the Mex were both fixed on Captain Jack's recital.

> *". . . I served with him in the Army*
> *In the darkest days of the war,*
> *And I reckon, ye know his record,*
> *For he was our guiding star.*
> *And the boys who gathered round him*
> *To charge in the early morn,*

War' jest like the brave who perished
With him on the Little Big Horn . . ."

Charley didn't know if he could wait it out. From where he was standing he could see Captain Jack's finger moving down the outside of the column. He'd read five or six verses, and was only halfway through. Bill and the Mex looked very solemn. The joints in Charley's hips and knees seemed to be locking into the bones. The Mex had tucked the Indian head into the crook of his arm, face forward, and somewhere in the achievement of its celebrity the Indian's face had been distorted, and half-looked like it was smiling.

Charley found a place on the bar to put his elbow and took some of the weight off his legs. The relief was instant, and when the pain ebbed he felt more patient. The poem was turning angry now.

"They talk about peace with the demons,
By feeding and clothing them well,
I'd as soon think an angel from heaven
Would reign with contentment in hell.
And some day these Quakers will answer
Before the great Judge of all
For the death of daring young Custer
And the boys that around him did fall . . ."

"Damn right," someone shouted. Captain Jack held up his hand for quiet, but there was a demonstration before he could finish. With interruptions, the poem lasted another five minutes, and at the end of it one of the miners drew his pistol and shot the smiling Indian out of the Mex's arm. The Mex was slightly wounded— more burned than shot, but a little of each—so they gave him the money right away, without teasing him.

He accepted it with the same solemnity he'd accepted the poem, and then he turned to the bartender and gave three of the bills to him, and pointed at the empty glass in front of him.

"Da-me," he said. The bartender filled his glass, and then Bill's glass, and then he picked up a glass that was sitting on the bar in front of a sleeping miner, threw what was in it on the floor, and set it in front of Charley. "Da-me," the Mex said, and the bartender filled it too.

Captain Jack refused even before the Mex offered him a drink.

"No *da-me*," he said, more to the room than the Mex, and began another oration. There was something about his voice that nobody else wanted to talk at the same time.

"After the war," he began, "in which my father was killed and I myself was twice wounded, Battle of Spottsylvania, 1864, Forty-seventh Regiment of Pennsylvania Volunteers, I returned home to New York to find my mother ravaged by sickness. As I wept beside her, she asked one last thing, that I never touch a drop of liquor, and I made that good lady that promise, and it is a promise I mean to keep." To Charley's knowledge, Jack Crawford was the only man in the West who spoke footnotes.

"*Da-me*," said the Mex, pointing to his glass. And when it was full he turned with it to Captain Jack and offered a toast. "*Tu mamá*," he said, and spilled some of it down the front of Captain Jack's buckskin jacket. Then he drank what was left and turned back to the bartender.

Charley moved closer to Bill. So did the poet-scout. "These are all good men," Captain Jack said to Bill, and pointed around the room. "Miners, paper-collars, even the greaser. But they don't know a thing about Indian fighting. Most of them can't use a side arm at all, except the ones that were in the war, and some of them don't have a stomach for it now."

Bill nodded. The war didn't leave anybody the same. Some of those in it came away too scared to live anymore, and some had spent all the time since looking for some excitement to match it. Captain Jack said, "They came here without the protection of the United States government, against the government, into these hills the Indians would claim for their own."

Captain Jack paused and gave the miners and gamblers a chance to agitate against the government. Charley had seen the same sort of thing a couple of times in Kansas, but he couldn't see the point here. There wasn't anybody around to hang.

"And so we have taken up arms to protect ourselves," Captain Jack said, and somebody shot a gun into the ceiling. "Forty-five volunteers, hard-working pilgrims of this territory, ride with me and patrol the mining camps on the outside of town. Three quick shots brings us on a run, and we are never more than a minute from the commencement of action."

Charley said, "Shit, they shoot off side arms in this burg like they used it to keep time." Bill turned and saw him there, and smiled at that.

Captain Jack nodded. "Discipline is always a problem," he said, "in any military situation. Compounded here by the fact that most of the Minutemen have no experience with arms or the military. That is why I would ask you"—he was speaking to Bill now—"to join me as a leader of the Minutemen. Together, we could make Indian fighters of these pilgrims."

"*Da-me*," said the Mex.

Bill looked at Charley, dead solemn. Charley said, "I already been shot by accident, once in each leg. I know where fate intends to put the third one."

The bartender filled the Mex's glass, and he offered another toast. "*Tu mamá*," he said again.

"No *da-me*," Captain Jack said. "We're discussing the protection of the miners."

That stopped the Mex cold. He had repossessed the Indian's head and was standing with his foot on one of its ears. As he considered Captain Jack's words to him, he rolled the head back and forth under his foot, the way a white man might stroke his chin. Finally he seemed to decide on something. He raised the glass toward Captain Jack again and said, "Pro-tess-shion." Then he smiled and killed what was in the glass.

"This greaser wears on you," Captain Jack said to Bill, "but he has proved himself in combat." The Mex set his glass on the bar and picked up the Indian's head. The eyes had shut, like it had seen the bullet coming that shot him out of the Mex's arm.

"*Mis amigos*," the Mex said. He hugged Captain Jack, then Bill. Then he turned to the rest of the bar and said it again. "*Mis amigos*." He started out the door, and the miners and reprobates cheered him, and some of them shot their pistols into the ceiling. The Mex smiled and blew them kisses. That caused more shooting and cheering, and the Mex, in a moment Charley considered inspired, stood at the door to the Green Front and blew the room a kiss from his own lips, and then one from the Indian's.

Then he went outside, got on his horse, and drew his pistol. He rode back through town the way he had come in, holding the Indian's head by the hair so it could bounce, shooting his pistol into the air so nobody would miss it. He went out of the badlands into Deadwood proper, where he was arrested by Seth Bullock and escorted out of town.

The citizens of Deadwood did not wring their hands over the workings of the badlands, but they drew the line at being shot in the course of their daily affairs by ambassadors of that part of the city, particularly a greaser carrying a human head.

SHERIFF BULLOCK WAS JUST BACK FROM SEEING THE MEX OUT OF town, and was sitting down behind his desk when Boone May walked into the office. The office was at the corner of Main Street and Wall Street, and the sign across the front of it said DEADWOOD BRICKWORKS, INC. Beneath that were the words QUEENSWARE, FUR-NITURE, HARDWARE, LAMPS, WALLPAPER, ETC. And beneath that, in smaller letters, SHERIFF SETH BULLOCK.

Bullock's partner was a single-minded man named Solomon Star, who had come to Deadwood with him from Bismarck and put up the money for their business. He was tighter than Seth Bullock, and worried they were ordering too much, and too many different things. He had a wife back in Bismarck, but he had never loved anything but business, and did not see yet how much there was in Deadwood for the taking.

When Boone May walked in, Solomon Star was sitting at an-other desk, going over an ordering form. He had been against it when Bullock agreed to take over the unofficial duties of town sher-iff. He'd said they hadn't come to Deadwood to end up as statues in the town square. He took off his reading glasses and looked at Boone May, then he looked at Bullock.

"You see where this road leads, Mr. Bullock?" he said. "You can-not leave your door open to all God's creatures in the blind faith that they were made by God, and somehow reflect His image."

Solomon Star had a facility for that. It always sounded like he was quoting the Bible. Boone May walked across the room, track-ing mud, and sat down in the chair beside Bullock's desk. He was carrying a leather bag, and smelled like everything he'd touched or eaten in two months.

Bullock said, "Solomon, would you give us a few minutes?" He always spoke politely to his partner. The little man stood up and put his glasses in his shirt pocket. He took his coat off the hanger and held on to his shirt cuffs as they went into the sleeves of the coat. He stepped in front of the mirror and retied his necktie. His hat went on his head as carefully as you set dynamite.

Boone May watched him walk out of the office and close the door. He shook his head and smiled. "Paper-collars," he said. He didn't push that too far, though, because he wasn't sure that Seth Bullock wasn't part paper-collar himself.

Bullock sat still, looking at him in a steady, unfriendly way that made him forget the way he intended to put the case for collecting on Frank Towles's head. Seth Bullock was the hardest man to talk to that Boone May ever met.

"Lookie," he said, patting the bag, "I got Frank Towles's head that's worth two hundred dollars in Cheyenne. I shot him myself in a legal, fair fight, and did the public's welfare. So I don't see why you couldn't jurisdict this matter to give me the two hundred dollars here, so's I don't have to ride all the way back to Cheyenne."

Seth Bullock leaned closer. He was big through the arms and shoulders, as big as Boone. "Frank Towles's head isn't worth a nickel in Dakota Territory," he said.

"You could arrange it," he said.

Bullock shook his head. "I just paid a Mexican two hundred and fifty dollars gold for an Indian's head, out of the Board of Health funds, because that is municipal law. There is no such reward for Frank Towles." He didn't mention that he'd fined the Mexican the same $250 for endangering public safety, and taken his fifty percent collection fee.

Boone May covered his eyes. "You paid a Mex two hundred and fifty dollars?" he said. "And a white man's got to sit here and beg for what's comin' to him?"

"I never asked you to shoot Frank Towles," Bullock said.

"I don't need nobody to tell me to shoot Frank Towles. Where you find a dollar, you pick it up." He crossed one leg over the other and put his hands behind his head to wait. "I got a legal warrant."

Bullock said, "I don't know Frank Towles or what he looks like. That could be anybody, and you bring it in here tracking mud and say the town of Deadwood owes you two hundred dollars."

Boone May stared at Bullock a long minute, trying to decide what he meant about mud. Everybody tracked mud. He untied the bag in his lap, took the head out, and put it on Bullock's desk. "This here is what Frank looks like," he said. "You can ask Lurline Monti Verdi."

Bullock never acknowledged the head. Boone was watching to see if he was squeamish at heads, but it didn't do a thing, any more than it had for Lurline. Boone didn't know where the fault lay, but socially, Frank Towles's head was a failure. "You come and talk to me and W. H. Llewellyn fast enough when you need somebody killed," he said. "You never mentioned muddy when you wanted somebody tracked down. All I'm askin' here is fair treatment for a white man."

"I never said 'killed,'" Bullock said. "I always said 'apprehended.'"

Boone pointed to the head on the desk. "That's apprehended as you get."

Bullock still wouldn't look at it. Boone thought he must of practiced self-control. Then Boone thought of something else. "You seen Wild Bill yet?" The sheriff stiffened. "You plannin' on usin' him now, instead of me and W.H.? You tryin' to insult me and W.H. to get rid of us?"

"There's enough work to go around," Bullock said.

"Well, he ain't muddy," Boone said, "I admit that. That dandy with him, he might keep canaries."

Bullock shrugged. He'd been thinking about Bill that afternoon, trying to decide how to fit him into Deadwood Brickworks, Inc. It wasn't a question he could be useful. Anybody could be useful when you decided where they fit. That was what business was.

Solomon Star didn't fathom that. He saw the trading end of it clear enough. He saw the holes where money fell through and he knew ways to catch it before it hit the ground. But he didn't have a view of the future. He couldn't see that everything had to go somewhere.

Solomon came back into the office carrying a bag of roasted peanuts. There were peanut-sellers on every block in the city. He took off his coat and hat and straightened his vest and checked his pocket watch. It was an Elgin. Then he saw the head on Seth Bullock's desk.

"I wouldn't believe all them stories about Wild Bill," Boone May said to the sheriff. "I heard stories about Frank Towles here, and he went off crying like a baby . . ."

"What insult to God is that?" Solomon said, pointing at the desk.

"It's Frank Towles," Boone said. He watched Solomon Star, and was grateful to see there was still somebody that cared about a human head. He didn't know what the paper-collar was to the sheriff, but they had the same office and he decided to make his case to him too. "Sheriff don't want to pay me the reward on him, and I think he's got an obligation."

Solomon Star sat down at his desk and looked at the papers on top of it. Not like he was studying them, like he was trying to remember what they were. "He give a greaser two hundred and fifty dollars not more than an hour ago," Boone said.

Seth Bullock reached into a desk drawer and came out with a

pair of fireplace tongs, made in Baltimore, Maryland. To Boone they looked like giant tweezers. The sheriff worked the small end, and the big end opened, wider than Frank Towles's head, and then closed around it. He picked the head up with the tweezers and dropped it in Boone's lap. "When I need you for something," the sheriff said, "I'll come find you."

Boone thought it was just like Seth Bullock to have a head-mover in his desk. "I'll be in Cheyenne," he said. He put the head back in the bag and pulled the cord that closed the top. "And I ain't forgettin' who caused the inconvenience." It didn't have the right sound for a warning, though. It sounded half like a question.

Seth Bullock didn't move a muscle, he just stared. Boone stood up, looking for something more to say. He didn't like things to end sounding like questions. He didn't like nobody looking at him the way the sheriff was. "I wouldn't be countin' on Wild Bill too much," he said. Bullock still didn't answer. Boone said, "I wouldn't be countin' on nothing." But it still didn't sound like it should.

Boone walked out, passing the paper-collar, who was still sitting there staring at the top of his desk, and brushed him across the ear with the sack. He jumped about half a foot.

When the door shut, Solomon Star got up and went to the back of the store. He kept a pitcher of water there, and a bowl and some black soap on a cabinet, the only furniture he'd brought from his office in Bismarck. Seth Bullock had promised they would return for the rest of it.

Bullock followed him back now. Solomon poured water into the bowl and then worked the soap into it until the top was dark and bubbly. He got a washcloth out of one of the drawers in the cabinet, wet it, and centered it over his hand. He made the hand into a fist and began to scrub his ear.

Bullock looked at the faded yellow picture Solomon had hung on the wall. It was his mother, holding him on her lap. She had a jawline, the only one he'd seen like it was attached to Pink Buford's bulldog.

"Boone May is a fact of nature," Bullock said after a while. "There's worse than him around, ones that you can't aim in any direction at all."

Solomon quit scrubbing long enough to say, "He came into our place of business with a human head."

"Once something's dead, Solomon, it's dead."

Solomon began scrubbing again. His ear and all the skin around it were turning red. "It was a wanted man," Bullock said. "A killer of some kind . . . a thief. He could of robbed the stage we sent the payment for the kilns." Bullock saw that carried more weight with his partner than just being a killer. They'd put up sixty thousand dollars—Bullock had borrowed his end of it from Solomon—for three kilns. They were on the way now from Sioux City. Bullock saw a day coming when the whole city would be brick.

The soap had gotten up into Solomon's hair, and the gunk he used to keep it slick ran down his neck into his collar. "It isn't like there weren't hangings in Bismarck," Bullock said.

Solomon took the washcloth away from his ear, which was now the color of two-day-old frostbite, and began to dry himself off with a towel. "That's hanging," he said. "It's civilized. A proper gallows is a comfort to the aggrieved, but he came into our place of business with a human . . . head."

"Dead is dead, Solomon," Bullock said. "What you're talking about is manners." Solomon finished with the towel, which was black every place it had touched him, and picked up the mop. He followed Boone May's steps from Bullock's desk to the door, washing what he could off the floorboards. They were pine—there wasn't any hardwood to be had in Deadwood yet—and already warped and uneven. The office was one of the first three buildings erected in the gulch.

Then he washed the door handles, inside and out. When he had finished, Solomon threw the dirty water into the street and went back to the papers on his desk. He didn't say another word to Seth Bullock, and Bullock didn't say anything to him. Solomon Star's talent was money, Seth Bullock knew other things, principal among them when to leave things alone.

Not counting tents or the Chinese establishments, where Captain Jack said he would not set foot, there were sixteen barrooms in the badlands. Some of them had been thrown together in a day, and the ceilings would shift in a wind or a fight. Some of them, like the Gem and the Green Front, were built more slowly, with a stage and a bar and little rooms upstairs closed off the hallway by curtains, and a girl's name written in chalk above each one. The prettiest ones and the singers got rooms with doors.

Charley followed Bill and Captain Jack from one place to another, all that night. Captain Jack would drink only milk, Charley had quit after the Mex left the Green Front, but everyplace they went Bill accepted all hospitalities.

He drank and listened to stories of gunplay. There wasn't a pilgrim in town that didn't have a story to tell Bill Hickok about something he'd done with a gun. Some of them had shot the eyes out of Indians at a hundred yards, some of them had turned the tide of battles in the war. Captain Jack Crawford told the account of his own injuries at Spottsylvania three different times that night, which to Charley was unforgivable for a man drinking milk.

Captain Jack said it was while he was recovering in the hospital that the nurses there came to like him, and taught him to read and write. "If it hadn't been for that Reb ball that found me in the midst of combat," he said, "and knocked me unconscious so I could not continue fighting, I would never have learned to write a word." By then he had read the poem he wrote in the paper about Custer six or eight times.

"Burn the South," Charley said.

Captain Jack shook his head and signaled for silence. "The wounds of war heal," he said, "and we must heal with them, pards. We're all of one skin and one country, and it's best forgotten."

Charley couldn't see what it was about Captain Jack that Bill tolerated so long, but he wasn't giving off any signs to be left alone. Bill's parents had been shunned in Troy Grove, Illinois, before the war for keeping a station that smuggled runaway slaves to the North, and he wasn't normally receptive to the reasons that people decided they fought for after the war was over.

They went from the Green Front back to the Gem, and then to the Senate, then to half a dozen places that didn't have names, at least not on signs in front. They went to Shingle's Number 3, then to Nuttall and Mann's Number 10, where Bill met Pink Buford and his famous bulldog, Apocalypse. Bill and the dog were love at first sight. The dog sat at Bill's feet, licking himself, and followed him every time he went outside to relieve himself.

Pink Buford made a place for Bill and Captain Jack at the card table, and they played draw poker and drank gin and bitters until Bill had lost thirty dollars. Charley could see Pink Buford was as drunk as Bill—you would have thought drunker because Bill never lost his deportment—but Bill wasn't in a class with him at cards.

Bill miscalculated himself at the card table, but it was harmless. He didn't have any money to speak of—mostly it was just what Charley gave him—and he would put the game behind him as soon as he quit for the night. There wasn't anybody Charley knew who didn't miscalculate himself one way or another—the main categories were guns or understanding women—and cards was a better blind side than most.

Charley wondered sometimes where his own blind side was. It wasn't the kind of thing you came out and asked your partner, though, not if you respected keeping a distance.

Bill was still at the card table when Boone May came in the door. Charley was looking in that direction at the time, supporting his weight against the bar with his back and elbows, and he took one glance and thought of the way the Hills had looked to him on the day the boy had shot Bill's horse. Something out of the Devil's dreams.

"Oh, shit," the bartender said. "It's Boone and that damn head."

He came in carrying a bag by its drawstrings, half a foot taller than anybody else in the room. He was bug-eyed, and his head was a size to be noticeable even if it wasn't up there above anybody else's. As he walked past the card table, his look stopped on Bill, but only for a moment. Charley had never seen a human being with eyes like that who wasn't in the throes of strangulation.

Boone May moved through the crowd to a place next to Charley at the bar. He didn't push anybody out of the way to get there, he just took over the air they were using, and they moved to establish breathing room somewhere else. He put his hat and the bag on the bar in front of him and ordered a gin and bitters. The bartender, Harry Sam Young, did not know where to put the glass when he came back with it and was reluctant to touch the hat or the bag. And so he stood there until Boone slid them apart and made room.

Charley smiled at the sight of a monster drinking pink-colored concoctions. Then the man was looking at him, eyes like a scared horse, like there was too much juice in there for even a head that size to hold it. Charley kept his smile where it was.

Boone May studied him with one of his eyes. "Little fancy," he said, "you got a hundret and seventy dollars in gold?" Charley squared himself and set his jaw.

"A dandy with pearl-handled guns, he must got a hundret and seventy dollars." Charley's guns were .36 caliber Colt Navy revolvers, designed in 1851, and modified in Chicago to take modern cartridges. He cleaned them after every use, and made no apologies for how they looked. Them or himself. Charley gave people their distance, and did not give up his own to strangers. ". . . And fine linen," Boone May said. He reached for Charley's shirt, and Charley dropped his left hand to his side. There was a boning knife in back of the gun there, pearl-handled and sharp. If it touched you, it cut you. It cost Charley seventy dollars, having the handle remade to match the Colts.

The fingers stopped before they got to the shirt, as if the hand had thoughts of its own, and went sideways to the sack on the bar. Boone May said, "Here's your chance to get rich in the Hills, fancy. Thirty fast dollars." He opened the sack and pulled the head out by the hair. "This unfortunate goes by the name of Frank Towles. I got a legal warrant for his arrest, dead or alive, with a reward of two hundret dollars for the apprehendor."

The noise at the poker table had stopped. Charley turned to Bill, who was sitting straight and solemn with his back against the wall and the bulldog in his lap, and said, "You notice something peculiar about this town?"

Bill nodded, never changed expressions. "I never been anywhere," Charley said, "that so many people were walking around carrying spare heads." Bill smiled at that, Captain Jack Crawford began to lean away from it. It wasn't any contest who would be first under the table.

Charley turned back to Boone May to see where it would lead. It was a pattern to his life that he didn't understand. Things would stop before they happened. Like this man's fingers. If his fingers had touched Charley's shirt, the clean-up boy would of found them in the sawdust tomorrow morning. But at the last minute, they'd seemed to sense it—Charley had watched animals do the same thing at traps—and gone some other way.

That was a difference between Charley and Bill. Bill didn't give off the same warnings, or maybe it was that by the time somebody decided to aggravate Bill Hickok they'd quit listening to what their private voices were telling them.

"All you got to do," Boone May was saying, "is take the head in tomorrow and pick up the reward. Thirty dollars for no work at all." He smiled at Charley. "It ain't heavy, even for a fancy."

Charley looked him in the eye, motionless. Boone May pushed the head toward him, Charley stepped away. "You ain't afraid to touch it," Boone said, "it ain't nothin' but a head." He slid it another six inches. "You git the head and the bag both for a hundret and seventy dollars, I'll even put it inside for you. All you got to do is take the package in and pick up the reward, make yourself thirty dollars."

He waited for Charley to answer, then shook his head. "Frank Towles is been nothing but trouble since I kilt him," he said.

Harry Sam Young mixed Boone another gin and bitters. "Maybe you shouldn't of cut off his head," he said. "Maybe it's bad luck."

Boone turned one eye on the bartender, the other one looked adjacent. Charley felt his own weight change with the bug-eyes settled on something else. "I didn't have no choice," Boone said. There was a whine in his voice now. "The way it happened was a shotgun, blew most of Frank's neck off, so's he was only attached to himself by a thread. It just didn't make no sense to bring it all in together, especially now I got to go all the way to Cheyenne to collect on him."

"Must of been close range," the bartender said.

"About two inches," Boone said. "But nothin' to do with it has been right since I pulled the trigger."

"You believe in the spirit world?" the bartender said after a while. "There's a faro dealer over to Jim Persate's place, a French woman named Madame Moustache, who talks to the spirits of the dead. Maybe she could talk to Frank for you."

"What the hell am I going to say to Frank?" Boone said. "I shot him. Besides, I seen that French girl, and Frank's got too much pride to talk to somebody looks like that."

"You could tell him it was just business, nothin' personal between the two of you," the bartender said.

Boone May looked at the head. "No," he said, "he took it personal." The barkeep shrugged and returned to his duties. Boone May seemed to have forgotten Charley was there, and Bill went back to his cards, holding them up where the bulldog could read them too. Once in a while Boone would steal a look in that direction, but something told Bill when he was being watched, and he caught him every time.

When he thought it over later, Boone decided it was the dog giving him signals.

CHARLEY WOKE UP SUNDAY MORNING LISTENING TO A METHODIST. HE was brought up in the faith and recognized the sound before he could pick up the words.

He'd kept his sleeping quarters in the back of the wagon. Clean sheets, blankets, a pillow. He took his clothes off at night, even on the coldest nights, to keep the bed clean. Charley had spent as many nights on the ground as anybody, but when he got into a bed he didn't like to smell a previous sleeper, even himself.

He sat up and looked out the back of the wagon. The preacher was standing on a wood box in the middle of the street, not fifty yards from the wagon. His suit must have been a hundred years old. "Jesus loves you, every one," he said.

There was a small group of men collected in front of him, most of them holding their hats in their hands, and staring at the mud they were standing in. There was a way clothes hung when you left them on a year that looked like old people's skin.

Charley rubbed his face and leaned his head out of the wagon. Bill was asleep on the ground, next to him was the dog, and next to him was the boy. "Dear Lord," the preacher said, "deliver us from evil, find us with Your love in this place and protect us . . ." From time to time, a dollar would drop into the hat that he'd put on the box next to him.

If the preacher saw the donations, he did not acknowledge it. "Keep these miners in Your thoughts, Lord, just as they keep You in theirs . . ." Charley got into his pants and climbed slowly out of the wagon, easing himself to the ground so not to jolt his legs. Morning after was always a bad time for his joints.

He got his toilet kit from the front of the wagon—soap and razor, bicarbonate of soda, and a mirror—and walked up the street to the bathhouse. The place was built of wood and leaned downhill, to the north, at a subtle angle that would make you look twice to see if the roof was tilted or you were. A man in rags and a black Eastern hat was sitting on a stool outside, beside a burlap bag he had gathered and tied at the top. There was something wrong with his neck, the way he held his head. "Clean water is fifteen cents," he said. "Hot water is another dime, but there ain't none today."

Charley saw he was soft-brained right away. "It's a nice business you got here," Charley said, looking around.

The man shrugged. "The man that built it is a doctor," he said. "Dr. O. E. Sick. He give it to me on the promise I'd quit my suicides."

Charley nodded politely, as if that was the way they did business everywhere. "That was a smart thing, to take it," he said.

The man shrugged. "Ain't nobody uses it but whores," he said.

"Dr. Sick said he didn't have time to be overlooking the bathing habits of upstairs girls, he was too busy cleaning up their mischief. It didn't make him no money anyway. Did you say clean water?"

The building was about twenty feet square, with a bathtub in each corner. There was a stove in the middle. Two of the tubs were half full. The water was dark, the surfaces speckled with insects. Some were swimmers and some were floaters. "Clean water," Charley said.

"Hot's an extra dime," the man said, "but there ain't any." He took two buckets out the back door and filled them in the Whitewood Creek, then emptied them into the tub nearest the front door. He repeated that until the water was a foot from the lip of the tub. Charley got out of his pants and slipped in. It took his breath. The man stood at the door, smiling. "Water this cold is supposed to be ice," Charley said.

The man went out the door and came back in with his sack. He stayed in one spot and watched while Charley scrubbed himself with soap. The soap was hard and grainy; it felt like sand against his skin. Charley foresaw the invention of a more agreeable soap, and there wouldn't be room in the bathhouses for all the customers. "What you got in your sack?" he said.

"My bottles," the man said. "I got more at home. Eleven hundred and sixteen, and eight today."

"Well," Charley said, "you got a business and a hobby."

"Doc Howe wouldn't work on no suicides," the soft-brain said. "He says ain't nobody going to make deliberate work for him, so Dr. Sick always had to come . . ."

"I meant the bottles," Charley said. "Suicide's no hobby."

The man gave him a soft-brained grin and shrugged. "Whenever I thought of it, I did it," he said. "I don't know how many times." Charley settled into the tub. He liked a man that knew he had 1116 bottles at home, but didn't know how many times he'd attempted suicide. "Sometimes I et poison eggs," the soft-brain said, "sometimes I put morphine in me, onct I tried to hang myself." He pulled the collar of his shirt away to show Charley the disfigurement.

"I already seen," he said. Charley did not like to look at scars or goiters or club feet. He thought of his wife's body then, white and slender, not a mark on it. She liked to touch the places on his legs where the bullets had gone in, he never understood that. His right leg, the wound was like half a star, the color of ketchup, about three inches below the hip. His brother Steve had shot him and took the ball out himself. He used Charley's hunting knife, and every time Charley had moved, Steve said he was sorry.

The other leg, the ball had gone in from behind, farther down than Steve's. It was a Ute Indian who did that while they were climbing a tree outside a bear den. It went in the back and came out the top, which did not leave as clear a reminder as Steve's surgery. It was just two dents, one black and one the same red color as the half star. He didn't hold it against the Utes, or even that Ute, but he never went up a tree ahead of an Indian again.

Matilda Nash was attracted to those spots from the time she was fourteen, when she first saw them. She would touch his scars, and his legs and his testicles, as if she knew what it felt like to be a man. At first when she touched him, it didn't seem possible that she was only fourteen years old.

On the other hand, sometimes she would take his peeder in her small, white hands and talk to it, and Charley would promise himself to marry her because if he didn't, he was a child molester. She would encircle the head with one hand and squeeze, and then, with her finger, work the opening in it up and down like a little mouth. She called it "Baby Chipper," and invented it stories.

She talked with Charley's peeder from the first time they undressed, through most of their wedding night, and all the nights after. Sometimes the stories were exciting to the imagination. She talked with his peeder right up until the time Bill came through Empire, a month late for the wedding, and walked into their bedroom drunk one night by accident.

He'd never said a word about what he saw or heard, but she never talked to Charley's peeder again. Charley thought she might pick the stories back up again after Bill was gone, but it never happened.

The world was not without make-believe long, however. A few months later, there was an eyewitness story in *Harper's Weekly* of how Bill had wiped out all ten of the M'Kandass Gang, and after that, everything he did got immortalized. If he ate pork, he shot the pig at high noon in the street. He had been famous before, but after *Harper's Weekly* the reporters came out from San Francisco and New York and Boston and Philadelphia. Bill saw where it was leading, and let it take him along.

He adjusted to being famous. He encouraged the stories; he helped make some of them up. It led to more reporters, and women, and now and then a fight, which was no great inconvenience. There was something in him that turned cold in a fight, and he would kill what was in front of him without a thought, and walk away from it afterwards like it wasn't his business. It was a kind of purity.

He was the best pistol shot Charley ever saw, and the only shootist there was who would fight with his hands. There was no question God had given him uncommon gifts, and he went where they took him.

Charley's gift was harder to put your finger on. When they were alone, it didn't seem like a hair's difference between them, but somehow in public Bill's cork floated one way and Charley's floated another. People told things to Charley. He thought it might have been because he was short. A man who doesn't mind being short is everybody's friend.

This soft-brain, for instance, standing in the door telling him about his suicides while Charley sat in ice water. "Poison eggs is turrible," he said. "It's better to hang than to eat poison eggs."

Charley ducked his head under the water and came up with his hair pressed all around his face. He worked the soap into his head, feeling for ticks and anything else that might of crawled in there since he'd been in Deadwood.

"How come a good man like yourself would want to cash in ahead of schedule?" Charley said.

"When I thought of it, I never thought that far," he said. "Just to the doing part. A lot of others done it since I been here. A man hung himself and set a fire underneath, so there wouldn't be no remains for this world." The soft-brain looked at Charley. "I never did that," he said. "I wouldn't want to do nothing strange for people to talk about afterwards. I want them to talk about the Bottle Man right."

Charley made a note to keep Malcolm away from the bathhouse. He ducked his head under the water again, to rinse the soap out of his hair, and climbed out of the tub. The soft-brain handed him his pants. "I stopped," he said. "Dr. Sick give me this business to make me promise. That's how I got into this career."

Charley shaved in the tub water, brushed his hair, and scrubbed his teeth with bicarbonate of soda. He rubbed a little of that under his arms too, and then put on a clean shirt. He gave the soft-brain a dollar. "Hot water tomorrow," he said.

The Bottle Man's head went even farther off center, to see if he was teasing. "You comin' back tomorrow?"

"Every day," Charley said.

The soft-brain said, "That's good, I like you to come here." Which was the direction of Charley Utter's talent.

When Charley got back to camp, Bill was sitting bare-chested on a tree stump, writing a letter. The Methodist was still at it in the street, saying the same things to a different flock. Bill had put his saddle on the ground in front of him, and was using that to hold his stationery. His nose was about an inch over the pencil. Charley marveled at the angles his body went. The boy was still asleep, and now that Charley was clean he could smell the liquor on both of them.

Charley climbed into the wagon to straighten his bed, and when he came out Bill handed him the letter. Bill always liked to have Charley check his letters because he believed they would end up famous after he was dead. Bill never wanted to be embarrassed, especially after he was dead and couldn't right it. He had a beautiful penmanship, Charley thought, maybe what a doctor's hand would look like.

My own darling Wife Agnes
I have but a few moments left before this letter Starts
I never was as well in my life but you would laugh to see me now
Just got in from Prospecting will go a way again to morrow will write In the morning but good newse
My friend will take this to Cheyenne if he lives I don't expect to hear from you but it is all the same
I no my Agnes and only live to love hur never mind Pet we will have a home yet then we will be so happy
I am all most shure I will do well hear
The man is huring me Good by Dear Wife love to Emma.
                                                    J. B. Hickok
                                                    "Wild Bill"

Bill watched Charley while he read it. "How does it sound?" he said.

"Prospecting?" Charley said.

Bill shrugged. "You got to put down something, that's what a letter is. I mean the tone. Is the tone true?"

Charley gave it back to him. "You know Agnes's dispositions," he said. "How do you talk to her?"

"What's that matter?"

"The way to write letters to somebody," Charley said, "is the way you talk."

Bill was embarrassed. "What kind of sweethearts do you send Matilda?" he said. "I'd like to see one of those letters."

"I don't put down anything personal," he said. "I write business letters. Everything I ever said to Matilda she took three different ways, and wondered what did I mean by each of them. I don't say anything I don't have to, and I sure as Jesus don't put it down on paper. There is such a thing as looking for trouble."

Bill looked at the paper in his hand. Charley said, "Of course, I've been married a long time."

Bill said, "Me and Agnes never started out from the same place. That makes it harder. I can't live like a paper-collar in St. Louis the rest of my life, and I can't bring her here. She isn't used to a place like this."

In the street, the Methodist was asking God for protection. Bill and Charley listened to him a few minutes. The letter to Agnes was still in Bill's hand, between them. "Did you know that preacher left his wife behind too?" Bill said. "Jack Crawford told me that. He came out here to find gold and left his wife and four babies back in the States. Sends them every cent he earns at the sawmill, and lives off what he makes standing on that packing crate."

"A minister that works?" Charley said. He looked at the Methodist closer and noticed he was preaching with his eyes shut now. And Charley loved God for many things, among them not calling him to the ministry.

BOONE MAY SLAPPED HIMSELF AWAKE. HE COULD HAVE SLEPT ALL morning, even with the snoring, but Jane Cannary had rolled in her sleep and come to rest with her mouth next to his ear. As she snored, she blew, and the breath in his ear felt like insects to Boone, who reached out in his sleep and slapped himself across the side of the head. The hand was cupped and caught his ear, and there was an empty, numb feeling inside there, along with a sort of ricochet noise that he associated with the sound of going deaf.

He opened his eyes and saw calico-pattern walls. Half the tents in town had the same walls, it was the only material you could get at Farnum's until there was a new shipment. The tent was open, and he looked out to the street, thinking of how easy he could of got robbed in the night.

He sat up at the thought, and began looking for Frank Towles's head. His guns and pants were beside him on the ground, but the bag was gone. He got his underwear on and crawled out from under his blanket. He picked up Jane's pants and then her shirt and then her boots, throwing everything out the front of the tent. Nothing.

He didn't want to, but he pulled the cover off Jane and looked underneath that too. Her skin was pale and bruised and old. She was a big-boned girl, but fat. Spindly legs, soft-looking arms, no chest to her at all. He had never seen a woman black and blue so many different places. It looked like they'd dragged her all the way from Chicago. And she was as ripe as a live body gets.

"Whatever you got on your mind," she said without opening her eyes, "furget it."

He looked at her face then, a man's face. Not a man you'd want to know. Flat eyes, no lips to speak of, she had a nose similar to the outlaw Big Nose George. Boone stuck his head out of the tent and took a few breaths of fresh air.

"It wouldn't hurt nothing," he said when he came back in, "you was to visit the bathhouse once."

"I give it a bath once," she said, pulling the blanket back over her body, "and a Cheyenne peeder come floating out." Boone felt himself getting sick.

"Where is Frank Towles's head?" he said. "You're the only one could of took it."

"The buck was about twenty-two years old," she said, "handsome for that breed. He was desirious to make a papoose with Calamity Jane, and it wasn't till the last minute I changed my mind. But shit, a lady's got a right to change her mind." The Indian story was something Jane said in the morning to the ugliest ones and the youngest ones, to keep them from falling in love.

Boone went back outside and lost what was in his stomach. It was mostly pink, from the gin and bitters. "So whatever you got in mind this morning," she said from inside the tent, "think of that redskin. It's Sunday morning and I save that for the Lord."

When he felt better, Boone looked again, this time without moving anything. Sometimes things was easier to see if you wasn't looking as hard. And there it was. Jane sat up and spit, and the bag was where her head had been. She'd been using Frank for a pillow. He picked it up before she could lie back down. "You got no respect for personal property, Jane," he said.

She laughed at him, and said, "Gee," and "Haw," which was the words she'd used when it was still Saturday night, to tell him which way she wanted him to move.

Jane had arrived in Deadwood that same day from Fort Laramie, where she'd been hired to replace a bullwhacker that had come down with torpid fever on the way out from Cheyenne. He was yellow-skinned and depressed by the time Jane saw him, and she doubted if they'd got him to town in time to save him. The cure for torpid fever was Tutt's Pills and Phosphoric Air. You took the pills in the morning and took Phosphoric Air at night, and the pain in your head went away if it was in time, and you went soft-brained if it wasn't.

Jane was a natural nurse. The sight of a sick man brought something out in her. She knew cures for all the diseases that had cures, which worked for what, and she took the sick bullwhacker's job with a sorry heart over the circumstances.

The man who owned the bull train had a sorry heart too. Jane had done some bullwhacking for him before. She could swear with the best, but where a man would use a whip to influence the oxen left or right, Jane would get drunk and abuse their hides. It wasn't intentional, but whenever Jane ran a wagon, the cattle came in scarred. Open scars were collecting spots for grubs, and grubs would cripple the oxen until they were only good for slaughter and hides. Not that scarred hides were worth much.

But Jane was the only unemployed bullwhacker in Fort Laramie at the time the train came through, and the man who owned it offered her thirty dollars to take the sick driver's team the rest of the way into Deadwood. She wanted to go back to the Hills, and swore to stay sober.

She had been there before with Lieutenant Colonel Richard T. Dodge's expedition in 1875, when all the boys got the summer complaint drinking bad water from Beaver Creek. Jane dressed like a soldier and rode like a soldier and panned the creeks like a soldier, until she was finally discovered by California Joe Milner, who had guided the expedition into the Hills, getting lost sometimes for two and three days at a stretch. He'd caught her doing business. She was charging the Army boys a dollar a turn, half the regular rate. Jane was never one to exploit the U.S. Army, which, to her thinking, was a damn sight more than you could say for California Joe.

He came into her tent—there was two or three boys waiting outside—and caught her with a corporal. Recognizing her, he called Jane a notorious harlot. The corporal was trying to put all his clothes on at the same time. She lay back, her Army uniform open here and there, and congratulated California Joe for finally finding something he knew what it was.

Lieutenant Colonel Dodge decided against sending her back because of the Indians, but they watched her every minute after that, and it was never in Jane's plans to be watched except at her invitation.

They were five weeks in the Hills and she was glad to leave, but later she pined to return. It wasn't that the Hills had looked that good the first time—Jane never cared much for scenery—but the stories made it sound brand new.

And it was someplace to go. She had about wore out Fort Laramie.

There was another reason, too. She'd heard Bill was headed there. That he'd come through Fort Laramie with a wagon train not four days before the bull train. Jane had told more lies about Bill Hickok than *Harper's Weekly.* She had said they were pards, she had said they fought Indians together, she had said they were married. Calamity Jane Cannary felt like there was a link between them, and that when they finally met, Bill would see that they was two of a kind. She never saw herself embraced with him, she had visions of saving his life.

On her first night in Deadwood, though, she'd run into Boone May at Nuttall and Mann's Number 10, and bunked down with him. She was comfortable with Boone. She had the feeling that nobody homelier than herself would notice how she looked.

She got up now and dressed, leaving the front of her shirt unbuttoned, and crawled out of the tent. The preacher was still out there on his packing crate, his arms reaching into the air now, pulling at the air while he asked God's protection. It reminded her of a child pulling on its mother's skirts, trying to get her to notice it was there.

She stood up and tucked her shirt into her pants. She strapped her gun belt around her waist, and then slid it to the left until the buckle was in back and the pistol lay at an angle across her lower stomach. She thought it fit her, to wear her protection over her womanhood. She tied a wide yellow scarf around her neck and pulled her hat down right to her ears. The hat was perfectly round. She thought it softened her face.

She walked from the tent to the preacher in long strides, unmindful of the mud. "Let this day be peaceful, Lord," the preacher was saying, "so that we may preparest ourselves for the hardships we have found in this place . . ."

Jane pushed her way through miners, paper-collars, tourists, even a few ladies—not upstairs girls, but ladies—and got to the packing crate. She picked up the preacher's hat and screamed her eagle scream. It was a noise that nobody but Calamity Jane could make. She caused it by pulling air into her voice box instead of blowing it out, and nobody who ever heard it denied it sounded like an eagle.

It was a noise that stopped people from whatever they were doing, particularly talking with the Lord. The congregation looked up from the mud, almost in unison, to see what it was. Then, together, they took a step back. There wasn't many of them who had come across anything this remote.

She closed the distance with an exaggerated stride and pushed the preacher's hat at the first miner she reached. "Limber up, pilgrim," she said. "The old mountain goat looks broke, and I intend to collect about ninety dollars for him." The miner stood still, looking at her, and she kicked him in the leg. "I said git down into your pokes now and come up with some cash."

The miner reached into his pocket and found his purse. He picked a tiny piece of gold out and put it in the hat. A few of the miners who panned in the Whitewood had claims that could make them fifty dollars a day. Most of them sat on their heels in the water all day for two or three dollars, enough to find something to eat.

Most of them already knew that they weren't going to make a go of it placer-mining. Their hopes went a different way now, that the little pieces of ground they'd staked out and claimed would be worth more to somebody else.

Jane passed through the miners, getting money for the preacher. He had stopped when she'd done her eagle scream, but now, even while she was walking through the crowd with his hat, he started again.

THE PREACHER'S NAME WAS HENRY HIRAM WESTON SMITH, AND HE had been in the Hills almost a year. First in Custer, then Hill City, then Deadwood. As the gold strikes moved north, Preacher Smith moved with them. He'd wintered in Deadwood, and it had taken the life out of his face. The weather, or the things he'd seen.

He had reasons besides preaching for coming to Deadwood, and he was ashamed of them. There was gold here, and in her whole life his wife had never had comforts.

But the reasons had faded in the winter, and now there was nothing but the Lord. Who he realized he'd misunderstood. No man understood the Lord. Henry Hiram Weston Smith had read the Bible from one end to the other. There were nights he dreamed whole chapters, but where he used to see God in those dreams, now he just felt Him. Preacher Smith was afraid to look on Him, even in his sleep, for fear of what he would see.

He had cast aside portions of the Bible, and never read from it now when he preached, although he never preached without it in his hand. Once or twice in a service, a little piece of it would slip into his sermon—there was comfort in the New Testament, and the miners needed comfort—but he didn't hold it out for them, like it was a gift they could take if they wanted it. The greatest misunderstanding in the world was that salvation was there for the asking.

Preacher Smith was thirty-one years old, and he looked fifty.

"Thou created us in Thy image," he said now. "Grant us Thy strength for the tests ahead . . ." It had come to the preacher lately that the image was closer than he had previously thought. He had watched men go soft-brained from the winter's cold and hate, kill themselves and each other, and he had begun to see the Lord in that too.

"Keep us to the good, Lord," he said. "Do not let us stray." As he said that, Jane Cannary set the hat on the crate next to his feet. He saw her there, but never looked down. He was coming to the important part now, to the idea of an evil side to the Lord. It wasn't two different things, the Lord and the Devil. He had been on this spot all morning getting to it, and now it was coming. They were one and the same.

Jane made a noise in her throat and spat. He didn't look down, but she had distracted him, and he was losing track of it. There was a way the Lord could be evil and still be the Lord, and he had almost gotten to it. He closed his eyes and tried to concentrate.

"Look down here, you old fool," Jane said. When he didn't answer, she made another eagle scream, which opened the preacher's eyes. He stared down, and the homeliest woman he had ever seen was standing at his feet, open-chested, like a messenger from the

Lord's bad side. "There's plenty of time to preach," she said. "Now pick up this damn money before these sheep-lovers change their mind and take it back."

He looked in his hat then, and saw there were several dollars in folding money and gold dust. He didn't know what kind of message it was, but something was still changing between him and the Lord. And even with all he had seen, there was something the Lord had to show him yet.

BOONE MAY WENT LOOKING FOR LURLINE MONTI VERDI. HE HAD BEEN with Jane twice before, in Cheyenne and Sundance, and both times he hadn't felt right until he'd been with a regular woman to wash out the taste. It was something about her that made him feel little. He needed to smell Lurline's toilet water and feel her underneath him again, where he decided things right down to when she breathed.

Lurline wasn't in her room at the Gem. He walked in without knocking, and it was just as he'd left it the day before. She hadn't made the bed, or even swept the pieces of mirror glass off the floor. Lurline was always cleaning something, picking some speck of food off his coat or face. She hadn't been back.

He thought of Wild Bill then, and the way she'd looked at him out the window. Boone felt bad. He didn't like the idea of his own woman—which she was whenever Boone wanted her to be—running off with Bill and his fancy friend. He wondered if she'd done them both, and the feeling that started when he woke up with Jane got worse.

He sat down on her bed and took Frank Towles's head out of the sack. What had the bartender said? Maybe Frank's spirit was angry and he ought to see Madame Moustache about it? He thought about that and decided to live with the ghost a while longer.

"Goddamn you, Frank," he said, staring into the face. It was looking less like Frank every day. As a matter of fact, it was looking less like a face.

Boone began to see a plot. He'd take the head all the way back to Cheyenne, and every day it would change a little more, look a little less human, until the day he got there it wouldn't look like nothing.

"Goddamn you, Frank," he said again. "You'd do that to me, wouldn't you?"

And that is how it happened that Al Swearingen came to the door of Lurline Monti Verdi's room, meaning to hit her in the eye for missing her obligations the night before, and found Boone May instead, talking to a head. He stood in the door until Boone looked up.

"Where's Lurline?" Swearingen said. Boone May didn't try to put the head away or hide it behind him; there wasn't an ounce of social grace in his body. "Boone? You seen Lurline?"

"The last I seen your sorprano," Boone said, "she was running skirts-up down the stairs in the direction of Bill Hickok. That was yesterday."

Swearingen looked around the room, then walked over the window and looked there. "She didn't sing last night," he said. "I paid her to sing, and she didn't set foot in the Gem all night long."

Boone shrugged. "Well, I ain't got her under the bed," he said, "besides which, I got business problems of my own."

Swearingen didn't ask what problems, because it might of had something to do with the head. He didn't trust Boone May; there wasn't nobody he wouldn't kill. Swearingen included. He pictured what that would be like, trying to talk him out of it. Floating his words out toward that monster head, they'd get as far inside as snowflakes.

Boone was telling it anyway. "The sheriff won't give me my two hundret dollars from Frank Towles," he said. "Going to make me ride all the way to Cheyenne." Boone shook his head. "I don't know what's got into him, thinking I got nothing to do but ride to Cheyenne. He's quick enough to come running when he needs something done."

Swearingen said, "Seth Bullock ain't nothing different from me, except his business location." Swearingen didn't like Boone May or Seth Bullock either, but with Bullock it wasn't because he couldn't of talked him out of killing him.

He was beginning to think that Bullock was smarter than he was, that Bullock had figured out something about Deadwood that he hadn't thought of. Swearingen couldn't imagine what it was. The money came to the badlands. If a pilgrim had a hundred dollars, where else did you want to be to get it away from him?

There was something about Seth Bullock, though, that wasn't in a hurry. Swearingen didn't trust anybody that didn't scramble for spilled money. It was like he knew he would get it all later.

"Maybe he thinks he's got Wild Bill now, he don't need W.H. and me," Boone said.

"Wild Bill ain't going to change Deadwood," Swearingen said.

"Well," Boone said, "he's been here one night, and you lost your sopranie, I can't find nothing to fuck on a Sunday morning, and Seth Bullock won't give me two hundret dollars for Frank Towles's head. That ain't bad for a start."

"I come in the same time he did," Swearingen said. "I was eight days on the train with him and about twenty wagons of China whores, and he never touched none of them or none of mine."

Boone May looked at him a long time. "That don't sound normal," he said.

"He drinks," Swearingen said, "but he don't have nothing to do with the girls."

"I heard he got married," Boone said.

"I'm talkin' about his health here," Swearingen said. "I don't think he intends to live long."

"He eat?"

Swearingen nodded.

Boone said, "And I seen him drinking."

"I told you that already."

Boone closed his eyes and thought. Swearingen felt relief to be out from under his stare. Those were terrible bug-eyes, and they didn't even operate together. "Well," Boone said after a while, "it ain't a cancer. If he was to fuck and drink but not eat, then it could be a cancer. Or just drink, but not to fuck or eat. But this . . ." He rubbed his chin, going over the symptoms. "It could be torpid fever," he said.

"He don't look like that," Swearingen said. "His carriage's good. Torpid fever's yellow-skinned and swoped posture."

"All I know," Boone said, "if he don't intend to live long I wisht he'd hurry up with it. It's a lot of wasted thought he's already caused if he's about to die."

"There's a time for everybody," Swearingen said. He was thinking of the boy. He had been thinking of the boy, one way or another, since they hooked up at Fort Laramie.

Boone stood up and put Frank Towles's head back in the bag. "How much did you say?" Swearingen said.

"Two hundret dollars," Boone said, and sat back down. Al Swearingen was one of maybe four people Boone knew who had two hundred dollars. Probably had it in his pocket. "I could let you have it for less," he said. "You could take it back with you when you went to Cheyenne again."

"I just been to Cheyenne."

"I'll take a hundret and fifty," Boone said. "I ain't anxious to see that place right now."

Swearingen smiled at him. "Sitting Bull been visiting you in your dreams?"

"Shit," he said.

"What about Wild Bill?" he said. "You scairt of Wild Bill Hickok?" Boone didn't see where it was going. "All the things I ever heard about you," Swearingen said, "nobody ever mentioned scairt."

Boone put one of his bug-eyes on him then, full weight. "If there was a legal warrant for Wild Bill," he said, "I'd put his head right here on the bed next to Frank Towles."

Swearingen looked back and believed him. He remembered the way his oysters tried to climb back up inside when Bill ordered him into his own wagon and made him hand the reins to a whore. "What if it wasn't a legal warrant?" he said.

"What if it wasn't?" Boone said. He'd forgotten the cool feeling in his own balls the night before, when Bill had caught his eyes in the bar. He wished Al Swearingen would get to what he was going to say about the two hundred dollars. Wild Bill had took enough of Boone's time already.

"I heard that he come to Deadwood to the same purpose he went to Abilene and Cheyenne," Swearingen said.

"He ain't got the authority here," Boone said.

"Not yet."

"Don't play the larks with me," Boone said. "Say what you're going to say."

Swearingen said, "If you was to put two heads there on the bed, what would that cost?"

"Frank's worth two hundret dollars, at least," Boone said. "I already told you that."

Swearingen shook his head. "If he was there with the other head we was talking about, that might be worth two hundred dollars," he said.

"To who?"

"If it was the head we was talking about," he said, "to me."

"A hundret dollars each," Boone said.

But Swearingen saw what he was thinking. "No," he said, "two hundred for both of them, and you can keep Frank Towles."

It seemed different to Boone, put that way. The line between right and wrong was the law, and once you was on the safe side of it, there wasn't much you couldn't do, if you used common sense who you done it to, and kept it out of view. The thought he could end up staring at the sky through tree limbs never entered Boone's mind while he was working, because he stayed on the safe side of the line.

Taking Wild Bill seemed to cross that. If worse came to worse, you couldn't even say you mistook him for somebody else, with that head of hair. Boone had never killed anybody popular before. He wondered if you took their place afterwards. He was considering that when he happened to look down at Frank Towles's head in his lap. "You only take somebody's place," he said out loud, "if they're a better class than you."

Swearingen nodded, like he'd been thinking the same thing. Boone didn't like that. He wished there was some way to kill Al Swearingen instead, and collect two hundred dollars for that. He pictured Swearingen trying to talk him out of it. It didn't make sense to kill Wild Bill instead of a whore man.

Like everybody else in Deadwood, Boone May sometimes wished the world was a more logical place.

THE FIRST RESPECTABLE PEOPLE CHARLEY UTTER ENCOUNTERED IN Deadwood, unless you counted Captain Jack Crawford, were Jack Langrishe and his wife, Elizabeth. They came to Charley's camp on the Whitewood about five o'clock Sunday afternoon to meet Bill. They said they'd been rehearsing all day.

"Yes, ma'am," Charley said. He took off his hat to make her acquaintance. She was a confident-looking woman, half a foot taller than her husband, with hair like a barn fire. Mr. Langrishe wore a suit and a string tie. He had a handshake that could of cracked Brazil nuts.

"I have come to Deadwood," Mr. Langrishe announced, "to bring cultural matters to the Black Hills." His voice resembled Captain Jack's.

"The place could use some cultural matters," Charley said, and realized he was still staring at the missus.

Jack Langrishe smiled. He said, "My wife, as you can see, is an actress. The rest of my troupe is still at the theater, preparing for tonight's performance." Langrishe pointed up the street and Charley nodded, as if he knew exactly what Langrishe was talking about.

"When we heard that Mr. Hickok had arrived in the city," Mrs. Langrishe said, "it seemed an act of providence." She smiled at Charley and a humming began in his peeder. Her being an actress, he guessed it was nothing personal.

"Well," Charley said, "Bill will surely be glad to hear you came by. He enjoys a good play more than most." They seemed to be looking behind him now, so Charley stepped out of the way.

"I was wondering," Mrs. Langrishe said, "if Mr. Hickok was about. We would like to invite him—invite you both—to tonight's opening. It just seemed too fortuitous that you had arrived in time."

"I'm afraid Mr. Hickok is attending some business," Charley said, "but I'm sure he'll be back." Freckles floated down into Mrs. Langrishe's blouse like sparks from the roof. "I will be glad to forward your invitation."

Mrs. Langrishe was looking at him again in a way that would have been uncomfortable if she wasn't an actress. Maybe her husband didn't care if you entertained his wife, as long as he'd got to break your knuckles first. As a rule Charley did not entertain married women, but he was human.

Her skin was as white as Matilda's, her teeth were white another way, and set off the tip of her tongue. He thought there must of been bones in those bosoms to hold them up. He moved his eyes off her, an act of will. Mr. Langrishe offered his hand again, which Charley took. "We will save you two seats in the orchestra," he said.

As soon as Charley got his eyes off Mrs. Langrishe, he began to smell her. Her perfume had to come from a thousand miles away. He smelled the perfume, but he couldn't smell her underneath it, so she didn't use it instead of soap. He thought he could feel the heat of her body. Jack Langrishe was crushing his hand again; he noticed that and squeezed back just enough to get his knuckles off the top of each other.

It was a class of people that squeezed you like that. Generals did it, the governor of Colorado did it too. Charley had taken the governor elk-hunting in the mountains near Middle Park and ended up carrying him twelve miles back to camp, through two and three feet of snow, after the governor had stepped into the fire and broke his ankle. At least he said it was broke. The governor of Colorado weighed close to as much as an elk himself, and one hundred yards out of camp he got down off Charley's back and limped in, using Charley's shoulder for support. Then he'd shaken hands with Charley for his official photographer, who was disappointed not to get a shot of the governor with a dead elk. The governor paid Charley and said he'd send him a copy of the picture. The bones in Charley's hands were sore for days, and he guessed the picture got lost in the mail.

"Are you and Mr. Hickok partial to Bronson Howard?" Mrs. Langrishe asked. He looked at her again, and she'd gotten prettier while her husband was shaking his hand. "Or do you prefer the classics?"

Before Charley could think which side he and Bill took in the matter, she was saying they did both. "Tonight we're offering Mr. Howard's *Banker's Daughter*," she said, "but next week we have Shakespeare's *Macbeth*. I'm sure we'll find something to your taste, Mr. Utter. And Mr. Hickok's."

"Shakespeare is one of our favorites," he said. And then he bowed. He was thirty-seven years old, and that was his first one.

He watched them walk back in the direction Mr. Langrishe had pointed. They went maybe two hundred yards and then crossed the street where the boards were laid across the mud, and disappeared into a wood building. Two carpenters were hammering nails into the roof, which was made mostly of canvas.

Charley studied the building and saw that the carpenters had hung the canvas from the top beam and then run it to the lowest point of the roof, securing it there with different-sized pieces of board nailed to the frame. Charley discovered early on that he was not put on the earth to build things—giving him a hammer was like handing a drunk Indian your scattergun—but he knew better than that. It was like packing a wagon wrong, there were some things you just looked at and knew better.

And some things you didn't. Mrs. Langrishe hadn't struck him that way at all.

Charley found Bill back at Nuttall and Mann's Number 10, shooting glasses off the head of Pink Buford's bulldog. The bulldog was fearless. As soon as Bill set a shot glass between the animal's ears, the dog would put his tongue in his mouth so his head wouldn't jiggle, and sit dead still while Bill drew one pistol or the other and shot it off.

Bill was careful at first, aiming, but the dog proved steady, and by the time Charley came in looking for him, Bill was lining up a left-handed, over-the-shoulder shot in the mirror. The dog was sitting near the door. "Well, well," Charley said, "Wild Bill Hickok."

Bill nodded at him in the mirror; a low growl came out of the dog, who didn't want the shooter disturbed. At the same time there was the sound of Bill's shot. The glass exploded, and the dog's tongue rolled out of his mouth, slapped against the flat, wet nose, and then hung there, like a tree leaf in a bad wind.

The sound was softer than most pistols. Bill used about two-thirds the regular load. It gave the pistol less kick—less correction for a second shot—and Bill couldn't see far enough to need a regulation load anyway. Besides, when he shot somebody, he didn't want his lead passing through the body. He wanted it inside, where it would stop up the machinery.

The smell of powder filled the room, and several tourists ordered drinks for themselves and Bill. He was drinking pink gin again. Charley moved in next to him at the bar and said what had to be said. "We are obligated to attend the theater tonight, Bill."

Bill nodded and picked up one of the glasses of gin and bitters. He received all news, good and bad, the same way. Stoical. "We allowed a last meal?" he said.

Charley noticed Captain Jack Crawford then, standing on the other side of Bill, in front of a glass of milk. The bulldog pushed in next to them, and Bill gave him an egg. It was amazing how Bill collected friends.

A drink later, Captain Jack first proposed a hunt back into the Hills. He looked at Charley and said, "I been told you're the best hunter in Colorado."

Charley didn't answer, but he loaded up a look for Bill. "I know a place," Captain Jack said, "a child with a squirrel rifle could get all the moose he wanted."

Charley didn't say anything to that either. He was more particular about who he hunted with than who he drank with. Captain Jack seemed to back away a little. "Just in case you and Bill were to get restless in the city," he said.

"It takes us longer to get restless than it used to," Charley said. "For today, we've still got to investigate the local culture." He thought of Mrs. Langrishe and wondered if she would be in the play.

Bill set an empty glass side by side with another empty glass, starting a new row. "Then we'll go to the theater," he said.

Captain Jack held up his hand for quiet and began a story about his mother. There were dates and illnesses and vows, which Charley ignored and Bill listened to like it was directions to the Lost Saloon. By the end of the story, Jack had promised her to stay away from theaters too.

An hour later, while Bill and Charley were still preparing themselves at the bar, a horse man from Belle Fourche came into the place, a celebration unto himself. He'd sold twenty of his animals to a paper-collar from Cheyenne who ran the Pony Express. The paper-collar had paid him twice what they were worth.

The horse man's name was Brick Pomeroy. He said there was no feeling in the world like stealing from a paper-collar. He bought drinks for Bill and Charley and several of the upstairs girls, who all agreed with him. "How does this paper-collar operate?" Charley said. The Pony Express was a sort of local joke, like bad weather, and he had contemplated getting into the business ever since he'd heard the first complaints. He thought he might bring his brother Steve into it with him, to prove he'd forgiven him for shooting his leg.

"Damn if I know," he said. "What the man knows about horses is that the legs is supposed to be the same length. He don't have reliable stations, or riders, which is a collection of the sorriest roughs in the countryside. Pays them money in advance. You can't blame roughs for taking a paper-collar's money."

Brick Pomeroy noticed then that Bill was drinking gin and bitters, and asked what it was. He'd never seen anything pink served in a public saloon before. As an answer, Bill pushed one in front of him, and Brick Pomeroy drank that and his mood improved again.

He said, "Some days is so perfect nothing can touch you." He toasted Bill to that, then spotted the glass of milk sitting in front of Captain Jack Crawford. "What kind of sweet poison is that?" he said.

"Milk," Captain Jack said. Then he cleared his throat and the room got quiet. Charley wondered how he did that. "After the war," he said, "in which my father was killed and I myself was wounded . . ."

Brick Pomeroy waited a respectful time after the story ended and then looked at Charley and said, "The main consideration about a pony express is the Sioux. This paper-collar's got white men stealing from him legal, the Indians is going to take everything he's got . . . I caught one of them my own self, three days ago, running off with two of my mares."

"I hope you dealt him out of the game," Captain Jack said. There was hooting in the bar, a couple of gunshots into the ceiling. The dog nuzzled Bill's leg.

"You can rest assured," Brick Pomeroy said. "I shot him, and then my Mex cut off his head. I ain't seen the Mex since." He shrugged. "I guess a man can always find another Mex to clean out his livery."

Brick Pomeroy and Bill toasted to that, too. And then Captain Jack said, "There was a greaser come through here yesterday with an Indian head."

Pomeroy held his hand about shoulder-high and considered the drop to the floor. "Was he about this high?" he said. "Quick eyes, dirty, drunk? Did he have half an ear?"

"I believe we got the right half-eared Mex," Charley said.

Brick Pomeroy nodded. "That would be him, all right."

"He collected about three hundred dollars for the Indian," Captain Jack said. "They passed the hat at the Green Front, and then Sheriff Bullock gave him the legal town reward, two hundred and fifty dollars."

Brick Pomeroy was drinking a glass of sloe gin when Captain Jack said that, and he put it directly on the bar. In three seconds everything changed but his underwear. "You mean that Mex got three hundred dollars for my Indian head?" he said.

Everybody but Bill took a half step back to give Brick Pomeroy room to receive the news. "At least three hundred," Captain Jack said. "He rode into town holding the head in the air, rode out the same way, only richer."

Charley watched Brick Pomeroy's hands curl into fists. The veins came out on his forehead. It was the way ordinary people got when they found out a Mex had beat them out of three hundred dollars, but it was useless. Brick Pomeroy couldn't have fought two minutes in that condition, he certainly couldn't hit anything he was shooting at. He could stand on the banks of the Rio Grande and miss Mexico.

It was one of the peculiarities of life that the moment common men went into a fight was the moment they were least prepared.

Brick Pomeroy lifted one of the fists shoulder-high, almost like he was guessing the greaser's height again, and then brought it down in the middle of his glass. "Which way did he go?" he said. His hand was still a fist, dripping blood all over the bar. It looked like there was something inside it that he was squeezing.

"North," Captain Jack said. "He rode back toward Belle Fourche."

"I'll bet the son of a bitch is in Crook City," Brick Pomeroy said. "He's got a Mex whore he goes to see there. They love to hear each other make that fast talk."

Captain Jack nodded. "It could be Crook City."

Charley looked at Bill and said, "We could forget moose and just hunt the Mex."

Captain Jack said, "Stealing is stealing, and it's a code we live by that separates us from the savages. It's got to be on the up-and-up when there's gold for the taking in the streams."

Brick Pomeroy wrapped his hand in a bar towel and headed out the door. He walked across the street, shin-deep in mud, and then beat his horse half to death just getting him turned around. Charley had gone to the door to watch him leave, and when he came back Bill was accepting more free drinks from the tourists. They had been frightened at Brick Pomeroy's blood and temper, and were relieved to have him gone.

Bill drank and looked at himself in the mirror. Charley knew he couldn't have been paying attention to the here and now, not and entertain thoughts of a moose-hunt with somebody that made public speeches about milk-drinking and the code of the West.

"What do you suppose will happen," Captain Jack said, "if he tracks down the Mex?" He was smiling.

Bill stirred from his fix in the mirror. "What happens to any of us?" he said.

"I believe I'll have another shot," Charley said to the bartender. When he'd finished it, he turned to Captain Jack and said, "It's not a matter of if he tracks the Mex. That man's as hard to find as the full moon. For what will happen, you saw them both when they left, what did you think would happen when you told him where the Mex went?"

Captain Jack would not meet his gaze. He turned to the room and said, "Stealing is stealing."

BILL AND CHARLEY LEFT NUTTALL AND MANN'S AT SEVEN-THIRTY, TO give Bill time to relieve himself before the play. The wind had picked up and the canyon turned cool. Charley had never been anyplace, including the Rockies, where the weather changed so fast.

They went to their camp and got clean shirts. Bill stood behind the wagon with his eyes closed, holding on to his peeder until he finally began to empty. Charley sat on the stump on the other side of the wagon, combing his hair, waiting. He didn't talk or whistle. Bill liked it quiet so he could concentrate.

Charley went through his hair, first with his fingers, then with a brush. Smoothing out the tangles, then parting it in the middle and pulling it back over his shoulders. He rinsed his mouth with baking soda and whiskey and waited, fifteen or twenty minutes, until he heard Bill sigh, and then the sound of piss hitting the mud. Not a steady sound, it came and went, weak and strong, and then not at all. Bill came back around the wagon, tucking himself in. He borrowed Charley's brush, which Charley was not ordinarily disposed to lend out, and ran it through his hair. Bill's hair was thinner than Charley's; it lay flat naturally and collected less insects.

Bill had removed his guns to piss, but now he put them back in his sash and regained his public posture. He set his chin at an intelligent angle, put on his hat, and he and Charley started out toward the theater.

On the way Charley said, "Are you thinking things, Bill?"

"I got to write my Agnes," he said. "Set my affairs straight."

"The place is brand new, and full of old obligations," Charley said.

Bill stumbled into a crate. It looked like the one the Methodist had been standing on that morning, and nobody but a blind man could have missed it. "There's Custer, or Hill City," Charley said. He had never seen Bill stumble over anything before. "This doesn't have to be where we are."

Bill stepped over the crate and they continued uphill toward the theater. "It's the time of day," Bill said. "This half-light, it isn't one way or the other, is why a person can't see."

There was a boy sitting at a table near the front door of the theater, collecting a dollar and a half a customer, but Mrs. Langrishe herself met Bill and Charley at the door and told the boy they were her guests.

The Langrishe Theater was lamp-lit, the back was pitch-dark, and Bill's confidence seemed to change as soon as the contrast allowed him to see again. The stage was built of pine slats, maybe half an inch between them, and was not likely to support anything heavier than a tenor. Stakes had been pounded into the ground for seats, and small pieces of four-by-eight had been nailed to the tops to make them more comfortable.

Mrs. Langrishe walked them down to the front, a hand on Bill's arm, a hand on Charley's, and showed them to their seats. She had changed perfumes to something you couldn't take two ways. Charley thought it might have been gypsy.

"I hope you enjoy Bronson Howard," she said to Bill. "Mr. Utter has told me of your affection for the great Bard, and I hope this small amusement we offer tonight will distract you enough to bring you back for something more weighty."

"Well," Bill said, "if it isn't the great Bard tonight, maybe next time around. You can't live in the past." And he gave her a formal smile.

"I had no idea," she said, a little color coming into her cheeks now, "what a . . . gracious man you were, Mr. Hickok. The reputation pales beside the man."

Bill nodded politely. "This very afternoon," he said, "I shot ounce glasses off the head of Mr. Pink Buford's bulldog, Apocalypse." Mrs. Langrishe nodded, the same nod Bill had used on her. She had forgotten Charley was there, and Bill had already forgotten her. He closed his eyes and swayed. A line of sweat crossed his forehead.

Charley could hear the wind picking up outside. The canvas roof had a foot or two of play in it, and billowed out and then in, like death-bed breathing.

Mrs. Langrishe climbed a wooden scaffold to the stage. "Good evening, ladies and gentlemen," she said. There were sixty or seventy seats in the room, every one of them occupied. She waited while the audience gave her a small round of applause. Some of the finest clothes Charley had ever seen were assembled in that theater.

"Tonight, as you know, is the premiere performance of the Langrishe Theater, and it is our pleasure to bring you a light comedy of manners, Bronson Howard's *The Banker's Daughter.*" There was more applause for that, and then again when she announced the players. Her husband, Jack, was the banker. He had powdered his face and stuck on a moustache, but he still looked short.

When the introductions were over, Mrs. Langrishe talked for a moment about the importance of theater to a community, and then, looking right at Bill, she said she hoped to see them all again soon.

When the audience clapped this time, as she left the stage, Charley joined in. He didn't know why, but it seemed like she had done something brave. He looked sideways then, just in time to see Bill's eyes jump open at the sound of the applause. That was the only way you could have known he was already asleep, if you saw his eyes. Bill sat dead still, figuring things out, and then, just before the daughter came on stage to begin the play, he slowly stood up, turned to the room, and nodded.

Then he sat back down and nodded to Charley.

The daughter was too old to be a daughter, but they'd dressed her in skirts and painted her cheeks pink. Charley saw they had done the best with what they had. He applauded with the audience again.

The daughter twirled once, showing bloomers, and then put the back of her hand against her forehead and said, "Alas." She had the playbook in her hand, but said that from memory.

"Shit," somebody in back of them said, "I hate it when it starts with 'alas.'" The sound of the wind covered the voice then. The wind and the rain. The canvas slammed up and down, gaining more leverage as it loosened the boards.

Jack Langrishe came on from the other side of the stage, reading from a book. "What is it, my pet?" he said. "Why do you look so sad?"

And at that moment the roof blew off the theater. There was a long rumble of thunder, and then a noise like an explosion, and then the rain was coming in as thick as bear piss, blowing sideways with hats and leaves and sawdust and little pieces of board that were left by the carpenters.

On the stage, Jack Langrishe stopped what he was doing and stared straight up. Charley had the feeling he was looking a long way beyond the roof. Hats rolled across the floor, and some of the ladies made blinders of their hands to protect their eyes.

Lightning flashed, and froze the audience in green light. On the stage, the banker's daughter was fighting the wind for her skirt. The rain beaded up on Jack Langrishe's face and rolled down his cheeks without streaking his powder.

Charley and Bill had grabbed their hats at the sound of the explosion, and they sat and watched the scene while the rain made little gutters of the brims. There was a fair amount of noise in the theater—mostly thunder and the popping sound from the torn canvas—but nobody screamed, and nobody left.

And then Jack Langrishe cleared his throat. Being an actor, he could do that loud enough to be heard over a thunderstorm. As much as was possible, the audience turned themselves away from the wind and looked up. About half the floor lamps were still lit, and that and the lightning gave the actor's motions a jerky look that struck Charley as theatrical. Jack Langrishe took the banker's daughter by the arm then. "What is it, my pet?"

The daughter stared at him. "What is it, my pet?" he said again.

"Oh, shit," she said.

There was a long crack of thunder, and when it died people were laughing. Ten minutes later it began to hail.

The play lasted most of an hour, the storm quit about halfway through. The wind died, the rain stopped, and before it was over there were stars in the sky. That's how fast things turned in the Hills. At the end, Mrs. Langrishe stood in the door and shook hands with everybody who had come. The street behind her was under half a foot of moving water. Her dress was soaked through and stuck to her person everyplace there was a hold. Her hair had come loose and her eyes seemed to be bleeding black. Charley had never seen a woman look more beautiful. She thanked him for coming, and then Bill, but she used two hands to shake with Bill.

"I hope we can have something more amusing for you next time," she said.

"Drier," Bill said. "Next time make it drier."

Mrs. Langrishe put her hand over her mouth and began to laugh. "You are clever, Mr. Hickok," she said. She gave him that peeder-hummer smile, but Bill didn't notice. "Perhaps sometime you would like to take part in one of our plays," she said.

Bill shook his head. He said, "I did acting three months in a production of Buffalo Bill Cody's Wild West Show, but it didn't suit my disposition."

"Perhaps it was the selection of material," she said. Charley noticed that everything Mrs. Langrishe said sounded like it meant two things. "We could offer you something more suited to your tastes. Perhaps the great Bard . . ."

"Well," Bill said, "if it was the great Bard, me and Charley might be interested."

She touched Bill's hand, just the tips of her fingers against his wrist. That was something Matilda did too, when Charley was leaving Colorado on business. He wondered if he was beginning to miss her. "*Taming of the Shrew?*" Mrs. Langrishe said.

Bill said, "It would be our honor."

BILL WAS SITTING ON THE TREE STUMP HOLDING A GLASS OF GIN AND bitters when Charley woke up in the morning. Bill was wearing his guns and his pants. His body was silver-colored, and there was a little bottle on the ground next to him, with a silver-stained rag next to it. "That reprobate with the head and the bug-eyes," Bill said, "you remember him?" Bill always knew when Charley woke up, it was like he could hear his eyes open.

Charley got up slowly, feeling the weather in his legs. "Did you shoot him?" Bill had gone back to the badlands after the play, Charley had gone to bed. There was something about getting rained on that always made him tired.

Bill shook his head. "Not yet," he said.

Charley said, "What's the circumstances?"

"Everywhere I went last night," he said, "he was standing off to the side or in a corner, studying my habits. A man that size trying to hide in corners, it's unseemly." He touched his shoulder and then checked the finger, to see if what was on him had dried.

"Mercury?" Charley said.

"It's a safety measure," Bill said. He drank some of the pink gin and stood up. "I got an idea about him," he said, "that he's somebody I have to watch."

"Then shoot him," Charley said. "Give him fair warning and finish it. You can't have someone in the corners every minute."

Bill picked up his shirt and put his arms into the sleeves. The way he dressed when there was trouble, there was never a time when both hands were away from his guns. "Captain Jack mentioned it too," he said. "That there were scoundrels looking for all our scalps."

"What scoundrels?" Charley said.

"He didn't say, except they were close at hand. Captain Jack doesn't talk specific."

Charley climbed out of the wagon, Bill finished his drink. "He talks like a woman," Charley said. "A gossip that won't name names."

Bill smiled at that. "I wish there was a general reluctance to bring my name into things," he said. "The trouble is accuracy. You can't explain what you did to anybody, especially a reporter, because things don't come out the same in words. And the words you give them, they get it wrong. I tremble to think what the writers do after a body dies."

"The only ones you can trust to know what you mean are your pards," Charley said.

Bill shook his head. "Women know you best," he said. That led his thoughts a different way, and he picked up the bottle of mercury and stared at it. "Agnes sees me better than I see my own self."

Charley let that settle, and then he said, "What about this corner-hugger?"

"He doesn't know me at all," Bill said. "If he did, he'd let me alone."

Charley reached into the back of the wagon and came out with a clean shirt and his toilet. Bill went with him to the bathhouse, and they sat in hot tubs while the soft-brain told them about poison eggs and hangings. Bill listened to it without expressing judgment one way or the other. When the soft-brain was finished, though, Bill said, "If it was me, I believe I'd burn myself up. I don't want my picture taken after I'm gone."

"They took my picture once," the soft-brain said.

"They do me alone at first," Bill said, "and then the man that operates the machine always sets things up in back so a volunteer can pull the trigger on it, and he stands in next to me, like we were pards."

"It don't hurt to get your picture took," the soft-brain said.

"Not too bad," Bill said.

"I seen my soul when they did it," the soft-brain said. Bill sat up in the tub. He was interested in the soul. "It's true," the soft-brain said. "There's little floating circles, all pretty colors, and inside them was my soul. When you die, they float up out of your body to God."

Charley said, "You believe there's circles inside you?"

"That's where I seen them," he said. All three of them were quiet then until the soft-brain said, "I got to get my picture took again."

"I wouldn't advise it," Bill said. "You don't want to do something like that unless there's a reason, like if you were famous and had to. A picture is the beginning of misstatement and misunderstanding.

You got people looking at it with all different opinions, and they make up stories to go with them."

The soft-brain nodded, like he could see the problem. "There's stories on me already," he said.

"Like what?" Bill said. He was saying more than he usually did, but there wasn't anybody there but Charley and the soft-brain to hear it.

"Soft-brained," the soft-brain said. "I heard people say the Bottle Fiend was soft-brained."

Bill smiled. "Who's this Bottle Fiend?"

"Me," the soft-brain said.

"They just call you soft-brained because of your hobby," Bill said. "They don't see how anybody would eat poison eggs or hang hisself, so they say you're soft-brained."

"I shot myself once, too," the soft-brain said. "It took the wrong angle, though. That's what Doc Sick said. I heard people say, though, 'A soft-brain shoots himself in the head, so what?'"

Bill stood up and reached for a towel. "Listen," he said, "there's some soft-brained in everybody."

"That can be proved in federal court," Charley said.

The tone of his voice made Bill sit back down. "Was there something happened last night?" he said. Bill had memory lapses when he drank which he didn't like to acknowledge.

"I came to bed after the flood," Charley said, "but earlier in the festivities you put it in Captain Jack Crawford's head that we were going on a moose-hunt."

"That's not so bad," Bill said.

"It's not all," Charley said. "When we get back from the hunt, you volunteered us for *Taming of the Shrew.*"

"Under what conditions?" he said, calm and even. Bill accepted all news the same stoic way, that's what made him who he was.

"There were no conditions or attachments," Charley said. He stood up in the tub and gave Bill a bow, to show how he'd done it. "You said, 'It would be our honor.'"

"Son of a bitch," Bill said.

"I could see it if you had designs on the lady," Charley said, "but you hardly looked." He got out of the tub and wrapped himself in a towel.

Bill closed his eyes and thought. "Did I say when?" Charley shook his head. "That's to the good side," Bill said. "We'll leave it like an accident, like your bun fell off the dinner table."

Charley said, "I believe Mrs. Langrishe is not slow to bring fresh buns."

Charley had just pulled on his pants when the first of the upstairs girls came in for her weekly bath. Not all of them took baths, but the ones that did came in on Monday mornings. In the afternoon they did their shopping. It was understood the ladies from the good part of town stayed off the streets on Monday.

The girl was young and blue-lipped and skinny. She walked past Bill and Charley and the Bottle Fiend and began to undress next to the tub in the far corner. The way she did it, it was nothing. The Bottle Fiend went over for his money. "Clean water's fifteen cents," he said. "Hot's another dime." Her shirt came off, and she was skinnier than she'd looked. Her skin was somewhere between white and light blue, and you could see the shape of the bones in her arms and ribs. She was shaking now, cold.

She looked through her purse for change, setting the things inside it on the stool next to the tub. There was a locket shaped like a heart, a man's ring, a shot glass, a comb, perfumed soap. Charley knew firsthand that perfumed soap left an eight-day rash. "Shit," she said. Bill covered himself with a towel and got out of his tub. He didn't need to cover himself, though, she had no interest in that side of the room at all. "I'll git you later," she said. "I left my money back in my room." She pulled her skirt up over her head and then dropped her underthings in a pile around her feet.

You could see the bones in her butt, too. Charley knew it couldn't be healthy when you could see the bones there. He also knew no upstairs girl in the world would leave her money in her room. But it wasn't his business. He tucked his shirt in while Bill got into his pants. "Cold water or hot?" the soft-brain said.

"Hot," she said.

"That's a dime extra," he said, and held out his hand.

"I already told you," she said, "I left my money in the room." Her legs were as thin as her arms, and Charley noticed the needle marks along the veins. He'd thought it was insect bites at first.

The Bottle Fiend looked at her in an uncertain way. Charley took a dollar out of his pocket and handed it to him. "For her too," he said. Charley had pity for anybody attached to morphine, and that heart-shaped locket had caught him by surprise.

The girl climbed in the tub and waited. She never said thank you, she never glanced at Charley or Bill. It looked like it had been two weeks since she ate, but there wasn't anything to do about that. Charley had been around morphine victims, and they just weren't interested. In food, or anything else but morphine.

He thought it must be the worst way to go there was.

THE BOY COULD NOT FORGIVE HIMSELF FOR SHOOTING BILL'S HORSE. He left the camp and staked an abandoned claim a mile south of Deadwood, in the direction of the city of Lead. Number 12 Above Old Hope. It ran three hundred feet along the Whitewood Creek in shallow water. He registered the claim with the district recorder in Deadwood. It cost him two dollars. The recorder gave him a certificate that said, *"Personally appeared before this official, Malcolm Nash, and recorded undivided right title and interest to Claim Number 12 Above Old Hope of 300 feet for mining purposes. This here is July 20, 1876."*

The boy's sister had given him sixty dollars before he left Colorado. He bought his tent and equipment from the old man who worked Number 11, and who had bought them himself from the previous owner of Number 12. The old man had rheumatics of the back and was always cold. His hands were twisted from the work and cold water until they were almost useless.

He sold the boy rubber boots, a pick and a pan and a shovel. A small leather bag made from a bull's scrotum. A frying pan, a fork and a knife, and the tent, which was lined with old calico. He charged him twenty dollars. It was twice what he'd paid the previous owner, who had quit the Hills and gone back to his family in the States.

The mining pan was about a foot and a half across, and five inches deep. The sides angled in to the bottom, which was less than half the diameter of the top. It was made of soft steel and rusted top to bottom. The boy shook his head at its condition. "I intend to buy a new one," he told the old man, "and keep it clean." He had watched Bill and Charley cleaning their guns after hunts.

The old man was patient with him. It was the rust that held on to the specks of gold, which was all there was left in Old Hope, specks. "Don't use it to cook," he told the boy. "You get slick in there, you might as well throw it away."

The old man was patient. He worked his claim one day a week, as the law required to keep title, and the rest of the time he sat on a box in front of his tent, resting his back, trying to rub some of the coldness out of his hands and wrists. The old man was waiting for the mining companies. They could get the gold out of quartz, and he thought they would buy him out.

He watched the boy all afternoon Monday. He saw that he had never worked a placer before—he handled the pan like it was another shovel—but it was after he'd been at it all afternoon and hadn't improved that the old man knew he had no talent. Before dark he walked down the bank into the boy's claim and took the pan out of his hands.

He filled the pan with gravel from the side of the creek, and then walked out into the water and sat on his heels. It hurt his knees to get down. The boy came with him, watching over the old man's shoulder.

The old man put the pan underwater and moved it gently side to side, cleaning out the dirt. He brought it back up and picked out the biggest pieces of rock, rinsing them, then tossing them into the water. Then he dipped one side of the pan into the creek and carefully rocked the contents back and forth until the sand began to spill over the side. "Look for it now," he said. "If there was a nugget, you'd see it now."

The boy watched, thinking of ways to do it faster. The old man rocked the pan until most of the sand was gone. What was left then was a small pile of red and black minerals, heavier than what had been washed out. Red garnets, iron, tin.

"Now watch," the old man said. He moved the pan suddenly. The boy thought he was throwing it away, but the old man held on and then peered into the bottom. The minerals were sprayed out there like the moon at crescent, and the old man poked his finger into the tip, and came out with a speck of gold. He put it in the boy's pouch. "It's always at the fartherest tip of the moon," he said.

The boy took the pan and did what the old man had told him until dark. In the morning, the old man watched him again. The boy had no talent at all. He had a strong back, though, and the old man saw it would be a long time before he gave up. He liked the boy, and was glad for the company.

BOONE MAY HAD THOUGHT IT OVER, AND DID NOT WANT TO HAVE business with Wild Bill. He'd decided that while Bill was shooting glasses off the head of Pink Buford's bulldog. It wasn't the shots themselves, it was something in the way the dog trusted him. Boone May had watched Bill for two days, and knew by then all the stories he'd heard about him was true.

Bill Hickok was not born to be killed by his peers. Nobody ordinary would survive trying. That was something Boone May felt, and he trusted it.

He lay awake next to Lurline Monti Verdi all night Monday, and was awake in the morning when Bill came up the street toward Nuttall and Mann's for his morning cocktail.

He thought about Bill, and about dying. Several times he also thought about Calamity Jane, which was somehow tied into it too. His thoughts were circular. First there was Bill and the dog, and then it was Bill and him in that half second when you realized you was killed but it hadn't happened yet, and then it was him and Jane. Every time he got to that part, he woke Lurline up and tried to wash himself in her again. He wasn't rough or humorous with her, and each time he was done she went back to sleep disappointed.

He got up at the sounds of activity in the street and watched Bill walking to the bar. He wished it was the sissy he had business with. He carried himself straight enough now, but Boone pictured him without Wild Bill.

He removed himself from Lurline's bed for good sometime toward the middle of the day. She was gone, but he could still smell her toilet water on the pillow. It was hot in the room, and he took off his underwear before he put on his pants and shirt. He did that fast, afraid someone would come in the door.

His peeder rubbed against the sewing in his trousers, and he noticed it was tender. He tried to remember how many times he'd took Lurline during the night, but when he considered them one by one they embarrassed him because he hadn't really took her at all. It wasn't like bedding down with Jane, of course, with her trying him out like a new saddle, but in the whole night with Lurline, he'd never once done anything manly.

There was time for that, though. Boone May was never one to let his peeder do the thinking. He had seen where that led, and when Boone cashed in, it wasn't going to be his member that got him into it.

He was looking out the window, thinking of the man he had

hung in Hill City, when the Bottle Fiend came walking down the street dragging his flour sack, poking through the mud with a stick for bottles.

Boone had never had reason to talk to a soft-brain, but he saw something in this one, and called to him. The Bottle Fiend looked up, found him in the window, and came in the door downstairs. A minute later he knocked on the door. Boone guessed soft-brains wasn't afraid of nothing.

He opened the door. The Bottle Fiend walked in and took off his hat and put that and his stick on the bed. He held on to the sack. The bottles inside made stirring noises whenever he moved, then seemed to settle down when he stopped. The thought hit Boone that the soft-brain might think the bottles was his babies.

The Bottle Fiend looked around the room, then out the window. He seemed happy to look down where he'd been before. Boone watched him, not knowing how to put things so he would understand. "You're the one that commits suicide," he said after a while.

The Bottle Fiend held out his shirt collar to show him his neck. "I hanged myself and et poison eggs," he said. "And tried to shoot myself onct, too."

"I heard about you," Boone said. He sat back down on the windowsill and the soft-brain took the chair over by Lurline's dresser.

"A soft-brain shoots himself in the head, so what?" the Bottle Fiend said.

Boone shook his head. "I never said nothing like that. What I heard was that you wasn't afraid." The Bottle Fiend stared at him and waited. "How many bottles you got there?" Boone said.

The Bottle Fiend pulled the sack close to his chest. The sound was fragile and nervous, but it settled. "I ain't going to take them from you," Boone said, smiling the way he'd seen other people smile when they talked to children. "I just wondered how many you had."

"Eleven hundred and forty-seven," the Bottle Fiend said.

And that made Boone smile for real. "Where did you hear a number like that?" he said. He thought bottles must be like money to soft-brains.

The Bottle Fiend shrugged.

Boone took his pistol out of its holster and held it up for the Bottle Fiend to see. "You ever shot a gun?" he said.

The Bottle Fiend nodded his head, but he didn't try to touch the gun. "I promised to Dr. Sick to quit," he said. "So he give me the bathhouse instead."

Boone smiled and nodded. The muscles in his jaws hurt. "What I meant was did you ever shoot anybody but your own self. Not that that don't count . . ."

The Bottle Fiend turned in his chair and looked the other way. It was quiet in the room. The Bottle Fiend ran his finger over one of the little bottles on Lurline's dresser. It was clear glass with a red cap, shaped like a drop of sweat. Boone thought it was her France perfume, but he wasn't sure. "You like them little bottles?" he said.

The Bottle Fiend moved his hand from that bottle to the next one, which was larger and regular-shaped. And then to the toilet water. It came from San Francisco; Lurline told him that when he'd first commented on her smell. Lurline was proud to have things from foreign places.

When he had finished touching the toilet water, the Bottle Fiend turned back around in his chair and looked at Boone again. "I ain't stupid," he said.

"I never said you was," Boone said. "I just asted if you liked them little bottles, because if you did, maybe I could let you have one if you did something for me." Boone tried to think of which one Lurline wouldn't miss.

The Bottle Fiend shook his head. "Not one," he said. "I need six."

Boone started up off the windowsill after him, but he made himself sit back down. He could almost feel the Bottle Fiend in his hands. It wasn't his peeder that led him around, but sometimes the feel of breaking somebody's bones did; it rushed over him in a way that he couldn't hold himself back.

He smiled, showing too much teeth. "I might could give you two," he said, "if you could do something for me at the bathhouse." Boone moved the gun closer to the Bottle Fiend, who gave no sign of taking it.

"I promised Dr. Sick," he said.

Boone said, "I ain't sayin' to shoot yourself. I'm talkin' about something else."

The Bottle Fiend turned back to the dresser and picked up the perfume from France.

Boone moved over next to him, still holding the gun in his hand. "There ain't but seven here," he said. He took the bottle out of the

Bottle Fiend's hand and looked at it closer. It had little bumps in the bottom and a picture of an angel on the top, where it smoothed out. The Bottle Fiend looked up at him, wanting it back. "This here's a damn fine bottle," Boone said. "I could give you this one and some of the others . . ."

The Bottle Fiend picked up the toilet water, which came in a quart size, and moved it away from the smaller bottles on the dresser. He said he needed six.

Boone put his hand over the Bottle Fiend's mouth. The Bottle Fiend didn't move or try to get it away, he just stood still and stared at him, not even a little fearful. It wasn't the way Boone thought soft-brains would be.

"All right," Boone said. "If I was to give you this France bottle right now, that means you got to do something for me with the gun." He took his hand off the soft-brain's mouth and put the bottle back on the table to see if they had an agreement.

The Bottle Fiend looked at the other bottles and shook his head.

Boone studied him, trying to decide. What it came down to, if the soft-brain messed it up and told about this, nobody would listen. If he got Bill, they might not even hang him, figuring he didn't know better. There was an asylum for soft-brains in Bismarck full of killers that didn't know better. Boone had heard they painted pictures with their fingers in there all day long. In some ways, Boone thought, he wouldn't of minded being a soft-brain himself.

He took the cap off the toilet water and left it open on the dresser. Then, one by one, he opened the other bottles and emptied them into it. No sense in getting Lurline mad at him if he didn't have to. The Bottle Fiend watched everything he did.

When he'd finished, the toilet water was pink and about an inch higher in its bottle than it had been. Boone's fingers stunk in a way that wouldn't wash off, he knew that without trying. There was something chemical in all those perfumes that didn't agree with each other. He put the caps back on the bottles—starting with the toilet water—and the fumes wasn't as strong. "Now," he said, sliding all six of the empties across the dresser to the soft-brain, "all these here is for you."

"I need six," he said.

"Goddamnit," Boone whispered, "that is six." Boone felt himself reaching for the soft-brain's throat, but stopped himself again. Instead, he moved the empties into a new spot on the dresser, counting each one as he moved it so the soft-brain could see he wasn't cheating. "One, two, three, four, five, six."

"That's what I said," the soft-brain said.

Boone said, "Good," showing teeth again. "That's good. You got what you want. Now here's what you got to do for them." He went into Lurline's dresser drawer and found the .44 caliber Smith & Wesson derringer he'd given her. It was about the size of a canary. Boone had shot it once, and it had felt like he was holding a firecracker when it went off. He put the gun in the soft-brain's hand and wrapped his fingers around the handle.

"It's little-bitty, ain't it?" Boone said. The Bottle Fiend looked at the derringer. "Now what you got to do is when a certain party comes into your bathhouse again, I want you to put this little-bitty gun up next to his ear and pull the trigger, so they can hear it."

For the first time, the soft-brain looked scared. "Don't worry," Boone said, "it's just little-bitty. You walk up behind him, like you was bringin' water, and put it just behind his ear. Up close . . ." He stood the soft-brain up and took his seat, then he moved the hand holding the derringer until it was right behind his own ear. "You see?" he said. "Right there, and then you pull the trigger."

The soft-brain's hand dropped as soon as Boone let go of it. "And then," Boone said, "all them bottles is yours, fair and square." The Bottle Fiend looked at the bottles. "You can take them now," Boone said, "but they ain't yours until it's done."

"What's done?" the Bottle Fiend said.

Boone got out of the chair and went back to the window, thinking how to put it. "For the bottles," he said. "You like them little bottles, don't you?"

The room was suddenly quiet.

Boone quit trying to be polite. "You and me made a deal," he said, "and nobody backs after they made a deal." He took the knife off his belt and held it up where the soft-brain could see it. "If they back out," he said, "they get their gizzard cut." He watched to see if the Bottle Fiend was scared of a knife. Everybody was scared of something, it was just harder to locate in a soft-brain.

He moved in for a better look at the knife. He touched the blade with the tip of his finger and smiled.

"Git away from there," Boone said. The Bottle Fiend pressed on the blade—Boone could feel the pressure—and then ran his finger the length. It happened before Boone understood what he was doing, and for all the things he had seen and done, including cutting the head off Frank Towles and spending the night with Calamity Jane Cannary, nothing had ever made him feel the way he did when he looked down at the blade and saw the tip of the soft-brain's finger hanging there, half on, half off, next to a smear of blood.

"What in Jesus' name?" he screamed.

The Bottle Fiend was holding the finger in his other hand, along with the derringer. The blood was running down both of his arms and dripping on the floor, and he had a look on his face that was somehow the opposite of Boone's feelings.

"I don't want to shoot nobody with a little-bitty gun," the Bottle Fiend said.

Boone took the derringer out of his hand and put it back in Lurline's drawer, spotting her things with blood. "Don't do nothin' else," Boone said. "Just wrap your finger up . . ." He looked around the room and found a pair of Lurline's lace panties near the closet. They were the color of Key lime pie and manufactured in New Orleans, Louisiana. She'd told him about that like New Orleans was someplace he should of been, and Key lime pie was something he should of ate. He picked them up off the floor and wrapped the soft-brain's finger.

The blood was down the front of his shirt now, and on his pants and face. Boone had never seen as much blood from an inconsequential opening. It was on the windowsill and the floor and the walls. Every time the soft-brain moved, he left blood somewhere new.

Boone doubled the panties back over the finger and squeezed. "Here now," he said, "you squeeze this." The soft-brain smiled and tried to unwrap the finger.

Boone slapped him once, to bring him out of it. The look on the soft-brain's face changed then, went completely dead. "Now listen," Boone said, "git yourself down to the bathhouse and clean up. If anybody asts, you don't remember how that happened, but you was sawin' wood."

"I don't want to shoot nobody for you," the Bottle Fiend said.

"I don't know what you're talkin' about," Boone said. "You're a soft-brain, cuts his own person and eats poison eggs, I never had nothing to do with it."

The soft-brain seemed to understand that. "Do I get the bottles?" he said.

Boone took his arm and pulled him to the door, dripping blood as he went. "You don't get nothin' because you wasn't here," he said. "And if you said elsewise, I'd tell Doc Sick what you done." He picked up the sack of bottles and wrapped the top of that around the hurt hand, then he pushed the Bottle Fiend out the door.

"I don't need them bottles anyway," the soft-brain said. That stopped Boone for a minute, and before he closed the door the soft-brain said something else. "The thoughts in them bottles, every one of them is about little-bitty guns."

Boone listened at the door while the Bottle Fiend went down the stairs, dragging the bag on the steps behind him. Then he looked at the room, covered with blood, and the dresser with all of Lurline's perfume bottles sitting empty in a line. He didn't see there was anything to do about the blood—when it dried you didn't notice it much anyway—but he did sit down at her dresser and fill up the little bottles again, replacing the caps as he finished each one. It was a long job, and Boone held one hand in the other as he poured to stop the shaking in his fingers. It took most of an hour, but he stayed with it.

There wasn't no sense in getting Lurline mad for nothing.

THE MAN WHO WOULD KILL WILD BILL HICKOK HAD BEEN IN DEAD-wood since late winter.

His name was Jack McCall, and he had come to the Hills from Cheyenne with Phatty Thompson and eighty-three cats. Phatty paid twenty-five cents a cat in Cheyenne, and meant to sell each of them for ten dollars in Deadwood. There was a rat problem in the northern Hills, and some of the upstairs girls wanted cats for company. He correctly surmised that once one got a cat, all of them would want cats.

Phatty found Jack McCall begging nickels and running errands for whores at the Republican Theater in Cheyenne, and told him he looked like just what he needed. "Yessir, I am," McCall said. Nobody had ever said he was what they needed before. He was a weak-looking Irishman with narrow shoulders and no butt end and a face like a rodent, which was something Phatty Thompson noticed when he picked him out of the crowd of hobos that stood outside the Republican begging change.

Phatty thought a man that looked like a rodent would have a way with cats. He had constructed a two-hundred-pound wooden crate that fit into the back of his wagon, and he kept the cats there as he collected them. In the four days he spent buying cats, the crate became the most popular attraction in the city. Every time Jack threw a new tom inside, it was life or death until the animals decided where the new one fit into the order of things. Sometimes one wouldn't fit in at all.

Jack McCall loved the sounds of a cat fight, he recognized the screams from his own secret thoughts. His job was feeding and care of the cats, and removal of the dead. They killed each other about two a day. Phatty Thompson bought chicken heads in twenty-pound sacks and Jack McCall would toss them to different parts of the cage. Sometimes he threw a head between two of the toms so they would fight. He had favorites among the cats, and made sure they always got fed. Others—the smallest ones and the ones that were scairt—he left them huddled in their corners and never tossed them nothing.

At the end of each day, Phatty Thompson gave him a dollar, which he used to buy whiskey. It was the best job Jack McCall ever had. He was sorry to leave Cheyenne for the Hills.

Jack McCall rode on the floor of the wagon, in back behind the cage where he could keep an eye on the cats. That's where Phatty put the extra sacks of chicken heads too. Jack did not mind the smell of chicken blood or the ride. For distraction, he would grab an occasional tail through the bars of the crate, and when the cat complained the others would attack it, at least the ones that wasn't fucking.

That was the only thing Jack McCall didn't like about the job. The cats were fucking all the time. When he saw them at it, Jack would bang on the cage with his shoe. The noise stopped them at first, but the cats soon accustomed themselves and paid no attention. Phatty didn't like cat fucking either. He said it ruined future business.

They rode unmolested through Wyoming and then up into the Dakota Territory. It was five days to Laramie, and another five into the Hills. The Indians had not yet officially got into their war paint, and it was not considered brave or foolish to travel alone.

Two days into the Hills, on the north side of Hill City, Phatty drove over a stump on the bank of Spring Creek, hit some ice, and tipped the wagon over. He had been drinking at the time. The crate broke open and the cats ran into the woods. Jack McCall was knocked unconscious and came to in a pile of half-frozen chicken heads.

There was a cat licking his fingers, another one at his feet. Jack picked them up and put them back in the crate. "I knew you was a cat man the minute I saw you," Phatty said. He was sitting on the ground against a tree. The cats came out of the brush and Jack picked them up and dropped them in the crate. Phatty and the miners slapped him on the back when he was finished and called him a natural cat man, and Jack McCall understood it was the best thing he had ever done.

In the end, they got them all back but eleven. Phatty gave another five to the miners, and camped there on Spring Creek overnight. The miners built a fire and called, "Oh, Joe . . ." into the night. They talked about their women and children back in the States, about the Indians, about gold. And they talked about Jack McCall. Nobody had ever seen such a natural cat man.

They got drunk and one of the miners named his new cat "McCall" in Jack's honor. They slept on the floor of a miner's cabin, and in the morning they tied the crate to the wagon and headed toward the northern Hills. Spring Creek was the second place in Jack McCall's life that he was sorry to leave.

They got to Deadwood in two days and Phatty sold twenty cats for ten dollars each, just getting drunk at the Senate. There were a few Maltese, which went for twenty-five. "You and me are going into business," he said to Jack that night.

The next night somebody pried the wood planks off the crate and all the unsold cats escaped, and were claimed by upstairs girls and miners, or anybody lonesome or had rat problems.

On the same day news of Indian trouble arrived in Deadwood. Norman Storms and Eddie Rowser were killed south of Cheyenne, William Ward killed and mutilated four miles north of Belle Fourche.

Jack McCall went looking for Phatty that night to ask when they were going after more cats. He found him in the Senate. They had a chair from England in there three feet across, and they saved it for him to sit in. Phatty shook his head. "We ain't in business no more," he said. "The pilgrims vandalized my cats, and I sure as hell ain't goin' back to Cheyenne now, the way things is with the redskins.

"The way things is, I'm staying right here until the U.S. Army comes in and kills every one of the red sons of bitches, so we can live safe." He patted his seat when he said "right here."

Jack McCall said, "I'm a natural cat man." Phatty gave him twenty dollars and bought him a drink.

"I hate to fire a man as good as you," he said, "but we ain't got a business now."

Jack McCall waited out the winter in a pine shack on the east side of town. The roof caved in twice under the weight of snow. During the days he moved from one tavern to another, until he was known and avoided all over the badlands. He ran errands for the upstairs girls and sometimes swept out their rooms. He was a natural cat man, but Deadwood was the wrong place for specialists.

In the morning he woke up on the floor and made a fire. He felt good in the morning, not like hurting nothing. That was when he ran his errands and swept out rooms. Sometimes the girls sent him into Chinatown to pick up their laundry. He went, although he didn't like nobody to talk fast or point too much with their fingers.

One of the upstairs girls had tried to fuck him once. Ten o'clock in the morning. He had run out of her room and never gone near her again.

He started his own drinking in the afternoon, and it changed him. It caused him to think about Phatty Thompson—who had gone back to Cheyenne without him in April—and it turned him ugly, to think he'd been left behind. He talked when he turned ugly to those that would talk to him, which was mostly tourists, and then, as he drank, it changed again, and he quit thinking about getting left behind, and began to think about the one that did the leaving.

He'd quit talking then, his head would start to sweat, and he would imagine himself cutting Phatty Thompson into pieces and feeding them to cats. And before long it wasn't only Phatty Thompson. The upstairs girls who paid him to run errands, the slant-eyes, the sheriff, all the tony bartenders that wouldn't advance him the price of a drink.

Jack McCall was a weak-looking man, but nobody teased him after his head begun to sweat. He was the kind that went soft-brained, and you either found them one morning sitting in the mud quacking, or they poured lamp oil all over the floor and set a hotel on fire.

Jack McCall would drink until his money was gone and then walk up the hill to his cabin and lie in his blanket on the floor, and after a while he could remember the night at Spring Creek when Phatty and the miners had told him they had never saw such a natural man with cats.

When he had got himself back to Spring Creek, he could let himself sleep. He did not believe in going under with the black thoughts still in charge. They grew in the night when he did.

WEDNESDAY MORNING WHEN CHARLEY WOKE, BILL WAS SITTING ON his stump with Pink Buford's bulldog in his lap. The dog was torn on both legs and there was a piece of his nose that hung down from the rest, hinged there by a little bit of skin. "I don't know why Pink wants to fight this dog," Bill said.

Charley straightened his legs, which weren't too bad that day. "It's enough of that in this place without bringing old Apocalypse into it too," Bill said. "It isn't like there's nothing else to do . . ." The dog heard his name and began to wash Bill's throat with his tongue. Bill held still, looking serene.

"Maybe it's his nature to fight," Charley said. "Maybe he'd kill chickens if Pink didn't let him fight."

Bill pushed the dog back to look him in the face. "He might at that. He might have two natures that don't know each other is there." Bill shrugged. "At least that way, he doesn't need to go around all the time forgiving himself."

Charley went into the back of the wagon and got his razor and soap and towel. When he started up the street for the bathhouse, Bill came with him. "I could use a little soak," he said.

The soft-brain was sitting on a chair outside the bathhouse. Not whittling or whistling or watching the street, just sitting. He didn't look at Bill or Charley until they spoke. "Hot baths," Charley said.

The soft-brain said, "Hot's an extra dime." Charley expected he had forgot who he was. The soft-brain heated buckets of water, and in a little while Bill and Charley were both sitting in tubs. Somehow, Bill produced a bottle of pink gin. Charley found a copy of the *Black Hills Pioneer* on the floor next to him and noticed the motto written across the top. *"Everything published on our own authority may be strictly relied on."*

He looked through the pages. There was a story about a fish tournament in Philadelphia, one about foreign travel entitled "Inland Africa Is a Marvelous Land," and a discussion of the dangers and advantages of telephone poles. He read "Inland Africa" to Bill, but went through the rest without much interest until he got to a first-person account by Mr. A. P. Woodward, "How It Feels to Be Scalped."

Mr. Woodward, formerly of Boston, now of Custer, had accompanied Mr. Herman Ganzo of Milwaukee on a trip into the Valley of Hat Creek, seventy miles north of Fort Laramie, and there encountered Indians.

"I felt a sharp, stinging pain in my left shoulder and left leg," he wrote, *"and I fell. One of them put a knee in my back while another hit me a clip with a club or a butt of a gun.*

"My hair was held tight. I felt a hot, red hot, stinging sort of pain all around the top of my head, as though the hair were torn out.

"Thirteen men got up just in time to keep the red devils from finishing their work. But I came to again and my scalp was laid back again. It was only half torn off as you will see, and is growing again nicely."

Charley cringed reading that, more than if he'd run into A. P. Woodward and heard it firsthand. For Charley, reading put things into his own voice.

He looked at a story about a new gun they had out in California that spit seventy rounds in four seconds. They called it the "Peace Conservator." They were always doing some damn thing in California that nobody had thought out the consequences.

The Bottle Fiend took a bucket of water off the stove and poured half of it into the tub between Charley's knees. The other half went into Bill's tub. Bill was reclined and looking at the ceiling, and never as much as flinched. Charley wondered if his peeder was damaged enough by the blood disease, he didn't care what else happened to it. Charley had almost read him "How It Feels to Be Scalped," but Bill was too far away and serious.

Charley turned the page of the newspaper and there was a report on the suicide of Mons Jensen, a part-time farmer, part-time miner who lived with his wife and boy on twenty acres just east of town.

Mons Jensen had written his note early in the morning, while the boy and the woman were out doing chores. It said, *"I wish what is left of me to be burned, and what will not burn I want buried right on the spot."* He nailed that to the door of his cabin, and then went outside and built a pile of logs around one of the smaller trees in the yard.

Charley looked up then, and noticed the Bottle Fiend was watching him. "What's in them pages?" he said.

"News," Charley said. "What's happened lately."

"Does it tell what's next?"

Charley said, "Nobody knows what's next."

"Madame Moustache does," the Bottle Fiend said. Charley went back to his paper. The Bottle Fiend said, "Sometimes me, too." Charley looked up again, waiting, but that seemed to be all the soft-brain was going to say. A minute after he looked back at the paper, though, the soft-brain said, "Are you going to tell me what it says in there, or I got to read it myself?"

"There are some things that don't do you any service to hear them," Charley said. "It just gives you bad ideas . . ."

The Bottle Fiend nodded, as if he understood that, and sat down on the bench and watched Charley read. Mons Jensen had poured kerosene and gunpowder on the logs. Then he'd harnessed a span of horses so his boy could come to town, and he'd carried a crock of butter from the cellar for his wife to sell at Farnum's.

Then he'd gone back to the tree and chained himself there by his leg, and then he'd dropped his match. Charley went back and read the note again. *"I wish what is left of me to be burned, and what will not burn I want buried right on the spot."*

Charley read the words and heard them in his own voice. He pictured the events again, trying to keep the hand from dropping the match. He couldn't make it come out that way, even in his own head. Once Mons Jensen got the chain around his leg, there wasn't a thing that could stop the match from dropping. He imagined that was the way it had happened too, that there was a place the farmer couldn't turn back even if he wanted to. Charley put the paper down to get the scene out of his head. Reading was personal to him; he always found himself in the words. Sometimes that was good, and sometimes it wasn't. Some of the letters Bill wrote, for instance, were killers.

He closed his eyes and after a while Bill began to talk. "I never been interested in things after I done them," he said. "The past is the past, but there is something now that I regret like I was about to do it."

Charley did not like the way that sounded. He opened his eyes and saw Bill was still staring at the ceiling. He always looked up when he talked about love.

"It's the matter of Agnes Lake," Bill said. "I remember the day I first put my eyes on her, walking the high wire in Cheyenne, the look on her face while she was up there, feeling every little stir in the air. You have to be perfect for that, there can't be a bad thing inside you to get in the way . . . I never saw such legs, more muscle than my own . . ."

Charley had seen Agnes's legs, and Bill was right. They were springy, too. She could jump from the floor to the back of a horse without warning. She could jump backwards, over herself, grabbing her knees, and land on the same spot she left. Charley had seen her do these things and thought of his own legs, and how useless they were by comparison.

"She was the most perfect sight I ever saw," Bill said. "That day on the high wire. I decided on the spot it was Agnes Lake and Wild Bill. I don't know if I mentioned it, but there was a while when I was damn near a perfect sight myself."

When Charley looked, Bill was smiling at him. Charley didn't want to comment on the perfection of Agnes Lake, who was five years older than Bill after the circus makeup came off. Charley liked his perfection younger and softer.

"Of course," Bill was saying, "there's no such thing as perfect. And even if there was, it doesn't mean that one perfect thing ought to have another one . . ."

While they let that settle, the Bottle Fiend brought Charley a new newspaper. "Her thoughts about me weren't necessarily true," Bill said. "She believed I was as good as she was because I was as famous. She still doesn't know me through and through."

"Maybe you don't know her through and through either," Charley said.

Bill sat up in his tub. "Like what?" he said.

"I don't know," Charley said. "But there's a lot goes into getting this old that doesn't necessarily show." He felt himself getting somewhere he didn't belong, but didn't know how to get out. Bill was still looking at him. Charley said, "I meant she's been as many places as you or me, she can't of missed the whole world."

Bill took another drink from the bottle and looked back at the ceiling. "She never saw things the way other people did," he said. "There's something innocent in her, she doesn't see anybody's motives."

"What motives were yours?" Charley said.

"None," he said. He looked back at the ceiling. "All I ever wanted from her, from the day I saw her walking across the wire in Cheyenne, was to be included, and be in the back of her mind when she went up on the wire."

"Well," Charley said, "that's what you got."

Bill shook his head. "I did something to her," he said. "That was the perfectest sight I ever saw, and I took it, and now I changed it."

"How do you know?" Charley said. "She's in St. Louis."

It was quiet in the room for a little while. "I know it," Bill said, "because I did the same thing to myself."

Charley said, "There's a sawbones named Wedelstaedt I heard of, a specialist in diseases of passion."

"That's all he does?" Bill said.

"That and care for the Chinese," Charley said. "He's the only one that will set foot in Chinatown." Bill thought about it, and changed moods.

"I never saw how Chinese were worse than anybody else," Bill said. "Maybe a little jumpier."

Charley was grateful to be off the subject of Agnes Lake. "They got a peculiar language," he said. "I listened to it on the trip out here, and couldn't pick up as much as 'fornicate' and 'eat.'"

"I heard they can't file claims, that the sheriff has said they can't."

"A fact," Charley said. "Sheriff Seth Bullock, the miner's friend."

Bill took another drink of the gin. "Do you believe one sawbones is different from another?"

"It has to be," Charley said.

In a while Bill said, "What does a blood disease do? To a woman, I mean."

"I heard they don't notice," Charley said.

Bill fitted his head back into the wall of the tub and looked at the ceiling. Charley looked through the paper the Bottle Fiend had brought him, and saw that Mrs. Langrishe had announced monthly meetings of the Deadwood Social Club, in which members could partake of the waltz, polka, schottische, or quadrille.

Charley had been a long time without a female, and the image of the sparks falling into Mrs. Langrishe's blouse jumped on him like something out of a tree. It hung all over him, right through an editorial that said, *"The hostile Sioux should be exterminated, and the white men engaged in trading ammunition to them should be hung wherever found."* And another one concerning the spreading of stories about murderous encounters with the Indians. *"We wish to say that a man cannot be guilty of anything more craven and contemptible than to willfully and deliberately put out stories of Indian massacres among the friends of the reported victims, and we would advise that fellow 'Just came in from the scene of the massacre' to keep himself shady."*

Charley was in agreement with that, but he was more in agreement with Mrs. Langrishe's chest. Then he turned the page and saw an article entitled "The Cremation of Baron Van Palm." When he saw what it was, he read it out loud. Disposal of the deceased was one of Bill's constant interests. It wasn't morbidity. Bill believed he was different and wanted to be treated that way, in life and beyond.

"*The Cremation of Baron Van Palm*," Charley said. "Listen to this."

"Who?"

"Baron Van Palm."

"Who is that?"

Charley skimmed the article and shook his head. "It doesn't matter. It starts at eight-twenty-seven, when they inserted his body into the oven." Bill put the bottle against his lips again, but slower.

"*Eight-forty-five*," Charley read, "*vapor cleared and body was seen plainly against the red background of the retort. Flue mouth white hot and there seemed to be a radiant crown floating over the old man's head.*"

"Well, he was old," Bill said. "That's good."

Charley continued reading. "*A sheet enfolds the corpse, the alum experiment being a perfect success in preserving elements of decency.*"

Bill stopped him again. "What's that? An alum experiment?"

"It's a sheet for preserving the elements of decency," Charley said, and picked it back up at "elements of decency."

"*Nine-fifteen; sheet charred at the head, and stood up black and ragged. The body's left hand raises and points upward, as if the dead were ascending from the remains. At this point, the eye-hole was opened to test for oxygen.*

"*At nine-twenty-five, the hand fell again. Dr. Otterson, in charge of the experiment, notes a glorious rose-colored light about the remains, and there is a faint mint odor through the eye-hole.*"

"Mint?"

"Mint," Charley said. "It's a damn sight better-sounding than worm food, isn't it?"

"It sounds better than life," Bill said.

"*Ten-twenty-five*," Charley read. "*Feet incandescent and semitransparent. Body surrounded by gold mist . . .*"

"Then what?" Bill said.

"That's the end of it," Charley said. He turned the page to make sure. "Right after that it says, '*reported by Colonel Olcott.*'"

Bill said, "Did you notice that everybody we met in this place is a colonel or a major or a professor?"

"Or a captain," Charley said, meaning Jack Crawford.

The Bottle Fiend pulled another bucket of water off the stove and divided it between Bill and Charley. "I never tried to burn myself," he said. "I just et poison eggs and shot myself in the head. And I tried to hang."

"It isn't dignified to burn yourself," Charley said. "People talk bad about you afterwards. This story in the paper, the deceased was already dead, and it was the family and friends that did it." Charley had a vision of the soft-brain chaining himself to a tree and dropping a match in a pile of wood, like Mons Jensen.

Bill had closed his eyes to concentrate on the heat in the water. The Bottle Fiend was nodding, as if he was thinking over what Charley said on burning, but when he spoke again, it was as if they were still talking about newspapers.

"I know something's going to happen next," he said. "The newspaper don't know it, but I do."

Charley said, "Nobody can predict the future."

"I know something's going to happen," the soft-brain said. Charley waited and finally the soft-brain told him. "It's somebody wants to shoot Bill."

Charley was looking at Bill, and he never opened his eyes. He did smile. "Who told you?" Charley said.

"A man with little bottles," the soft-brain said. "He give me the little bottles and then took them away when I cut myself. He give me a gun too, and said to shoot Wild Bill when he was sitting in the bath. A little-bitty gun, little-bitty bottles. I know who he meant."

Bill had stopped smiling and opened his eyes. He was drunk and tired, but he could always put it off to do what needed to be done. "What was this man's name?" Bill said.

The Bottle Fiend shrugged. "I don't know names," he said.

"Where was he?"

The Bottle Fiend looked at the ceiling. "In a room," he said after a while. "There was little bottles, and he had a knife. He give me the bottles, fair and square, and then took them back when I got cut."

"Where?" Bill said.

"My finger," he said, and held it up. It was wrapped in a piece of dirty cotton.

Bill said, "Will you do something for me, sir?" The soft-brain nodded. "When you see the man again, you tell him Wild Bill said there's about to be a cheap funeral in Deadwood."

The Bottle Fiend looked at the ceiling again, maybe picturing it.

Bill settled back against the tub and closed his eyes. That fast, he was drunk again.

"You know," Bill said after a while, "we got to study cremation. That sounds like the ticket." He took another drink of the gin, and the Bottle Fiend sat quietly and watched them.

Once, maybe twenty minutes later, he said, "I don't remember what you said, about the man with little bottles."

"Don't concern yourself," Bill said. "I'll get you some bottles. It's no consequence at all."

THE OLD MAN'S HANDS HURT HIM AT NIGHT AND KEPT HIM FROM sleeping much, but even so, the first thing he heard every morning was the boy, banging around his camp in the dawn light, making breakfast. He wondered how a person made that much clatter lighting a fire.

Before the sun broke the hills, the boy was in the creek. Every morning. He sat on his haunches in an uncomfortable way, and none of the ordinary panning motions was ordinary for him. He was jumpy, and he tried too hard. He panned gold like there was somebody watching him.

Which in fact there was.

The old man saw him on Friday, sitting on a horse above the trail that followed the Whitewood into the city. The old man only saw him for a moment, but he recognized the beard and the posture. It was the man from the Gem Theater. He sat on a horse the same way he stood on his feet. It was him. There was nothing wrong with the old man's eyes.

He had been to the Gem six times in the last six weeks, but not regular, like every Saturday morning. He went when he wanted. Sometimes he paid the girls, sometimes he paid the man.

There was nothing wrong with his peeder, either.

He was there again on Sunday. He came in the afternoon with two others, and stayed in the trees away from the trail, not to be seen. When they had gone, the old man walked down to the water. The boy was as grim as the creek he was panning.

He had froze his mind on keeping on, and had forgot what he was keeping on at. He had worked Number 12 seven days then, taken maybe five dollars' worth of gold out of the claim. If a luckier man was to fall in, there might be that much in his pockets when he climbed out. The boy had no luck, though. That was as clear as the fact he had no talent.

Not that the two were unrelated.

"Even the Lord rests on Sunday," the old man said.

The boy was slopping gravel over the sides of his pan and never looked up. "I don't care about religion," he said. "I care about what I can see."

The old man sat down on the bank and watched him work. "It ain't that clean a line, sometimes," he said, "what you can see and what you can't."

The boy shook his head, like he had been accused. "I ain't seen nothing lately," he said, "but silt and gravel." The old man saw the skin on the boy's hands was cracked at the knuckles, and he knew how it hurt to work with broke skin.

"You ought to go slower," the old man said. "Look around more, get the feel of what's around you . . ."

"I know everything about this wet bastard creek I need to," the boy said. "I know I staked a claim, and I intend to work it until it gives up its gold."

"It ain't no hurry," the old man said, seeing he would not be warned.

"Maybe not for you, old man," the boy said. "But I got things to do." The old man stood up and walked back to his camp. He would have told the boy about the man who come out twice to watch him, but he could see the boy didn't want him there, and wouldn't listen anyway. He would have told him, but the old man did not like to be called "old man."

The man from the Gem Theater was back again that evening, with the others. The old man was in the trees, collecting kindling, and heard their horses. The boy had stayed in the creek until dusk, and then gone up the hill and taken off his boots. He'd gone to sleep without supper.

The men on horses stopped in the trees above the boy's camp again, but only for a few minutes. They tied the horses there and walked down. The old man moved to a place where he could watch. He had a scattergun in his cabin, but there was nothing he could do with it but get himself shot.

They moved down the rocks to the tent slowly, trying not to make noise. They needn't have bothered, the boy slept like he was buried. They came slow, and when they were a few yards from the tent two of them took the guns out of their holsters. The old man thought they would shoot the boy in his sleep and take what they wanted, but they stopped at the entrance to the tent, and the man from the Gem Theater held on to the roof and kicked inside. There was a grunt, but nothing else. The man from the Gem kicked again.

"Wake up, boy," he said. "Al Swearingen is here to collect his debts."

The old man could hear the boy talking inside the tent, but he couldn't tell what he said. The man from the Gem Theater kicked again, and then backed up several steps in a hurry as the boy came out after him. One of the others hit the boy across the back of the head—the old man thought he'd hit him with his gun, but the light was going fast and he couldn't say for sure—and the boy dropped on the ground.

The man from the Gem Theater walked away, and the other two dragged the boy after him. They had him under the arms. They draped him across the boy's firewood and took off his trousers. There were no sounds at all from the boy, not even a groan. The man from the Gem Theater unbuttoned his own pants and got down on the ground behind the boy. "Now," he said to one of the men, "put that knife in his mouth so he'll notice it when he wakes up."

The old man turned away and sat on the other side of the tree. In a few minutes he heard the boy. He never groaned, the old man was surprised at that, it was a gagging noise. "That's Mr. Bowie in your mouth, boy," the man from the Gem Theater said. "Don't move nothin' . . ."

The boy made that noise again, strangled, like he was trying to get out the words. Then he cried out—half a cry really, something had cut it off—and the man from the Gem Theater was talking. "Where's Wild Bill tonight, boy?" he said. The boy made the strangling noise again. "No, no," the man said, almost gentle, "I brung *my* friends tonight . . ."

The old man stood up, quietly, and made his way back into the trees, trying to get away from it. The farther he went, though, the louder the boy's cries got. He had walked fifty yards before it was quiet again, and he sat down there. There was a scream a few minutes later, a long, scairt scream, and then it was quiet.

The old man thought of his scattergun again, and that maybe there were things that signaled you were supposed to get yourself shot. The scream was the last of it. The old man waited in the trees, and a long time later the men came back up the hill. "We ought to finished it," one of them said.

The man from the Gem Theater said, "I know it."

"I wouldn't had nothing to do with this business," the first one said, "if you said you was going to leave him alive."

The man from the Gem Theater said, "There's things you give away without knowing why. We give that boy his life."

"You give him his life," the first one said. "If it was me, I'd go back down there and finish it."

The old man heard them get on their horses. He thought of the scattergun, but he didn't want to kill anybody. He was sixty-seven years old, and didn't want that over him now. He didn't know what he did want, except to wait for the mining companies, and sell them Number 11 Above Good Hope, and then move into town and eat his breakfast in the hotel. Maybe visit the Green Front once a week. He didn't expect he would be going back to the Gem.

He made his way to his cabin in the dark, stumbling over tree roots and rocks, but he moved quiet. He didn't want to make noise now. The air was dead still; the only sound from the boy's camp was the creek. He made a fire so the boy could see he was there, and sat down in his chair by the door. There was still no noise from the boy's direction, nothing but the creek. He tried to act natural, like he had just got back from town. He made himself a pot of coffee and ate half a pound of New York cheese. It was thirty cents a pound at Farnum's, and he ate it for dinner every night. He sat on his chair holding coffee in a tin cup in one hand, the cheese in the other. The mosquitoes never bothered a man that ate cheese every night.

He looked in the direction of the boy's camp, but there were clouds that night, and no light at all from the sky. The thought hit him that the boy might be hurt serious. The old man didn't want to bust in uninvited—the time for that was past—but if the boy was hurt . . .

He walked to the edge of the fire's light and stared down toward the boy's tent. He listened; he thought it over. It wasn't likely the boy had gone back to sleep, so he was either hurt or morose. The old man decided to wait. He let the fire die, and when it was gone he went inside his shack and lay in bed. The scattergun leaned against the door, and he thought again that he might of been supposed to go down there and get himself shot.

He woke in the morning at first light, put on his boots and his trousers, and walked outside. The clouds were still there, heavy and low, and the air smelled the way it did before a storm. He looked down to the boy's camp and saw it was empty.

The old man walked down the gravel slope and looked inside the tent. He had took his clothes and personals, left the pan and shovel and the rubber boots. There was dried blood all over the cot. The old man pulled his head outside the tent; he'd already seen more than he wanted. There was blood on the ground, too. It led from the firewood to the tent. The old man wondered what they had done to him that bled this much and didn't kill him. He wondered that, and he wondered what it had to do with him. "What was a body supposed to do?" he said out loud.

He walked back up the little hill to his own camp. "All I could of done," he said, "was to get shot myself." He sat down on the chair near his door and looked out at the Whitewood Creek, where the boy would have been by then, ignorant and clumsy and strong, holding his silent argument with the nature of how things were. He missed the boy, and felt the loss. And he had lost something besides the boy, sitting in the trees, listening to the sounds of what they did to him.

THE BOY WALKED ALONG THE CREEK BACK INTO TOWN. HIS TONGUE was cut deep and swollen, and the metal taste was as strong as when the knife was inside his mouth. He did not let himself think about the rest of it.

He'd done too much of that after what had happened in the whore man's wagon on the way out, thought about it until it crippled his talk and his feelings, until he stuttered and couldn't decide what to say. He'd felt himself close to something bad then, and he knew if he thought about this now, he would find it.

He walked past half a dozen miners on the way in, most of them sitting in chairs outside their tents or shacks, usually with a rifle or scattergun propped against a tree nearby. The boy saw something humorous in that, men worried that somebody would steal their ground, something that was always there. Only one or two of the miners were working their claims; the boy saw there wasn't much left in the stream.

He came into town downhill, along the same path the wagons had took the first day he had ever seen Deadwood. He didn't know where he was going, he hadn't thought about it. He did know there wasn't anything for him sitting on his heels in the Whitewood Creek, looking for specks of gold. He could have sat in front of his tent with a rifle, like the old man, and waited for the mining companies to buy him out, but the boy did not have a waiting sort of disposition.

It was nine-thirty. He could hear shooting down in the badlands, but he was in no hurry to get there. He had lost his interest in shooting. A woman in a flower-pattern dress came out of the Deadwood Brickworks, Inc., carrying a chamber pot, and spoke to him. He was standing in the mud. "Good morning," she said.

He started a reply, but his tongue suddenly felt too big for his mouth, and he was afraid if he tried to talk, it would come out and he wouldn't be able to get it back in. He smiled at her instead, and the blood leaked out a corner of his mouth, and her face changed.

"Are you shot?" she said.

He shook his head no. She ran back into the Deadwood Brickworks, Inc., calling for the sheriff. The boy stood in the mud and waited, he didn't know what for.

She came back, pulling the sheriff by the arm. He was a big man with eyes like a bad dog. He said, "Is something wrong with you, boy?"

The boy wiped at the front of his mouth and turned away from them to drop a line of blood out of his mouth into the mud. "What's wrong with him?" the woman said.

"Something," the sheriff said, "but it isn't serious."

"He can't speak," she said. "He's bleeding from the mouth."

The sheriff seemed to soften. "All right," he said, "I see what it is now. I'll take care of it."

"Thank you, Sheriff," the woman said. "If you need first-aid techniques, you know where I am . . ."

"I'll take care of it now," the sheriff said. He took the woman by the elbow and walked her off his porch. When she was gone, the sheriff turned to the boy. "Where did you come from?" he said. The sheriff took a step closer. The boy didn't feel afraid, but something was causing the blood to flow from both sides of his mouth now.

"Where did you come from?" the sheriff said again. He reached out and grabbed the boy by the neck. It was almost gentle, the way he reached for him. The boy saw that the sheriff didn't want people to see that he was hurting him. His thumb pushed into the nerve at the bottom of the boy's neck, and the movement started his tongue bleeding for real again, and he opened his mouth to let the blood out.

The sheriff watched him, reconsidered, and let go of his neck.

"If I was you," he said, "I wouldn't come here. This is a business area, son. Ladies walk on the street. If I was you, I'd go to the badlands, or back where I came from."

The boy did not let himself think about where he had come from. And when the sheriff finished, he walked away, toward the badlands. The sheriff stood out on the porch of the Deadwood Brickworks, Inc., watching him. The boy felt him back there. He had a stare you could feel on the back of your head.

He walked into the bathhouse, thinking Charley might be inside. There was nobody there but a soft-brain, though, who wanted to see inside his mouth.

He walked north, downhill, until he saw Charley's camp. There wasn't anybody around. He looked inside the wagon and saw the sheet Charley had laid out for himself, the blanket, the pillow. Everything clean and white. He realized what he wanted was to sleep.

He took off his boots and his shirt. The shirt was heavy from his blood, some dried, some fresh. He walked to the creek and splashed water over his face. He didn't want to soil Charley's bed. The feel of the water on his face made him thirsty, and he poured a little of it from the heels of his hands over his lips. Some of it went into his mouth—he felt it—and then it disappeared. There was nothing to swallow.

He crawled in the back of the wagon and fit himself into the sheets. He lay still a long time, leaving his thoughts empty. He looked at the canvas roof and kept himself still. That was the way you mended, he thought, keeping everything still. He fell in and out of sleep all that day while the sun moved across the canvas top. It was hot, and then it was cooler. The flies were all over him, but he threw his shirt out the back of the wagon, and most of them followed that.

The light was dim when Charley came back to camp. The boy heard him coming in, heard him stop when he realized something was in his wagon. Charley didn't like anybody but himself in his bunk. He called it a shooting matter.

The boy listened to Charley's steps, slow and careful, and then he saw his head at the front end of the wagon, the opposite place he expected it to be. The boy thought Charley would yell, but he didn't. He stood there a minute, looking in, and then he climbed in too, and sat backwards over the driver's seat and looked at him.

"Malcolm?" he said.

The boy smiled. A line of watery blood came out one corner of his mouth. His tongue had swollen now where he couldn't close his teeth. "Good Jesus," Charley said.

The boy shrugged, but his shoulders were under the sheets, where Charley couldn't see them.

Charley wiped at the sides of the boy's mouth with his handkerchief. "What kind of accident was this?" he said. He moved the boy's jaw, seeing if it was broken, and fresh blood ran down into the sheets. Part of the boy's tongue lay between his teeth, the color of the Hills themselves. The tongue was sliced through in front, Charley couldn't see how far back the cut went.

"What in the world?" he said.

The boy smiled again, keeping himself still. He wasn't going to think about that now, he wasn't sure he could remember. When it happened, the boy knew every detail. No matter what assault was made on him, there was something that accepted it, and knew what it was. And walking back to town, even after what had happened, things had a normal feel. Now, though, lying in Charley's bed, it began to slip away from him, the normal world. The boy did not struggle against that, it didn't seem like something you needed to fight.

CHARLEY CONSIDERED WRITING MATILDA A LETTER. HE BEGAN IT ON the evening of the third day the boy had been lying in the wagon.

My Dear Wife,
I do not wish to upset you, there has been a small accident with your brother, the nature of which remains a mystery. Has there been tongue-biting in your family?

Charley got that far and decided against a letter. Even if he told her everything he knew, which wasn't a thing, it wasn't going to satisfy her on anything, except the fact that she had made a terrible mistake trusting him with her brother in the first place. On the other hand, he could conjure a picture of his wife coming in unexpected one day on the stage and finding Malcolm with his tongue swollen half out of his mouth, lying in the wagon with brains like a barbecued squirrel's.

"It isn't likely Matilda would show up unexpected," he told Bill later, "but not impossible. She's done it before."

Bill thought about it half a minute. "If it was me," he said, "I'd write her the letter and keep it on my person at all times. If she showed up and the boy wasn't improved, I'd hand it over and say I didn't have the heart to worry her before."

There was some practicality in that. Charley never considered himself the captive of true love, but there was something about Matilda beyond her skin that he liked, especially when he'd been away, and he didn't like to see her disappointed in him.

"See," Bill said, "you married on a different level. A girl like that can't understand people like us."

Charley nodded, even though it was never what Matilda didn't understand that worried him. Bill said, "My own Agnes, you never saw her short-tempered, because being famous herself, she knows the situations you can get into. It's understanding that makes her different. There's nothing Agnes won't understand."

And Charley heard the wishing in that.

The boy went downhill. He lay still, looking at the ceiling, and except to drool or shrug, did not respond to noise or movement.

Charley bought milk from a widow woman, whose husband had been hit by lightning the week they got to the Hills. She had four children—all girls, one of them too young to talk—and they'd run to Charley when he came for the milk in the morning, and grab his hands and walk him to the back, where the widow kept her cow. Charley wondered what kept her in the Hills, but he never asked. He'd get his hands loose from the little girls, overpay for the milk, and leave. He would feel their hands wrapped around his fingers all day.

In the wagon he'd lift Malcolm's head and pour the milk into the corner of his mouth, a tiny bit at a time. Some days Bill would return from Nuttall and Mann's Number 10 and attend the feeding. That's where he went for his morning drinking and a daily exhibition of his skill at shooting bottles off the heads of soft-brains and drunks.

He would take off his shirt and wash himself in the Whitewood, then cover his chest with mercury, slipping his hands down into his trousers to his privates. Then he'd put on a clean shirt and stand at the back end of the wagon and watch Charley feed the boy.

"How is it?" he'd ask.

Charley would shake his head. "I don't know."

"Well," Bill would say, "he isn't bound for the other side yet."

And then, like his saying it made it so, he'd head off into town somewhere, to play cards or tell stories to the tourists. Some days Charley gave him twenty dollars, and some days Bill didn't need it. Charley never minded the money, he'd never in his life had trouble finding more.

It took him an hour to move a quart of milk from inside the bottle to inside Malcolm. It spilled, of course, and Charley kept a wet towel close by to wipe it as it slid down his cheeks and neck. Even so, the wagon began to smell sour. For smells, Charley hated sour worse than anything up to decayed fish.

He washed the boy after he fed him, and changed the sheets. The first time he did it there was a spot of blood from the boy's backside, but he never saw that again. He took the dirty sheets, along with his own clothes, to a laundry in Chinatown and picked up the clean.

He walked through the two blocks of Chinese slowly. He was interested in their cooking and their language and their ways. One day he saw the girl the Chinese whore man had kept to himself on the wagon train. Another day he saw her picture in the door of one of their theaters. Her name was the China Doll.

Whenever Charley had been to Chinatown, he went to the bath-house. It was later in the day than he liked to bathe, but he waited because it didn't make sense to take a bath and then to go to China-town. Sometimes he sat in the tub and talked to the Bottle Fiend, sometimes he didn't. It was funny with the soft-brain. You could say what you wanted, sorting out your thoughts, because he couldn't understand what things meant, but then the next day he might repeat the whole thing back to you.

"It don't seem right," the soft-brain told him one morning, "that the boy ought to be getting between you and your life, but there it is. You marry, you carry."

Charley gave him a dollar and said, "Forget you heard that, Bottle Man."

The Bottle Fiend said, "What?"

In the afternoons, Charley looked into business. He spent two days in the district recorder's office, going over placer claims. He had bought and sold claims in Colorado, but it was nothing he liked. If you wanted to know who somebody was, set them down next to a gold claim. Charley had seen common people cheat their brothers and fathers, abuse their wives and leave their children to get close to gold. Mostly, they acted on the assumption they could come back and straighten it all out after they were rich. They believed gold healed, too.

And there wasn't a man in a hundred who doubted he could handle it. The softest-brains in the Hills, the kind that couldn't buy new boots without having their own dog piss all over them, would all assume they could handle money.

It was easy enough, then—buying and selling mining claims— to take what money those people had, but the feeling was related to the one he sometimes got the moment a black bear came out of her den in the morning, and he was sitting in a tree forty feet away with a needle gun waiting for her. It always felt like it was too early.

Of course, trading mining claims, you didn't have a Ute Indian shooting your ass out of the tree while you were sitting there waiting.

Charley studied the placer claims and declined to enter the business. There were other things he understood as well. Transportation, hauling, if worst came to worst he could trap for a living. He had something over $30,000 in Colorado banks, there was no hurry. Money had always come to him like he was standing downhill.

By the end of the week, he had decided to run a pony express from Fort Laramie into the Hills. A transportation line was too encumbered, Charley was not married to this place yet. He had been partners in such a line before, and there was more to it than mules and wagons.

The financing was not incidental. Teams of two mules or American horses went for three hundred dollars each. Broncs were eighty dollars, pack mules were sixty dollars, where you could find them. Charley didn't know what he would do with his yet, but he was grateful to have them. Then there was food for the animals, and horseshoes, and a blacksmith's tools, and guns and ammunition and shovels and hatchets. Oats were $1.40 a hundredweight, baled hay was twenty-five dollars a ton. And some of the drivers ate too.

And sometimes they stole, but more often they lightened their loads by throwing part of it away. Charley's experience in the transportation business was that the only way things operated right was when he rode the wagons himself, and there was no future in that for a man with painful legs.

The pony express looked cleaner. Of course, he had never operated one before. There was already a twice-weekly service run by Enis Clippinger, but it took a letter two weeks or less to get from

Boston or San Francisco to Cheyenne, and that long again to find its owner in the Hills. And then, depending on the rider—some could read and some couldn't—the seals on the letter would be broken and the letter stuffed wrong into the envelope.

Sometimes the letters didn't get to the miners at all. Enis Clippinger wrote public notices blaming the Indians and the outlaws. He said the miners were ungrateful of his efforts. He also said nobody could do better, which was when Charley decided to take his business. On Thursday he sent letters to the *Black Hills Pioneer* and the *Cheyenne Leader* announcing his new service.

> *Messr. Charles Utter has established a pony express between Deadwood and Cheyenne and will make round trips hereafter. All riders are hired illiterate. The pony express must prove a great convenience and we hope it may be adequately patronized.*

It took him one minute to write. Bill stood over him, watching. "I don't know how you do that," he said. "Like the words are already inside the pen."

"It's just what's in your brain," Charley said. "The way the words come to you naturally is the best way to put them down."

Bill said, "The things in my head don't come in words."

THE BOY STAYED THE SAME, OR MIGHT OF LOST GROUND. IT WAS HARD to say. Charley fed him milk until he refused it, washed him, changed his sheets. He'd almost given up talk, the boy wasn't listening. And the boy didn't know him from the blanket. He thought he might hire someone to care for him until it went one way or the other. The thought came to Charley then that if you stayed one way long enough, that was the way you were. He wished he could explain it to the boy.

By the end of the week, the boy's tongue had turned colors. It was lighter now, greens and blues and purples, and didn't look so swollen. "What in the world could of happened to you?" Charley said, more to himself than the boy. The boy shrugged. He always shrugged when he heard talk.

Calamity Jane Cannary came by on Friday afternoon. She had stopped three times previous, looking for Bill. Once he had hid under the wagon. Friday afternoon was the first time Charley had ever seen her sober.

"He's in the wagon, ain't he?" she said.

"No, ma'am," Charley said.

"There's something in there," she said.

He said, "It's my wife's brother." He tried to mention his wife at least once every time he saw Jane. "He's been sickly all week."

Jane took off her hat and ran her fingers through the knots and tangles and burrs in her hair. Charley looked for bats. "What is it?" she said. "Torpid fever?"

Charley shook his head. "I don't know," he said. "I found him in there early this week, and he hasn't moved since." Jane closed her eyes, thinking.

"I'll take a look at him for you," she said.

"There's already been the doctor here," Charley said. He'd found Dr. O. E. Sick at his office one afternoon and brought him back to the wagon. He went to him because of his association with the Bottle Fiend, which somehow struck Charley as connected to the present case. Dr. O. E. Sick had run his fingers through the boy's hair. "In some ways," he'd said, "it resembles snakebite."

"Doctors don't know nothin' about healing," Jane said. She walked past Charley to the wagon, washing him in her smell. She was wearing buckskin trousers and a fringed buckskin coat, an old Colt .41 that must have weighed eight pounds, an ammunition belt, and a wool scarf around her neck. It was the middle of a summer afternoon.

She leaned into the wagon, staring. "Why, he ain't nothing but a boy," she said when she had come out.

"He's eighteen," Charley said. "My wife's brother." She climbed into the wagon then, and Charley heard her in there, talking to him, moving things. He didn't try to stop her; it took a shock sometimes to bring a person out from under a spell.

She asked Charley for water, which he got her, and then a towel. She stayed in there with him most of an hour. "His tongue is swole," she said when she came out, "but it's more serious than that."

"I don't know what it is," Charley said.

"I could come by," Jane said, "and look after him. I nursed the sick all my life. Smallpox, torpid fever, consumption . . ."

Charley did not see how it would hurt the boy to have a little more company. There was a temptation to picture the unexpected arrival of his wife again—finding Malcolm fork-tongued and molested of his senses in the care of Calamity Jane Cannary—but he fought it off.

He saw that she wanted to be in Bill's camp, but it was something else too. She cared for the sick. Charley left her there with the boy and went looking for Enis Clippinger.

HE FOUND BILL INSTEAD, OUTSIDE THE BELLA UNION. PINK BUFORD'S bulldog had just killed a wolf in the street. Pink collected five hundred dollars, and was inside, buying drinks. Bill was sitting on the steps with the dog. The dog had lost an ear in the fight, but was otherwise unmarked.

"I wish Pink Buford wouldn't fight this dog so much," Bill said.

Charley said, "It must be what he likes."

Bill kissed the dog on the muzzle and looked him in the eye. "I can't see it," he said. He moved the animal's head and looked at the place where his ear had been. "That isn't going to grow back," he said. The dog licked Bill's chin. The wolf lay in the street, opened wide at the throat.

Charley sat down next to Bill. "I decided to run a pony express," he said.

"They already got a pony express."

Charley shook his head. "I'm going to race him, Cheyenne to Deadwood, for rights to the mail business."

Bill said, "Why would they race you?"

"I'll issue a challenge," Charley said. "When you issue the challenge, they always come around to race."

Bill smoothed the bulldog's ear back on his head, trying to make both sides look the same. When he spoke again, Charley heard something coming. "I located a dead Chinaman half a mile north of here," Bill said. "Near the mules."

"A dead Chinaman."

Bill shrugged. "They didn't have a cause of death, or even a name. Nobody claimed him, so he's ours."

"Lucky day," Charley said.

Bill looked at the dog while he talked. "There was a delivery today, from Sioux City. A kiln, a great big bastard, to the Deadwood Brickworks. They left it north of town."

"Who left it north of town?"

Bill shrugged again. "Whoever. They weren't ready for it yet at the Brickworks, so they left it. Cast iron, it must weigh four tons. I removed the crate myself."

"Slow down," Charley said. The Deadwood Brickworks belonged to the sheriff, and Charley saw where Bill was pointed in this.

"We could go out there tonight," Bill said. Charley thought it over, remembering the newspaper account of Baron Van Palm. Bill said, "A Chinaman's got a right to decent disposal too."

The part that came back to Charley was when the baron's hand pointed toward his ascending soul, and a holy light glowed around his feet. He had to admit it was something he wouldn't have minded seeing for himself. "The Chinaman didn't have a family?"

Bill said, "All they intend to do for him is dig a four-foot hole in the ground and roll him in. Chinese don't even get a box if nobody claims them. He's better off with us."

"You know whose vessel that is you propose to use to float this slant-eyes to heaven? You know who the Deadwood Brickworks is?"

Bill was not interested. "What difference does that make?"

"Bullock," Charley said. "It's Sheriff Bullock's kiln."

Bill looked at him, waiting for the rest. Charley waited too. That seemed like enough. Bill said, "You think this might be against the law? You think they got a law about Chinese in kilns? This place barely has laws against crucifixion . . ."

Charley edged away from him, not to confuse the Lord over which one of them said that. "Besides," Bill said, "all that's left when we're done is a few ashes. The sheriff won't know it's been tested."

Some time passed before Charley spoke again. Their conversations were like that, they would let the words settle between them before they added to them.

"How did you come into possession of this slant-eyes?" he said.

Bill shook his head. "Dr. Wedelstaedt gave him to me. He said the Chinese was ostracized from the rest. They wouldn't talk to him if he came in the front door, they wouldn't see him if he was standing in front of them. He wasn't allowed to live in Chinatown or attend the Chinese rituals."

"You been seeing Doc Wedelstaedt?" Charley said. He didn't like having more people in it than needed to be there. "What's he said?"

"He says the Chinese got their ways and we got ours. He isn't much of one to make judgments."

"I mean about yourself."

Bill looked away. "He's got treatments, but nothing that would appear to be better than dying. One thing is a wire that he sticks up your weasel and heats it."

Charley tried to see how bad Bill had taken that news, but he couldn't read it one way or the other. "He gave me more mercury," Bill said, "and then he told me about the Chinese, and what his own people did to him. He's the kind of doctor that if he can't fix what's wrong with you, he's got a story about somebody that's worse off."

Charley nodded. There were a lot of that kind of doctors. "Did he say why the Chinese did that to one of their own?"

Bill stood up and stretched and smoothed his hair back off his face. "It had something to do with a girl," he said. "More than one, maybe. He knows their names, which all sound sing-song to me. It was money and weasel and promises, one depending on the other, and there wasn't anything they could do in the end but ostracize him or admit they might of been wrong about the way they had things set up for about three thousand years. The slant-eyes say 'Sorry, sorry' all the time, but among themselves they don't like to be wrong."

"Nobody spoke to him, over a girl . . ."

"Not a person," Bill said. "They sent him off into the trees, I guess he'd been there since spring. The doc says he never heard of him until he was dead. When that happened, the Chinese were more conciliatory, at least to the point they would mention his name out loud."

Charley stayed on the step, looking up at Bill. He thought of how the Chinese liked to talk, how they couldn't seem to get it out fast enough. "That must have been a lonely slant-eyes," he said.

"Well," Bill said, "it's taken care of now."

THE CHINESE WAS LYING UNDER A SMALL PILE OF BRANCHES AND PINE needles, back in the trees beyond the field where Charley had tethered his mules. Bill went right to the spot, even though in the fading light he couldn't have seen the length of his arm. Charley followed, putting his feet in the same places Bill's had been, out of habit.

Before they got to the Chinese they passed his lean-to, and Charley stopped to look inside. There was a book he took to be some sort of Bible, a pair of U.S. Army boots, a bone knife, an empty money pouch. They were set out neatly along the straw mat the Chinese had used for a bed, as if they were things he meant to sell.

"There isn't even a picture in there," Charley said.

Bill said, "Maybe he didn't want to see them, either." A little later he said, "There's white men do cruel things too."

Charley could see the Chinese before they moved a branch. He was lying face-up, not much bigger than a boy. He had on loose pants, sandals, and a U.S. Army coat. His mouth was open half an inch and there was dirt on his front teeth. Bill began to pull the branches off. "Is this where he died?" Charley said.

Bill said, "I found him on this spot, and never touched a thing."

The more Bill uncovered, the less of the Chinese there was. Charley suddenly didn't want to know about the Chinese, any more than he had to.

When the branches were gone, Bill borrowed Charley's handkerchief and brushed the pine dust off the face. "He wasn't much more than a boy, was he?" Charley said. Bill stopped cleaning the Chinese and said he wished he'd brought a bottle of pink gin along.

Charley said, "I wish you did too." Bill picked up the body as if there were no more weight to it than the clothes it was wrapped in. He draped it over his shoulder and they walked around the edge of the field, keeping just behind the trees. It was a half mile that way over fallen limbs and singed tree stumps, but Bill never even broke a sweat. Charley followed him, watching the Chinese's head bounce against Bill's back.

The kiln was a monster. The doors must of weighed two hundred pounds themselves. It was built on two tiers. There was a bottom compartment for wood or coal, and a top for what you intended to heat. The compartments were separated by a steel grating and a flat piece of metal that might have been tin.

The crating Bill had removed lay in a pile nearby, as tall as the kiln itself.

Bill said, "What do you think about that metal? You want to take it out, and lay him on the grating?" Charley didn't have an opinion on it one way or the other. "In the paper," Bill said, "did they have the baron on a sheet of tin or was it open fire?"

Charley put his head inside the kiln. It was as hollow and dark as bad dreams in there. "It didn't say," he said. Charley pulled his head out. "The problem with the grating," he said, "is if you wanted to keep the ashes separate from the wood. Without the tin, ashes is ashes, and we'd be guessing which was which."

Bill thought it over. "If it was me," he said, "I'd want the tin. You might need time for the soul to ascend from the remains. I think they probably used the tin with old Baron Van Palm . . ."

The tin slid out of the oven like a shelf. They laid it on the ground and put the Chinese on top of it. Bill straightened the clothes and did what he could to get the arms to lie at the sides. They tied the feet together to make it look neater.

Charley started the fire. He used dried pine branches and the crate the kiln had come in as kindling, and then went back for the Chinese's own firewood for the rest, walking straight across the field now he wasn't moving bodies. There were two flues in the top of the kiln that controlled the heat. Charley set them wide open, and when he looked in through the eye-hole twenty minutes later, the kiln had begun to glow.

The Chinese lay on the ground with his feet tied together.

"I do wish I'd brought along a bottle of pink," Bill said. They waited another ten minutes, neither of them talking. Then Bill said, "You think it's time?"

Charley looked into the eye-hole again, and the insides of the kiln were orange-red, he could see every detail of the seams. "If we're going to do it," he said.

Charley opened the top door, and the heat backed them both away. They picked up the piece of tin with the Chinese on it. Bill took the end with the head. "You're going to thank us," he said to the Chinese, "when we meet on the other side."

The Chinese wasn't heavy, but the tin was. "You think we ought to say some words over him first?" Bill said.

Charley said, "I think we ought to put him in the oven or put him down."

They put him in. Neither one of them was much for false starts once events were in motion. The tin fit into a groove in each side of the oven, and they slid it in and closed the door.

The heat of the kiln watered Charley's eyes, and he and Bill stood there for the first minute after the door was closed, looking at each other. Then Bill opened the eye-hole and stared inside.

"What's he doing?" Charley said.

Bill moved away from the hole and Charley looked in. The Chinese's clothes were on fire, and his hair. Little fires that started and then went out. His skin turned dark, and blistered, but he didn't catch fire himself.

Charley closed the eye-hole and moved away from the kiln. It felt like the heat had wrinkled his face. He and Bill sat on a log. "Sometime I'd like to know," Charley said, "what he did, that they would treat him like that."

Bill shook his head. "The doc explained it, but I don't think the celestials tell him the truth. To them, everybody's a foreigner." They sat quietly for a few minutes. There were popping noises inside the kiln. Bill said, "If they'd hung him, that's at least admitting he was there."

Charley went back to the oven. It felt hotter than it had. The Chinese was still intact. The edges of his ears were burned, and there was fluid from his eyes that bubbled on his cheeks but didn't seem to evaporate. And the feet were pink. "How's he doing?" Bill said.

Charley scratched his neck. "It's a time for patience," he said.

"This has got an empty feel," Bill said after a while. "It might not be a fair test, on account of the circumstances. That isn't an ordinary man in there, even an ordinary celestial. He was nobody so long, maybe the point's lost in the send-off now." Charley stared at him. Bill said, "How long could you go like that, nobody would admit you were there, before you began to wonder yourself?"

"He must have known when he was hungry," Charley said. "He built a lean-to, he must of looked at that and seen somebody did it." Bill went to the kiln now and looked inside.

"I'm talking about his spirit," Bill said. "This one, maybe his spirit was already departed, and we're sitting out here wasting our time."

"Either way, this is where we are," Charley said.

It got darker, and then the air turned cold, like it had the night they went to the play. Charley thought of Mrs. Langrishe dry, and he thought of her wet. He couldn't make up his mind which way he liked her best. Lightning broke overhead, then thunder.

The first drops of rain fell on the kiln. Frying noises. Bill and Charley stayed where they were. "What I meant," Bill said after a while, "was there's a part of you that anchors to what common people think. There's a body of opinion that you can't get away from, even if you lived by yourself twelve months a year."

Charley adjusted his hat so the rain would run off the front of the brim, and not down his back. "What's being famous," Bill said, "but somebody's opinion? It's the same as love. That doesn't make it false. If there is love in this world, then there are opinions, and one is as good as the other."

The rain on the kiln was smoking now. Bill was still working something out. "When the Chinese took away their opinions of this boy, they took away the biggest part, and he might not have been strong enough to keep his spirit by himself. It might have already left."

Charley looked in the kiln again. The lightning was hitting up in the hills. "I think it's going to take longer than the baron," he said.

"You see what I'm saying to you?" Bill said.

Charley nodded. "That you been loved," he said.

They sat in the rain and waited. After a while Bill said, "We could sit this out in town."

IT STARTED TO HAIL JUST AS THEY GOT TO THE DOOR OF NUTTALL AND Mann's Number 10. It looked to Charley like a hundred people inside. They went to the bar and Bill ordered a gin and bitters. Like magic, Pink Buford's bulldog was standing at his feet, and a minute later Captain Jack Crawford was there too.

Captain Jack was with Brick Pomeroy, the horse man from Belle Fourche. Brick had caught up with his Mex in Crook City and shot him in the street. Captain Jack told the story and bought drinks for Bill and Brick Pomeroy. Charley bought his own, a nice brown shot of whiskey from the United States of America. There was a professor at the piano, and every kind of whore known to man, except a clean one.

Charley thought of Mrs. Langrishe, fresh out of her bath. He thought of the way her hand had felt when she took his arm. Captain Jack was discussing dead moose again. Charley had stepped away from the milk-drinker, but he heard him just the same. The man's voice carried like a bad taste in food. Presently Captain Jack stepped around Bill and addressed Charley.

"Bill and me are ready to hunt," he said. "Take a few horses up into the Hills and kill some moose. I know a place where they've never been bothered, they'll walk right up and nuzzle your ear."

Charley looked around like he'd just woke up in the middle of the Red Desert. "The Indians never hunted them," Captain Jack said, "sacred ground." He smiled when he said that, and some of the tourists laughed. "Of course, that never kept them from spilling white men's blood."

"What about the Minutemen?" Charley said. "Who's to keep this settlement safe from the blood-spillers if you're up in the hills killing moose?"

"Two days, and we'll be back," Captain Jack said. Charley looked him over, happy-mouthed and innocent. All in all, Charley would rather have gone moose-hunting with the Ute that shot him in the leg. "Wild Bill says you are the best hunter in Colorado," Captain Jack said.

Bill shrugged and reached for another glass of pink gin. There was a line of them waiting for him now as long as his forearm, and Charley knew he would drink them all with no visible effect. "You don't need the best hunter in Colorado to shoot moose that kiss you in the ear," Charley said.

"There's grizzly up there too," Captain Jack said, like that was free dessert.

Charley covered his eyes and tried to picture scrambling up a tree in front of Captain Jack Crawford, armed. "It isn't a good time of year to be encountering grizzly," he said. "A she-rip with cubs, the Indians'll be kinder to your body."

Captain Jack turned back to Bill, who had finished the gin in his hand and was reaching for another. "I predicted he wouldn't want to go," he said. The hail was coming heavier now, and with the noise of it on the roof, Charley could barely hear them.

Bill looked at Captain Jack, then back at Charley. "A hunt might not be so bad," he said. "The exercise relieves the shakes in your blood."

"We always hunted alone," Charley said.

"Just us and Jack," Bill said. "Jack's hunted moose with Custer . . ."

Charley saw that Bill was asking him for something now, and he'd never told Bill no in his life. He said, "I suppose I could use some fresh air," and it was settled.

Captain Jack called the bartender over and bought Charley a shot of brown whiskey. He stationed himself on one side of Charley, Bill was on the other, and offered his glass of milk for Bill to toast. That left Charley in the middle, and he didn't have any choice but to join them. "To the moose," Captain Jack said.

Bill touched the glasses and killed another gin and bitters. "To ear-kissers everywhere," Charley said.

The storm lasted. Bill won fifteen dollars playing poker and drank free all night after shooting a beer glass off Pink Buford's bulldog's head. When things quieted, Captain Jack told the story again of Brick Pomeroy catching up with the greaser in Crook City. "Shot him four times, right, partner? Four?"

Brick Pomeroy was drinking pink gin too. He said four was the right number, but he wasn't anxious to tell it again. "I ain't even sure the greaser ought to be dead," he said.

Captain Jack bought him a drink and got himself another milk. "Modesty is a rare virtue in this country," he said, "and a welcome one."

They stayed at Nuttall and Mann's until the storm quit. Until Bill was half asleep and Charley was so drunk he'd begun to see what Bill liked about Captain Jack Crawford. He didn't know what time it was, but somewhere late in the night Charley noticed the sound of the wind and rain was gone. He walked outside and the hailstones had melted.

"If we're truly going to hunt moose tomorrow," he said to Bill, "we ought to close our eyes a while first." Bill never said a word. He just got up off his chair and walked back to camp. They went single file, Bill, Charley, and Pink Buford's bulldog. Bill climbed into his bedroll without taking off his boots. The dog curled up into his chin. One of them began to snore, and then the other. Charley couldn't tell which snore belonged to which party.

Charley took off his guns and boots and clothes, and washed. The creek was ice cold from the storm. He put his face a few inches above the water and rinsed it again and again, cupping the water in his hands. He did that until his cheeks went numb. Then he quit, and it felt like needle points all over his cheeks, and the life began to come back.

He brushed out his bedding in the small tent he was sleeping in now, with the boy in the wagon. Thinking of the boy, he looked in to make sure he was covered. It was darker in there than outside, reminding him of the kiln, and it took Charley's eyes a minute to adjust. Then he saw the boy, lying open-eyed in the dark, staring at him. His head was cradled in the armpit of Calamity Jane Cannary, who was sound asleep, and looked happier than Charley had ever seen her before.

It was a few minutes after daybreak when Captain Jack came for them. He was wearing two guns on his belt, and had packed a Springfield needle rifle and a scattergun in his saddle. He was wearing more ammunition than a Mexican.

The sound of the horses woke Charley up, but Bill was already awake, sitting on the stump he favored, rubbing himself with mercury. If Captain Jack noticed Bill had silver skin, he didn't say so.

They went from Charley's camp to the north end of town to pick up two of his mules. It wasn't until they were in the grazing field that Charley remembered the celestial they'd left in the kiln. He got off his horse and handed the reins to Captain Jack. "You wait here," he said. "Bill and I got something to talk over."

Bill looked at Charley a minute, then got off his horse too. They walked off in the direction of the mules, and the kiln, which was black and undeniable in the corner of the clearing. Behind them, Captain Jack was in a hurry to get on with the moose-killing. "We don't need pack animals, boys," he said.

Charley turned around and said, "Are these creatures of yours friendly enough to accompany us back so we can shoot them here?"

He and Bill walked the rest of the way without a word. The ground was soaked, and their moccasins made wet noises as they went. The mules were tethered about a hundred feet from the kiln, and when they got to the animals Charley allowed himself a look back at Captain Jack. "How could we forget the celestial?" Bill said, no more than a whisper.

"It was the drinking," Charley said.

Bill nodded. "I wish to hell I had something in my hand right now," he said. Charley untied two of the mules, Bill stood looking at the kiln. He said, "I never forgot something of this nature in my life."

They walked the last hundred feet to the kiln and Charley opened it. First the top door, then the bottom. He stared inside for what seemed like a long time, then he closed the doors in the same order he'd opened them. He took one of the mules from Bill and started back toward the other end of the clearing, where Captain Jack was waiting.

"Somebody's watching," Bill said.

Charley didn't argue or ask who. He fell in next to Bill and walked. "You know where they are?" he said, into his shirt.

Bill looked straight ahead. "No, just that they're there."

"Who is it?"

"I don't know," Bill said.

Before they got to Captain Jack, Charley said, "The kiln's empty."

Bill said, "There has to be ashes."

Charley said, "No there doesn't."

THEY FOLLOWED THE WAGON TRAIL SOUTH INTO THE HILLS, KEEPING to one side or the other, more to stay out of the mud than to hide from Indians. At noon they left the trail and went east. "An Indian showed me this place," Captain Jack said. "I expect he's gone bad too, like the rest." He looked around at the Hills. "I wouldn't mind running into a redskin or two today," he said.

Bill hadn't spoken since they left the clearing and the kiln. They came to a flooded creek and followed it south most of the afternoon. When they stopped, Bill walked off into the bushes for half an hour.

Captain Jack got off his horse and pointed south. "About a mile down, it widens," he said to Charley, "just a few hundred yards. The water gets deep, and there's a little island out in the middle of it, all by itself. That's where the moose are."

"You didn't say anything about an island," Charley said. It was a queer thing for a man who spent so much of his life in water, but Charley couldn't swim a stroke. He thought his body sank because it had inner heaviness.

Captain Jack smiled. "I got a canoe," he said. "The same redskin showed me this place sold me his canoe."

The word *canoe* set off a panic in Charley. "If you wanted," Captain Jack was saying, "you could pick them off from this side with the Springfield, and then paddle over and pick them up. They'll come right to the edge of the island to see what we are."

"Some sport," Charley said. "Canoes, moose that come to watch you shoot them . . ." Captain Jack smiled in a certain way, and Charley thought he was probably composing an epic poem on it right now.

Captain Jack was looking in the direction of the bushes. "What's keeping Bill?" he said.

"He'll be along," Charley said.

Captain Jack shook his head. "He hasn't appeared well," he said. "All morning long I've wondered was he sick." Charley looked at him but didn't answer. Captain Jack said, "Sometimes when you look at Bill he looks right, and sometimes he doesn't. But he never complains a word." The way he put it, that was a question.

Charley held silent.

"I always thought he'd be different," Captain Jack said. "From the stories, I thought he'd be wild."

There was some movement in the bushes now, Bill coming back. "When the time comes," Charley said, "he's wild enough."

Bill's mood had improved now that he'd passed water, and Captain Jack felt the difference and engaged him in conversation. Charley rode behind them, attached to the mules, and the water, thinking of canoes. More than most, Charley hated to be helpless.

They rode through a stand of evergreens so thick that the trees seemed to change color inside. Everything in there turned dark. Charley heard Bill's voice up ahead, steady and calm; nobody would have guessed he'd just gone stone blind.

When they came out of the trees Charley saw the island. The creek widened to maybe seventy yards, and the island was two thirds of the way across. The water was dark, no white in it at all, and he wondered what act of nature had occurred there to cause deep water this high in the Hills.

Charley tended to think more about how things got the way they were when he was in the mountains than he did when he was in the flats. He believed the world had once been bigger than it was now, and that in the squeezing down, parts of it had been forced up, between God's fingers. And God had left it like that, left the testing places for those that needed testing.

Captain Jack got off his horse and tied her to a sapling. Bill leaned in the saddle and dropped a line of spit to the ground. "It's right down here," Captain Jack said. He'd hidden the canoe under some branches fifty feet from the water, where it wouldn't wash away in a flood. The branches were arranged in such a way that you'd have to be blind not to notice something was hid there. The canoe was stub-nosed and narrow, not really a canoe at all. It was fastened together with nails and rawhide and baling wire. It looked exactly like half a dozen Indians had built it all at one time, without checking to see what each other were doing. The Sioux were not a great nation of boat-builders.

Captain Jack pulled the branches off, and the more Charley could see, the worse it looked. "What do you think?" Jack said to Bill.

Bill shrugged. "Why ask him?" Charley said. "He can swim."

Captain Jack flicked at some insects that had burrowed into the wood, and then pushed his thumb through the hull.

"Rotted," Charley said.

Captain Jack shook his head. "Just one spot," he said. "It's up over the water line." The sun went behind the hills in back of them, and the place began to feel dark. Captain Jack said, "If we get to it, we can be across before nightfall."

"We got to feed the horses and mules," Charley said. "We'll stay on this side tonight." The way he said that, it wasn't up for a vote. Bill got off his horse and pulled a bottle of gin and bitters from one of the saddlebags. Charley hoped he had something brown in there too, although he'd been meaning to cut back. Matilda disapproved and was still in the back of his thoughts. He had not given up on her. There was something about sitting in a bathhouse, for instance, and seeing a rail-thin morphine addict come in and take off her clothes that made him crave his wife's company.

On the other hand, Mrs. Langrishe had replaced her in his regular, conscious longings.

"Did you bring anything to imbibe that isn't colored pink?" he said.

Bill shook his head. "You ought to give pink its chance," he said. "It's a different taste on your breath the next morning, and it doesn't leak out of your skin."

Captain Jack took the saddle off his horse and began on Bill's. "You still got to put it in your mouth," Charley said.

"It's a first time for everything," Bill said. The mare he'd been riding had a blind right eye, and was nervous to that side. Captain Jack never noticed until he'd walked behind her and she kicked him in the leg. It wasn't much of a kick—it glanced off the side of his thigh, where it could have just as easily broken his kneecap—but it dropped him to the ground. He lay where he fell, cussing. Charley was embarrassed for him, lying on the ground crying when he wasn't hurt. Bill pretended he hadn't seen it.

Captain Jack got up slowly, flexing the leg at the knee. He walked around to the front of the animal, giving her plenty of room, and then jerked her reins twice. He said, "You ingrate whore," and then did something more ignorant than walking behind a one-eyed horse on her blind side. He hit her in the head. He made a fist with his right hand, still holding her reins with his left, and hit her square in the forehead. The poet-scout.

This time Captain Jack didn't cuss. He just sat down and

watched his hand swell. The worst of it was the knuckle of the little finger, which puffed three times normal size. Bill took a drink of the gin and bitters and offered the bottle to Charley.

"All right," Charley said, and he took it. "I like a drink after a good fight."

"I think she broke my hand," Captain Jack said.

Charley said, "In any battle, there's winners and losers."

Captain Jack's face got damp and moldy-looking. "I never broke anything before," he said.

Bill took the bottle back and said, "Would you look at his hand for him, Charley?"

Charley leaned over to get close to the hand. "You still haven't broke anything," he said. He put Jack's hand on top of his, gently, palm to palm. He pointed to the knuckle and then touched the finger connected to it.

"See this here," he said, closing his hand around the finger, "when it makes a pop sound, that means it wasn't broke."

Charley sat still a minute, until Captain Jack began to understand what he was going to do, and then he pulled the finger straight out. There was a popping noise as the bone slipped back into the joint, and then the color returned to Jack's cheeks. He looked at Charley with new respect.

"That's sharp," he said, moving the finger.

Bill said, "Charley's always been medicine sharp. He learned it from Calamity Jane."

Charley took the pink from him and had another swallow. It did have a different weight in his stomach, it felt sillier than whiskey. "It isn't anything," Charley said. "Me and all my family have been nursing horse-fighters since time begun."

CHARLEY WOKE UP STIFF. IT ALWAYS TOOK HIM A FEW DAYS TO GET used to new sleeping arrangements. Bill was still asleep, wrapped around an empty bottle, drooling. Captain Jack was propped against a tree with his needle gun across his lap.

He jumped when Charley sat up, the gun moving toward movement. "Easy," Charley said. "Let's see how bad I feel first, then you can go ahead and shoot." Gin was a different business, all right. It settled higher up in the head than whiskey, and Charley's mouth, instead of tasting bad, like it would have from whiskey, had turned combustible. Captain Jack began to smile.

"You don't look too good yourself, horse-fighter," Charley said.

"I been awake all night," he said, as if that were somehow better than hung over. "I tried to wake you and Bill for your watches, but it might as well of been an opium den . . ."

"Opium?" Charley said. "You been visiting celestials?"

"I have never been to an opium den in my life," he said. "All I know is what I heard." Charley shrugged and stood up. He was dizzy and weak and thirsty. He took off his shirt and pants and walked naked out into the water. Captain Jack looked the other way, embarrassed.

"Kick that legend on the ground awake," Charley said. The water was making him feel better. "Tell him he missed his watch." Captain Jack looked at Bill, but he didn't move to kick him. Charley held his breath and dropped completely under the water. It pressed in on his ears, panicking him, reminding him of being buried. He stood up and walked back to the camp and kicked Bill himself.

Bill spoke without opening his eyes. "I have been dreaming," he said, "that old women were profaning my legend."

"It wasn't me, Bill," Captain Jack said. Charley got back into his pants slowly. The discouragement of leg trouble was that the first things you did in the morning—dress and stand up—reminded you of it. Bill sat up and checked the bottom of the bottle for gin.

They loaded their rope and guns into the canoe. Bill sat in back because he liked to steer, and Captain Jack sat in front. Charley was in the middle, faced backwards toward Bill, holding on to both sides. When they were halfway across, he said, "You know, you do appear legendary in this light."

Bill stopped paddling and got that look like they were going to have to rassle. He spit between his knees. He was sweating pure gin, Charley could smell it. Charley didn't want to rassle anybody in a boat. "Of course," he said, quoting from *Harper's Weekly*, "it could just be the sun playing in those steely blue eyes."

The words touched Captain Jack, who quit paddling too and turned around to stare at them. Charley noticed the canoe starting to move sideways. "Pay attention to the damn boat," he said. In his experience, anything you rode, if it was going sideways you were in some kind of trouble.

"That had a poetical quality, what you said," Captain Jack said. "I might use that sometime."

Charley said, "If you get me to land, you can use every word I ever said. I give it all to you now, with Bill Hickok, a legend, as my witness."

They pulled the canoe thirty feet up the bank of the island and left it under a pine tree. Charley got out, taking his time straightening up. It killed his legs one way to be cramped and another way to be straightened. "Are you hurt?" Captain Jack said.

Charley shook his head. "Give me a minute to put my bones back together," he said.

"If you want, you could wait here," Captain Jack said, talking to him now like Charley was somebody's wife that tagged along and couldn't keep up.

"I said give me a minute," Charley said. "I don't want to miss your shoot-out with the moose." They climbed a hill and found rocks where something tall had molted. They sat down in some trees a few yards away and waited. Charley stretched his legs straight out in front of him, and that stopped the worst of the pain, the part that shot up into his hips. It was a relief, like bad news that proved untrue. That's how he thought of the onset of pain, like bad news. Once you weren't afraid of it, it came to you like reported facts.

The moose came from the low side of the gully, a bull and two cows. Captain Jack flattened out on the ground and sighted down the barrel of the needle gun. Charley could hear his breathing change.

The bull lifted his head into the air and stopped. "He's caught our scent," Captain Jack said. The bull looked directly at them then and stood dead still. The cows waited behind him, swinging their heads. The bull blew air through his nose and moved a few steps closer.

The cows stayed with him, nervous now. They'd caught the scent too. The bull kept coming, looking at the opening in the trees where they were. Captain Jack pulled the hammer back on the needle gun, his hand shaking like he'd been drinking all night.

The bull was fifty feet away and heard the hammer cock. He stopped again, looking right at them, as if it was something there he couldn't quite figure out. The ball tore open his throat and he turned around, as if he could just walk away from it, and then dropped onto the rocks. The cows stayed where they were. One of them touched him with her nose.

"The others," Captain Jack said. Bill and Charley looked at each other, and then Charley broke cover. He picked up a rock and walked down the gully, keeping himself between Captain Jack and the cows, and when he was close enough he threw the rock and shouted. The cows turned and ran.

The bull's head lay cockeyed on the ground; the smooth, heavy antlers wouldn't let it rest flat. His eyes were open and his heart was still beating, because the blood pumped out of the hole in his neck in spurts, but there wasn't much power driving it now. His nose was coated in dirt, but the dust in front of it didn't stir.

"We could of took the other two," Captain Jack said. He and Bill were standing behind Charley now.

"Some hunt," Charley said. He said it to Bill; there wasn't anything he wanted to say to Captain Jack. Bill stared at the animal and then closed his eyes, like he was praying. Captain Jack went back to the trees for the ropes. "Some hunt," Charley said again.

"It's nothing but a sad-nosed horse," Bill said. "Not worth the case you're building. The circumstances don't matter, he ended up the same as a thousand others."

"It doesn't matter to him," Charley said, "but if we left the etiquette of it up to the animals, they'd probably just as soon we did something else in the first place."

Captain Jack tied a rope around the bull's neck, just behind the antlers, then climbed to the top of the gully, playing the rope out as he went. He walked behind a pine tree, making a pulley, and then came back down the gully to Bill and Charley.

"Once we get him there," he said, pointing at the tree, "we can slide him down to the water easy." Captain Jack held on to the rope and waited to see if they were going to help. Bill took a deep breath and grabbed the rope at the very end, where he could steer. Captain Jack took the spot in front of him and Charley looked at them both for a minute, and then moved in front of Captain Jack. He couldn't see just leaving the bull out there for the flies.

They pulled together, on the count of three. The moose moved half a foot. Bill counted to three again, and half a foot at a time they got him up the gully. It took all morning. Once, the place where the ball had gone into the bull's neck began to tear, and Captain Jack had to retie the rope. They dragged him up the rocks. They sweated and counted and breathed through their teeth. Without knowing how, Charley sensed Captain Jack wasn't pulling his share. The smell of gin coming out of Bill got stronger and more distinct. It struck Charley that the cows would come back after they were gone, and smell pink gin and think that was the scent of death.

They got the moose up over the lip of the gully, and Bill walked, purposeful and erect, back into the trees, where he threw up. Charley was half-stomached too, and reflected, as he listened to Bill, that the only difference in the way they felt was the amount of pink gin they'd drunk the night before.

Captain Jack had hardly broken a sweat. "There isn't a more peaceful feeling in the world than the aftermath of a hunt," he said.

Like magic, Bill came back from the trees with a bottle of pink and sat down under the trees next to Charley. It was as if he'd been everywhere on God's earth before and left himself a bottle for later. He offered Charley a drink, which he refused. "I got to get some water in me first," he said.

Captain Jack went down the hill toward the canoe and came back a few minutes later with a U.S. Army canteen. He sat down and took a long, noisy drink. Charley guessed he'd waited until he got back to prove he'd done his part in the pulling. When he'd finished, he offered the canteen to Charley, who ignored it.

Captain Jack took no offense. He lifted the canteen toward Bill, who obliged him, and touched it with the side of the gin bottle. "To the hunt," Captain Jack said.

They pulled the moose downhill to the water and Captain Jack tied the rope to the back end of the canoe. He left about six feet between the moose and the boat. "I don't like this," Charley said.

Captain Jack smiled at him. "I've done it a hundred times," he said.

Charley looked at the bull, twice as big as a horse, and then at the canoe, then at Bill.

"It's just a sad-nosed horse," Bill said, and took another drink of the gin.

"I know what you're contemplating," Captain Jack said to Charley, "that he's too heavy." Charley looked at him. Captain Jack shook his head. "Soon as it gets in the water, he's just like a cork," he said. "He'll float like another boat . . ."

The next time Bill offered him a drink, Charley took it. They pushed the moose and the boat into the water and, good to Captain Jack's word, it all floated. "See there?" Jack said when they were in the canoe. "What did I say? The secret's the gas, that's what keeps him up."

They started back across the water. The gas made the bull float, but it didn't do anything to make him easier to drag through the water. Charley sat in the middle, watching Bill, and the bull behind him. The bull's tongue lay out one side of his mouth, purple-blue and a foot long, and one of his eyeballs had rolled up into his head, leaving the socket white, and he still looked better than Bill. "You want me to take a turn at that paddle?" Charley said.

Bill didn't answer. He just stood up, bringing the bottle of gin, and let Charley crawl under his legs to the seat where he'd been. Captain Jack turned around to remark on the quiet satisfactions of hunting one's own food. "I love the city as much as anyone, pards," he said, meaning Deadwood, "but sometimes I think we're losing something in all this civilization."

It sounded to Charley like another poem in the works.

They were two thirds of the way across when the moose sank. One minute Charley was pulling his paddle against the water, and the next minute there was a sound that he recognized even though he'd never heard it before. They all recognized it, because there wasn't anything else it could have been. The moose passed air.

It rolled out as sudden as bad weather, and lasted until the back end of the animal submerged, when it was replaced by the sound of bubbles. Captain Jack turned around, panicky.

Charley turned around too, and watched the moose sink. He went straight down, butt first. Charley reached for his knife, but the moose was too fast for him. Before he could get to the rope, the front end of the canoe had started to come up in the air. That threw Charley off balance, and while he grabbed the side of the boat to steady himself, the front end went further up, and then Captain Jack—wild-eyed now, and shouting something Charley couldn't understand—fell into Bill, who was trying to get the cork in his gin bottle. Losing the forward weight, the canoe went straight up. Charley saw the Springfield fall into the water, and then the ropes, and then he was in the water too, fighting too many directions at once, losing ground with every move he made. He couldn't see where he was. Something was pulling at him in a way he couldn't pull back.

He fought and lost, and then he calmed himself. The air went out of his chest and the water came in, almost by itself. He calmed himself and opened his eyes. He couldn't remember shutting them. Then he was forcing them open again—when did they shut?—and he saw the light, a halo. Then, as he watched, a dark angel came through the light after him. The angel had the face of the Chinese in the kiln. He pushed out his hands to hold him off. They'd gotten heavy in the water, though, and were useless against an angel anyway.

The angel brushed his arms aside, and took him by the head, and took him away. "I have loved you, Lord," he thought. He wanted to get it on the record. He was moving now, he couldn't tell where. He calmed again, too heavy to help himself, and waited. The light got brighter and bigger—he thought it would have taken longer to get where they were going—and then shattered, warm and clean over his face. And he knew his soul was saved.

BILL GRABBED HIM UNDER THE ARMS AND DRAGGED HIM OUT OF THE water. Charley began to cough. Bill left him flat on the ground, and then lay down next to him.

"Charley?" he said. "You hear me?"

A convulsion shook his body—it felt like a release in his peeder; was that possible?—and Charley felt water coming up out of his chest. Warm water. It happened again and again. In between, he could hear Bill's voice, asking if he could hear him.

Even when Charley could answer, he didn't. He didn't have anything to say just then. The convulsions made him weaker, but after each one passed he gained more than he'd lost. It resembled healing. He opened his eyes and the sun was like spider legs through the needles of the pine tree Bill had pulled him under. He moved his hand to shade his eyes.

"Charley?" Bill was still on the ground next to him, white-faced and wet and sickly. Charley sat up and vomited water.

Captain Jack was sitting with his back up against another tree, maybe ten feet away. "You should of cut the rope," he said. "If you'd of cut the rope, we'd still have the boat and guns."

Charley lay back and began to shake. His whole body felt ice cold and ashamed of being saved. "I never saw a moose sink like that before," Captain Jack said. "There must of been something wrong with him."

Bill said, "I hope he realizes how disappointed we were in him." He got up then and walked into the bushes. He was gone half an hour. Captain Jack talked about the rope that Charley should of cut, Charley never said a word. What happened was mixed up with angels and the Chinese in the kiln, and he was confused. He didn't feel like talking to anybody.

Particularly Bill. He saw him then, incomplete. One half of a perfect man. He was brave, strong, loyal, handsome, and a swimmer.

And inside he had as much feelings as a hawk.

There was something between them that had never been there before, and Charley couldn't picture things ever being the same.

Bill came out of the bushes, drooling blood. Charley saw clearly that the disease had taken his strength, and didn't have any left inside himself he could borrow against.

Charley didn't think either one of them were worth much when they were weak.

BOONE HEARD ABOUT THE CAT MAN FROM LURLINE MONTI VERDI. SHE told the story to cheer him up, the little pilgrim that looked like a rat and called himself a natural cat man, and had dreams about cutting Phatty Thompson to pieces.

She thought he would laugh, but he sat up in bed and began to put on his underwear. It was nine o'clock in the morning, too early for Boone to be on the streets. "Where are you going?" she said. The truth was, since Boone had got depressed over the two hundred dollars, it wasn't any fun to be with him. He'd quit scaring her, but he'd quit everything else too. Last night he just wanted to lay up close, talking about Frank Towles's head. She was hoping he'd be better in the morning.

If Lurline needed to cradle something, she would of borrowed Pink Buford's bulldog.

Boone hadn't taken Frank's head to Cheyenne. He regretted it, but the longer he went without doing it, the less possible it was to happen. To Boone the head was getting heavier, or the distance to Cheyenne was getting longer. She was tired of listening about it. How the sheriff was treating him unfair. That was why she'd told him about the cat man, to get his mind off Frank Towles's head.

"What did you say his name was?" Boone said. He'd got his underwear on over his privates and stood up next to the bed to button it up the front. His head looked bigger than usual, and there was an ache in her shoulder where he had laid it to talk.

"Jack McCall," she said. "But it ain't nothing to get out of bed for." He pulled his pants on, fastened them with his belt, and then tucked his shirt in a fistful at a time. She wondered what would make a man dress himself in that order.

"Where would I find this cat man?" he said. He strapped his gun belt around his waist and put his hat on top of his head. There was room in that hat to grow strawberries. She let the sheets fall off her breasts, but he didn't notice. When Boone May wasn't suffocating her, he was hurting her feelings.

"I don't know," she said. "What do you want with him, honey?" He didn't seem to hear. He just left her, naked, and disappeared. He didn't even close the door. She wondered sometimes why she liked him better than the others.

HE FOUND JACK MCCALL ASLEEP ON THE BACK STEP OF THE SENATE bar. He was curled to accommodate the shape of the step. Boone noticed his gun and his clothes and his shoes. Total, he wasn't worth five dollars. He put the toe of his boot in Jack McCall's stomach and rolled him off the step.

The cat man looked up at him from the ground. He didn't try to get up, he just stared at Boone's face, like he was trying to place it. "Cat man?" Boone said.

Jack McCall nodded. Boone sat down on the step. McCall backed away, reminding Boone of a crab.

"I understand," Boone said, "that you been looking for employment amongst the upstairs girls at the Gem Theater."

"I run errands," the cat man said, "just until I get back to Cheyenne. After that, I'm strictly cats."

Boone nodded. "I heard you was good with them," he said.

"That's true," Jack McCall said. "I was partners with Phatty Thompson, but he went back to Cheyenne . . ."

Boone held up his hand and the cat man stopped. "I don't care about no Phatty Thompson," he said. The cat man waited. "What I care about," Boone said, "is your employment. What a white man's doin', running errands for whores."

"It's only temporary," the cat man said. "When I get back to Cheyenne and find Phatty Thompson, I'm strictly cats. They come up to me, even in the wild, and let me put them in the cage."

"I heard you wanted to cut Phatty Thompson's throat," Boone said. "Is that what you want him for?"

Jack McCall shook his head. "Either that," he said, "or go back into partners with him."

Boone said, "Maybe I got the wrong man."

"What man are you looking for?" Jack McCall said.

"I'm looking for the one that wants to cut a man's throat." The cat man stared at him again, thinking, and then he nodded his head. Boone got off the porch and picked the cat man up by the back of his collar. He brushed mud and pine needles off the back of his shirt, and then took the gun out of the cat man's holster and looked to see if it would fire. There was dried mud in the barrel and rust in the mechanisms. "Can you shoot this?" Boone said.

Jack McCall nodded. Boone pointed at some dead trees up the hill. "Go on up there and show me," he said. Jack McCall walked up the hill and stopped. He raised the gun over his head, closed his eyes, and pulled the trigger.

He disappeared in a cloud of smoke. When it cleared, he hadn't moved a muscle. The gun was still pointed at the sky, his eyes were still shut. That's how he stayed.

Boone went up the hill after him. "Can you do it without shutting your eyes?" he said. "You got to see what you're shooting to shoot."

Jack McCall was looking at the gun. "It hurt my hand," he said. "Like 'lectricity."

Boone put a finger in each ear and pretended to clean them out. "Who told you about 'lectricity?" he said.

"They got it in Cheyenne," the cat man said. Boone smiled at that.

"A gentleman like yourself must get invited to a lot of fancy places," he said.

"It's a man in the street who has a machine," the cat man said. Boone looked at him to see if it was true. He couldn't tell. This was the kind that could lie as easy as tell the truth, sometimes they didn't know the difference. "He charges a nickel, and you put your fingers in the holes to see how much you could take." The cat man looked up at him. "I only done it twict," he said, "but some did it all the time."

Boone said, "I heard it's like fire."

The cat man thought it over. "No, it ain't hot," he said. "It's fast, and there's bumps run through your skin and bones. I only did it twict because I don't like things fast."

"You ever shot a man?" Boone said, just like that. Jack McCall watched him but didn't answer. "I thought a man like yourself would of done that," Boone said. "It ain't nothing to it, you just point the front end and squeeze the back. Most men done that . . ."

"I shot people before," McCall said.

"I thought you had," Boone said. "A man like you don't want to be remembered for kitty cats." He smiled at the cat man, the cat man smiled back. "I got somebody for you to shoot, they'll remember you for it," Boone said.

THEY CAME BACK INTO TOWN SINGLE FILE FRIDAY AFTERNOON, strung out over twenty yards. First Bill, then Captain Jack Crawford, then Charley. Charley led the pack mules, which were as empty as when they left. It was embarrassing.

Bill was straight and tall and looked purposeful. Nobody but a student of his carriage would of known he was drunk. They had been wordless all day. Bill and Charley didn't have the least interest in conversation, and Captain Jack, who was always interested, didn't have anybody to conduct it with.

Bill rode directly to the camp on the Whitewood and got off the horse. He handed the reins to Captain Jack without a word and opened a bottle of pink. Charley took the mules north of town and tied them with the others. Then he checked into the Grand Union Hotel. He felt like sleeping indoors.

The room was on the ground floor and cost fifteen dollars a week. There was a hotel saloon, tended by the famous Alphonso the Polite, and a dining room offering the cooking of the also-famous Lucretia "Aunt Lou" Marchbanks. There was a lock on the door and a bath at each end of the hallway. Charley sat on the bed, feeling the new springs, and thought about Colorado. He saw it was a mistake, coming north again.

There were springs on his bed at home.

The way he thought of it then, his wife had expected things of him, and he had expected things of himself. She wanted to be comfortable—how she lived, and in the way people thought of her. He saw that he must have wanted some of that too, he didn't marry her for nothing. He'd joined the Congregational Church and then the Temperance Union. There had to be some reason for things as unnatural as that.

But there was something he wanted more. And his sense of that wasn't trading mine claims and real estate in Middle Park or Empire, Colorado, forty years after the ones who found it had moved someplace new. Bad legs and all, he needed to be there when things were fresh.

And the Black Hills were as fresh as it got, and it was a mistake. He lay on the bed and stared at the ceiling. He tried to picture how he would like things to be, but nothing came to mind. He thought he might need a freshness of spirit, that he had been chasing new places too hard to find it.

There were five bullet holes in the ceiling, and the hotel was only two months old.

He thought about the boy then, lying in his wagon. And the Chinese in the kiln, and Bill shooting glasses off the head of Pink Buford's bulldog for the tourists, and drooling in his sleep from the poison in the mercury. Charley had seen the mercury cure before; the next step, Bill's teeth would loosen. He began to think about the hunt, but he stopped himself before he got to the part where the moose took his revenge. There was a moment in the water he was still afraid of, when the angel came through the light for him.

His legs began to ache.

He sat up and went to a desk in the corner of the room. There was writing paper and a pen and ink in the top drawer. He wondered about the letters that had been written from this room, if the writers told things the way they were, or if they tried to make it sound the way they wanted it to be. He guessed that the kind that would shoot holes in the ceiling wouldn't be the writers, but if they were, they'd tell it the way it happened. The hearts and flowers would of been written by the paper-collars and salesmen.

He took paper out of the drawer and composed a public challenge to the Clippinger Pony Express Company. It took his mind off Deadwood. *"As owner of a newly established pony express,"* he wrote, *"I now propose a race, from Cheyenne to Deadwood, Dakota Territory, to be initiated on the second day of August, 1876, between the Clippinger Pony Express and the Pony Express of Charley Utter, previously of Middle Park and Empire, Colorado, who has successfully dealt in the transportation of goods all his life. The purpose of the race is to decide, once and for all, who is best able to deliver the mail to the miners and the pilgrims of the Black Hills, who deserve a damn sight better than they've got."*

He signed the letter and made a copy. He left one at the Clippinger office, next door to the Big Horn Grocery, and gave the other to A. W. Merrick, editor and publisher of the *Black Hills Pioneer.*

A. W. Merrick was soft-faced, gray-haired, and he had a twitch. He was twenty-nine years old. He had come to Deadwood from Custer, and before that from Omaha. There was a story that he'd made camp in the southern Hills one night and woke up in the morning with his head propped against a gravestone, and his hair had gone gray. Charley didn't know if that was true, but he knew a man that shouldn't of left Omaha when he saw one.

The newspaperman put on a pair of spectacles and read the challenge. He said, "You write with style, Mr. Utter."

"Thank you," Charley said.

He read it again. "Quite exciting," he said. "Did you ever consider working for a newspaper?"

"I was thinking of running a pony express line," Charley said.

A. W. Merrick shook his head. "It's a pity to waste talent," he said. "A paper like the *Pioneer* offers grand opportunities."

Charley said, "I think I'll save it to fall back on." The newspaperman took the pencil from behind his ear and made marks on the paper that Charley couldn't read.

"I'll have to remove the word *damn*," he said. "Our readers bring the *Pioneer* into their homes, where there's women and children."

"All right," Charley said, "*damn* goes."

A. W. Merrick studied him across the desk. "An editor has to make decisions like this all the time; nobody else can do it."

There was a trapper Charley knew back in Colorado who ran lines deep into the mountains and sometimes didn't see a human face, white or redskin, for six months at a time. He wasn't a hermit by choice, it was business. And that trapper let go of a conversation easier than A. W. Merrick. All the newspapermen Charley ever met were the same way, it was like something depended on you knowing what they did.

Charley had been interviewed a dozen times, had his picture taken twice. They asked you questions, and then wrote answers in the paper that you didn't say. The lies were worse about Bill, who, of course, participated in them, saying any damn thing that came into his head to a reporter, figuring his imagination was as good as theirs.

A. W. Merrick discussed the thankless nature of an editor's job, the price of newsprint, when you could get it, and humorous headlines he had seen in newspapers all over the country. He had begun a description of a printing press he had seen in Boston when Charley stopped him. "Mr. Merrick," he said, "if you would excuse me, I've got to prepare myself for the race against Clippinger."

The newspaperman looked like Charley had slapped him in the face. "I didn't realize preparation was needed," he said. "What do you need besides a horse?"

That's how newspapermen were. When Charley walked back outside, it was dusk. His feelings on Bill had changed, and it made him sad and tired. He started back to the Grand Union, thinking he would try the famous Alphonso the Polite for company, but at the door he thought of the boy in the wagon, and went back to his camp instead. Jane was sitting on Bill's stump, drinking coffee and whiskey, half and half.

Bill was gone to his appointments in the badlands. He was weak and sick, but not weak and sick enough to stay there in the moon-light with Jane Cannary. She stared at Charley without seeming to recognize him.

"How's the boy?" he said.

"Asleep," she said. "He's a good boy, he don't say a word." Charley leaned against one of the wheels of the wagon and looked in. Malcolm was right where he'd left him. "I took care of him while you were gone," Jane said. "Don't worry about that."

"Thank you," Charley said.

"Shit," she said. Jane was never much at accepting appreciations.

"Did he eat?" Charley said. The boy looked thin to him, and pale, but it was hard to say in that light.

"Milk," she said. "Corn soup."

Charley sat down on the ground with his back against the wheel. Dark came fast in the Hills, and he was having trouble seeing Jane's face. "Bill come back," she said. Charley didn't answer. "I was in the wagon with the boy. When I come out, he was rubbing hisself with silver."

"Mercury," Charley said. "The doctor prescribed him that for his treatment."

"I wisht he'd of come to me," she said. "Doctors don't know nothin' about illness." She drew in the dirt with a pointed stick while she talked. "I been nursing the ill all my life, never asked a thing in return."

"You did good by the boy," he said.

"Shit."

"He's lookin' better," Charley said.

"His tongue got unswole," she said. "Anybody looks better, they can get their tongue back inside their mouth. He ain't spoke a word yet." She finished what was in her cup, and then filled it again. Coffee and whiskey, half and half. She stirred it with her finger. "Bill don't like me," she said.

"He's consternated," Charley said. "Things are changing too fast for him, and he's trying to stay the same." Saying that, he saw that it was probably true for them both. "It doesn't have a thing to do with anybody, except maybe his wife."

"Shit," she said. "Wild Bill Hickok ain't got himself married."

"I was there," Charley said. "The woman is Agnes Lake, the famous trapeze artist and equestrian."

"I don't believe it," she said. "What does Wild Bill need with a circus lady? That ain't his kind of people, tricksters and illusionists. Elephants . . ."

"He didn't join the circus," Charley said. "He just married a trapeze artist."

"Shit," she said. "It probably ain't legal. They was probably playing the larks with you . . ." Charley saw that she loved Bill. It was some strange ripples they got when God dropped Bill Hickok into the pond. It was darker now, and he could see her better. Dirt poor and homely, she sat on a stump poking at the ground with a stick, crying for the most famous and handsome man in the West. The moon picked up the streaks on her face. Charley didn't blame Bill—he'd never done a thing to Jane but run away—but it seemed like he ought to of known about this before Charley did. "Elephants," she said, shaking her head.

"He took her back to St. Louis," Charley said. "So maybe they aren't married in the common way." Jane finished the coffee and sighed. A long, hoarse sigh, and then she stood up and threw the stick.

"Shit," she said. Her movements were mannish and heavy. She wiped at her eyes with the back of her hands and sighed again. Charley sat still, giving her time to compose. "Well," she said after a while, "I still got the boy to take care of."

"You did good by him," he said again. "Here's something for you." He reached into his shirt pocket and found twenty dollars.

She took a few steps toward him and saw what it was. "I don't take pay for nursin' the sick," she said, and he thought she was about to cry again. "It's my duty. I'll take pay for driving a bull train or scouting or accommodating a gentleman—everything I do, I'm the best—but not for nursing the sick."

Charley studied the woman, and could not imagine it. Not on the drunkest night of his life, not with somebody else's peeder. "It's for the food," he said. "Somebody's got to pay for milk and corn." Jane took the money and the bottle sitting on the ground next to the stump.

"Anything that's left over, you'll get it back," she said.

"I might be gone a while," he said. "I got to travel to Cheyenne to set up a pony express . . ."

"You need riders?" she said. "I can ride with any man, and I have killed more redskins than I could keep count of." He watched her in the moonlight, and he'd never felt sorrier for anybody in his life.

"Not right away," he said. "I won't know what I need right away."

She climbed into the front of the wagon using one hand. The bottle was in the other. She was clumsy and lacked balance. It seemed to Charley that she didn't have strong enough traits either way—man or woman—to get by. When she was in the wagon, she sat down in the seat and pulled the cork out of the bottle. Charley saw her close her lips against the mouth of the bottle when she drank, but she threw her head back like there wasn't enough liquor in the world.

"Well," she said, "I still got the boy."

She climbed over the seat and disappeared into the back of the wagon. It creaked and complained as she settled. Charley was back in the street, headed for the hotel, when he heard her singing to Malcolm. She had a sweet, high voice, nothing like the way she looked. She sang "The Battle Hymn of the Republic."

BOONE MAY TOOK THE CAT MAN BACK UP INTO THE HILLS TO PRAC-tice. He set Frank Towles's head on a tree stump to shoot at. The head was worthless now, unrecognizable even in Cheyenne. Boone had set it on the floor at Nuttall and Mann's while he watched Wild Bill play cards, and the bulldog that followed him around had chewed into the sack and mauled the identifying features.

Boone had been studying Bill's moves at the time. It seemed like he had been doing that ever since Bill arrived in town, and he had decided the reason Bill was famous was that he could feel every current in the room. The cat man would probably run off when he saw him in person. Boone watched him, noticing what he drank, watching for him to spill cards or stumble on the way outside to piss. Which never happened.

He took forever outside. He'd tilt his chair into the table to save his spot and disappear for half an hour. Nobody ever complained. Boone decided if it was himself that had to do business with Wild Bill, that's where he would do it. Out in back, with a shotgun. That's where he would do it, but he had no confidence it would go his way.

He had the feeling the gunfighter saw as well in the dark as he did in the light.

He would have the cat man do his work inside, though. He was not the kind you could trust in the dark.

It was while Boone was figuring that all out for maybe the tenth time that the bulldog got into the bag and changed Frank Towles's features. Boone never noticed until he heard the bones cracking at his feet, and then the dog didn't want to give it up. Frank's head was soaked with dog spit, and Boone's hands kept slipping off when he tried to pull it away. The dog growled and held on. It was Wild Bill himself who called the animal away. At the sound of his voice, he let go of Frank's head and padded over to the card table, trailing saliva, and lay at Bill's feet.

Boone set the head on the stump now and stood beside the cat man. The cat man sighted down the rusted barrel of the gun he was holding, and then turned his head away and pulled the trigger. "You scairt of guns?" Boone said when the smoke cleared. "I didn't figure a cat man to be scairt of guns."

"I killed men," Jack McCall said. "I ain't scared of guns." Boone pointed at Frank Towles's head, and the cat man tried again. This time he didn't close his eyes.

"Get closer," Boone said. "You ain't going to get but one opportunity to die famous." Jack McCall stepped closer, then closer again. He was almost touching-distance before he hit the head.

"That feels peculiar," he said to Boone. "Shooting a head."

Boone shrugged. "It wasn't peculiar when I shot him." He picked the head up off the ground and put it back on the stump. "Do it again," he said.

"What for?"

"That's what practice is," Boone said. And the cat man pointed his pistol at the head again, and hit it again. He shot the head off the stump again and again, until it broke into pieces so small there wasn't anything big enough for Boone to put it back up there.

Boone took the cat man to the Gem Theater and bought him a bottle of J. Fred McCurnin swoop whiskey, which was as thick and sweet as molasses, and about as expensive. He sat him at a table with the bottle and a glass, and left him there while he went to talk to Al Swearingen. "Don't do a thing until I tell you," he told the cat man. "This is touchy business."

Boone found Al Swearingen in his office with his missus. She was crying, which was how Boone knew who it was. Swearingen did not like her to show herself in public. Boone walked in without knocking, and found them with their faces so close they might of been kissing, except he had the front of her shirt in his fist.

Boone stood in the door and waited. He didn't leave, he didn't interfere. The way he looked at it, anybody that married Al Swearingen must of liked to bawl. It was the same way with him and Lurline, who kept asking was he going to kill her someday, and kept coming back just the same. There was something in them that craved it.

Al Swearingen saw Boone wasn't going to excuse himself, and let go of his wife. She sat in a chair and cried. The crying sounded pitiful to Boone, who was used to an angrier kind. Swearingen sat down on the desk. "What is it?" he said.

"Two hundred dollars," Boone said.

Swearingen changed expressions. "It's done?"

Boone said, "As good as. I got the man to do it, but when Wild Bill's laying in his brains, I don't want you sayin' it was no accident. I got a lot of time and effort in training the right man, and I want my two hundred dollars. I already lost Frank Towles's head in this, and I want you to know right now that you and me are in business."

Al Swearingen's wife looked up, blinking tears. Boone stopped himself, then he nodded. "Ma'am," he said.

"Don't pay no attention to the woman," Swearingen said. "She don't talk unless I tell her what to say." She found a hankie in her dress pocket and blew her nose, and Boone could tell just from the sound of it that what Swearingen said was true.

"I see that," he said.

Swearingen smiled. "I got all my girls broke," he said. Then he said, "Who is this man you trained?"

Boone shook his head. "That's nothin' you need to know," he said.

"How am I supposed to know he's the one that does it then?" Swearingen said. "For two hundred dollars, I want to know it was me that paid for it."

"You ain't paid nothing yet," Boone said.

"After," he said. "After it's done. I don't pay good money to have somebody to run out on his obligations. That ain't the way I do business."

"The way you did this was to offer me two hundred dollars for Wild Bill's scalp, and that's what I'm here to announce."

"How?" Swearingen said.

"What's the difference, as long as he's kilt?"

"I told you," Swearingen said, "I want to know I was the one that paid for it."

His wife made a noise then, someplace between gagging and a laugh, and ran for the door. Swearingen shouted at her, but she ran past Boone and out into the bar. Swearingen scratched at his head. "I've about give up trying to understand that girl," he said.

AL SWEARINGEN'S WIFE RAN OUT OF THE OFFICE AND THROUGH THE bar. A miner caught her around the waist and put her on his lap, but she stuck her thumb in his eye until he let go. She went out into the street, crying, and fell in the mud.

She was wearing a dress Swearingen had brought her from Omaha. She knew he'd let one of the whores wear it on the trip back, and then given it to her used. She could smell other women on all her clothes. When she stood up, the dress stuck to her legs in front, and it embarrassed her the way it showed her off. She shook some of the mud off her hands and then started south, up the street. She was crying and wet, and once she was out of the badlands people in the street turned and stared at her.

There was nothing unkind in it. The cold part of town was where she'd come from, where they didn't look twice at a crying girl. She ran from the Gem all the way into town proper, and then tired and began to walk.

She was still crying when she came through the door of the Deadwood Brickworks, Inc. Seth Bullock and Solomon Star were on the way outside to inspect the rock flooring they'd commissioned to hold their new kilns. An enclosure would be built over them, after they were all in place.

They both looked at the door when she came in, then Seth Bullock tipped his hat. "Yes, ma'am," he said.

"I am Mrs. Al Swearingen," she said. Bullock nodded. He knew every permanent resident of Deadwood on sight, even the ones that kept out of sight. She said, "I am here to report on my husband."

Bullock looked at the woman carefully. She was covered with mud and she'd been crying, but didn't appear to be bleeding, or even show new swellings on her face. The sheriff had seen her black-eyed and petal-lipped more often than not. There were a large number of married men in Deadwood—most of them hadn't brought their wives in yet—and Bullock was not anxious to begin stepping into the middle of family disputes. There were too many of them, for one thing, and it was a good way to get shot, for another.

"Mrs. Swearingen," he said, "I respectfully can't allow my office to become involved in family business. A man's house is his castle, and it isn't the business of the law."

"I am here to report on my husband," she said again. Bullock saw that she was about to cry. He got her a chair and helped her sit down. He wasn't in a hurry to get in the middle of family troubles, but crying, muddy women walking out the front door wasn't going to do anybody any good, either.

He took a handkerchief and wiped some of the mud off her face. She sat quietly and allowed herself to be cleaned. When he had done what he could, he gave her the handkerchief and let her wipe her front and hands for herself. "The way the law is," he said, "it's public. It doesn't apply in private life." Solomon Star had moved to the floor in back of him, and had a hammer in his hand and half a dozen nails in his lips. Bullock was glad that Solomon's mouth was occupied.

"What I'm here about ain't private," the woman said. "My husband and Mr. Boone May plan to have Mr. Wild Bill Hickok shot."

The sheriff smiled at her. "A man like Bill Hickok," he said, "there's bound to be stories . . ." Hickok had been in town a little over two weeks, and there was already talk of making him sheriff.

The woman shook her head. "These two ain't just talking," she said. "I know them better." Seth Bullock patted her hand. It wasn't the talk of Bill becoming sheriff that troubled him—the office wasn't anything Seth Bullock wanted to hold on to any longer than he needed to—it was the way people spoke of him, like Bill would save them from Indians and thieves and cold weather. Bill had done nothing but drink gin and lose at cards, and he'd already begun to take Seth Bullock's claim. Not just in the badlands, everywhere in the city. Nobody knew what Bill Hickok was like, but that's where popularity lay, in the idea, not the fact.

Nobody ever got his statue built because the public knew him over breakfast.

"Mrs. Swearingen," Bullock said, "I want you to go back to your husband and don't say anything about coming here."

"I come here to report him," she said. Bullock shook his head no.

"The law is public," he said. "People's private problems, they ought to settle them at home. In fairness, you married him, missus. Try to remember all the things you saw in him then, and see if they aren't still there."

She looked for something in his face, to see if that was a joke. "You ain't going to do nothing about this, are you?" she said.

"No," he said, "no, I'm not."

FRIDAY, CHARLEY LEFT FOR CHEYENNE. THE CLIPPINGER PONY EX-press Company had accepted his challenge as it was laid down. It had surprised Charley, and told him the business was not worth as much as he had surmised.

He left without talking to Bill. He checked on the boy, who he now believed would never improve, and gave Jane another twenty dollars for groceries. Then he got on a rough-looking gray gelding that he bought for $450 from Brick Pomeroy, and rode out of town. It felt wrong to leave without speaking to Bill, but the longer he'd stayed at the Grand Union, the more distance there was between them, and he didn't have the way to narrow it.

It was going the other way, in fact. He'd begun to judge him. He found himself thinking of Bill in ways that weren't any of his business. Like why he couldn't make money, or why he married a woman he didn't know. It was small and wrong, but he thought of those things anyway.

He tried talking to himself out loud. He said, "All Bill did was pull your ass out the river once—how long are you going to hold it against him?" but it was empty. There was something that happened in the water that day that Charley couldn't forgive.

He took six days to get to Cheyenne, stopping here and there to make arrangements to care for his horses later. There were two- and three-family settlements that the Indians had left alone, a few ranches. Texans, mostly. They were the least humorous people Charley had ever been among, Texans. He thought it was probably the dust storms. But they were reliable too, not likely to run at the sight of Indians. Not likely to run at all.

For purposes of the race, he decided to use four riders, with his brother Steve riding the longest stretch, which ran from a house full of Mexicans sitting unprotected out in the middle of eastern Wyoming into the settlement of Camp Collier in the southern Hills.

He would have taken the hardest ride himself, but he wanted the last leg. He thought it would be better for business if the miners saw him in the saddle, so they would know his express was trust- worthy. Nobody had ever seen Enis Clippinger, or knew who he was. Charley surmised that was why the miners objected that he read their mail.

He met his brother in Cheyenne, and they spent the day hiring riders. The Street brothers, Brant and Dick, Herbert Godard, H. G. "Huge" Rocafellow, and Bloody Dick Seymour. Two were cu- riosities. Bloody Dick was a full-blooded Englishman, who had settled on the Niobrara River in Nebraska and then come to the Hills. Most of the English stayed where they settled. He wasn't much good on a horse, and useless with a side arm, but Charley liked his accent.

The other oddity was Huge Rocafellow, who was nearly as big as his horse—a dark, sorry-looking animal that Huge swore would run forever. "Where did you find that one?" Charley said to his brother, when Huge had left them.

His brother was so much like Charley that they had to stay apart from each other to avoid bloodshed. He said Huge was the best- humored man in Cheyenne, and he'd hired him for that. Steve was smart, and understood how his brother ran a business. If there wasn't some fun in it, Charley wouldn't do it.

Charley would waste his money, but not his time.

They spent the early evening in the bar of the Republican Hotel. Steve had two drinks and asked after Matilda, and then Bill. He had bee-homing instincts for what Charley didn't want to talk about.

"Is something come between you and Bill?" he said.

Charley shook his head. "It's nothing," he said. "Bill is Bill. There isn't anything written down that says we have to be together every minute of the day."

Steve couldn't have looked more surprised if his feet disappeared. "You and Bill are still partners, ain't you? I never seen partners as close as you and Bill . . ."

Charley stood up and stretched. "I got to get some sleep," he said. And he left him there in the bar and went to his room. He loved his brother, but he couldn't be around him.

He lay sleepless for most of the night. He mounted the bed on his stomach with his head hanging over the side, trying to find a comfortable way to position his legs—which ached from the time in the saddle—and stared for a while at a cricket on the floor. The cricket's movements were mostly in his whiskers. Charley believed God was in every creature on earth, even people, and waited about ten minutes for Him to reveal Himself. It didn't happen. He rolled over on his side and closed his eyes. There were no lessons for him in crickets.

He imagined the cricket and himself were something akin to Bill and Matilda, who after all, were both God's idea, but could stare at each other forever and never recognize a mutuality.

THE BOY HAD LOST TRACK OF DAY AND NIGHT. HE'D ALMOST FORGOT what it meant. Sometimes the canvas top was light, sometimes it was dark. When it was dark, she was always with him, holding his head against her body while she snored.

He watched her sleep and wake up, he watched her drink whiskey from the bottle. He heard her outside, talking to Bill. "You and me," she would say, "we're two of a kind, Bill. We got the same blood in our veins."

He never heard Bill answer. She would drink and talk, and then Bill would go away. Sometimes she would crawl into the wagon with him afterwards, and he would watch her cry.

She never knew he was watching.

He forgot why he was lying down. Something had happened, he knew, but it wasn't with him anymore, at least not at hand. It was someplace else. He didn't try to find it, he didn't try to get up. He was weak, but it was comfortable. She sang to him when it was dark.

He had no sense of time passing, just that it had passed. He knew he couldn't lie in the wagon forever. He heard people on the street, and knew that sometime he would have to go out there himself. He was in no hurry. He lay in the wagon and waited for the things that would come to him.

She washed him at first light, talking to him as she scrubbed dark soap against her washrag, and then the washrag against his skin. She washed his chest and his arms. She held his peeder in a milk bottle and he would let go of his piss. He watched everything she did, and listened to everything she said.

She began to call him her baby. "When are you going to talk to me?" she said. And, "You ain't going to die on your momma, are you? You're all your momma's got . . ."

It never entered his thoughts to answer. She fed him milk and soup, a spoonful at a time, holding his head in the cradle of her elbow. His mouth did not hurt now to have things inside it.

And then one morning there was a voice outside. Louder than the usual voices in the street. He was lying against her shoulder when he heard it, and he recognized right away that it was for him. "Dear God," the voice said, "help the sad and the weak and the lost among us. Lend us Thy strength, so that we may do Thy work better, and find our way back to You from this place full of Thy enemies . . ."

He sat up, out of her lap, and looked out through the opening in front of the wagon to the street. A thin, gray-faced man was standing on a box in front of a cluster of miners, holding a Bible in front of his face, like he was talking to it.

The boy got on his hands and knees and crawled to the front of the wagon. "That's a preacher," she said behind him. "He's trying to save these sinners from hell."

The boy began to climb out of the wagon. He was the weak and the lost and the sad, and the preacher had come for him. She grabbed him from behind. "Whoa, my baby," she said. "You ain't dressed for church." But he was too strong for her and pulled away. He climbed out the front of the wagon, buck-naked on shaky legs, and then dropped himself onto the ground.

The preacher stopped when he heard the upstairs girls scream. There were a few of them scattered among the miners; most were there to catch the early service before they went to bed. They had spent Saturday night naked with these same miners, or ones like them, but at the sight of the boy, pale and naked and skinny, walking out of Charley Utter's camp, they screamed.

The boy came toward the Methodist, and the miners moved apart to give him room. The truth was, they weren't overly comfortable around an uncovered boy either. The boy did not seem to hear the screaming or notice the miners. He was looking at the Methodist on the packing crate.

The Methodist spoke first. "What is it, boy?"

The boy started to speak, but his throat was dry and unreliable. Half the noises he made could of come out of a hawk, but finally he made himself understood. "I'm the one you come for." This set off a new round of excitement among the upstairs girls, but the Methodist took it serious. He stared down at the boy, and then seemed to decide. "One of you get him a blanket," he said. When nobody moved, the preacher got down off his box and walked to the boy and wrapped him in his own coat.

The boy allowed himself to be wrapped. The Methodist looked into his eyes and the boy looked back.

The Methodist said, "Maybe so."

Jane watched it from the front seat of the wagon. She had four inches left in the bottom of a bottle of whiskey—she'd made it last half the week—and she pulled the cork now with intentions to finish it. The preacher got back on his crate and led the miners and whores in the Lord's Prayer, and then dismissed them without even asking for the collection. He took the boy away.

Jane felt herself crying. It seemed like that's all she'd done for two weeks. Unless she got hold of herself, somebody would catch her at it. She drank the bottle and watched the street from the seat of the wagon. After a while the crying passed, and she thought she might go to Rapid City and get drunk. She had once ridden a bull on Main Street there and got her picture in the newspaper. She thought about that day, how good her future looked, and wondered how she'd got so unhappy so fast.

She guessed it was from listening too much to her heart. "That boy was mine," she said out loud, almost finished with the bottle now. "I collected that Methodist about thirty dollars, too."

She stood up in the wagon and shook the last few drops of the bottle out on the ground. Then she threw it in the air and drew the Smith & Wesson Russian model she carried butt-first in her gun belt to shoot it. Then she lost the bottle in the morning sun and fell off the wagon.

The ground was drier there than the street, and hard. She heard the sound of her breath leaving her as she landed, and then lay still until she could tell that she wasn't hurt. That was a disappointment too, and she began to cry again. She curled into herself right there next to the wagon, in plain view of the public, and bawled.

"He was mine," she said.

THE METHODIST TOOK THE BOY TO HIS CABIN NEAR THE SAWMILL. HE sat him in a rocking chair near the door, naked except for the coat. "What happened to your shoes?" he said.

The boy looked at his feet longer than it took to see he didn't have shoes on. "I got clothes," the preacher said, "but shoes ought to fit."

The boy accepted that like a first lesson. Shoes ought to fit. He nodded and waited for whatever the preacher would say next. "Can you work?" he asked. The boy looked at him. "Are you deaf?" he said. Not reproachful, a question.

The boy shook his head and cleared his throat. "I heard what you said. 'Help the sad and the weak and the lost among us. Lend us Thy strength, so that we may do Thy work better, and find our way back to You from this place full of Thy enemies . . .'"

Henry Hiram Weston Smith smiled. "That's more attention than I pay myself," he said. The boy did not smile back. The preacher said, "You're not soft-brained, what's the nature of your affliction?"

The boy shook his head. He wouldn't think about the nature of his affliction, something kept him from it.

"Have you been hurt?" the preacher said. "Are you on the mend?"

The boy turned in the chair, avoiding the preacher's questions. "I'm the one you come for," he said. Preacher Smith took those words seriously. He found a pair of old black pants among his things, and a shirt big enough for two men to wear at the same time. His initials were sewn into the pocket. A present from his wife, who always thought of him as bigger than he was.

He gave those to the boy, along with his spare underwear, and went outside while he dressed. He had no thought that his obligations to the boy were satisfied. He had no thought of what else he was supposed to do.

He skinned a rabbit he had killed the day before, and made a fire in a circle of quartz rocks he'd arranged on the ground. The little house had no fireplace, but was protected by trees on three sides. Still, there were nights in the winter when he dreamed he was freezing, and the dreams would wake him, and he would lie in his blankets knowing that the place where his dreams met the world was the place he would die.

Preacher Smith was afraid of his dreams.

The boy came out of the house and watched him run the spit through the rabbit and lay it across the fire. He was wearing the pants, which quit above his ankles, and the shirt. He nearly filled the shirt out; the boy was bigger than the preacher had thought.

The boy watched everything the preacher did. "You never prepared a rabbit before?" he said. The boy squatted on his heels to get a closer look, but he didn't answer. Something in that posture was familiar and bad. "Well," the preacher said, "there isn't nothing to it. You kill the animal, gut it, skin it, then you burn it." He pointed to the rabbit's skin—still attached to the head—that was lying on the ground. The boy looked at it, without interest.

"You put the stick through, front to back, and lay it over a fire," the preacher said. "When the meat pulls off, it's done . . ." He looked across the fire at the boy. He had intelligence; the preacher wondered how he had stayed so innocent. "You never did any of this before?" he said.

The boy slept innocent and peaceful on blankets on the floor of the cabin, the preacher kept the bed. His own sleep was interrupted by frightening dreams he could not remember after they woke him up.

It came to him early in the morning that the boy was intended to be his disciple. That God was ready to speak through his mouth, and the boy was there to learn the words, and then teach them to others.

ON WEDNESDAY AFTERNOON, AUGUST 2, BILL WROTE HIS LAST LETTER to Agnes Lake. He had been to the doctor that morning and reported loose teeth in addition to his regular problems passing water. The doctor had stuck a hollow rod into his peeder to drain his urine. He felt it clear to his stomach. The doctor had given him powdered sulfur, which he'd taken with Hood's Sarsaparilla ("*Spring medicine, a True Blood Purifier*"), and Phosphoric Air, which was labeled "*to ease the pain of spermatorrhoea, seminal weakness, loss of vitality, impotency, and all diseases arising from the errors of youth or the excesses of adult age.*"

He'd taken Tutt's Pills too, and rubbed his skin with mercury.

Thus medicated, he sat down on the stump near the wagon and began the letter. Jane had left the camp two days before, when the boy did, mentioning Rapid City. He would never have written Agnes with Jane Cannary anywhere in the vicinity.

Agnes Darling,

All is well in the Hills. Charley Utter and I stakd claims on the Deadwood and Whitewood both, and prospeck daily. We have done what we cud, and evrthing else is up to The Lord.

I do not no what He has planned yet, but this is a Wonderful cuntry, as rich and wild as Inland Africa, which is a marvelous place. We will go there to one day, but the Hills will be our home. When it is safe from Indians. I must end this now, as the man is impatent to start for Cheyenne. Be in good humor, pet, in the nowlege that we shall be together again soon, once and for always.

J. B. Hickok
"Wild Bill"

P.S. Brave once, if such shud be we never meet again, while firing my last shot, I will gently breeth the name of my wife—Agnes—and with wishes even for my enemies I will make the plunge and try to swim to the other side.

He folded the letter and took it to the Pony Express office. Then he walked into the badlands, wondering what had happened to Charley. He didn't remember talking to him since the hunt. He wondered if Charley held what happened to the moose against him.

Harry Sam Young was behind the bar at Number 10, and fixed Bill a gin and bitters without being asked. Pink Buford and his bulldog were at one of the poker tables, along with a retired Mississippi River pilot named William R. Massie and three or four pilgrims who had made themselves colonels or captains when they arrived in Deadwood. The dog saw Bill and came over to sit at his feet.

"I'd sell you that dog," Pink Buford said, "if you'd let me keep fighting rights." Pink was suffering a losing streak. Bill leaned over and kneaded the loose skin on top of the bulldog's head. Pink made a place for him at the table, but Bill shook his head.

"There's no luck in here today," he said. He sipped the pink gin in front of him, and it didn't taste right either.

"It must of been some in here last night," Pink said. He was playing draw poker for quarters with the pilgrims and Massie, winning their quarters and giving them back, so he'd have somebody to play with. "You took two hundred dollars out of my pocket . . ."

Bill hadn't counted what he had, and was surprised at the amount. The wound over the dog's missing ear had crusted, and little pieces of scab came off as he ran his hands over his head. "You oughtn't to fight him so much, Pink," Bill said. He felt uncomfortable, telling other people how to treat their dog.

"He gets moody if he don't fight," Pink Buford said. "He could turn on a body in the night, from the frustration." Bill shrugged, and scratched the dog under his ear. Pink said, "Besides, the animal was intended to fight. Look at them jaws, you believe he's built like that to no reason? It ain't no favor to him to keep him from it."

Bill bought a pickled egg and dropped it into the jaws. The dog swallowed it without chewing, and Bill got him another. "He could find his own fights, if that's what he wants," Bill said. His voice was flat and quiet. "It's no favor, betting him to kill other dogs."

"He's a killer," Pink Buford said. "That's what he is, just like I am a gambler." He was holding a deck of cards in his hands, and as he spoke they divided in half, almost by themselves, and then merged into each other and were one deck again. "Come over here, and I'll demonstrate it beyond question."

Bill stayed with the dog. The Mississippi pilot was sitting in Bill's regular chair anyway, the one in the corner. Bill had taken a few dollars from him the night before too, and he had come in early to claim the lucky seat.

"A dime-quarter game doesn't spill enough blood," Bill said. "I'd just as soon drop eggs into this monster all day."

"If it's the price of the game," said the Mississippi pilot, "I can correct that with a visit to my hotel." Bill made no reply, which the pilot took the wrong way. "I think he's scared because I got his lucky chair."

Bill was about to feed the dog another egg, but his hand stopped an inch above the animal's mouth, and for a few seconds nothing moved. Then the dog's head began to rise toward the egg, slow as a snake. A line of drool spilled from one of the folds that covered his teeth.

Bill looked at Massie. "A pilot ought to respect limits," he said.

The pilot saw he had overstepped himself. "I didn't intend to insult your courage, sir," he said. "I questioned only your skill at the card table . . ."

"The water's getting shallow, pilot," Bill said. The dog came up slowly, off his front legs, and took the egg out of Bill's fingers. For a bulldog, it was a delicate thing, and it changed the gunfighter's mood. "Look here," Bill said, "this dog just picked my pocket." He looked at his hand. "Didn't even get my fingers wet. Pink, your bulldog is embarked on a life of crime . . ."

Bill and the dog walked toward the door. "Will you return today, Mr. Hickok?" the pilot said. Bill stopped and looked at him again. "I'm at your service," the pilot said. "In this seat, with sufficient funds to keep you entertained."

Bill walked north through the badlands to the clearing where he and Charley had cremated the slant-eyes. The dog was drunk with pickled eggs, and ran in circles out in front. The mules were still where Charley left them, in deep grass. A rancher had brought forty or fifty head of cattle through town the day before, and they were in another part of the clearing, while the rancher made his deals with the grocers in town.

The cattle had been left with two boys, seventeen or eighteen years old, who sat squint-eyed on their horses, holding rifles across their laps, and watched while Bill and the dog crossed the field. If they knew who Bill was, they didn't show it.

The dog ran a few steps toward the cattle, but Bill called him back. "There's nothing here for you to assassinate," he said.

He went right to the kiln, without a consideration that the boys were watching, and looked inside. It was as shiny in there as the bulldog's peeder. Not a speck of ash. He wondered where Charley was, and tried to remember the last time they had spoken.

Bill and the dog walked up one of the hills east of the clearing and found a smaller clearing, overlooking the town. He couldn't see Deadwood from there, but he felt it.

It was there like his illness. Nagging, something he couldn't put off.

The bulldog buried his nose under one of Bill's hands, wanting him to scratch the place he'd lost the ear. Bill accommodated him, thinking of the slant-eyes they had put in the kiln. His whole life, Bill had walked away from what he'd done, good or bad, like it wasn't there because it was past.

He'd even walked away from the lie he knew that to be.

He thought of his wife, trying to change the troubled feelings in himself, but unless it was walking a high wire, he had no idea what she would be doing that afternoon. He didn't know what she did when she was alone.

He remembered their wedding night in Cheyenne, as awkward a time as he'd ever had with a woman. They were afraid to find out about each other, even that.

He couldn't remember what stage the blood disease was in then. It wasn't like it was now, where the doctor had to fit a tube in him to drain his piss, he didn't think it hurt then to piss for himself. He did remember there wasn't any power behind it. That had been gone a long time, and he privately believed that was the first sign that he'd caught it.

He couldn't remember if he knew the disease was there when he married her or not. He did remember that later he'd thought it didn't matter, that they were joined for better or worse. He still didn't know what blood disease did to a woman's apparatus.

And he thought of the letter he'd written her that morning.

. . . if such shud be that we never meet again, while firing my last shot, I will gently breeth the name of my wife—Agnes—and with wishes even for my enemies I will make the plunge and try to swim to the other side.

He tried to picture her reading that, but it wouldn't come. He could see her this way or that—happy or crying—but it didn't ring true. At the bottom of it, he didn't know what she thought of him. If he took care of her, or she took care of him. He didn't even know who was more famous.

It still seemed to him that famous people ought to marry each other, but it wasn't for the practical reasons he'd told to Charley. It was more instinctual, like people from Ohio liked to marry other people from Ohio. It seemed to him there was more to talk about that way. He tried to think what he would say to her now, if she was sitting next to him on the hill.

It wouldn't of been "If such should be that we never meet again . . ." No, even the simple things were uncomfortable between them. He'd probably be talking about the dog. Telling her about his fights and his appetites, how he ate pickled eggs whole. And that he liked Bill better than his own master. Bill wouldn't of said so, but he was proud of that. He would show her where the dog got his power to bite—it was in the back legs—and have her lift him off the ground. He was like a suitcase full of rocks.

Bill found himself smiling at that, thinking how it would sound to her. It occurred to him sometime later that he knew the dog better than he knew Agnes. He stood up and unbuttoned his pants and killed a quarter of an hour waiting for a small bit of relief. Then he made his way down the hill, past the hard-faced boys that squinted and sat on their horses with rifles across their laps, and headed back to Nuttall and Mann's Number 10, where a Mississippi River pilot was sitting at the card table with fresh money, and a belief that luck was tied to a chair.

It was dusk before Bill got back into town, walking sightless up the street, slow and straight with his eyes dangerous. The dog stayed a few feet in front of him, panting, and Bill followed the noise all the way to the bar. He thought the dog understood that there were times he went blind.

The place had filled up in the hours Bill had been gone, he could tell that from the noise. He found the bar and Harry Sam Young brought him a gin and bitters. He tasted it, and his eyes began to see shapes again. The pilot shouted to him across the room, "We got you a chair saved, Bill."

Bill pushed the gin and bitters away. "Let me test something different," he said. "This is lost its bouquet."

The bartender moved the glass in front of a pilgrim a few feet down the bar—half of the badlands was drinking pink gin by then—and poured Bill a shot of whiskey.

The whiskey tasted healthy and familiar, and Bill wished Charley would come in the door so they could drink one together. No matter what had gone wrong between them, they couldn't be so far apart that a bottle of American whiskey wouldn't bridge it. He waited while the bartender poured him another, and then picked the bottle up and took it with him to the table where Pink Buford, Carl Mann, Charles Rich, and the river pilot, Massie, were playing poker.

Massie was still in Bill's customary seat. The seat they'd left for Bill offered his back to the door. "I don't sit with my back exposed," he said.

"I got your lucky seat," the pilot said.

Bill looked at him unkindly. He had his rules, and his reasons. With all the local talk of Indians and bandits and poisonings, the citizens and visitors of the badlands visioned themselves as charmed men in dangerous times, but the truth was there wasn't a man at the table anybody had ever tried to kill.

Bill had been shot at frequently. Once he had believed he was charmed too, but that feeling had ebbed from the moment he shot the policeman Mike Williams in Abilene. He never mentioned the change to a soul, not even Charley, but killing Mike Williams by accident told him he could be killed by accident too. And he was accordingly careful in places accidents happened. He never filled his right hand in a bar, he never sat with his back to the door.

It was a strain, always watching for accidents, and he was tired.

Nobody at the table moved, and Bill saw they weren't going to. It was like a test. He set the bottle of whiskey in front of the empty chair and sat down. The river pilot winked at him and patted the dollars he had already won.

The bulldog lay at Bill's feet and sighed. Bill took the winnings from the night before out of his pocket and laid them next to his bottle. The room seemed wrong, he couldn't say why.

Pink Buford dealt cards. They played dollar ante, table-stakes draw poker. Bill couldn't catch a hand; the river pilot's cards continued their winning run. He drew one card into Bill's three tens, and caught his straight. He drew into Pink Buford's aces, and made three fours.

The more the river pilot won, the more reckless he got. And the cards still defied all the laws of probability and common sense, and stayed with him. "I can't lose, boys," he said. Bill had seen runs before, and waited him out.

In two hours, Bill lost close to a hundred and fifty dollars, and finished the bottle of whiskey. He was feeling the need to relieve himself, but he hated to leave the table and miss it when the laws of common sense caught up with the pilot. It wasn't anybody's time forever.

Number 10 had filled, as it did most nights, with tourists and miners of all kinds and quality. Captain Jack Crawford had come in and was standing behind him, just out of sight. There was a professor at the piano, and the upstairs girls took turns singing ballads of the West. The tourists paid them to sing, the miners paid them to stop.

It was a hot night and even with the front and back doors open, all the smoke and noise hung inside. Bill decided to leave the table. He began to stand up, but the dealer, Carl Mann, gave him the first card of a new hand, and he stayed to finish it.

Jack McCall came in through the back door and went to the bar. He picked up a glass of gin and bitters sitting in front of a tourist and drank it before Harry Sam Young could stop him. The bartender fixed the cat man a hard look. "A whiskey thief is unwelcome everywhere," he said. "Even thieves won't have a whiskey thief around . . ."

But there was something loose in Jack McCall's eyes that Harry Sam Young had seen before, and he stopped himself in mid-sentence. Jack McCall walked away from him, down the bar, pushing through whores and miners alike. He was holding a gun in his hand now, and the ones who saw it moved out of his way.

At the end of the bar was the poker table. Bill had picked up his cards and was holding them against his chest. Across the table, Pink Buford noticed the change in the way Bill protected his cards, and prepared to abandon his hand.

Captain Jack Crawford saw the cat man and the gun, and backed out of the way.

Jack McCall fired into the left side of Bill's head from a distance of less than a foot. The ball exited through his right cheek, then broke all the bones in the river pilot's left wrist. Telling it later, the pilot would say he saw smoke before he heard the shot.

A moment later, Jack McCall shouted, "Damn you, take that," and Bill's head, which had been turned to the left by the force of the ball exiting his cheek, lowered slowly to the table. He could have been taking a nap. William Massie fell out of his chair, covering his wrist with his body; Charles Rich sat frozen. Only Carl Mann moved, and McCall pointed the pistol at his face and pulled the trigger. There was a snapping noise, but no shot. Mann would sell his half of the business the next week and move to New Orleans.

It was a few seconds before most of the bar patrons realized what had happened—it was nothing out of the ordinary for somebody to fire into the ceiling—and in those moments Jack McCall ran out the front door, snapping his gun at Harry Sam Young and half a dozen others. He turned in the street and yelled at the bar, "Come on, you sons of bitches," and then ran south and tried to take the first horse he saw.

The bar emptied out after him, with no one in a hurry to be at the front. The horse belonged to Mayor E. B. Farnum, who was a considerate man and always eased the animal's cinch when he left him saddled. The saddle turned over, dropping McCall into the mud. He got up and ran into Farnum's store, and hid in back behind freshly butchered meat. The crowd followed him in and took McCall prisoner. Not as much as a piece of penny candy was stolen.

In the crowd now was Boone May, who assumed authority, being the closest thing to a law officer there. He took McCall to the Gem Theater, holding him by the back of the collar. He allowed anybody so inclined to cuff McCall in the face, and by the time they arrived at the Gem, the prisoner was bleeding from the nose.

A MINER'S JURY WAS ALREADY WAITING AT THE BAR. AL SWEARINGEN closed all downstairs activities and forbade howling upstairs while the trial was in progress. Howling had become as fashionable as pink gin. Two hundred men crowded into the establishment to watch, and that many again stood outside, unable to get in. Word of what happened was spreading everywhere in town.

Jack McCall testified that Bill had killed his brother in Abilene, and then threatened to kill him too, if their paths ever crossed again. "As soon as I saw Wild Bill, I knewed it was him or me," he said.

The jury took an hour to decide. Al Swearingen opened the bar while they made up their minds, and then closed down again for the announcement. The foreman was a soft-brain who had once been a Confederate soldier. He was called Swill Barrel Jimmy, and owned what was conceded to be the oldest coat and shoes in Deadwood, but always wore a clean white collar. "We find the defendant not guilty on account of his mortal grudge against Wild Bill, and self-defense," he said.

And Jack McCall was released. He took a horse that belonged to Al Swearingen and rode for Fort Laramie.

ELLIOT "DOC" PIERCE WAS CALLED FROM HIS HOUSE TO ADMINISTER to the corpse. He lived in the quarters behind his barber shop. He brought along his nephews, Mutt and Buster, to carry the body. They went into Nuttall and Mann's and found Bill lying on the poker table. The cards he had been holding were in his lap. Pink Buford's bulldog was asleep at his feet. There wasn't much blood.

Carl Mann, who had looked into the barrel of Jack McCall's gun, was still sitting on the other side of the table, drinking. Everyone else had gone to the trial. Doc Pierce felt for a pulse at the neck and the wrist, and noted to Buster that it was strange to find the most famous man in the West dead with so little company. There was about seventy dollars under him on the table.

He had the nephews carry the body back to the barber shop, and laid it on a table. Doc Pierce sent Buster to Charley Utter's camp for Bill's Sunday clothes, and any other personal effects that would be appropriate for the funeral, such as his derringer.

He shaved Bill and then closed the wound in his cheek and covered it with pancake makeup. It was a perfect cross. He cleaned Bill's nails and cut ten locks of his hair from the back, where it wouldn't show as Bill lay in his box. The nephew came back, and they dressed Bill in a clean shirt and the Prince Albert frock coat that was his favorite.

They laid him in the box with his guns on and the derringer in a coat pocket. The white handles of Bill's pistols looked beautiful against the green lining of the box. They combed his hair. They put Charley's carbine in the box too, trying it on both sides to see which way it looked best.

A. W. Merrick of the *Black Hills Pioneer* arrived sometime after midnight, out of breath, shaking. He asked Doc Pierce questions and wrote down the answers. "What was the hand he was holding?" the newspaperman asked.

"I didn't notice," the barber said.

"Some said it was aces," the newspaperman said, "and some said it was eights . . . Exactly how did you find him?"

Doc Pierce didn't have much use for the printed word. "Lookit," he said, "I got things to do here. How the hell do you think I found him?"

"How did he look?"

Doc Pierce sighed. "This is for the people who loved the deceased," Merrick said. "This is the last they'll hear of him, so it ought to be good . . ."

"Well," the barber said, "Bill was the prettiest corpse I ever encountered. His fingers looked like marble."

The newspaperman was looking at him, waiting. "What else?" he said.

"The place where the assassin's bullet come out, it was a perfect cross." Doc Pierce brushed past the newspaperman then, pretending there was more left to do than there was. "You want to make yourself useful," he said, "you could print up some funeral notices."

By morning, the notices were posted all over town.

The funeral was attended by four hundred people, including a large contingent from Crook City, so it was impossible to say later who stole Charley's rifle out of the casket.

All the town dignitaries were there, including Mayor E. B. Farnum, Sheriff Seth Bullock, and owners of all the large businesses. Mrs. Langrishe sang "I Know That My Redeemer Liveth," and then broke into tears.

Jane Cannary was in Rapid City, looking for a bull to ride on Main Street. Captain Jack Crawford had left town for Omaha, and would later swear he was a hundred miles away at the time of the killing.

And as Doc Pierce and his nephews were committing Bill's body to the earth, Charley Utter was asleep in Tigerville, between Hill City and Mystic, waiting to ride the last leg of his race against the Clippinger Pony Express.

The service was conducted by Preacher Smith, assisted by Malcolm Nash, whom he believed to be his disciple. The boy stood silently beside the preacher and stared into the sky, so lost in the preacher's words he could not remember who they were for, and he was the only one at the service who had ever known Bill at all.

PART TWO

THE CHINA DOLL

1876

She watched the funeral from the window of her room. It was afternoon, and she was not allowed outside. Behind her, the old woman combed her hair and talked of family problems. The old woman's breath was like swamp gas, and she talked too much. She was all that Tan You-chau had given her for servants.

The one they buried was Wild Bill. She knew he was honored by his people as a soldier. She did not know which war he had won or whom he had killed. The old woman told her one thing one day, another thing the next. She pretended to understand this place, but she lied by habit, as the women of her class did, and did not know herself what was true and what she had invented.

The old woman had told her, for instance, that the Red People had defeated Pudding, the greatest white warrior, and hundreds of his men, and that the white people mourned him and had sworn revenge. But she watched the white people from her window every afternoon while the old woman combed out her hair, and it was not true.

People in mourning did not laugh in the streets, or do business openly. She compared her own revenge to theirs, and saw theirs was false and unplanned. Not an intention, a comfort. "Hush yourself," she said now, and the old woman fell silent. They were moving the coffin from the camp where the man had kept his sleeping quarters. Four men lifted the box up onto a flatbed wagon, pulled by horses, and they took him south, up the street.

The cemetery was a thirty-minute walk to the southeast, and then a painful climb a hundred yards up one of the hills that marked the boundaries of the town. She had gone there herself, looking for a respectable place to bury her brother Song. First, of course, she intended to send the heart and eyes, and the bones of his arms, home. She did not care then that Tan You-chau had forbidden her brother's burial.

Burial did not matter now. The one in the coffin—together with a smaller man—had put Song's body into the oven, and what she had reclaimed could have as easily belonged to a dog. There was no heart, no eyes, no long bones to send home. She had come to this place to repay her brother's debts, but she had come too late. And she would never go home, either.

She watched the street for the smaller one, to see if it hurt him for Wild Bill to die. She was not white-skinned, and would not put away her revenge.

The old woman pulled the comb through her hair, starting at the scalp and traveling the length of her back. She began to speak of her husband again, who had quit his job and spent all his time in the opium dens. "He was always a dreamer," she said, "and now he dreams of his dreams. It is not my fault that he has changed."

"Hush yourself," she said, and the old woman was silent again. She went through the hair carefully at first, working out each tangle, and when it was smooth she pulled through with even, heavy strokes, grunting at the top of each one. The China Doll did not try to correct her manners. It was not possible to keep things here as they had been in Toishan. She thought of Tan You-chau, who kept only the customs which suited him. He wore the white man's clothes, but he had banished Song over a two-hundred-dollar debt, and Song had died in the hills.

She sat on her heels and watched the last of the white people turn the corner and follow the wagon to the graveyard. The little one was not among them. She wondered if he was dead too.

The old woman spoke of her daughters, who disobeyed her, and her son, who was a coward. He had been born the day after the slave ship docked in British Columbia, and refused the old woman a moment's peace since.

"Hush yourself," she said. Ci-an stood up and walked to her bath. The old woman averted her eyes while she undressed and stepped into the tub. Ci-an was the only Chinese in Deadwood with her own bath. She did not know about the whites. Even Tan's wife did not have a bath in her own room. Of course, Tan did not sleep with his wife.

Ci-an thought of her, fat and passive, as she studied her own body in the water. Her beauty gave her no pleasure now, except in refusing it to Tan. Even while he took her, she refused him. She would lie still on the bed and search the ceiling for the face of her brother. She would not smile or fight, even when he had threatened to sell her to the whites.

He would do that soon, and she welcomed it. Their skin had a rotted smell, and they were mannerless, but one day the little one who had put Song in the oven would come to her room. If he was not already dead.

She held one of her feet and washed between the toes. Her feet were smaller than her hands, and ached when she walked beyond the limits of her room. When she stayed in her room, as Tan wished, they turned numb, almost dead. That was the reward for obedience. She had walked once to the north end of town, and once to the graveyard in the south; and the curved, fragile bones in her feet had hurt until she had forgotten everything else, and lost herself in the pain.

And she saw then that she must wait in her room for revenge to come to her.

The old woman knelt beside the tub and began to wash her back. "A disobedient child pulls at a mother's heart like a child in the grave," she said.

"Hush yourself, old woman," Ci-an said. "You do not know what you are saying."

IN THE EVENING, TAN YOU-CHAU CAME TO HER DOOR TO TAKE HER downstairs. She was dressed in a silk robe and had made her face with rice powder and rouge. She had perfumed her palms. Most of Tan's girls had discarded formal dress. He had sold them all to the white men anyway. Only the singers—the Children of Joy—appeared in whiteface, but being ugly, they made themselves carelessly, more to fool the white men than to preserve themselves against this place. Tan had sold them to the white men too.

"Ah," he said when she opened the door, "the China Doll." That was the name he had given her, and it was written in two languages under the likenesses of her that hung outside. She did not like to be addressed in this way, especially by him who had given her the name. She bowed to him, expressionless.

"Perhaps before you sing for the creek miners tonight, you would like to lie with a man," he said.

She looked at him without interest or fear. "Do you want me to lie on the bed?" she asked. Her obedience angered him. He pushed her and she fell. The coarse wooden floor tore her robe. He picked her up by the sash and threw her, without effort, onto the bed. She lay still. He stood over her, staring, breathing through his teeth.

She did not change expression. Not when he tore her robe, not when he entered her, not when he slapped her face. She lay still and searched the ceiling for the face of her brother. In the end he spit on her breasts. "I will sell you to the cow-eaters," he said.

She lay expressionless on the bed, and did not move to wipe the spit from her chest. He stood up and buttoned his pants. He wore the clothes of the white people, and spoke words of their language. He laughed too much when he was with them, like a child with older children, and drank all the concoctions that were in fashion. He played their games with cards.

It was only among his own people that Tan You-chau was feared. She had seen Tan's two faces, and knew him to be empty inside. She did not need or want to kill him. His own life would be her brother's revenge.

"Do you want me to dress?" she said. "Or may I wash first?"

He said, "Have I made you dirty?"

"Yes."

He stood over her a long minute, until she thought he was going to abuse her again. "You are no use to me," he said finally. "To-night, after you sing, I will sell you to the creek miners. You are no longer under my protection."

"Then I should wash," she said. "I would not want your new friends to soil themselves, and think badly of your hospitality."

She washed the spit off her breasts, and then cleaned herself inside. She chose a fresh robe from a trunk under her bed and dressed. She never looked in his direction, not once. "Perhaps you will be wearing the clothes of the white people too," he said.

She offered no opinion. She tightened the combs in her hair and checked her face in the mirror. He had not disturbed her makeup, which was all she now saw in mirrors. She had lost the sense of her own beauty, and knew it would never return. That sense was a gift, like the beauty itself, and one without the other was useless.

He waited until she had finished in the mirror, and then stood up. He opened the door, and the sounds from the theater were suddenly close, as if they had been waiting just outside her room. At the top of the stairs she could smell the white men, a smell that made her think of the dead animals they ate.

But she was not afraid of lying with the cow-eaters. She had opened the door of the oven and found Song, and nothing in this life would sicken her again. That was gone too.

She walked behind Tan down the stairs, her head bowed. She heard the noise change when they saw her. She was as beautiful to the white men as to the real people, but the white men did not know that silence was expression enough. They whistled and yelped like wild dogs, they fired shots into the floor.

She did not raise her head.

She followed Tan to the stage and waited while he introduced her to the audience. He did it twice, once in the language of the white men, who laughed at his clumsiness with their words. Tan laughed with them. He was of two faces, and empty inside.

When he had finished, she stepped into the place he had stood and began to sing. The accompanist was Tan's uncle, who was blind. He had been captured when he first tried to leave Kwangtung, and blinded with acid. Such were the risks of leaving China.

The uncle played the white man's instrument, the piano, instead of his own. It was not an instrument designed to accompany singers. She looked out into the theater—half white, half real people—and sang her mother's song, of a young woman who had lost her betrothed in the war. It was a sentimental song—Tan had forbidden such tunes until late at night, after the white men had drunk many hours—but she ignored his stare and sang the words that came to her.

"He is missing tonight.
I am brave in the night,
But I am afraid of the morning
When I will see that he is gone."

The blind man followed her on the piano, unsure of the notes. The real people bowed their heads, perhaps to memorize the moment, or perhaps trying to remember something from the time before they came to this place. There was nothing so beautiful that it was not more beautiful on reflection. It was the purpose of rice powder and rouge to suggest other times.

Only the white men were unchanged by her singing. Some of them spoke as she performed, some called for drinks from the two bartenders, who were Tan's nephews. The nephews wore white men's clothing too, and sometimes sat in the white people's bars and watched which drinks were served and how they were made. She saw they were as greedy as Tan.

Later, as she sang, one of the white men climbed onto the stage, bowed, and took her into his arms as if to dance. She was grateful for his stink of liquor, which hid the odor of dead animals. The white men in the theater howled, and when she looked down—the bar stood between the theater and the stage—she saw one of Tan's nephews howling too.

The white man was clumsy and strong, and carried her off her feet. She had stopped singing, and now she closed her eyes and waited. She felt him put her down, his hands carefully avoiding her breasts, and then he bowed again, spoke a few words to her in his own language, and left the stage. The other white men applauded him, and he waved his hat in the air to return their courtesy.

After that, there were other white men. Crawling up over the bar onto the stage, each one picking her up off her feet and moving a few steps with her in his arms, and then crawling back down, smiling, while the others cheered. One stepped on her feet, another dirtied her robe. The white men grew more elaborate in their bows, and one fell into the pit where Tan's nephews mixed drinks, and broke his arm. This was also cheered by the white men.

After each interruption, she returned to her songs. She saw Tan at a table with one of the white men. This one had small hands and wore a tie and vest and a round hat. His nose was huge, even for a white man, and she knew from that he was wealthy.

Tan sat with a solemn look on his face, nodding at every word from the white man's mouth. Then they looked at her together, and she knew he was selling her. She put it aside, it was no longer her body, no longer her pain. Her life had become a tool, nothing more, and she would wait to use it. Until the friend of Wild Bill came to her, and she had revenged Song for what they had done to his body.

When she finished singing, she returned to her room and waited for the white man in the suit and vest. Tan brought him to the door, and bowed formally when she answered his knock. The white man bowed too. His nose recalled a tree root, part of something knotted and longer, exposed to view by accident.

"Perhaps you will not belong to all white men if you please this one," Tan said. "He is very rich." The white man held his hat in both hands and smiled. She saw he was afraid to be with real people.

"One is the same as a thousand," she said. She bowed to the man—who, of course, did not speak the language of real people—but did not return his smile.

"It is up to you," Tan said. "You have brought all your troubles to yourself."

"I have no troubles," she said. "Now leave us alone, and perhaps this rabbit will run away."

"Perhaps this rabbit is a fornicator," Tan said.

She shrugged. "One is like another," she said, looking into his eyes for a moment in an open and disrespectful way. "When you have laid with one, you have laid with a thousand."

Tan left the room without another word. The white man stood near the door, holding his hat. She had never seen a white man undressed, but the old woman had told her their shafts grew in proportion to their noses. She sat on her bed and waited to see.

The white man stayed where he was, awkward and afraid. She looked at him to ask what he wanted of her. "Shall I undress?" she said.

The white man pointed to his ear to show that he did not understand. She untied the sash of her robe and let it fall open on top. "Shall I undress?" she said again.

The white man nodded in an uncertain way, and put his hat on the chair near the window. Then he sat down and took off his shoes. He began to speak to her, words she didn't understand. She noticed that he had stopped undressing. He spoke in a soft voice, and asked with his eyes for her to understand him.

Presently he looked down at his hands and played with the wedding band on his third finger. She understood he was speaking of his wife.

She pointed to her ear, as he had done, to tell him she did not understand. That seemed to please the white man, and he straightened his back and pointed to his chest. He spoke the word "Bismarck."

She pointed to her own chest and said, "Ci-an." He smiled and began to speak again, less anxious now. She sat on her bed and waited for him to show her what he wanted. He stayed where he was, talking, until it came to her that the talk itself might be what this one wished.

A moment after she had thought that, though, the white man left the chair and came for her. She stood and removed the robe, and saw that he was struck by her beauty. There was a time when she had imagined all men struck in this way, but that was another time, and her dreams went a different way now. She lay on the bed, feeling the coolness of the quilt on her legs and back, and watched him remove his coat and unfasten the suspenders that held up his pants. When he saw that she was watching, he turned away.

She closed her eyes, not to embarrass him. She heard his breathing, she heard him stumble getting out of his pants. The room was still a long time. She felt him watching her, and then she felt his hands, as soft as a woman's, touching her ankles, then the curves of her feet.

When she opened her eyes, he was kneeling at the end of her bed, kissing her feet. She could not feel the kisses themselves, but the places where his lips had touched were wet, and she felt the coolness.

There was a circle at the top of the white man's head, barren of hair, and she saw that he had not removed his shirt or his tie. He pushed his face deeper into her feet, making eating noises, and she picked her head up off the pillow a few inches to watch more closely. The old woman had told her white people did not understand the beauty of bound feet.

He stayed at the foot of her bed with his face buried in her feet a long time, and when he emerged she saw that he was erect. The old woman was wrong about that too.

The white people's shafts were not in proportion to the size of their noses, they were the size of their noses.

The white man climbed onto the bed, as tentative as a pet who knows he does not belong there. He crawled, hands and knees, until he was over her face. His own face was pink and damp. She closed her eyes and waited. The white man lowered himself gently, again speaking words she did not understand, until his soft body was draped over hers like the final disease. He kissed her eyes and cheeks; she did not move. She felt the shaking in his arms and chest, and heard it in his voice. She thought she felt his tears on her cheeks, but the white man was naturally wet, and it was difficult to know.

He entered her more rudely than he had approached. There was a sudden jab, and then she could feel his small shaft working in and out, as if at the finish of the race. Which it was. The white man spent himself in the time it took to swallow a piece of beef. She wondered at the connection.

He left her body the way he had come to it, lifting himself slowly off until she felt the singing of her skin. She opened her eyes as he backed off the bed, and when she could, she swung her legs over the side, stood up, and wrapped herself in her robe.

The white man had turned away to dress, and stood on one foot as he put the other into his trousers. She went to her window and looked out, willing the friend of Wild Bill to come to her room soon. In this way she ignored the white man's shame, and her own. To acknowledge it was to feed it.

She waited for him to leave the room, but he stayed. When she brought her eyes back inside, he was standing against the door, wearing his coat and vest and trousers and shoes again, holding his hat in his hands. It was as if he had just come in.

He began to speak to her again, a rush of quick words that stopped as suddenly as they had started. The white men fornicated and spoke in the same manner. They had only one speed. She listened to the words with her eyes properly lowered. She had no desire to insult the pitiful or the lame.

When he had stopped speaking he came to her again. He knelt where she stood and kissed her hands, and then he stood up—his eyes had tears now, she was sure—bowed, and left her room.

A moment later, she saw him appear on the street, moving faster, hiding his face in the collar of his coat. She watched him walk a block west, and then turn left, to the south, in the direction of the cemetery. The white man's posture changed as he left Chinatown, his gait slowed, and as she watched him, she saw that he would return.

CHARLEY UTTER GOT BACK TO DEADWOOD ON FRIDAY AFTERNOON, A day ahead of the Clippinger man. He rode through town holding the pouch with fifty copies of the *Cheyenne Leader* over his head and delivered them to A. W. Merrick at the offices of the *Black Hills Pioneer,* and was told there of Bill's death.

His distinct feeling, from the moment he heard the words, was that one half of himself was gone.

"A common drunk?" he said. He remembered lying under the

pine tree after he had nearly drowned, realizing Bill was incomplete. Now, in Bill's absence, he saw the other side. It was a balance between them.

A. W. Merrick nodded, pleased to have a chance to tell it again. "Bill was holding aces and eights," he said, "and the coward Jack McCall came up from behind, pistol drawn, and fired once into the back of his head."

The newspaperman watched to see how Charley took it. "Doc Pierce said he'd never seen a prettier corpse, that Bill's fingers were just like marble." He paused again to see how that set before he went on. "The ball tore a perfect cross, coming out his cheek."

Charley stood dead still, feeling the newspaperman's eyes on him, feeling the words he'd said working on all the years of his life, pressing into them, changing them. Changing him. Not only what he was, but what he had been. The newspaperman had taken a pencil off the desk and prepared to record Charley's words.

Charley held on. "What are your feelings?" the newspaperman said.

Charley shook his head. "I don't have a thing to say in the newspaper," he said.

"This is for Bill," the newspaperman said. "He oughtn't to pass from this world to the next unmourned."

Charley looked across the counter. "Has anybody written his wife?" he said.

The newspaperman wrote that down, and then answered without looking at him. "There has been some conjecture that there was none," he said. "Can you verify a legal marriage?" Charley reached over the desk and took the pencil out of A. W. Merrick's hand. The newspaperman yelped.

"A common drunk?" Charley said again. A moment had passed.

"It happened in a split second," the newspaperman said. He cradled his wrist where Charley had touched him. "Before anyone could sense trouble. It was like lightning, or a flood. An act of God."

"It's no act of God to shoot a man in the back of the head," Charley said. "That's man-made."

Merrick shrugged and took a step away. "I think you fractured my wrist," he said, Charley having refused to notice he was carrying it.

"What happened to the assassin?" Charley said.

"Tried by a miner's court at the Gem Theater, and released,"

Merrick said. "His claim was upheld that Bill shot his brother in Abilene, and had vowed to murder the whole family on sight."

Charley remembered Abilene and swooned at the years that had passed, the things that were gone. "Where is this avenging angel?" he said.

The newspaperman held on to his wrist, insisting on his injury. "He took a horse and headed out alone in the direction of Fort Laramie," he said. "Jack McCall is his name, but he is known by his association with cats."

Charley turned and started out the door. His legs hurt, and he was tired and dirty. "Are you after him?" the newspaperman said.

Charley stopped. He breathed deeply before he answered, and waited until he was sure he could talk. "There is no hurry for circumstances to catch up with Mr. McCall," he said.

As Charley left, the newspaperman had overcome his injuries and was writing down his words.

Charley took the gelding to the livery stable and told the boy there to feed him and brush him down. The horse was good to Brick Pomeroy's word, and would run as long as you asked him. Charley thought he would keep the gelding, even though he now had no interest in the pony express. He thought he might give the business to his brother Steve. He gave the livery boy five dollars and walked back to his camp on the Whitewood. Malcolm was gone from the wagon, leaving only sour sheets and the smell of urine and aired whiskey.

He stood in front of the wagon, thinking of how things changed. The boy passed through his thoughts like a piece of A. W. Merrick's newspaper blown across the street. The killer Jack McCall appeared and disappeared too, weightless.

He held on.

He took the mattress out of the wagon and stripped the sheets. He filled a pail with water from the creek and scrubbed down the floor of the wagon. He took the sheets and his dirty shirts into Chinatown and left them at a laundry. He picked up fresh clothes. He was nauseated at the smell of Chinese food, and the sight of rows of dead ducks hung on lines outside the windows. He walked back to the wagon to collect his toilet, and then to the bathhouse. The Bottle Fiend was at his station next to the door, holding on to a sack of bottles.

"Hot water," Charley said, and handed him a dollar.

The Bottle Fiend did not seem to recognize him, and Charley

wondered if he had truer instincts than people with unmolested brains. If he saw inside Charley, and didn't recognize him.

Charley sat in the tub while the soft-brain heated water. After a while the Bottle Fiend spoke, and Charley saw he had been silent out of respect. "I don't believe nothin' I heard about Wild Bill," he said. "That he shot that man's family connections back in Kansas."

Charley said, "Bill shot six men in Kansas, including Phil Coe and the M'Kandass cousins. Nobody named McCall, in Kansas or anywhere else."

The Bottle Fiend said, "I don't believe nothin' I heard. I listen to my heart." Charley wondered again if the Bottle Fiend remembered him. He sat quietly as the tub filled, a bucket at a time.

"There is things in the future the newspaper can't tell," the Bottle Fiend said a few minutes later. "I told Bill right on this spot, and he said, 'If you see this man with the little-bitty gun, tell him there's about to be a cheap funeral in town.'" The Bottle Fiend shook his head. "I ain't seen him yet to tell him. It wouldn't make no difference if I did. Who listens to a soft-brain?"

Charley closed his eyes. He didn't inquire who it was with the gun. What was revealed was revealed, and you couldn't hurry it, asking a soft-brain questions. To learn, you had to see a thing on its own terms. And sometimes, understanding it, you came to love it.

Bill.

"I shot myself once," the Bottle Fiend said, "it's like having your picture took. You see them same colored bubbles, and one of them's got yourself inside it."

The Bottle Fiend looked at Charley then, and maybe into him. "Don't worry none about Bill, he just took one of them bubbles to heaven." For maybe two seconds there was a connection, brain to brain, and then as fast as it had come, it went, and the soft-brain was soft-brained again. "Don't ever eat poison eggs," he said. "Poison eggs is worse than hanging."

Charley washed himself with soap and sent the Bottle Fiend for two raw eggs, which he used to soften his hair. There was a condition that hair reached where it matted together so thick you couldn't even comb out the wildlife, where all you could do for it was to cut it off. He thought of Bill's hair, which was thinner than his own, and softer. It seemed to clean itself in the rain.

He held on.

He stood up and dried. He put on a clean white shirt, clean

pants, clean socks. The Chinese put starch in everything, and the pants went on like new boots.

"I don't expect you'll be back now," the Bottle Fiend said.

"I'll be back."

"When you ain't so sad," the Bottle Fiend said.

"There are some things I got to take care of," Charley said.

The Bottle Fiend nodded. "He's up on Boot Hill," he said. "He ain't marked yet, but it's the one with all the flowers."

Charley gave him another dollar, and walked to the cemetery. He followed the wagon road over the Whitewood on a little wooden bridge that shifted under his weight, and then he climbed about a hundred yards up the side of a 3500-foot hill on the east side of town. The cemetery was in a natural clearing. There wasn't a grave there that had settled yet. The newest ones, the dirt was still piled a foot above level. The older ones, the dirt had sunk below level, leaving a pocket in the earth, a place that looked like you might want to lie down there too.

Bill's grave was toward the north end of the cemetery, with a nice view of the gulch, where he could have looked things over and told the rest of them up there what was going on. Charley thought he would have liked the spot. The dirt was fresh and pieces of it still held the shape of the spades that had been used to dig it. There were wildflowers at the head and the foot, and a fresh-cut tree stump someone had written on.

A Brave Man; the Victim of an Assassin
J. B. (Wild Bill) Hickok, aged 48 years;
murdered by Jack McCall, Aug. 2, 1876.

Charley pictured Bill receiving the news that he'd just been memorialized into old age. He held on. "We should never have gone in that canoe," he said.

Children were coming up the hill now, and Charley stopped. It wasn't worth anything, talking to a grave anyway. He stood still and watched them, four little girls and their mother. The widow who'd sold him milk for Malcolm. He did not recognize them until the smallest broke from the others and ran to him, trailing ribbons. There were little folds in her legs and arms, and her cheeks bounced as her shoes hit the ground.

He waited, half inclined to run away. He did not think he could stand it now, a widow and four babies. The little girl skipped the last steps and grabbed his leg like she meant to eat it. As she hugged him, the others saw who it was, and they came too. He picked up the littlest one, and the others hung on to his fingers and arms.

The widow came last and slowest. She pried the girls off Charley's body but left the little one in his arms. "We was sorry to hear about your friend," she said, looking at the top of one of the blond heads.

"Thank you," Charley said. The little girl felt heavy and wet. "I was in Cheyenne . . ."

"The girls wondered what happened, you didn't come for milk." Charley shook his head.

"The boy got better," he said. "I think he did."

The widow smiled. "That's good news, ain't it."

"Yes, ma'am."

"There's always some good in the bad," she said. "Sometimes it ain't easy to find."

It was quiet then, both of them talked out. "Well," Charley said after a minute, "how is your cow?"

"Fine," the widow said. Then she looked north, to the oldest part of the cemetery. "We come up here to visit the girls' daddy," she said, "but I was going to say a prayer for your friend too."

"Thank you," Charley said.

"The prayers of the young are heard first," she said. "I believe that. They're unspoilt and pure." Charley handed her the child in his arms. The child did not want to let go of his neck, and complained when her mother took her. Charley reached into his pocket and found a twenty-dollar gold piece. He gave it to the widow, putting it in her hand and then closing her fingers around.

"I can't take nothin' like this," she said.

Charley looked one more time at the torn ground and the freshly cut stump. "There isn't anything in this world matters less than money," he said, as much to Bill as her. He looked back at the widow and saw that he'd made her ashamed. "All money comes down to," he said, "is who's holding it. And I don't need anything extra that way right now."

"I never thought of it like that," she said. "I never been the one holding it." The smallest child reached for him from her mother's arms.

He held on.

"Let me give these babies a kiss," he said, "and then I got to go." He kissed the smallest one first. He untangled himself from her arms, and knelt down and hugged the others. Kissing soft faces, getting hair in his mouth, he felt tears coming into his eyes and let them go.

One of the babies said, "Don't you want no more milk from us?"

"I'll be by from time to time," he said, "but I got to go now."

The widow pulled her children away. "We'll see Mr. Utter again," she said. Charley started back down the road off the hill. He heard one of the babies ask when that would be. The widow said, "We'll see him when he comes up here to visit his friend."

Charley walked back to his camp, stopping at the tent bar across the creek for a bottle of whiskey. The barkeep did not remember him without Bill, and took him for a tourist. "That spot you're standing on, friend, is the very place Wild Bill Hickok first set foot in Deadwood Gulch. You're on the threshold of history."

Charley gave him five dollars and picked up the bottle.

"You wouldn't like to try a bottle of pink?" the barkeep said. "That was Wild Bill's favorite."

Charley shook his head and started across the street. "Just a minute, pilgrim," the barkeep said, "a bottle's eight dollars." Charley gave him another five and waited for the change. The bartender kept his money in a cigar box, and when he came out of it he was holding a piece of hair. "Look here," he said, and showed Charley a lock of long, light-brown hair. "This come off Wild Bill himself." Charley looked closer and saw it was true.

He said, "How did you come into possession of this?"

The bartender leaned close. "I got it from Doc Pierce himself," he said. "He attended the corpse." The bartender saw something then in Charley's eyes. "This is all strictly legal," he said. "I bought it, so it's nothing shady . . ."

Charley took the bottle and crossed the street, and then the creek. He pulled Bill's saddle out of the wagon and put that on the ground in front of the tree stump Bill used to sit on while the mercury dried. He found paper and pen and sat down to write.

Nothing came. He tried to picture her standing there, and what he would say, but he couldn't get past clearing his throat. There was too much to tell, there was no way to get at it. He pictured himself hugging her like he did the babies, and that was as far as it went. And in the end, that's what he wrote.

Dear Mrs. Hickok,

I am Charley Utter, Bill's friend who signed the witness papers at the wedding. The short one. I have loved Bill like a brother—more than some brothers—ever since we first became partners back at the

*beginning of the war, and it has fallen to me now to write informing
you of his death.*

*I wish I could of come in person and told you this, but believe me
when I say that my regard for Bill reaches out from the Hills to all
that he loved, and more than anyone else to you.*

*The circumstances of this matter are not clear to me yet, as I was
out of town at the time it occurred.*

He stopped writing then and read the letter. He thought of explaining what had happened between them, but he couldn't see
how you told a woman her husband was dead one minute, and then
went into the particulars of a moose-hunt the next. There was
enough blood spilled as it was.

He pressed back into the saddle.

*The town has carved Bill's name into a tree stump, and his spot is
covered with fresh-cut wildflowers. I was there not more than half an
hour ago.*

*If there are any further instructions on the matter of his burial,
please write and tell me what to do. I hope to run into you soon, and
provide what context I can.*

> *Sincerely Yours,*
> *Charley Utter*

He folded the letter twice and put it in his shirt pocket. He
meant to read it again before he let it go. He put Bill's saddle back
in the wagon and began to drink. The sun had dropped behind the
hill where Bill was buried, and the air turned cool. Not an evening
cool, but similar to the cool before a storm. There was a threat
in it.

He thought of Bill's words on the day they had come down out
of the hills into Deadwood, and saw that they held that same coolness.

He took another drink, fighting off the chill. The way things
connected for Bill, he knew this was the place. He might of even
known how. What else was he doing with his back to the door at
Nuttall and Mann's?

Charley started for the badlands. He took the bottle with him,
and stopped first at the Green Front and then at the Senate. Then
he walked into Nuttall and Mann's. Harry Sam Young recognized
him and put a drink on the bar. Charley tried to pay, but Harry
Sam Young refused the money.

"Where did it happen?" Charley said, after a minute.

The bartender pointed to the table. Charley tried to imagine the way it happened, but it was just another room. He couldn't feel Bill there at all. He felt the coolness, though, and the threat, but he had brought that in himself.

"It wasn't a thing I could of done," the bartender said. Charley heard the lie in that, and noted it. You had to take what you found. You couldn't force the truth to reveal itself.

Charley finished the drink and filled the glass from his own bottle. There were tourists waiting for drinks now, but the bartender stayed in front of him. "After he did Bill, he pointed down at Carl Mann, then at me. But the firing pin had broke at the first shot. It was like somebody counting time . . ."

Charley waited.

"That's all I know," he said. "By now, every tourist in Deadwood is eyewitnessed it all. But the truth is, nobody seen it, not start to finish the way it happened." Charley heard something false in that too. "How could they?" the bartender said. "Bill hisself never knew what happened."

Charley finished half of the glass of whiskey. "Bill knew what he knew," he said. He was not as dependable a drinker as some, and it had already affected his thinking. He allowed for that, and held on. It felt like he was holding the door shut against all the years of his life.

"There was talk that you would revenge him," the bartender said a little later.

"I only came in to see what happened for myself," Charley said.

"To what use?" Harry Sam Young was a bartender, and that was a bygones-be-bygones business. Charley wondered sometimes what rules they must have broken themselves to end up in a life where the first thing you did every day, before you washed or counted your money, was to forgive everything from the day before.

"Could it be accidental, that he picked Bill?" Charley said.

The bartender thought it over. "I couldn't say."

Charley heard that for another lie, and noted it.

"There was a hundred people here, and a hundred stories of how it happened . . ."

Charley finished what was in the glass and put a dollar on the bar. Harry Sam Young shook his head. "No charges," he said. "I just want to let this event take its natural course."

Charley felt the whiskey crawling up the back of his head. He smiled at the bartender, a strange-feeling smile. "That part of it's already happened," he said.

CHARLEY DEVELOPED A PLAN.

Drink the whole bottle. He had drunk a bottle of whiskey in one night once before, in the mountains near Georgetown, Colorado, during a September blizzard. He remembered what that had done to him, and wanted it to happen again. He remembered lying on the floor of a cabin, looking up at the famous gunfighter Texas Jack Omohundro, who had come to Colorado to hunt grizzly with him, and clearly seeing there wasn't anything anywhere but the two of them, that they were the two parts God had made everything else out of.

He'd said, "Jack, you and I are what everything else is made of."

Texas Jack was working on a bottle of his own. He said, "You want the truth? I hate Texas."

And Charley said, "See there? That's just what I'm talking about."

And that's where Charley wanted to be again, back to the beginning of how things were made. Along the way there, he expected to see every living thing in Deadwood, on its own level, and in the end he would know what he needed to.

That was not his plan when he bought the bottle, but what developed as he sat in the chair by the window of Lurline Monti Verdi's room at the Gem Theater, looking outside. He had found her at Nuttall and Mann's, or she had found him. He followed his feelings, which told him not to sit still with Bill's murder so fresh. "You're the one that was partners with Bill," she said.

She had a peculiar perfume that Charley had never encountered before. Confused flavors. He remembered perfumes, and who went with them. "Yes, I am," he said.

She was clean-looking, he thought, and had plucked the hairs out of her eyebrows to make them thin and willowy. It always attracted Charley to a woman when he could see she had put some effort into her appearance. He liked those that tried.

"Are you in mourning?" she said.

"I'm married," he said.

She smiled at him and there wasn't a disfigurement anywhere. No broken teeth or dead gums. "Nobody has ever hit you in the mouth," he said.

She took that for the compliment it was. "I never allowed fists," she said. "The man that hurts my looks should never sleep comfortable again." She put her hand on his leg as she spoke, and left it there as she studied him. "You ain't the kind anyway," she said.

"No," he said.

"Not even your wife?"

"No," he said.

She pushed her hand up the inside of his leg. "A man that never hit his wife, that don't come up the street every day of the week."

"My wife was born lucky," he said.

"So I see," she said.

They got muddy walking to the Gem. "The owner here is likely to make remarks," she said before they went in.

"I have seen the whore man up close," Charley said, "and he has seen me."

"I didn't ast you for no money," she said. He saw that he had hurt her feelings, and gave her ten dollars.

"That's for your dowry," he said, and they walked through the bar directly to the stairs. Charley saw the whore man at one of the card tables. He looked up in time to see them on the stairs. There was half a second when the whore man was ready to bolt, but then he settled back into his chair and nodded at them both. And Charley noted that too.

"I never been with anybody famous," she said when they were in her room. She sat down on her bed and Charley took the chair by the window. There were miners outside, drunk, and a fistfight was starting in the street below him.

Charley had learned to fight watching Bill, and knew the secrets of relaxation. "I don't think you could count Big Nose George," she said. "They had two thousand dollars reward on him for a while, but Big Nose George wasn't known to be famous, except for his nose."

Charley smiled at that and took a drink from the bottle. He liked this woman, and determined to understand her as she was. He determined to understand the whole town. "Of course," she said, "I was with Marshal Cecil Irwin the night he hung George, but that was a temporary sort of famous."

"No," Charley said, "a lawman hanging the right miscreant isn't much in the line of a celebrity."

"I like the way you talk," she said. "It sounds English."

He said, "It is." Charley drank from the bottle and remembered the night in the mountains with Texas Jack Omohundro, and decided to finish every drop. He drank again, but when he checked the bottle it didn't seem to have altered its level. His own level was rising like the moon.

"I noticed this much," she was saying. "The more they tell you before, the worst it is after. I hate a man to come into my room and tell his personal business while he takes off his pants. It's weakness, and in the end they're ashamed and blame the girl."

Out in the street the two miners were circling each other, knuckles out, arms useless and stiff. There were other miners around them, calling advice. "Break his nose, Henry."

"Would you care for a bite of this?" he said, and offered the bottle.

"I drink gin and bitters," she said. "You get sweet breath and a sense of adventure. You ought to try it yourself."

"I tried it," he said, and drank again from the bottle.

"You ain't much of a drinker anyway, by local standards," she said. It made him laugh out loud. But then she said, "Bill drunk too much, didn't he?" and stopped him.

Charley looked at his hands and felt his brain tangle. "He drank what he drank," he said.

She said, "I heard he'd lost his functions."

"Where did you hear a story like that?" It always surprised Charley, the rumors that got around.

"He never come near an upstairs girl," she said. "Nobody ever seen him near Chinatown, which he wouldn't of sunk to anyway. Bill hated celestials."

"Bill didn't hate anybody more than a minute," he said. "He never let himself fall into that."

"Then how come he drunk so much?" she said.

Charley looked over at the bed, and saw that Lurline had got herself undressed, down to her undies. "It's a sure sign," she said. Her undies were black and red and attached to her stockings by garter belts. Charley loved accessories, and felt the start of a humming in his peeder, only it seemed distant, as if it were in another room.

"He had been let down a lot," he said.

"I never heard anything along those lines," she said.

"There's nothing you ever heard about Bill that's true, except by accident," he said. He took a drink, and then another one.

After a while he looked over and saw Lurline was watching him. "Tell me something true about Wild Bill," she said.

He looked through the hole in the top of the bottle and made himself dizzy. "I already did," he said. "He'd been let down."

Out on the street, one of the miners had slipped in the mud and the other one was sitting on his chest, trying to get his thumbs in his eyes. Charley knew that someone was about to get bitten, even before he heard the scream. The miners had closed the circle around the two men, now the men were rolling on the ground, and Charley noticed the bulldog then, standing behind them, watching the fight through their legs. He felt a wash of affection for the dog, and reminded himself to purchase the animal some pickled eggs the next time he saw him out drinking with Pink Buford. The dog watched the fight without enthusiasm. Charley expected he was not impressed with anything that bit and let go.

He heard Lurline come off her bed and cross the room. "What's you lookin' at out there?" she said. She did not go to the window, though. She stopped behind Charley, and he felt her breath behind his ear.

"A dog watching two men fight," he said.

She put her hands on the back of his neck and smoothed the muscles all the way down into his shoulders. She took the tip of his ear between her teeth, and bit him. He did not move a muscle, unless you counted his peeder. She said, "Are you a fighter too?"

He felt her take his ear in her mouth again, more of it this time. "It's never come up much," he said.

Her hands went around to the front of his neck, and her fingertips stroked his throat, soft, at the same time she bit down again on his ear. "You're too good-natured for fighting," she said.

He shook his head and she changed ears. "It isn't that," he said. "It's something else."

She bit his other ear, and then took a little of the skin beneath it between her teeth and bit that too. She bit hard, but not quite hard enough to complain about. "It don't matter," she said. "Everybody in this town's a fighter. You're different."

Charley sat still. "Yes, I am," he said.

She moved then, rose up behind him until he felt the warm press of her stomach where her teeth had been before. She cradled his head into her body, and he let himself be cradled. In a moment, he saw that her intentions were not motherly.

She reached down, still holding his head against her, and touched the outline of his peeder under his pants. She used one finger, and ran it the length. "You ain't that different," she said.

He found the bottle on the floor and took a long drink. "Let me have a look at you," she said. He sat still and watched her unbutton his pants, one-handed from behind. "There's some men that won't let a lady watch them undressed," she said.

She worked from the top down, no hurry at all, and the head of his peeder rose out of his trousers, a button at a time. It reminded him of Jesus rising from the dead, and he did not shake that thought from his head, but held on to it, so the Lord could see how bad he'd gone.

"Stand up," she said, behind him.

He stood up, and his pants dropped around his moccasins. He held on to his bottle, and when he took the next drink he saw it was about half gone. A bottle, he decided, was like a trip. You couldn't be stopping every mile to see how far you'd come. She ran her hands over his legs and found the scars where his brother Steve and the Ute had shot him. She put her finger in the darker scar, which belonged to the Ute, and looked into his eyes.

She didn't ask, and he didn't say.

She moved her hands again, around in back. It occurred to him then that they were standing in front of the window. When he tried to move, she sank her nails into the flesh at the back of his legs. She pushed deep, but not deep enough to complain about.

"Don't move," she said.

He stayed where he was. "You'll make a spectacle of us both," he said. She smiled, and he saw that's what she intended. In a moment, she lowered herself onto her knees. It had been weeks since Charley had spent himself, unless you counted the episode in the water, which he didn't, and at the sight of her on her knees in front of him he felt the beginnings of that sweet cramp before she so much as touched him. It began, and then passed.

A line of jizzom seeped from his peeder, strung half a foot, and then dropped onto the floor. He felt her hair against his legs, and then her teeth. This time he tried to pull away, but his feet were still encumbered in his trousers, and she had her arms around his knees. She moved her mouth and bit him higher.

He looked out the window and saw that the miners were still fighting, locked as still as sleep in each other's holds. He took another drink from the bottle and she moved to his other leg. It was not as painful as when she'd bit him before, it had lost the surprise. She moved up again, into the spot where his leg met his body, and bit him there too. She took his jewels in her hand and looked up into his face. "You're good-natured," she said, "and you keep your-self clean."

"You bite strangers," he said.

"You ain't no stranger," she said, and bit him again. Softer, though. More playful than before, like something had been agreed to that she could do what she wanted. Charley pulled on the bottle again. He still intended to drink all there was, but the reasons weren't as clear.

When he looked outside again, some of the miners were looking back. He tried to move away from the window, but she stopped him. She tightened her hand around his jewels and pulled him half a step to the side, and then she took the head of his peeder in her mouth.

She put her teeth in, not enough to complain about. He felt his legs begin to shake, and this time the cramp couldn't be headed, and then the jizzom was running out of him and down both sides of her mouth and dropping on the floor.

When she had let him go, he sat back down in the chair with his pants still around his ankles, and studied the little puddles on the floor. "There is something alive in that," he said, after a few min-utes.

She had wiped her mouth off on a pink towel and sat down on the bed. She stared at the floor too. "I never thought of it like that," she said.

"It's dying now," he said, and took another drink. The alcohol seemed to have lost its spark, and he thought the air might have killed that too. "It's similar to a polliwog," he said, "removed from its pond before it had time to grow lungs."

Lurline leaned closer to the floor. "I never thought of it, I swear."

"There," he said, "I saw it move."

She shook her head. "I never liked to see nothing suffer," she said.

"That's sweet talk for a biter," he said.

She smiled without looking up. She said, "It is alive, ain't it? It has to be, or elst nothing could come of it. I never thought of none of this . . ."

Charley wet his finger in the bottle and ran it over his eyelids. It was an Indian trick that gave you energy to keep drinking. She was lying on her stomach now, with her chin resting on her fist, still watching the floor. "I didn't see it move," he said. He didn't want to pass out and leave her there all night nursing his jizzom. "It's dead now, anyway," he said. "It can only last about two minutes in this heat . . ."

She would not let go of it, though. "I never thought of jizzom except something left behind, like a mark after they slapped your face."

"Who slapped your face?" he said.

She shrugged. "Everybody slaps upstairs girls," she said. Charley pushed another swallow down his throat and lost his balance putting the bottle back on the floor. He caught himself just before he fell off the chair. "You're too jumpy," she said. "Anybody else, they would of let themself fall where they may."

"I've been drunk on the floor," he said. "Myself and Texas Jack Omohundro, in a blizzard in the Rockies. He told me he hated Texas."

"Were you partners with Texas Jack too?" she said.

He shook his head. "I just took him hunting," he said. "He was more Bill's friend than mine, but neither one of us loved him."

"You're a strange one," she said. "Dying jizzom and true love." He smiled at her and kicked the moccasins off his feet. She said, "You planning to sleep in the window?"

She got off the bed and pulled his trousers off, untangling one foot at a time. She helped him up and over to the bed. He held on to the bottle. He tried to drink lying down and spilled cold whiskey over his chin and chest.

He lay on his back and she sat over him, one leg on each side, and unbuttoned his shirt. She was smiling again. She used her fingernails the length of his chest, down to his stomach. "Well, lookit here," she said a minute later. "I thought you was tired."

Charley looked. He picked his head up off the pillow and saw what she was talking about. "It's a death dance," he said. "Don't pay it any attention."

She adjusted her undies and fit herself over him. She began to move up and down, looking him in the eye. "If it pounds nails, it's a hammer," she said.

Charley watched her eyes until the movement made him dizzy. He took another drink, and saw that he was less than an inch from the bottom.

"I don't know what you got to finish that for," she said. "It's going to make you good and sick in the morning."

"Maybe blind," he said, and closed his eyes.

A little later she bit him again, on the chest. He opened his eyes and saw that they were still embraced in fornication. He knew time had passed, he didn't know how much. There was no feeling at all in his peeder.

"How come you bite so?" he said.

She pulled back until her face was almost in focus. He saw her shrug. "Somebody's got to squirm," she said, "that's what fuckin' is."

He put his hand around the back of her neck and pulled her down to him and kissed her cheeks. "How old are you, to think something like that?"

"Nineteen," she said.

HE WOKE UP SICK AND SORRY AND ALONE. LURLINE WAS GONE, HER black and red undies hung on the bedpost. He lifted his head to see them better, and it felt like something heavy and sharp-edged was balanced in there, and it fell frontwards as he moved.

He stood up slowly and looked at his body. There were dark blue bruises up and down the insides of his legs and on his chest. Scratch marks that slid down his stomach like rain on a window. He looked closer at his legs, and saw the imprint of her teeth.

His pants were over by the window. He broke a sweat getting into them. The bottle was on the floor, lying on its side. A fly sat on its lip. There was a puddle of liquor collected inside, near the neck. The whole room smelled like whiskey.

He found his shirt under the sheets, wrinkled and smelling of Lurline's perfume. He sniffed it, and the humming began in his peeder. His moccasins were back under the chair. As he bent to pick them up, the weight in his head moved again, and he froze until it settled. He found a comb in the dresser and ran it through his hair, and then walked out the door, down the steps, and into the barroom of the Gem Theater.

The whore man was standing behind the bar. He smiled at Charley, and there was a difference in him from the night before, as if he knew the condition of Charley's body, or as if somehow they were the same, now that Charley had sinned.

"The price for the night is ten dollars," the whore man said.

Charley stopped in the middle of the room. There were eight or nine tourists already drinking away the morning, but no whores—except one asleep on the piano—no gamblers of consequence. The whore man's words carried to every corner of the room.

Charley walked to the bar. "I don't recall your name," he said to the whore man.

"Al Swearingen," the whore man said. "We met on the wagon train you come in on."

"I didn't forget where we met," he said, "or the conditions. I forgot your name."

"Swearingen," he said. "I own the Gem and every girl in it." He smiled, and Charley remembered how his beard had looked, still wet with the boy's jizzom. He put that thought out of his mind, having done all the thinking about jizzom he cared to last night. "And you ain't got Wild Bill around to protect you now."

Charley took the pearl-handled knife out of his belt and held it sideways in front of the whore man's nose. For half a minute the only thing that moved was the whore man's throat. "I tell you this one time only, Mr. Swearingen," he said. "Don't ever ask me for nothing when I'm wearing a wrinkled shirt. I don't like to be addressed by a whore man before I get a bath and a change of clothing, so everybody can tell us apart."

The whore man didn't answer, and Charley let him go.

He walked out of the Gem and went to his camp. Nothing had been touched; the boy hadn't been back. He did not dwell on the boy or family entanglements. He picked up his toilet and a clean shirt and walked toward the bathhouse, thinking of Mrs. Langrishe.

In the aftermath of serious drinking, his peeder defied common sense and decency.

THE BOTTLE FIEND TOOK A DOLLAR FROM CHARLEY AND WATCHED HIM undress. He was transfixed by the bruises. He stood still, holding two buckets of hot water, and stared at Charley's chest and legs. "What kind of injuries is those?" he said after a while.

Charley sat down in the tub and waited for water. "Bites," he said. "Now start this bath and I'll find you a bottle later on."

"What bit you?"

"Teeth," Charley said. The Bottle Fiend put one of the buckets down and poured the other one into the tub. It was hot water, and Charley began to sweat.

"Heat's the best thing for drunks," the soft-brain said. "Hot water takes the poison out the skin. I don't know about bites . . ."

He poured the other bucket in the tub, and the hot water took what strength Charley had, all except his peeder. He dropped his chin into his chest and closed his eyes and thought of being bitten by Mrs. Langrishe. He wondered what sort of left turn his brain had taken.

"What bit you?" the Bottle Fiend said again. He brought two more buckets of water and poured them over Charley's shoulders.

Charley shook his head. "I bit myself," he said, and then he opened his eyes and saw the Bottle Fiend's mind at work. "Don't think it," Charley said. "You understand? Just don't think it . . ."

"I can't help what I think," the Bottle Fiend said.

Charley said, "There isn't a soul that drew breath on this planet so far committed suicide biting himself to death."

"You bit yourself," the Bottle Fiend said.

"It wasn't a suicide," Charley said. "It was something different."

The Bottle Fiend was standing over him, and the sweat ran into Charley's eyes and stung them when he blinked. "How is it different?" the Bottle Fiend said.

"It was different," he said. "God as my witness." He got a picture then of the Bottle Fiend sitting in his chair by the door, bleeding, holding a piece of his own shoulder in his mouth. Then he got a picture of Mrs. Langrishe sitting over him in the same attitude as Lurline last night.

The Bottle Fiend went for the last two buckets of hot water. "When you tell me something," he said when he came back, "is it true?"

"As much as you're ready for," Charley said.

The Bottle Fiend reflected on that. "That's what Doc Sick said."

"He looks out for your interests," Charley said.

"Sometimes," the Bottle Fiend said a few minutes later, "I wisht I didn't have nobody looking over me. Sometimes I want to know everything the way it is."

Something in that bothered Charley. "Don't ever wish for something you don't know what it is," he said. "You might get it." Then he handed the soft-brain five dollars and sent him out for a bottle of whiskey. "Nothing pink or clear," he said. "I want brown American whiskey. And when I'm done, you can have the bottle."

SETH BULLOCK HAD A NOSE FOR TROUBLE, AND THIS WAS IT.

Overnight, Solomon Star had lost his interest in business. Bullock had been business partners with him nine years, before Deadwood in Bismarck, and he noticed the difference from the morning Solomon quit complaining over the books. Two different days in the last week, he hadn't as much as sharpened a pencil.

On Monday, as a test, Bullock said, "You think we need a new porch on the place?"

Solomon Star shrugged. He never even asked how much porches cost. He was sitting at his desk, open-collared, looking at the ceiling. In nine years, Bullock had never seen Solomon at work without a tie. He couldn't remember seeing him star-gazing indoors either.

Before, his nose was always in the balance books. He knew where the money went and where it came from. He kept track of interest rates, and borrowed sometimes even when they didn't need capital. He argued with Bullock over orders and supplies, he argued over the money Bullock gave to widows and orphans and other public causes. He argued, but he gave in. Bullock had a long-range plan he never saw, and in the end he trusted that it was there.

And in that way Seth Bullock and Solomon Star depended on each other, and understood each other the way different people sometimes do—each of them thinking he saw the other better than the other saw him.

"We could ship some hardwood up from Colorado," Bullock said, worried now. Something depended on the balance between them, and he saw it had changed.

Solomon Star kept his eyes on the ceiling. "Whatever you think, Mr. Bullock," he said.

"Tropical flowers," Bullock said. "We could plant orchids and sell them May Day . . . Solomon?"

"I've been thinking," he said. "I might like to read a novel."

Seth Bullock did not own a nervous-type stomach, but that declaration sent it right to the edge of the cliff. "You haven't been yourself," he said.

"That's what I've been thinking too," Solomon said. "Exactly."

Bullock stared at his partner, trying to see what it was. "Are you sick with something?" he said. He was hoping he was sick.

Solomon stood up and went to the front of the store. He looked out the window. Solomon hadn't spent five minutes in his life looking out windows. Bullock followed him over. "You know what, Mr. Bullock?" Solomon said after a while. "Those hills are pretty. It's like I never saw them before, like this is the first day."

"Is it bad news from home?" Bullock said. "Did the mail come today?"

Solomon shook his head, still looking out the window. He took a deep breath and stood taller than usual. "I wonder what the sights are like from that hill," he said, pointing at one that formed the southeast boundary of town.

"You've been on top of hills plenty of times."

Seth Bullock moved closer, wanting a better look at Solomon's eyes. "We got two kilns somewhere between here and Sioux City," he said. "Twenty thousand dollars each. Another one north of town, exposed to the elements. We got a drawer full of contracts for bricks everyplace in the Hills. We got orders and shipments coming in from anyplace that ships out. We got men to hire and goods to move. There isn't any turning back . . ."

Solomon smiled at him. He never smiled over business, not in his life. He looked back out the window. "I think I might climb that hill," he said. And that fast, he walked out of the office, crossed the street, and started toward the south end of town. He didn't even close the door.

Bullock sat down at Solomon's desk. He looked through the papers there, seeing they were in some kind of order he didn't understand. He didn't understand how Solomon worked, he didn't know what he did.

He did understand it was Solomon that made it work.

Seth Bullock had been a successful businessman nine years without knowing how to balance accounts or keep books. He had never written an order form or argued price.

He put Solomon's papers back where he had found them and moved over to his own desk, where things were familiar. There were letters there from politicians, marshals, and widows with hopeless cases. Presidents of mining companies in California and Colorado. There was a stack of wanted posters, upside down, which he consulted when there was highwayman activity in the immediate area. Seth Bullock had been sheriff a little over half a year in Deadwood, and a deputy marshal in Bismarck for three years before that, and, reputation to the contrary, he was not anxious to clean up the Dakota Territory, or anything else. He did know where to go to get it done, though, when he had to.

He sat at his desk most of the afternoon, thinking about Solomon Star. He thought of all the things that caused sudden changes in men, which came down to losing their children or falling on their heads.

Or women.

No. Solomon Star was married the way one-legged people were crippled. Forever. He thought of Solomon's wife—she had expressions like a sullen child, and a hard edge to everything she said. He decided to write her if Solomon didn't improve. She hadn't wanted Solomon coming to the Hills alone in the first place, and was anxious to join him. He knew that from her letters, which Solomon left unlocked in the top left drawer of his desk. To Bullock's memory, his partner had never brought her name into a conversation. He was afraid of her in a way that distance didn't change.

Thinking of that, Bullock hoped he did not have to write the letter. He did not like to do that to a partner.

AFTER HE HAD SOLD HER TO THE WHITE MAN, TAN YOU-CHAU HAD forbidden Ci-an to leave the house, even in the morning. "Whatever you desire, you will have it here," he said.

She did not know how much Tan had taken from the white man, but Tan himself had not come near her since the bargain had been struck. She thought Bismarck must be very wealthy. "What if I desire to walk outside?" she said.

Tan had smiled at her. "I will give you another servant," he said. "And she will walk for you, and then return to your room and tell you what she has seen."

Tan had not struck her since the white man had come to her room. He had given her new gowns and combs. The combs she had seen before, in the hair of his wife.

Her meals were brought to her room by the old woman, who went with her to Tan's own privy in back, where she was allowed to attend to her personal needs. There was another privy, larger and farther from the house, where the others stood in line after their meals. At appointed times, the servants used the same building, and at other appointed times, Tan's own wife and relations. The old woman questioned his orders—believing she had misunderstood—and he told her he did not want his China Doll so far from his house again.

The old woman told this to Ci-an. Ci-an said, "This Bismarck is perhaps the richest man in the world."

After her morning toilet, Ci-an shooed the old woman away and stayed alone in her room, arranging and then sketching her artificial flowers. And so she was alone on the morning when she finally saw Wild Bill's friend in the street. At first, because of his pain, she had not recognized him. His clothes were wrinkled and out of place, and he walked without attention to the mud, or other men. Pain was the surest disguise.

But she was not mistaken. He had picked up one side of the metal that held Song's body, Wild Bill had picked up the other, and together—equally to blame—they had put Song into the oven.

In the afternoon, she spoke to the old woman. "There is a man," she said.

"There are many men," the old woman said, "none of them any good."

"Hush yourself," she said. "There is a man I wish to see." The old woman shook her head.

"Tan has forbidden," she said.

"I will see this man," she said. She reached out and took both of the old woman's hands in hers, an uncommon gesture toward a servant. "This man knows of my brother Song."

The old woman pulled her hands away and covered her ears. "There is no such person," she said. "He does not exist. You invite the same for us both. What would my children become if their mother had never existed?"

"Tan cannot decide who has existed," Ci-an said.

The old woman moved to leave the room. She was afraid and beginning to weep. Ci-an stopped her. "Please," the old woman said, "I am afraid."

"There is a man I wish to see," Ci-an said. The old woman was not listening now. Her eyes went from the window to the door to the ceiling, lighting like a bird, searching for a way out. She smiled and nodded, and could not stop her tears.

"Hush yourself now," Ci-an said kindly. "Soon I will ask you for something, and when you have done that thing, your obligations to me are over."

She watched the street all afternoon, but did not see Wild Bill's friend again. She closed her eyes and willed him to her room. She became his other person, and cried for him to find her, so they might be whole again. She did not know how long it would take, but this would happen.

She had senses that other women only pretended to possess.

In the evening Tan came to her room to take her downstairs. He knocked at her door before he entered. He did not insult her or try to touch her. He addressed her as Ci-an, not as China Doll, although that was still his name for her among his servants and family. The old woman had told her that.

"You are a very lucky girl," he said. She did not ask him why. "You have a benefactor of great wealth. You must continue to please him as you have . . ."

"I do not please him," she said. "He pleases himself." Tan winked at her, and watched while she perfumed the palms of her hands.

"There are some men who do not wish to be pleased by a woman," he said, as if this were the profound thought of an intelligent man. "Some wish only to give a woman pleasure. I think your white man is like that."

"He is not my white man," she said.

"You should be kinder toward the whites," he said. "They have many kind inclinations. They are very generous."

She said, "Perhaps when you have enough money, you will become one yourself." She thought Tan would strike her, but he only smiled. "Perhaps they will give you their smell as well as their money."

And still he only smiled.

He accompanied her downstairs, smiling at the voices, nodding at things the white men said. She watched the stairs, and then the floor. She did not acknowledge the men who had come to see her. She kept herself apart.

She sang happier songs that night, although there was no happiness in her. When she had finished, the white men howled and shot their guns into the ceiling and floor. Some of the real people howled too—she could hear single voices in the shouting, and knew which were Chinese.

She was beginning to know all things now.

The white man came that night with a gift. A gold ring. She accepted it, trying it on one finger after another until it fit, finally, on the thumb of her left hand. It seemed to please him that it fit, and he sat on her bed and smiled. She took off her clothes and lay next to him.

He talked for a long time, showing the mountains with his hands. He had bathed that day, she could smell the soap. His voice was excited, and then it calmed, and when he stopped speaking there were tears in his eyes.

She did not know what had turned him sad. "Bismarck," he said, pointing to himself. Then, with another finger, he pointed at her and said, "Ci-an." And then he crossed the fingers.

She closed her eyes and thought of Wild Bill's friend. In this moment, she suddenly knew, he would begin to find her.

She heard the sounds of Bismarck's undressing, and opened her eyes long enough to see him standing on one foot, pulling his pants leg inside out. He was not as careful with his clothing now as he had been before. He stumbled; she closed her eyes, and waited. His breathing grew louder as he fought with his pants, and then grew louder, a different way, as he came close.

He touched her hand first, the one she had put the ring on. He held it gently, cupping it as if it would spill, and then he spoke into the palm and kissed each of her fingers, beginning with the smallest and ending with the thumb, where he kissed the ring itself.

He spoke to her again, kissing her arm and then her shoulder. She smelled the beef he had eaten in his sweat. His voice became more melancholy as he spoke. She had no interest in what his words meant, but she thought that perhaps, like herself, he would be happier without his life. She thought that one day, if there was time, she would end his sadness.

Bismarck sat up suddenly, as if he had heard her thought, and walked across the room to the table where she kept the paper and charcoal she used to draw her flowers. He took a piece of the charcoal and several sheets of the paper and came back to the bed. He began to sketch. She watched his lines and saw white men had no talent for drawing.

He drew a picture first of a man. It was not an important man, for he placed him in the corner of the paper. The man had stick arms, a single line for a neck, and a mouth as narrow as a bird's. He drew hair and a tie and a hat. He drew shoes. Then he pointed to the man he had drawn and said, "Bismarck."

The next figure he drew was larger. He put it on the other side of the paper, in profile, so it watched the man. The second figure was sticks too, but on this one he drew fingers, and on one of those he put a ring.

He pointed at the second figure and said, "Wife." She did not know the word, but understood the meaning. Then he drew mountains between the figures, and stick deer, and water.

She looked at the drawing and said, "I will end your sadness, if there is time. But not now." He smiled at her, not understanding the words. He put the charcoal against the paper again and drew an X across the larger figure.

She thought Bismarck's wife was dead. She sat up against the bedboard, keeping the sheet over her breasts, and took the charcoal from his hand. She drew a likeness of Song on a clean paper. It took only a few seconds—she had drawn his face many times, and knew the tricks that showed the intelligence in his eyes, and the gentleness of his expression. And when she had finished, she drew an X over him too, to show that he was also gone.

The drawing pleased Bismarck, and he took the paper and charcoal from her hands and dropped them on the floor. His eyes teared again and he buried his face in her neck. The smell of the cows was stronger now, and she closed her eyes and held herself motionless.

It was a long time before he moved between her legs. She felt him tremble, and before he entered her, he had spilled himself on her legs. Like a boy. He stayed on top of her, with his head pushed deep into the curve of her jaw, until the trembling stopped and his breathing evened.

Later, after he had dressed, he returned to her on the bed and knelt on the floor. He was not sad now. He spoke into her hand again, and then kissed the thumb and the ring he had fit over it.

He left her a few minutes later, closing her door quietly behind him. She lay in her bed, and from there she saw the drawing of Song on the floor, and the drawing of Bismarck and his wife beside it.

Dead faces in her room.

She looked at the ring on her thumb and wondered what kind of ceremony that had been.

CHARLEY DID NOT SET OUT TO BECOME DRINKING PARTNERS WITH A soft-brain, but those things happened when you were kind to the underprivileged. Every morning he sat in his tub with the weight in his head and a weakness in his legs and arms. He sat there until it was time to begin drinking, when he would give the Bottle Fiend five dollars and send him for J. Fred McCurnin swoop whiskey. Charley couldn't do chores for himself until he had thinned out his blood.

The Bottle Fiend would return with the bottle and sit in his chair, remarking on Charley's new bites and bruises, until, a few swallows into the morning, it would suddenly seem cruel to Charley that anybody ought to have to go through life soft-brained and sober, and he'd pass the bottle back and forth with him half the morning.

And sometimes, after he'd dressed, he took the Bottle Fiend with him to the badlands and bought him drinks at Nuttall and Mann's. The Bottle Fiend didn't talk much when he drank. When he'd drunk enough, in fact, he didn't talk at all. It came to Charley one afternoon in the bar that Bill had never talked much either, and that from a conversational point of view, there wasn't much to choose one over the other.

He was not surprised. Drinking depended more on understanding than talk anyway.

Charley liked the Bottle Fiend for being straightforward, but had no idea what went on inside his head. And without that, there wasn't any understanding. It was more like drinking alone. But that had been done before too, somewhere in the history of the West.

And that is how it happened that the morning Charley finally ran into Mrs. Langrishe again, he was in the company of the soft-brain, both of them freshly bathed and drunk. Mrs. Langrishe was coming out of Farnum's carrying packages that pushed against her chest and distorted it in an agreeable way.

Charley took off his hat and nodded. He was holding an open bottle of J. Fred in his other hand. "Good morning," he said. She stopped, and took a moment to remember who it was.

"Mr. Utter," she said. "I thought you had disappeared."

"I've been laying low," he said. She looked into his face, and then into the Bottle Fiend's face. "This is my friend, the Bottle Man," he said. She smiled at the soft-brain, and he looked at his feet. Charley was not embarrassed.

"He is shy with strangers," Charley said. Then he turned to the Bottle Fiend and said, "Mrs. Langrishe runs the theater."

The soft-brain looked up from his feet at Charley, but would not acknowledge her. "Is she the one that bites you?" he said.

Charley smiled at Mrs. Langrishe, a horrible smile, and said, "Sometimes he gets things confused."

She smiled back at him, and the heat came into his skin. He had been with Lurline again the night before, at it one way or another all night long, but the heat was in him again. "I missed you at Bill's funeral," she said. "I never had the opportunity to tell you how sorry I felt." She was still holding the package. "He seemed like such a gentle man," she said.

Charley said, "He had a lot of sides." Then he handed the Bottle Fiend the whiskey and replaced his hat. He reached for her packages.

"I'll tote these for you," he said. She gave up the packages and— a peculiar gesture—she ran her fingers along the hollow of his cheek.

"I know how you feel," she said. And he wondered if that was true, and if it was, how far it went. He smelled the perfume on her hand—it was different from Lurline's—and every bit of blood in his body was congregated in his head or his peeder, pounding the tom-toms. He adjusted the packages and began to walk Mrs. Langrishe home. The Bottle Fiend followed them, a yard or two behind. Every now and then he would stop to splash a little whiskey into his mouth. The Bottle Fiend could not drink and walk at the same time.

Charley was not embarrassed. He refused to be embarrassed of his friends.

Mrs. Langrishe studied Charley as they walked. It was something about actresses that nothing they did ever seemed out of place. "I heard you had begun a pony express," she said. They had come to Shine Street, and turned west, uphill. The trouble with living in a gulch, besides floods and fires, was that every time you made a turn, it was uphill.

Charley shook his head. "We held a race for the business," he said. "Myself against Clippinger. We won by half a day, but Clippinger never quit his line, and my brother Steve got put in jail for thirty days for shooting somebody's pig back in Fort Laramie during the celebration." The news that Steve had been put in jail for shooting pigs had come in a letter, delivered by Clippinger Pony Express.

She smiled at him. "How ever did he come to shoot a pig?"

Charley looked behind him and saw the Bottle Fiend had just turned the corner. He stopped, waiting for him to catch up. "Excuse me," he said, "he gets confused."

"Your brother?" she said.

"Well, him too," Charley said. "But I was speaking of the Bottle Man. My brother Steve is thirty-six years old, and he's never shot anything on purpose yet." Mrs. Langrishe did not pursue the matter. The Bottle Fiend caught up, and they started back up the hill.

"So you abandoned the mail line?" she said.

Charley shrugged. "It's hard to say in these matters who abandoned what." She laughed at that and gave him that feeling he was clever in a way he didn't quite see. He smelled her and watched her all the way up the hill.

The house was two stories. It was whitewashed and had a porch and an ice-blue door. There were windows everywhere, more windows than house. It didn't look safe. She held the door for them, but the Bottle Fiend would not come inside. Even when Mrs. Langrishe offered him a glass for his whiskey, he shook his head and refused to move. "Relieving a bottle fiend of his bottle is no inducement," Charley told her.

"Well, perhaps I could find a bottle for him inside," she said.

The Bottle Fiend said, "Perhaps indeed."

They looked at each other for a minute, and then Mrs. Langrishe and Charley went inside. The Bottle Fiend stayed where he was. Charley followed her into a sitting room and put the packages on a chair. The walls of the room were covered with pictures and marquee signs from shows Jack Langrishe had done in the East. There were certifications of appreciation, and the key to the city of Gary, Indiana, hanging over the piano. The windows went from a foot above the floor almost to the ceiling, all of them closed. The room had a natural coolness.

"Mr. Langrishe must still be at the theater," she said. She sat down on the davenport and patted the seat next to her. The heat poured off Charley again. They sat so close her face was out of focus. "My husband has been consumed with the theater since the storm," she said.

"It was an opening night, all right," he said. He got that unintentionally clever feeling again. She tittered, and he saw that he was right.

"Poor Jack," she said. "He's there night and day. Rehearsing the players, overseeing the new roof. The reviews of Camille ruined his disposition."

"I don't believe I saw the reviews," he said. "I've been lying low . . ." She had a copy on the table, under a picture album. It was from the *Black Hills Daily Times*. "*Miss Flowers*," it said, "*is poor at dying, because she generally dies too hard. Her positions are not good in her passion scenes; when she should swell out like a mountain she sinks in like a gulch. That's wrong in this country—Camille is not her forte.*"

She leaned over his back as he read the review. "He is completely consumed," she said, in a way that made Charley think of eating, and then of the inside of Mrs. Langrishe's mouth. And then, against his will, he thought of her biting him.

He wondered if Lurline had turned him left-brained forever.

While he was thinking that, Mrs. Langrishe hung a short, soft hum behind his ear, a sound that could have been taken two ways. It seemed to Charley that everything about Mrs. Langrishe you could take two ways.

"What consumes you, Mr. Utter?" she said.

There, she did it again.

Charley swallowed and tried to think of what was consuming him. It wasn't much of a time to think. "Something," he said.

"But what?"

Charley shook his head. "It isn't one thing, like the theater," he said. "What's after me now doesn't have any focus." She left her hand on his shoulder, and moved it to the side of his neck. He felt his own pulse where her fingers touched him.

Nothing had any focus. Not himself, not her face. Charley saw that she was nodding. "I understand," she said.

He opened his mouth, wondering what would come out next, and at the same time he looked past Mrs. Langrishe's shoulder, trying to see something clear before things got more out of focus, and found himself staring at the Bottle Fiend, who was pressed into one of the windows in a way that had flattened his face.

The sight startled Charley—his nerves weren't good when he was drinking regularly—and Mrs. Langrishe felt the change in him, and looked back over her shoulder too. She issued a little cry then, and later on Charley would not be able to say for sure if it was the sight of the soft-brain pressed into the window that caused it, or the sight of him falling through.

He came into the living room and rolled across the floor. The glass seemed to follow him, maybe chasing him. The Bottle Fiend had been open-eyed and open-mouthed as he fell—that much Charley would swear on the Bible—but by the time Charley got to the place on the floor where he had finally stopped rolling, the soft-brain was drawn into himself, curled into a tight ball with his eyes squeezed shut. He looked like he expected to continue the fall momentarily.

There were small cuts on the Bottle Fiend's arms and hands, and one that looked more like a tear across his neck. Charley touched his arm, but the Bottle Fiend would not open his eyes. "Are you alive?" he said.

The Bottle Fiend did not answer.

"Are you cut somewhere I can't see?"

The Bottle Fiend lay motionless on his side. The glass spread out behind him like broken wings. Charley felt his eyes fill, he had no idea why.

Mrs. Langrishe bent over the soft-brain from the other side. "He's cut," she said.

Hearing that, the Bottle Fiend opened his eyes. He sat up and looked at his arms and hands while Mrs. Langrishe went into the back of the house for bandages. Charley said, "This is the last time I take you anywhere polite," but the soft-brain didn't seem to hear him.

He was staring at the cuts like a banker that had found six piles of money all at the same time. When he did speak, it was more to himself than Charley. He said, "I got inside."

"You might of used the door," Charley said, but then he saw the soft-brain wasn't talking about houses. He thought he'd broken into a bottle.

Mrs. Langrishe was back in a minute carrying a bowl of water, alcohol, and bandages. She sat on the floor between Charley and the soft-brain and began to wash him up. She cleaned the cuts one at a time, beginning at his neck and then working down. First with water and then alcohol, and then she wrapped them in cotton gauze. The Bottle Fiend watched her and from time to time, when he reached in to touch one of the openings in his skin, she pushed his hand away.

It was a thing about women and injuries that Charley had noticed before, that once you turned one over to them, it was theirs.

"I got inside," the Bottle Fiend said again. He looked around the room, and then at Mrs. Langrishe. He began to smile.

"This is a house," Charley said. "A bottle is a bottle." Mrs. Langrishe stopped working on the Bottle Fiend's arm and gave Charley a look. "He thinks it's a bottle," he said, and looked to see if that explained it. "My friend doesn't look at things the same as most people."

"I surmised that," she said, and returned to the cuts. She wiped away some blood and stared into the soft-brain's palm. Then she reached in, as delicate as fate, and pulled out a long sliver of glass.

Charley noticed her nails were painted red and thought of them on his chest. That's where Lurline put hers. She never did anything where you needed a mirror to see the mark.

"You see," Charley said, "to him, there's secrets in bottles."

Without looking up, the Bottle Fiend said, "There is secrets in bottles, sometimes I heard them." The cuts Mrs. Langrishe hadn't attended yet bled and ran down his arms to his elbows and fingers, finding the lowest places, and dropped from there onto the floor.

Mrs. Langrishe's floors, like anybody else's, were soft and warped, and the blood ran into the cracks between the boards. The Bottle Fiend was looking at the walls now.

"Do you like my pictures?" Mrs. Langrishe said.

The Bottle Fiend shut his eyes. "It's all right," she said. "You can come back sometime and look at them closer." As she said that, she smiled at Charley.

"Whence do they come?" the Bottle Fiend said.

"People paint them," she said. "Artists."

"No," he said, "I mean, whence do they come?"

Mrs. Langrishe stopped and thought. "From secrets," she said after a while. "Secrets inside painters." Charley saw that made sense to the Bottle Fiend. He wondered if Mrs. Langrishe knew about his secrets too.

"There's secrets inside me," the soft-brain said.

"There's secrets in everybody," she said, and looked at Charley. In the accident, his peeder had temporarily lost its sense of purpose, but it recovered itself now. She seemed to know that too.

"I knowed Bill was going to get shot," the soft-brain said. "But that ain't a secret now."

"No," she said, "not now."

Charley sat on his heels and looked at the Bottle Fiend's face. He waited for what had happened to Bill to reveal itself, but the Bottle Fiend shook his head. A line of blood appeared from the bandage on his neck and ran into his shirt. "A man with a little-bitty gun said so," he said.

"Does he take baths?" Charley said. The Bottle Fiend touched his ears.

"It wouldn't help nothing," he said. "It ain't a secret now."

And that was as much as he would say. Mrs. Langrishe wrapped him from the top down, the tip of her tongue working into her upper lip as she tied the little knots. Charley's legs had begun to hurt, and he took a seat back on the davenport. From there he admired her posture and her concentration, and he noticed the Bottle Fiend had relaxed and put himself in her hands. God had made him a soft-brain, but He'd given him instincts to protect himself. The soft-brain looked at the walls while she tied her knots. "Where is that from?" he said. He was looking at one of the marquee posters.

"It's from a play," she said.

The soft-brain scratched his head. "I never been to a play," he said.

"You'll have to come," Mrs. Langrishe said. "Perhaps Mr. Utter would come with you."

The soft-brain nodded. "We'd be delighted," he said.

THAT NIGHT CHARLEY GAVE THE BOTTLE FIEND ONE OF HIS SHIRTS. The Bottle Fiend's regular shirt was covered with blood from the accident, and it didn't have a collar anyway. They both took baths—he had to pay the soft-brain for them both before he would sit in the tub—and met Mrs. Langrishe and her husband at the theater door.

Charley stepped between Mr. Langrishe and the Bottle Fiend before they could shake hands. "He can't shake right now," Charley said. "He's injured his arm."

"Sorry to hear it," Mr. Langrishe said, and looked behind them for the next customers.

"Excuse my husband," Mrs. Langrishe said, as she walked them to their seats. "He is so absorbed in this place . . ." She walked between Charley and the Bottle Fiend, with a hand on each of them. She squeezed Charley's arm when she said that.

The program for the night was not exactly a play. Jack Langrishe had brought in some cancan girls from Cheyenne to fill the week between *Camille* and *Othello*, and among them was a woman named Fannie Garrettson, who had taken up living quarters with Handsome Banjo Dick Brown, the most famous singer in the Black Hills. Banjo Dick was known for the song "The Days of Forty-Nine," which he sang first and last at every performance. Sometimes he cried at the closing words:

> *My heart is filled with the days of yore, and oft I do repline,*
> *For the days of old, the days of gold, the days of forty-nine.*

The song had been written during the California gold rush, but miners were miners, and loyal to what came out of the ground, and not the ground itself.

While the theater filled, the Bottle Fiend turned in his seat, looking at the people in back of them, then at the walls, then at the ceiling. Jack Langrishe had constructed another canvas roof, although this one had less sag. It reminded Charley of the fine line between stubborn and stupid.

The ladies in the audience were dressed like they'd planned it from last week. Some of them had brought opera glasses. Charley smiled, thinking he might buy the Bottle Fiend opera glasses. The lights dimmed then, and Jack Langrishe came out onto the stage, comfortable in the wash of applause, and announced the evening's program and his plans for the cultural affairs of Deadwood. In the end, in a voice that hung in the air after he'd quit, he said, "No one will stop us from building a theater of the arts as great as the cities of Europe."

Charley leaned toward Mrs. Langrishe, smelling her evening perfume, and asked, "Who is it against him?"

"Critics," she whispered. "He means critics."

"Ours is the highest purpose," he added, "and it will not be denied or deterred by the naysayers." So it was the critics, all right. When he had finished, the cancan girls came out. Charley looked sideways and saw the Bottle Fiend was open-mouthed and spellbound.

Mrs. Langrishe moved in the dark, and he thought she was going to whisper again. When he leaned toward her, though, her hand dropped on the top of his leg, found a comfortable spot and nestled in.

She left her hand there through the cancan dancers, and while her husband introduced Handsome Banjo Dick Brown. It struck Charley as elegant, the way it lay there, light and graceful and still, while his peeder pushed up at it from underneath and her husband lectured from above.

She left it there through Handsome Dick's first number—"The Days of Forty-Nine"—and then the second. She left it there right up until a red-headed man in farmer's clothes stood up in front of them and shouted, "I'll have my Fannie back," and threw an axe past Handsome Banjo Dick Brown's left ear.

Handsome Dick was singing "Oh, Susanna" at the time. He stood up off his stool and pulled his pistol from underneath his coat, and fired five shots into the audience.

The red-headed man's name, it developed, was Ed Shaughnessy, and he had lived with Fannie Garrettson for six weeks on a farm outside Cheyenne before Handsome Dick had found her in town one night and taken her to Deadwood. Charley's first thought, as Ed Shaughnessy stood up and threw the axe, was that the soft-brain had more social graces.

Then Charley saw the first shot hit. It went in right under his eyebrow. The red-haired man fell back on his seat, and hung there while Handsome Dick, aiming carefully, put four more shots into his chest. Handsome Dick always got even, he bragged on that.

The screaming didn't start right away—nobody knows what's real in the theater—but then the ladies heard the balls going into Ed Shaughnessy's body, and they knew.

At the first shot, Mrs. Langrishe made the same noise that came out of her when the Bottle Fiend fell through her window, and she made it again every shot afterwards. Charley moved to protect her, but there was no need. Handsome Dick was a shootist; from the way he held his pistol high in his hand Charley guessed he had learned somewhere in the South.

Mrs. Langrishe's hand—the one that had been on Charley's leg—moved to her own throat. The skin there was soft-looking and took Charley's attention for a moment, even while the shots were still in the air. Charley thought of the Bottle Fiend then, but when he turned to look, the soft-brain hadn't moved a finger. His mouth was open half an inch, his head was still as a scared rabbit in tall grass. He hardly seemed to breathe.

Handsome Dick fired his fifth shot and sat back down on his stool, leaving one round in the chamber, and picked up his banjo. When the event was reported later in the *Times* and the *Pioneer*— the *Pioneer* also carried a letter from Fannie Garrettson pointing out that while she was notorious enough for living with Ed Shaughnessy, she'd never married him, so there was nothing wrong with running off with Handsome Banjo Dick Brown—it was treated as an act of heroism to pick up his banjo and finish "Oh, Susanna."

Charley did not see that it said much for a man to kill another man and then to give it no consequence at all.

When Charley looked again, Mrs. Langrishe had covered her face. Ed Shaughnessy's body had fallen off the seat and was lying now on the floor, eyes up. Charley had begun to feel sorry for him, looking at his clothes, and thinking of the work he must have done.

He reached over to pat Mrs. Langrishe's shoulder, but she pulled away from him and then left the theater. Charley checked the

Bottle Fiend. His eyes were still going from the stage to the man on the floor, and then back to the stage, afraid he might miss something, and Charley left him there and went after Mrs. Langrishe.

He was ashamed to admit it, but he wanted to get her hand back on his leg. He met Sheriff Bullock in the aisle, followed by Doc Pierce and his two nephews. Doc Pierce whispered to him, not to interrupt the performance, "Where is the deceased?"

Charley stepped out of the way, and the coroner and his nephews headed past him toward the front.

Charley found Mrs. Langrishe outside, standing against the door. He touched her arm, but it was tight against her side and would not be moved. She was not crying, but her breathing came in rushes, as if she were. "You've had a shock," he said.

She turned and stared at him. "What a wonderful eye you have, Mr. Utter," she said.

Charley did not know how to take that. "What I meant," he said, "a lady like yourself isn't used to a shooting, in your own place . . ."

She looked at him, and he thought he saw some of the red of her hair reflected in her eyes. "You're correct, Mr. Utter," she said. "I am not used to a shooting in my own place. I am barely used to soft-brains falling through my parlor windows, believing my house is a bottle."

"He didn't mean to," Charley said.

She continued to stare at him, and he was positive he saw the color red. It seemed to flare now, like a fire. "That is your whole idea of manners, isn't it?" she said. "*He didn't mean to.*"

Charley read women as well as most, but he hadn't come across any before that blew so hot and cold. He thought she must be scared to death of this place. "You've had a shock," he said again, and regretted it as soon as it was out of his mouth.

"I have been in shock all day," she said. "I have been in shock since the moment I came across your unfortunate person, walking the streets drunk at high noon, and tried to be kind to you."

"He isn't unfortunate," Charley said, "he's only interested in different things, and distracted."

She closed her eyes. "I was speaking of you, Mr. Utter," she said. Charley felt his cheeks flush. He had been called names before—after all, he was married—but nobody ever said he was unfortunate. It embarrassed him to think that he had appeared that way to her.

"I'm sorry for the window," he said, looking down at his clothes, "but I don't have anything to do with what happened in your theater."

That sounded weak, and he started back inside to collect the Bottle Fiend. Before he took a step, Doc Pierce came out the door. The farmer came next, carried by the nephews. One had the shoulders, the other had the knees. One of the dead man's hands was dragging along the ground.

Doc Pierce stopped long enough to nod at Mrs. Langrishe, and the nephew carrying Ed Shaughnessy's shoulders bumped him from behind.

"Is there any special instruction, something you'd like done with the deceased?" the coroner said to Mrs. Langrishe. She had been trying not to look at the body, but the nephew had lost his grip on the farmer's overalls, and now he was fighting not to drop him, and nobody could ignore that.

Charley saw her take it in—a long look—and then she covered her mouth. "Ma'am?" the coroner said.

Charley cleared his throat. "It isn't the lady's deceased," he said. "She only runs the theater, she isn't relations with everybody in it."

"It's somebody's deceased," the coroner said. "If he ain't local, the city don't pay and I don't work free." When Charley didn't answer, the coroner turned to his nephews and said, "Put it down, boys." And the boys dropped Ed Shaughnessy on the ground in front of Mrs. Langrishe.

The one who had held the shoulders rubbed his fingers. "Damn, he must of been two hundred pounds," he said.

"Not two hundred," the other one said. "Maybe one-eighty."

Mrs. Langrishe was still staring at the body, and Charley saw that she'd had enough. "I'll take responsibility," he said.

The coroner turned from Mrs. Langrishe and looked him over. "What might be your interest in this?" he said.

It was Mrs. Langrishe, but he didn't say so. "I am Charles Utter," Charley said, "and I will make good on the expenses if the city refuses to pay."

As he said his name, Charley saw the coroner change. "Would you be the friend of Wild Bill?" he said.

Charley nodded, remembering the barkeep with the lock of Bill's hair. "I am," he said, "and I have met a man who has a piece of Bill's scalp that rightfully belongs to his widow."

"I never did it," the coroner said.

"I know Bill's hair," Charley said.

"If I did," the coroner said, "it wasn't no place where it would show, just a few curls from the back."

"I will be by to settle this," Charley said, meaning the farmer's body, "and at that time I will collect all personal effects of Bill Hickok's in your possession."

The coroner smiled in a painful way. "I didn't mean to keep nothing like that myself," he said. "All I took was a few curls for the family and friends . . ." Sheriff Bullock came out of the theater then, and behind him Handsome Banjo Dick Brown. Charley saw that Handsome Dick was not under arrest. He expected there was paperwork connected with the shooting.

Bullock tipped his hat to Mrs. Langrishe, who nodded back, and then he looked at the body lying on the ground. "Mr. Pierce?" he said.

The coroner shook his head. "We was just discussing business," he said. "But we got it straight now, and Mr. Utter's agreed to make good the costs of burial if the city don't."

The sheriff looked at Charley and then at Mrs. Langrishe. Handsome Banjo Dick Brown also looked at Mrs. Langrishe. He took off his hat and bowed. "Let me apologize for the inconvenience," he said. He took her hand then, and Mrs. Langrishe let him have it. Charley saw why they called him Handsome, but he didn't see how it was any great trick to collect women if you were willing to go around kissing hands in public.

Doc Pierce said, "All right, boys," and the nephews picked the farmer off the ground and carried him up the street.

Charley noticed Handsome Dick still had Mrs. Langrishe's hand. They were looking into each other's skulls, like they could not get deep enough. "Come along, Mr. Brown," the sheriff said. And Handsome Dick went along. He kissed her hand again, and then let go of it a finger at a time.

"My apologies, once again," he said.

Mrs. Langrishe showed the beginnings of a smile. "Thank you," she said, and the sheriff and Handsome Dick headed off in the same direction as the dead farmer. The last member of this parade—Fannie Garrettson—came from the back of the theater on a dead run, still wearing her dancing accessories, and caught Handsome Dick from behind and took his arm.

Charley heard her say, "I knew he would come after me, Dick," but if Handsome Dick heard her, or even knew she was there, he gave no sign of it.

Charley turned back to Mrs. Langrishe. Inside, the music had changed and he could hear the stomp of the dancing girls' feet on the stage floor. "If I can be of any assistance," he said, and Mrs. Langrishe looked at him as if she'd just found a dead possum in the trash.

CHARLEY CROSSED THE STREET AND SAT ON A BARREL TO WAIT FOR the Bottle Fiend. He had never met a woman as contradictory as Mrs. Langrishe. The weather was more reliable. He thought he might love her.

The Bottle Fiend came out with the rest of the audience, half an hour later. Charley had a fresh bottle he'd bought at a tent bar. The Bottle Fiend refused a drink. "Bad things happened," he said. "Some of them ain't make-believe."

Charley walked him home, a little cabin on the south end of town. "I don't want to go home," the soft-brain said when they got there.

"You are home," Charley said. He was thinking of Lurline now, but the Bottle Fiend dug his feet in the mud and refused to move.

"You come in too," he said.

"I got things to do tonight," he said.

The Bottle Fiend laughed, at least it sounded like a laugh. It sounded like the voice in Charley's own head, and that was something like a laugh. "You get bit every night," he said.

"Not exactly bit," Charley said, and that was true. It was more than that now.

"Come with me and you can look at my bottles," the Bottle Fiend said. Charley took a mouthful of whiskey and followed him inside. He had wondered what all those bottles looked like together. The Bottle Fiend had no lamp, and they stood together in the dark while Charley patted himself for a match.

"You can't see them at first," the Bottle Fiend said.

Charley found his matches and struck one against the wall behind him. "Someday this place is going to burn up," the soft-brain said.

"You don't have matches of your own?" Charley said. The room was shallow and wide. There was a sleeping bag in the corner and old newspapers all over the floor.

"I don't have no matches at all," he said. "It ain't going to be my fire."

Charley held the match over his head and forgot it there until it burned his fingers. "It's a nice place," he said.

The next match he lit, he saw the soft-brain was smiling at him. "I got them hid," he said. Charley put the bottle back to his lips, being careful to keep it away from the fire. The soft-brain walked across the room and reached up, unhooking a piece of canvas.

The Bottle Fiend moved left to right, pulling the canvas after him, and then the light of Charley's match reflected back at him from a thousand places.

He took a step forward, but the Bottle Fiend stopped him. "Don't get close," he said. "They'll all fall down . . ."

Charley stood still and looked at the bottles. The pile was four feet high and stretched from one wall to the other. "There must be a thousand," he said.

"One thousand, seven hundred and forty," the soft-brain said. Charley looked at him and saw that he was telling the straight. The Bottle Fiend didn't have anything but the straight in him.

The bottles were stacked this way and that, in no order Charley could see. Some places the mouths stuck out of the pile, some places the bottoms. The bottles had settled under their own weight, and the balance was tricky. You couldn't take a bottle out anywhere without moving them all.

"How do you keep track of the number?" he said.

The Bottle Fiend looked at him, and the match went out. When Charley lit another, the soft-brain was still staring at him. The Bottle Fiend puzzled. "I keep track of *the bottles*," he said, "not the number." And Charley stood there lighting matches and sipping whiskey until he ran out of matches.

The Bottle Fiend put the canvas curtain back and lay down on the floor. Charley's eyes had accustomed themselves to the room, and he could see the outline of the soft-brain in the corner. He sat on the ledge of the only window in the cabin and sipped whiskey and slapped mosquitoes. "I'll wait until you nod off," Charley said, but the Bottle Fiend didn't answer. His breathing had already evened out, and in a minute he began to snore.

He was flat on his back, unprotected. Charley tried to remember if there was ever a time when he could go off to sleep like that, if there was a time when he wasn't covering himself up. "Little friend," he said to the corner, "you might have found yourself the ticket."

The Bottle Fiend's place had mellowed Charley, and he walked the length of Main Street, thinking of dropping his whiskey in the mud and going back to the hotel. He couldn't make up his mind. The closer he got to the badlands, though, the less inclination he felt to abandon the bottle.

He stopped at the Bella Union, which he ordinarily avoided because of the tourists. All the talk tonight was of Handsome Dick, who had already finished his business with the sheriff and returned to the badlands. The Bella Union was full of eyewitnesses telling each other they'd of done exactly what Handsome did.

Charley listened and had a drink, then he walked next door to Nuttall and Mann's. The talk there was about Handsome Dick too, but at least at Nuttall and Mann's the eyewitnesses were calling each other liars. Harry Sam Young saw Charley and set a brown-eye on the bar in front of him. Ever since Bill died, Harry Sam Young had been setting up free drinks for Charley anytime he came in. "I guess Handsome Banjo Dick Brown shot a farmer over to Langrishe's," the bartender said. "Everybody here seen it."

Charley said, "Everybody in this town saw God rest on Sunday." Charley put the shot glass to his lips and cocked his head. The bar whiskey was rougher than his own, and he fought himself to swallow it. He understood that Harry Sam Young needed to give him free drinks because of Bill, and he didn't want to spit that on the floor.

"It was self-defense, I heard," the bartender said. "It must of been on account Seth Bullock already let him go." He refilled Charley's glass.

"The way it happened," Charley said, "it won't take a hundred-dollar lawyer to get Handsome off. The farmer threw an axe."

"Self-defense," the bartender said.

Charley shrugged. "He put four shots in him, after he was dead."

A pilgrim leaned between them and said, "Somebody threw an axe at me, I'd shoot him too."

Charley drank the new shot, and then put his hand over the top of the glass so Harry Sam Young couldn't reload. "You ever notice," he said to Harry Sam Young, "the ones who know what they'd of done are always the ones who never did it?" He stood away from the bar then, tired of talking about dead farmers and Handsome Banjo Dick Brown, and walked out into the street. His moccasins sank half a foot, and it occurred to him that he hadn't noticed the mud once since he heard of Bill's death.

He was frightened at the things he got used to.

He looked at the Gem, undecided. Lurline had hurt him sincerely last night, and he had seen how the hurting fed on itself once he'd agreed to it. She had made him yip, biting his leg, and he had determined then to return himself to normalcy at the first opportunity.

He weighed the night, and it did not strike him as such an opportunity.

He walked into the Gem looking for her. Al Swearingen was sitting in a corner, and averted his stare the moment Charley's eyes came across him. The whore man had kept himself scarce since Charley had showed him his knife. Charley guessed you did not run a line of whores without learning something about what to leave alone.

Charley took a drink from his bottle and surveyed the room. He satisfied himself Lurline wasn't there; he climbed the stairs toward her quarters. On the way up, he glanced again at Al Swearingen's table and saw that the whore man was watching him, smiling in a way that set off a warning. Charley ignored it. He knocked at Lurline's door. There was noise inside, but no answer. He tried again, and this time he heard her voice. "Who is it?"

"Charles Utter," he said.

"Go away," she said. "I'm sick."

He took a drink of the bottle and stared at his feet. He felt himself sway. He heard her voice again, closer. "It ain't nothing contagious," she said. "Just let me rest, and I'll be fine . . ."

And suddenly Charley knew, as certain as his birthday was July, the whore man had beaten her up, and she didn't want him to see it. Charley started back down the stairs for him, but he stopped halfway and returned to her room. He wanted to see her for himself, to have that in his mind when he encountered Al Swearingen.

This time he didn't knock. He moved quietly, not to scare her, and turned the door handle without a sound. The floorboards had warped at a spot a foot and a half into the room, and the door hit there and braked. The room was half-lit, and at the sound of the door, two faces came up off the bed. They looked like ghosts. Hers stayed where it was, his rolled toward the bedpost. Charley saw the holster hung there, and dropped to the floor. He heard a chair break and found his knife in his hand. He found that he'd covered the distance between the door and the bed.

Charley never stopped, or thought, or saw it happen. One minute he was standing in the doorway, and the next minute he had Handsome Banjo Dick Brown's jaw locked in one arm and was holding the knife against the pulse in his neck. In the second that had taken, Handsome Dick had reached behind himself with his gun and the muzzle was pressed into Charley's leg. Charley held him dead still. "I been shot in the leg before," Charley said into Handsome Dick's ear, "have you had your throat cut?"

Handsome Dick could not answer, but he shook his head, an eighth of an inch, back and forth. It was all that Charley's purchase allowed him. "Let go, songbird," Charley said, "or I'll do it." The struggle had gone out of Handsome Dick's head, but he held on to the gun.

It was pressed into the very spot Steve's shot had found. Charley remembered the powder burns. For a while, that was what hurt him most. "Let go of it," Charley said again. "This isn't a dirt farmer that's on to you now."

It wasn't until after Handsome Dick's gun dropped and Charley let go of his jaw that Lurline spoke. "What in Jesus' name?" she said. Charley ran his hands through his hair in a way that Bill used to do, and waited for his dizziness to pass. Handsome Dick had dropped onto the foot of the bed when Charley let go of his jaw, and he lay there, stark naked, holding his throat with both hands. Charley kept an eye on him anyway, because Handsome Dick always got even. "I ast you a question," Lurline said.

"You didn't," Charley said, and he sat down on the bed next to Handsome Dick. "Just because it starts with *what* doesn't make it a question."

"I thought you was different," she said, and that was a question. She was sitting up in bed. He saw she was wearing her red and black undies, and felt a poke of remorse that she shared them with the others. He felt no such poke that Lurline shared herself. An upstairs girl was an upstairs girl, things were what they were. "I thought you was gentle," she said.

Handsome Dick was looking up at him now, as if that had been his understanding too. Charley shook his head. "It's not one way or the other," he said. "A person isn't all one way."

He noticed his bottle of J. Fred McCurnin then, over by the

door. It had somehow landed mouth-up when he'd dropped it. It hadn't broken, from what he could see it hadn't even spilled. He stood up, unsteady, and collected it. He held on to the door when he bent over to pick it up. It was hard to see how, three minutes before, the same human being could have covered the same distance in something less than a second and put a death-hold on Handsome Dick's head.

"You and me was different," she said. "It wasn't no business involved, and then you cut a man's throat on my bed."

Charley looked at Handsome Dick, who hadn't moved. A skirt of blood hung from a single pink line high on his neck. "His throat isn't cut," Charley said. Handsome Dick sat up slowly and looked at the blood on his hands.

"I think you damaged my voice box," he said.

Lurline looked at Handsome Dick when he said that, and then back at Charley. "See what you done?" she said. "You have damaged his voice box."

"I saw him put five shots into a farmer," Charley said, "four after he was dead. I don't stand still while a man with those sporting inclinations goes after his shooter."

"Self-defense," Lurline said.

"I saw it," Charley said, looking at the singer. "I know what it was."

"He threw an axe," Handsome Dick said. He patted the side of his neck and then looked at his hand. The blood had stopped running and was beginning to dry.

"You surmised he was going to reload?" Charley said.

Lurline did not give the singer a chance to reply. She got up off the bed, crossed the room, and pushed Charley out. He let himself be pushed. "Don't come back in here," she said, and she balled one of her hands into a fist and hit Charley in the chest. She hit him again and again, all the way to the stairs. Charley walked backwards, smiling. Lurline hurt you less hurting you than she did loving you. "This ain't funny," she said, grunting on the word *funny* because she was throwing a fist at the time.

Charley stood at the top of the stairs until Lurline was out of breath. "You was special," she said, and then turned her back and slammed the door.

He looked at the ceiling. "I never said that," he said, out loud. He started down the stairs, and before he got to the bottom he heard Handsome Dick singing scales, testing his voice box.

Charley sat down at a table and looked at his bottle. He thought again of how it had landed and tried to see the reason. He decided he was meant to drink it.

The whore man had gone behind the bar while Charley was upstairs, and Charley moved his chair so he could watch him and the stairs both. He did not expect to see the banjo player again soon, but he couldn't be sure that Lurline would hold his interest the way she did his. A man who named himself Handsome Banjo could not be counted on to stay long-term with any girl.

He was still sitting there an hour later, drinking and watching the whore man and the stairs, when it came to him out of nowhere to find the pretty little girl in Chinatown, the one Al Swearingen had wanted to buy.

It was the kind of thought, once you thought it, you wondered why you never thought of it earlier.

SOLOMON STAR STOOD NAKED IN HIS FIRST-FLOOR ROOM AT MRS. Grace Tubb's rooming house, slicking his hair. He dropped his comb into a jar of axle grease and spread it evenly over his head, then he parted it down the middle, testing the straightness with his finger. He pulled the comb straight down from the part, first the right side, then the left, then the back. He touched the crown of his head, looking for misplaced hairs, and finding none, he picked his hat up off the bed and centered it over his ears.

He put on his shirt next, a new shirt with the initials *SS* sewn into the pocket, and buttoned it from the collar down. When that was done, he lifted the collar and put on his tie. It was a bow tie, and he worked several minutes on the knot, checking with his fingers to make sure the ends were even. Then he reached into his top drawer for a tin of talcum—he knew without looking where it was—and dusted himself under the shirt. He pulled on his vest, then his underwear bottoms, and then his pants. He sat down to put on his socks, dark red with the initials *SS* sewn into the sides. People assumed Solomon Star was all business, they hadn't seen his socks.

He buffed his shoes on the bedspread.

Before he left the room, he picked up the wildflowers in a vase by the window. He had picked them north of town that afternoon. Seth Bullock was worried to death. "Picking flowers," he'd said. "You spent a whole day picking flowers?"

Solomon had smiled at him and left the office early.

He carried the flowers across the town now into Chinatown. He took the seat he always took at the theater, and smiled at the celestial. Solomon Star believed the celestial owned the business. He also believed the celestial was the father of Ci-an, the China Doll.

He came over now, all smiles and bows, and asked if Solomon would have a drink. Solomon thanked him, returning the smiles, and waited while he spoke to one of the waiters.

The celestial settled in next to him and said, "China Doll, she miss you."

Solomon Star nodded and sipped the whiskey that the waiters brought. "I know," he said.

"She think you special white man. She wants be only yours."

Solomon nodded and sipped. "Her wish is my own," he said.

"Good," the celestial said. "Very good." He looked around the room, uncomfortable, and Solomon took the envelope out of his pants pocket and put it between them on the table. In it were ten hundred-dollar bills.

"For her dowry," he said.

"Yes," the celestial said. "So she marry white man she wants." Solomon did not understand Chinese ways, but he knew they were interested in money, and that the girl did not have enough to marry.

"Not yet," Solomon said. "White men have only one wife. I must unmarry first." The Chinese smiled, as if that were a small joke between them, and put the envelope in his blouse. "Soon," Solomon said.

The celestial nodded. "Very soon," he said. "I get China Doll now, she sing for you and then you see her tonight, very soon."

Solomon handed the Chinese the flowers. "Take these to her," he said, "from Bismarck." The Chinese took the flowers, smiling and bowing, and made his way up the stairs. The room was full now, more miners than Chinese, sitting at all the tables, standing at the bar and along the walls.

Solomon knew they had come for Ci-an. The theater filled every night at the same time, and then emptied after she had finished. He looked at them now, unshaved faces, dirty and torn clothes, permanent squints. He wondered what methods the miners used, to ruin their eyes.

He did not like them there, in dirty clothes, waiting for Ci-an. They belonged with upstairs girls, which were convenient all over the northern Hills. He looked around the theater, face after face, red-eyed and drunk, and found himself looking at them as Ci-an would. Their faces became one face, and it came up out of the smoke open-mouthed for her as she stood on the stage.

He wiped his mouth with his hand and thought of taking her away that night, back to Mrs. Tubb's rooming house. In all, he had paid the celestial three thousand dollars. If he understood the Chinese, the money would be returned to him as her dowry.

He thought he would have a house built on the west side of town, where the sun would touch it in the morning while the rest of town was still in the shadows of the mountains.

Then he thought of his own wife, in Bismarck. And Seth Bullock, and the business. Two twenty-thousand-dollar kilns were on the road somewhere between Deadwood and Sioux City. He didn't know why, but it did not seem possible to keep a Chinese woman in his house and a brickworks in town. It seemed like too much for one man. He decided to turn the operation of the kilns over to Bullock.

He imagined what he might write in the letter to his wife. He did not consider telling her in person. He had changed, but he had not lost his senses. He would write that he had worked all his life, and missed things he could not get back, and it was time now to do the things that were left. And she could have half of the brick business.

He did not know how to explain the Chinese woman. To his wife or to Seth Bullock, who depended on him as much. The difference being that Solomon was not afraid of Seth Bullock.

The miners began to hoot now; the celestial was bringing Ci-an onto the stage. She walked with tiny steps, head bowed. He thought he could see something tremble inside her. He looked at her hands and saw the ring he had put on her thumb. Her fingers were like a child's.

She went straight to the center of the stage and stood alone while the piano player began. The room went quiet, and she started to sing. The words were like baby talk, they had that sweetness to them. In her mouth, even the chopped sounds were soft.

She sang for almost an hour, and at the end the miners hooted and shot off their guns. Some of them whistled through their fingers. They belonged with whores. She belonged someplace away from them.

She waited on the stage until the celestial came to get her.

Solomon had another drink, giving her time to prepare herself, and then walked upstairs. He knocked at Ci-an's door; she did not answer. He waited. He knocked again. An old Chinese woman came toward him in the hall, talking to herself in a bothered way. She was carrying towels, and when she was close to Solomon she said, "You shoo now," and walked around him and through Ci-an's door.

He knocked again. He heard the old woman talking, then Ci-an. In a few minutes the old woman came back out, still carrying the towels, and spoke to him again. "You shoo now," she said. "China Doll sick."

"Sick?" he said, and moved around her and into the room. Ci-an was lying in bed, staring at the ceiling. She looked weak and pale, and he thought he saw her tremble. He was always seeing her tremble. "What is it?" he said. He stepped toward her, but Ci-an held up her hand to stop him. The old woman came in behind him and pulled at his arm.

"You shoo," she said.

Ci-an smiled at him and then closed her eyes for a moment, to show that she wanted to sleep. She put her finger over her lips, and he put his finger over his. Something in the movement touched him. The old woman was pushing him out. "You shoo," she said.

He walked down the hallway, away from the stairs, and sat in the window at the end. He wanted to watch over her. From there he could see the hall without being noticed himself. Solomon did not show more of himself in Chinatown than he needed to. He had changed, but he had not lost his senses.

A breeze came through the window and cooled his neck and head. He realized he was sweating. It was not uncomfortable, though, and for a long time he sat still, thinking of a morning he and Ci-an might have in the house that would catch the sun earlier than the gulch. It felt like he was protecting her now, and keeping her company. He wondered if she felt him there.

The old woman left the room a few minutes after Solomon. She was speaking to Ci-an in a frightened way even as she closed the door between them. It sounded frightened to Solomon, anyway, but that was how the Chinese always sounded. He smiled and waited, and thought of the house. He was happy to be close to her.

In ten minutes the old woman was back again, bringing a small man, who carried a bottle of J. Fred McCurnin swoop whiskey. Solomon saw that the man was drunk. He was freshly shaven and wore clean clothes, but he was drunk. The old woman looked up and down the hall, but did not notice him sitting in the window. The man did not look one way or another, and Solomon wondered if he had paid to lie with the old woman. Stranger things happened.

No. The old woman opened Ci-an's door and pulled the man inside. Solomon thought the man must be a doctor. But then, a few minutes later, the old woman came out alone, and Solomon realized he hadn't been carrying a medicine bag.

The breeze stopped, and in the stillness the sweat on his neck began to tickle.

Solomon waited. Staring down the hallway until it seemed to weave, like the flats in the summer heat, and he began to hear voices in his head. Some of those voices were his and some of them weren't, and he could not tell one from the other.

CI-AN HAD SENSED THE FRIEND OF WILD BILL WAS THERE BEFORE SHE saw him. At the head of the stairs, as she descended into the theater, she knew he had come to her.

She found him quickly in the audience, and then averted her glance. She kept her eyes on the floor as she sang, and bowed her head between her songs, while Tan's uncle sat trying to remember the notes to the next. The uncle had difficulty remembering one song from another, a sign of his age.

It did not matter. She sang her songs slowly, knowing their effect on the man, all men. He would believe he had been forgiven. She sang to him and held him with her songs, and drew him toward her. And she looked another time, as she finished, and again met his eyes. A small promise.

When she had finished she returned to her room, sent Bismarck away, feigning illness, and sent the old woman for the friend of Wild Bill. "His hair is long and clean," she said, "you will see he is different from the rest."

When the old woman had left, she moved from her bed to the closet, and searched the trunks of clothes until she found a small, black-handled knife. The knife was sharp on both sides and heavy at the top. A tiny piece had been broken from the tip, an accident in throwing.

She put the knife on the table next to the bed, where the man would see it, and lay down. An unconcealed knife threatened no one. She looked at it from her pillow, fixing on it in such a way that the black of the handle became an opening, a door she would pass through leaving this place.

But the friend of Wild Bill would pass through first. She did not move, but thought of the instrument's weight in her hand. She wondered if Song had felt the weight of the instrument of his own passing. She trembled, remembering the oven.

The old woman came back with the white man. He was not as small in her room as he had seemed on the street. The friend of Wild Bill was holding a bottle, and she saw that he had drunk much of what was inside. She did not think that would slow his mind, or slow his hands.

The death of his friend had hurt him, but there was no pleasure for her in his pain now. He smiled at her and stood at the spot where the old woman left him. She had thought he would come to her, that the momentum of this event had begun and would bring him to her bed.

He spoke to her instead, softly, and she held out her hand. He crossed the distance between them and sat down on the bed. Ci-an moved and the sheet fell off her body. The man looked into her eyes. She held still, afraid that she would give herself away. Afraid that the man already knew.

But he was not cunning. He was unpracticed in deception, and so did not easily see it in others. Song had been blind to pretense too. She unbuttoned his shirt, allowing her fingers to touch his chest. She felt the movement of his heart. He watched her face as she undressed him, as if he were searching for the meaning of it. There was a kindness in his eyes that she had not seen before, and it comforted her for what was ahead.

When the shirt was unbuttoned, she sat up and pushed it back over his shoulders, and then his arms. She saw the place she would put the knife. He still looked into her eyes, and when the shirt was on the floor she took him in her arms and held him. Another comfort.

His back was hard and she could feel each muscle and tendon and bone. She moved her hands, learning his back, and sensed that he had released himself to her. She began to love him.

"I will take you away soon," she said.

He pulled back, smiling now, and made a motion with his hands for her to speak. She said it again. "I will take you away soon."

And he repeated the sounds back to her. In her lifetime, no white man had ever tried to speak Chinese to her before. The words came back to her, a prophecy.

There was a narrow space between their bodies now, and she reached across it and unbuckled the belt to his pants.

He sat very still, watching her, perhaps sensing that the things of this room did not harmonize. She went on with it, unbuttoning his pants. She was graceful in all things she did with her hands, and in a moment she held him in her fingers. His penis strained, like a blind old man.

"Men are led by the blind man inside them," she said.

He tried the sentence in Chinese, and she smiled at his pronunciation. He had dark eyes, the color of real people's, and patience. He tried again. She had meant to put the knife between his ribs at the first chance, but when the chance came, as he leaned over the side of the bed for the bottle, she could not bring herself to act.

She felt there was something to be done first.

He offered her the bottle, which she refused. He drank a long time, as if it were difficult for him to swallow. He removed the bottle from his lips and began to speak, his own language. She took his penis in her hand again and listened. Presently, he touched her shoulders. His fingers were soft and clean, and she held still, afraid again that he would see her purpose.

But he spoke quietly, without stopping, touching her shoulders. Then her sides, then her back. He moved behind her on the bed, and from there he touched her breasts. He held them carefully and then moved closer, until she could feel his mouth on her shoulder and neck and his penis pressing into her back. She stared at the knife on the table.

The pull was gentle, like a current. He was speaking behind her ear, and it pulled her. She bent herself forward until her face rested on her pillows, and he bent with her. He pushed into her slowly, as slowly as she had bent to the current, and it filled her in that same insistent way. One of his hands covered her belly, and she wondered if he wished to feel himself inside her.

She lifted herself and pushed back into him. She closed her eyes and then, in the contradictions of all the things he was to her, the penis was suddenly gone and the door to her room splintered and slammed against the wall. She heard the wood break.

The penis was gone, and then the man was gone too, and she

felt the absence in all the places he had pressed against her back. There was a shot, and the man shouted.

Words, not a cry.

AN OLD CHINESE WOMAN HAD COME TO CHARLEY IN THE BACK OF THE theater and pulled on his sleeve. "You come," she said.

And he went, because he had drunk most of the bottle, and because the old woman was afraid. He thought there might be a snake somewhere. But she led him up the stairs to a room and left him inside with the China Doll. He had seen glimpses of the woman on the wagon train from Fort Laramie, and watched her sing that very night on the stage of the theater, but neither of those looks prepared him.

Her face had the Chinese quality, but none of the weaknesses. It didn't look anything like a squash. Her skin was soft, and whatever her troubles—and there was something—she seemed single-minded enough about what to do for them. And Charley liked her. Something was reserved, and did not ask too much.

She was as pretty as Mrs. Langrishe, in her Chinese way, and Charley saw that she was normal and wasn't going to bite.

And so he let himself be undressed and handled, and then he saw she was unhappy, and he'd spoken to her as he kissed her from behind. "Don't be unhappy," he said.

Yes, Charles Utter could sweet-talk the ladies.

He did not crave her the way he craved Mrs. Langrishe, but there was enough craving left over from sitting in the theater with that lady's hand in his lap—her touch there had curled his peeder like salt on a caterpillar—so that by the time things developed with the China Doll, it felt like what he needed.

And then he slid himself inside her—it was soft and slow and normal, and it was a relief too, to find out he wasn't tangle-brained forever after all the nights with Lurline—and more than that, it felt good, the way it had a long time ago, before he knew what to expect. And he thanked her, not worrying himself over the phrasing because she didn't understand anyway. "You're real normal," he said.

And she lifted herself up and pushed back into him, and at that moment Handsome Banjo Dick Brown kicked open the door, holding his Colt in his hand, following him with it as Charley disengaged himself from the China Doll and rolled off the bed. He noticed again that Handsome Dick held the gun higher in his hand than most. Charley remembered the shooting at the theater.

Handsome Dick took his time—he was a calm one facing an unarmed man—and then fired a shot that broke a piece of the bedboard. "Son of a bitch," Charley said, "you *do* always get even."

Charley landed on the floor and rolled, left and right. He could not remember where his own guns were, or where he had been when the China Doll took them off. So it was an act of providence, somewhere in his drunk rollings, that his feet touched them. Not only touched them, but delivered them. He did not know how, but his feet put the gun belt in his hands.

He was still moving on the floor and had glimpses of Handsome Dick trying to draw a bead on his head. Vanity kept the singer from spraying bullets all over the floor. Handsome Dick was a shootist and hated to miss. Charley rolled under the bed and stopped. He took one of the guns out of its holster and cocked it. Above him, the mattress sagged, and he thought of the China Doll's bottom, almost as close to him now as before Handsome Dick came in the door.

Charley's head was swimming, much the same way that Charley himself swam, and he was out of breath. He found Handsome Dick's legs, though, and drew a bead of his own. "You want to call this off?" Charley said. He did not like to shoot a man in the leg unwarned. He waited but Handsome Dick did not answer. "You want to call it off?" he said again. Then the China Doll moved on the mattress, and it sagged between Charley's gun and his eyes, cutting off his view.

Handsome Dick said, "What?" and Charley shot him in the shin.

Handsome dropped to the floor and Charley rolled out from under the bed. For a long, uncomfortable minute they were eyeball to eyeball.

"You crippled me," Handsome said. He held on to the front of his leg, a little above the shoe. He had broken out sweating, and he spoke without opening his teeth.

Charley got to his feet and then sat on the bed over him, looking down. He was still holding his own gun in his hand, and the swimming in his head had changed at the sound of the explosion, and he felt more like he was floating now. The China Doll sat as still as the moon in the sky.

Charley looked from one of them to the other, and then at the gun in his hand. "I never shot a human being in my life," he said.

"You did now," Handsome said.

Charley saw he was afraid. "Move your hand and I'll have a look."

Handsome Dick let go of his shin, and Charley lifted his pants leg up over the wound. The shot had gone in dead center and exited the back. The bone had splintered, and there was a little piece of it caught in the torn skin under the calf. "How bad is it?" Handsome said.

"I don't understand it," Charley said. "I never shot a soul in my life, never had to."

"Am I crippled?"

Charley shook his head. "I don't know," he said. Handsome Dick covered his eyes and his face sparkled with sweat. "I don't feel anything," he said, "but I'm cold."

Charley turned back to the China Doll. "I never even pointed a gun at anybody," he said. She did not move. On the floor, Handsome Dick began to moan.

"I'll get a doctor," Charley said, but he didn't go. He wanted somebody to understand that he'd shot a human being.

Handsome Dick hissed. "Not here," he said. "I can't be caught with a China whore."

Charley looked at her again, but she hadn't understood. He thought of Bill, and then of the farmer at the Langrishe Theater. He wondered what they would say about this in the bars.

Charley said, "I could remove you back to a white whore and bring you a doctor there."

Handsome Dick was pale and he began to shake. "I'm freezing," he said. And Charley picked him up from behind and got his head under one of Handsome's arms for support. "This is fair and square of you," Handsome said, "but no more than I'd do for a Christian myself."

"I saw what you did for Christianity earlier tonight," Charley said.

Handsome Dick leaned on Charley and they walked out the door. As Charley left, he turned to the China Doll and bowed about four inches, which was as far off center as he could get without falling over. "I will return directly," he said.

At the stairs Handsome tried to hop, which caused him true pain. It came higher in the leg than Charley had shot him, and it stopped him where he stood. He choked Charley until it had passed.

"Hell," Charley said when Handsome had relaxed his hold on his windpipe, "I've got to carry you, don't I?"

Handsome did not seem to be paying attention. When Charley looked into his face, his eyes were unfocused and shiny. Charley moved out from under Handsome's arm and stood on the step in front of him.

The singer draped both arms over Charley's shoulders and brought them together under his chin. Then he moved his weight off his feet and onto Charley's back. Charley took Handsome's knees in his arms and carried him down the stairs. The theater had closed, and except for two celestials cleaning glasses off the tables, it was empty. Charley wondered if they had thought the shots were just miners, upstairs celebrating with the Chinese whores. They took no notice of white men carrying each other piggyback out the door.

When they were in the street, Charley tried to put Handsome Dick down, but the singer would not have it. "You'll aggravate the injury," he said, and held on to Charley's neck. And so Charley carried him out of Chinatown and back to the Gem Theater. His feet went to the bottom of the mud—he presumed there was a bottom to the mud—and it reminded him of carrying the governor of Colorado, who weighed three hundred pounds, through the snow. Anything you carried through the mud weighed three hundred pounds.

Charley had killed most of his bottle, and talked more than he normally would, repeating himself on the matter of having shot a human being.

Handsome moaned and held on. "Don't leave me alone," he said.

"If I was going to leave you someplace," Charley said, "would I be carrying your ass all over town in the mud to do it? When I leave something, I leave it." And Handsome moaned again, until Charley almost felt sorry for him.

There were still customers at the Gem, so Charley carried Handsome Dick around to the back. There was another set of stairs there which led to the opposite end of the hallway. Al Swearingen had instinctively known that a whorehouse was more comfortable with two ways out. The back stairs were narrower than the ones in front, and dark, and the wood bent and complained under the weight of Charley and his load. They complained, Handsome Dick complained.

"It hurts worse now," he said. "It comes in pulses."

"Yes, it does," Charley said. He was breathing hard, and there didn't seem to be air to talk with.

"Am I going to die?"

Charley saw the red-headed farmer lying across the stake in front of him while Handsome Dick put four shots into his chest. "Maybe," he said.

He took the singer to Lurline's door and eased him to the floor to open it. Handsome cried out at the change of positions and broke into a fresh sweat. "We'll put you in a chair," Charley said, "and tell it was Lurline instead of the Chinese. Lurline keeps a secret."

He opened the door to her room then, quietly, and found her lying in bed under Boone May. Charley recognized the head by its size even before it turned and stared at him and the ceiling at the same time. Boone May looked, and then Lurline looked.

Charley stood still, Handsome Dick moaned.

It was Charley and the whiskey that spoke first. "Outward appearance," he said, "you're beginning to look easy, Lurline."

Boone looked from Charley to Lurline. "Have you took up with this pretty?" he said.

"He ain't a pretty," she said. "He's intelligent."

"Thank you," Charley said.

"What's he doing now?" Boone said to her.

"I don't know," she said.

"Well," Boone said to Lurline, "he'd best do it someplace else. It's situations like this people get shot."

Handsome Dick moaned and fell into a chair. "What's wrong with him?" Boone said to Lurline. He still hadn't spoken to Charley.

"I don't know," she said.

Charley said, "Shooting is an unpopular subject right now," and Handsome grabbed his leg and began to rock back and forth.

"It's bad again," he said.

"What did you do to him?" Lurline said. She sat all the way up, disentangling herself from Boone May, and stared at Charley like Handsome was a blood relative.

Charley looked at the ceiling, wondering if, because of his eye, Boone May might not know more about ceilings than anybody alive. "It has been a star-crossed day for me and this singer," he said.

"Did you shoot him?" she said. Charley scratched his neck,

thinking of a way to explain it. "You did, didn't you?" And she came out of bed naked to look at Handsome's leg.

"It happened in Chinatown," Charley said.

Boone sat up and began dressing himself under the covers. Seeing he was suddenly polite, Charley realized Boone might have to be shot too, after he was decent.

"I can smell it on you," she said. "Nobody has to tell me they been in Chinatown. The whole goddamn place smells like a buffalo robe."

"Well, that's where it happened, but on account of his career, Handsome had me bring him here before I got him a doctor. Seeing how this is where it started anyway."

"What was the two of you doing in Chinatown?" she said.

"It wasn't me," Handsome said. "I just followed him there to get even." Lurline stared at Charley until he felt like it was himself without clothes.

"You used to be clean," she said. "Next thing I know, you got your peeder in some slant-eyes washee."

Charley nodded at the bed, where Boone was still trying to get his feet into the right sleeves of his long underwear. "Are you lecturing to me on cleanliness? The last time he got wet, he pissed himself in the night."

Boone did not seem to hear that, which Charley, on reflection, saw was just as well. Boone May was nobody to insult when you'd spent yourself carrying a shot singer out of Chinatown. Lurline said, "You ain't going to leave him here."

Handsome moaned. "It's horrible," he said, meaning his leg.

"This is where I found him," Charley said. "And this is where I brought him back. Now I got to go get him a doctor to give him some morphine before he dies on us."

Lurline looked at him a long minute. "I liked him better before you shot him," she said to Charley. "He don't act like he's famous now."

Boone had gotten into his underwear and buttoned it up the front. He stood up by the bed now, barefoot, taking up half the room. "There ain't nobody famous," he said to her, stepping into his pants. "Not the way you think of it."

"The hell there ain't," she said.

Boone looked at Charley. "Tell her, pretty. About famous. They die like anybody else."

Charley thought it over. "There's some die better than others," he said.

Handsome began to cry. "Some die quieter too," Boone said.

"Get me a sawbones," Handsome said, and then he fainted.

Lurline stared at Charley. "There," she said, "see what you done? You killed him."

IT WAS THREE O'CLOCK IN THE MORNING WHEN CHARLEY GOT DR. O. E. Sick out of bed. He hated to wake him at that hour, because the man had been kind to the Bottle Fiend, but for that same reason Charley tried him instead of one of the others. It was not a world that rewarded the kind.

Dr. O. E. Sick was old, and he took the story Charley told him and centered it again and again in his head, as if he were balancing it in there. "The man was shot in the lower left leg," he said on the way over, "and he is unconscious?"

"He was when I left," Charley said.

"And it was just the leg. You're sure . . ."

"I was there."

Dr. O. E. Sick had tucked his nightshirt into his pants and tucked his pants into his boots. Anything that spilled down his neck would end up on his feet. "Everyone's a shootist," he said. "Bang, bang."

Charley stopped in the mud. "In my life, I never shot a human being before, or wanted to," he said, "but it was a Christian thing, under the circumstances, not putting one in his head."

"Christianity," the doctor said.

They walked quietly a few yards, the doctor balancing his thoughts. "Could he be dead?" he said after a while.

"No."

They walked farther into the badlands. "I wouldn't like it if he was dead," the doctor said.

"I wouldn't like it either," Charley said. "That's why I came and got you."

The doctor did not seem to hear. "They come and got me early this morning for Preacher Smith," he said. "Woke me up at daybreak to ride three miles to view the Indians' work. He was shot forty times if he was shot once. I said, 'What is it you think a doctor does, fill holes?' It was more holes there than preacher."

It took Charley a few seconds to remember Preacher Smith,

standing out on his packing crate on Main Street, asking the Lord for protection, while Charley sat in that stale wagon, worrying over the boy.

Charley wondered how it happened that men of the cloth always seemed to misunderstand the ways of the Lord. If you wanted protection you had to ask for money or love, and He would give you protection instead. Prayer was a study in misdirection, but none of the Methodists Charley ever met paid enough attention to notice, and spent their lives praying the wrong way.

"The boys on the killing site thought it was a fine thing the Indians didn't mutilate the preacher," the doctor said. He shook his head and pushed through the mud. "You'll be hearing that for a while now," he said. "'At least they didn't mutilate him.'"

"Well," Charley said, "that's something."

The doctor stared at him. "I hope this man isn't dead," he said. "I'm too old to be getting out of bed to view corpses. I seen enough now, I can wait until business hours to look at the next one."

"He was speaking right up until the moment he passed out," Charley said, getting worried now.

"Coherent?" the doctor said.

"Hell yes, he can hear," Charley said. "I didn't shoot him in the ears."

And they looked at each other—the two smartest men awake in the Black Hills—each of them wondering what he had stumbled across now. The doctor had a theory soft-brain was caused by the climate, and before they got to the Gem he said, "You was caught out in the April blizzard this year, wasn't you?"

Handsome Banjo Dick Brown had regained consciousness and was lying on Lurline's bed. He was soaked through with sweat, and the expression on his face reminded Charley of the first times he had been hurt himself. Pain was its own teacher, and there wasn't any way to learn how it worked but to be visited. If the visits weren't right on top of each other—if they were far enough apart so you could forget the way it came but close enough to remember it went away—you could learn to ride it out.

Handsome Dick moaned, deep and helpless. His lips were pitiful. When he saw Dr. O. E. Sick he began to cry. The doctor sat down on the bed with him and put his hand on Handsome's forehead. "I never felt nothing like this," Handsome said. "I didn't know nothing like this existed."

The doctor lifted Handsome Dick's eyelids, one after the other, and then he pressed the nails of his fingers to see if the blood would come back after he let go. Then he moved down the bed and looked at the leg. Handsome's pants leg was pushed up over his knee as high as it would go, and Dr. Sick reached into his bag and came out with a knife.

Handsome closed his eyes and sobbed. Dr. Sick paid no attention. He cut the pants leg, bottom to top. Handsome Dick opened his eyes. "That feels better," he said, blinking tears. "You're a wizard."

The doctor paid no attention. He poked the skin around the entrance wound to see if the blood would return when he stopped. Then he rolled Handsome Dick over and looked at the other side. It was swollen now, and blue, and the blood had caked black in the opening. The swelling was such that you could not see the splinter of bone. "The bone's broke bad," the doctor said.

Handsome Dick moaned. "I ain't going to lose the leg . . ."

Charley was reminded in some distant way of Captain Jack Crawford. The doctor shook his head. "We got to clean out the wound," he said. "Remove bone fragments and splint you up."

Handsome Dick nodded at all that, and the doctor reached into his bag for the needle. He gave Handsome a shot of morphine, pushing it in at the vein in back of his knee. Charley watched, and in one minute Handsome's face uncontorted itself. Then a sly look came into his eyes. A moment later he winked at Lurline, who had been sitting by the window, looking like she could use a shot of painkiller too.

"Don't smile at me, either of you," she said. Boone had left mad. "I been disillusioned."

"I shall suck thy breasts," Handsome said.

Handsome's eyes closed around his thoughts. He was smiling now. "Pay him no attention," the doctor said to Lurline. "He don't know what he's saying now."

"Well," she said, "if he ain't responsible, I don't guess I can blame him."

The doctor looked through his bag and found a tin of black powder. He loaded some onto the blade of the knife and sifted it into the wounds, front and back. Handsome Dick opened his eyes and watched.

"Is that medicine?" Handsome said.

The doctor paid no attention. He went over the wounds twice, making sure each of them was covered with powder. When he had finished, he told Lurline to wet a towel. There was a pitcher of water in the corner, and she dipped a towel into it and then wrung it out.

"You hold him over there," he said to her, "and you hold him there." He pointed Charley to the far side of the bed. Charley did what he was told, but it brought him into it farther than he wanted to be. What he wanted was to leave the doctor with Handsome Dick and find his way back over to Chinatown. He put his hands on Handsome Dick's narrow shoulders, realizing the singer had never done a day's work in his life. He pictured how Handsome would have looked to the farmer he killed, whose whole life was work.

The doctor bent Handsome's knee until there was six inches between the wound and the bed. "What is that medicine?" Handsome asked. "Am I cured?" Then he rolled his eyes until they settled on Lurline, who was holding the other shoulder. "I shall taste thy loveliness," he said.

Lurline smiled at him and then looked at Charley. "You can't blame him for honest passions," she said. "He ain't responsible."

Dr. O. E. Sick found a match in his pants pocket and lit it against the bedpost. Handsome Dick moved his gaze from Lurline's loveliness toward the sound of the strike. He was late, though. By the time Handsome focused on what the doctor was doing, the match was already in the powder. There was a small sound when it lit, like somebody blowing out a candle, and then his leg was smoking.

The doctor had done the leg, front and back, before it hit Handsome's sensibilities. When it did, he screamed and bucked and buckled, but there wasn't a muscle in his body, and they held on to him. Dr. Sick waited five seconds and then wrapped the smoking part of Handsome's leg in the towel. It did not seem to stop the pain, and every time Handsome yelped there was surprise in it.

Dr. Sick looked into his bag again and found a pair of tweezers. He used them and the knife to look into the hole where the bullet had left the leg. Twice he located little pieces of bone, which he removed and dropped on the floor next to the bed. Handsome passed out.

Charley felt dizzy and dry. When the doctor stopped to examine his work, Charley said, "I believe I'll have a drink, unless you think he's about to confess . . ."

The doctor paid no attention. He wrapped the wounds in gauze, and then pulled the leg straight and built Handsome a splint from two pieces of the chair Charley had broken when they'd fought. He wrapped it with wire from his bag.

Then he brought out a small bottle of morphine and gave it to Lurline. "Don't administer this but three, four times a day," he said.

"He ain't staying here," she said.

"He can't be moved," the doctor said.

"The hell he can't," she said. "Somebody's got to move, so's I can conduct my business affairs."

The doctor looked up at her, interested. He said, "I was told that you were a musician."

"I am," she said. "Shit, singers need to sleep too." Handsome groaned and moved.

"If that wrapping starts to stink," the doctor said, "come get me and I'll change it." He looked at Lurline in a sympathetic way. "You might save this man's leg, miss," he said.

"How come he can't stay with Charley?" she said. "He was the one that shot him."

Charley got up then, lame in his own legs. He thanked the doctor, who paid no attention. "If he dies," he said to Charley, but without taking his eyes off Lurline, "I'll send you the billing."

Charley smiled at Lurline and stumbled out the door. When he got to the street he stopped and looked back up at Lurline's window. The light went out, but Dr. O. E. Sick stayed. He waited five minutes in the mud to make sure.

Lurline was sweet, but she would break your heart if you let her.

Charley walked through the mud, feeling tired. Too tired to go back to Chinatown. He passed Wall Street, which led there, but then he thought about bedding down alone, and he was too tired— in a different way—for that too.

And so he turned around, and followed Wall Street until he came to their theater. It was dark from the outside, not a lamp on anywhere. Charley let himself in the front door. There were no windows on the first floor. The Chinese, now he thought about it, didn't have much use for windows at all. He walked slowly through the theater, bumping into chairs and a piano, things he would have felt in front of himself sober.

He found the staircase and headed up. Somewhere, a long way off, a woman was snoring. The China Doll's room was third on the left, facing the street. It had one of the two windows in the whole building. Charley ran his fingers lightly along the wall, counting the doors. At the third one, his fingers came away wet. He stopped, dead still, dead drunk, and listened. Snoring, a long ways off.

In the dark, he thought he saw the farmer's face. And then Handsome Dick's face, pained and sweaty, and then Charley heard what Handsome Dick said. "Will it grow back?" From what he'd seen, the joke was not far from losing its humor.

Charley turned the door handle, thinking of the extra weight that would be to carry around. He had never wanted to shoot a man, and making one a cripple was no great favor either.

And with his mind still on amputations, he pushed open the door and saw a human leg on the floor.

He took a step in, and noticed a stickiness to the floor when he lifted his moccasins. He moved more carefully now, not feeling anybody else in the room, but doubting himself. He stepped in and to the side, and then went flat against the wall. Nothing moved.

He waited a full minute and then looked again at the floor. The leg lay on its side, smaller and smoother than Handsome's. He stared at it for another minute, seeing there was something wrong with the proportions. It seemed to him that the foot was missing, but moving closer he saw it was no such thing. Moving closer, he saw that the leg had a foot, but it was tiny. It could have belonged to a seven-year-old child. He looked around the room then, seeing her hand first, then the rest. From the blood, the killing had started in her bed and then moved across the room toward the window.

From the blood, that was where it ended.

There was a knife on the stool in front of the painting easel. Paper drawings of artificial flowers lay on the floor next to the flowers themselves. The room was motionless, and he was motionless in it. It seemed like it was already a memory. He walked out the door and sat down on the stairs. Where were the Chinese when the girl had screamed for help? Of course, she might not have screamed at all. Charley cradled his head in his hands and remembered her. There was something held back, and something sad. He did not understand what went on in a Chinese heart, that something like this could happen. The Indians made more sense.

He found the door and walked down the stairs, and then outside. It was five o'clock in the morning, and when Charley turned the corner at Main Street, he saw the sky in the north was lit the color of peaches. Deadwood was the only place Charley had ever been where the day broke in the north. He stared that way for a minute and then turned his back on the sky, and headed south, uphill, toward the Grand Union Hotel.

SETH BULLOCK HEARD SOLOMON COME IN, SO LATE THAT HIS FIRST thought was that Solomon was getting up. His second thought was that something had happened. Bullock listened to his partner, waiting for familiar sounds. Outside, it was dead still. There wasn't even a cat in the street. He knew Solomon, right down to the number of steps he took between his dresser and his closet; he knew the order he hung up his clothes. But the steps from the next room lacked purpose. Solomon did not go to his closet or his drawers; he wandered the room, from the window to his bed and then back to the window.

Bullock got out of his own bed and put on his boots. He slept in his pants, in the event of late-night emergencies. For late-night emergencies, the sheriff liked to be punctual enough to take the prisoner from the citizenry before they hung him, but late enough to miss getting shot at in the capture. Seth Bullock did not intend to die on the caprice of a common drunk.

He walked out into the hallway that connected his room to Solomon's, feeling heavy-legged and slow. He had not slept well during the night, thinking of the letter he had written to Solomon's wife. *"My confidential advice in this matter,"* he'd said, *"would be for yourself to join us in the Hills, for I am sure your sobering influence will return Solomon to his sensibilities, if anything can."*

He had laid in bed thinking of Solomon's sudden affliction with views and flowers, and what the letter would do to that. He told himself that business partners had obligations to each other. Bullock settled that for himself a dozen times, but it would not let him sleep.

He knocked once on Solomon's door, not wanting to wake Mrs. Tubb. Then he tried the door. It was unlocked. In fact, it hadn't been closed. Solomon was sitting on the floor in the corner, cross-legged and naked, dark-faced and dirty. The sight affirmed the decision to write his wife, and Bullock felt himself relieved to have it off his conscience. "Look at yourself," he said.

Solomon didn't look. At himself, or at Bullock or at anything else. His eyes were shut tight. "Solomon?"

Solomon shook his head slowly back and forth. Bullock stepped closer, noticing his clothes scattered here and there on the floor, as if they had fallen off while Solomon was walking around the room. His shirt was by the bed, as muddy as Solomon himself. "Solomon, look at yourself," he said again. "This isn't you . . ." As he spoke, he reached down and picked the shirt up off the floor, and then he saw that the stains weren't mud. He took the shirt to the table where Solomon wrote his letters and lit the lamp. The lamp turned the room orange, and even as the match struck, he saw it was blood.

Bullock looked into the corner again, and saw the blood there too. It was all over Solomon's face, caked in his hair and hands and in the hair of his body. He got closer and studied his partner's head. It had to be a head wound, blood didn't flow uphill. He couldn't see the opening, though. "Solomon," he said slowly, "where are you hurt?"

Solomon opened his eyes, but not to look at anything in that room. From the expression on his face, Bullock half expected to hear him invent a new language, but when he finally spoke it sounded reasonable. Particularly coming from a man sitting naked and blood-covered on the floor at five o'clock in the morning.

"Something unspeakable has happened," he said. Bullock sat down and waited. In the history of their partnership, Solomon had never used the word "unspeakable" except as it referred to money. As in, "This merchandise, sir, is an *unspeakable* aberration of our contract, and we hereby refuse delivery."

That's what it was, *unspeakable* meant Solomon would not accept delivery.

"Unspeakable," he said again.

"What?" Bullock said. He had visions of drunk miners vandalizing the new kiln.

Solomon stared into the wall, seeing the unspeakable. Bullock took his partner's shoulder in his hand and shook it. Solomon's head bounced, like a man asleep in a stagecoach. When Bullock had stopped, Solomon said, "There are pieces of Ci-an all over the floor."

Bullock closed his eyes. "You been to the opium dens," he said. "Seen things that weren't there." Solomon shook his head slowly, back and forth. "There isn't a Cheyenne in three hundred miles," Bullock said.

"She's cut to pieces," Solomon said.

"Where?"

"Chinatown," he said.

"What in the world, Solomon?" Bullock said. "What in the world are you doing in Chinatown?"

"That's where she is," he said. And then he closed his eyes again, as if he had seen all he could stand.

Bullock had a further thought then, that the blood had to come from somewhere. He stood up and went to the drawer, where Solomon had laid out a shallow bowl of water, a cake of black soap, and a washing rag before he'd left. He set the bowl on the floor beside Solomon and rubbed the soap back and forth against the washrag until it made a dirty-looking lather. Then, beginning with his head and working down, Bullock washed off the blood.

It had dried, and even in the cool early-morning air Bullock began to sweat. He worked a small section at a time, cleaning in circles a few inches wide, then washing out the rag in the water and lathering the soap again. It was slow, hard work. Solomon let himself be moved and cleaned, but did nothing to help. To scrub the blood from under his arm, Bullock had to hold the arm up with one hand and work with the other. It was something like brushing a horse, and something like scraping paint.

"Whatever it is that happened," Bullock said, "don't say a word to anybody. You can tell me when you're ready, but as far as anybody knows, you were here in your room since supper."

Solomon opened his eyes at the sound of Bullock's voice, and seemed to understand what he said. "Unspeakable," he said.

"That's what I mean," Bullock said, "unspeakable." He washed Solomon's stomach, but left the blood on his privates. He could take care of that himself when he regained his senses. Nobody would see it there, at least Bullock didn't think so. With Solomon's new interests, you couldn't tell. "You hear what I told you?" he said.

Solomon looked at him, and returned to the here and now. His voice lost its passion; it seemed to have lost its direction too. "I won't say a word," he said.

"Not a living soul," Bullock said. "Except me, when you're ready."

"Nobody," Solomon repeated. And Bullock looked at his partner and saw there wouldn't be any more talk of novels, or flower collections. The game had passed fast enough, he thought, and unless Solomon had stumbled into something tonight that couldn't be ignored, Bullock's problem was over.

"Who saw you tonight?" he said.

"Ci-an," Solomon said. Bullock still didn't know what Ci-an was, but he didn't think there was anything that happened at three or four o'clock in the morning in Chinatown that couldn't be ignored. And even washing the blood off Solomon Star, and listening to what was probably a report of a Chinese butchering, it never occurred to him that Solomon could have had a part in it.

Bullock felt happy, as if it were himself who had been sick and cured. "You see," he said, "what happened to you, Solomon, you forgot who you were for a little while. That's all. A man is one way or another, and it can't change reading a book."

Solomon stared at him, listening.

"What I mean is, there's some people that weren't meant for books and flowers," he said. "There are some that weren't meant to do any damn thing that looks good at the time."

Solomon stared and listened, as if Bullock still hadn't hit the chord.

"You weren't meant to *enjoy* things," he said. And when he looked again, he saw that he had finally hit home. Solomon was nodding, understanding, rocking back and forth on the floor. And then, without a sound, he began to weep.

Bullock felt sorry for him, but he knew it was in Solomon's own interests. That's what he told him. "It's in your interests to know it," he said. "Now you can go back to work."

THE CHINA DOLL WAS FOUND IN THE MORNING BY THE OLD WOMAN. The servant had argued the night before with her husband, and had begun to talk even before she entered the room with her towels and broom. She was two steps inside before she saw what was on the floor, and another two steps in before she realized what it was.

She screamed then, a high, hollow scream that brought other Chinese from every corner of the house. The servants came first, then the whores and Children of Joy, then Tan's nephews and wife. The servants held their hands tight against their mouths, and some of them cried.

The whores and Children of Joy did not grieve. The China Doll had lived in a room of her own with a window to the street, she had been given a servant. She was beautiful, while they were plain, and she had taken her meals alone in her room. And they had heard of the white man, Bismarck, who was rich and wanted to buy her from Tan.

It was not spoken here, in her room, but the China Doll's loss was not their own.

After several minutes, Tan himself entered. He was dressed in Chinese clothes, not the American pants and coat he seemed now to prefer. All the servants were suddenly quiet.

Tan crossed the room slowly and picked up the girl's head. He held it close to his chest and called her "little sister." "I will avenge you, little one," he said, and then looked around the room in a way that scared even his wife, who had seen him come into their apartment early in the morning, and had seen the blood on his hands. And who knew his only true passion was money. She was a wise woman, as old as Tan, and understood men well. She understood it was in this acting that they were most dangerous.

So she stood quietly while Tan spoke of his love for the dead girl. He spoke of her drawings and her songs and her beauty. "Where will we find another so lovely, little sister?" he said. The servants and whores and the Children of Joy stood with their heads bowed until he had finished speaking.

Then he sent a servant for pillows, and placed the parts of Ci-an's body on them and ordered the servants to carry them to the death house. The death house was a small, eight-sided building on the Whitewood. It was supervised by Tan's blind uncle, who also played the piano. Inside were the ribbons and plumage and horns and drums for funerals. And the zinc-lined boxes that were used to send the dead's bones back to China.

In the seven months since the first Chinese set foot in the northern Hills, only nine had died—ten, if you counted the disgraced Song. But he never was counted, or remembered aloud. All of the dead had been poor. Servants of one class or another, and unable, even in death, to pay for more than a few ribbons on a pine box and a short ride to the cemetery.

It disheartened the others to see this, as they were poor too but assumed against reason, as all real people assumed, that they would someday return to China to be buried. It disheartened them too because a long funeral was as important as a long life. They all hoped to please Tan in life, so he would take care of them afterwards.

The China Doll was brought to the death house by four servants. Tan himself carried her head. He instructed his uncle to arrange the funeral as if he himself had died.

The uncle obeyed. He removed the girl's eyes and heart, and

placed them in one of the zinc-lined boxes for shipment home. Then he took the bones of her arms and laid them in the box too. The rest, including all the flesh he had cut away from the bones, went into a small gold-colored coffin. It took the uncle an entire day to prepare the box and the coffin, and Tan stayed in the death house with him until it was finished.

The funeral began early in the morning. Six horses led the march through town, each carrying feathers of a different color. They were followed by a band of silver horns and drums, and then by the coffin itself, which was carried by four men. The rest of the Chinese followed, even the emaciated old men from the opium dens, some of them believing it was their own funeral. Each Chinese wore a pink ribbon tied to his sleeve.

They took the box from one end of the town to the other, stopping for demonstrations, and then finally to the graveyard. Several dozen white men had joined the procession by then, and walked behind the Chinese, applauding the horn-players and the speeches.

At the grave site a pig was butchered and skewered over a fire. Before it was eaten, Ci-an's coffin was lowered into the ground and covered with dirt. The women lay tiny flowers on the grave, believing the dead could smell them there at night.

Tan spoke then, for more than an hour, of his love for Ci-an. He cried and threatened and vowed revenge. The Chinese stood quietly while Tan spoke, although almost to a person they believed by now that Tan had killed the girl himself.

They were respectful, though, not wanting to anger him. They could see for themselves the rewards for staying in Tan's graces.

PART THREE

AGNES

1876

Barring episodes of the road, the Northwestern Express, Stage, and Transportation Company stage ran from Cheyenne to Deadwood in six days. The charge was forty-four dollars. It was forty-four dollars from Cheyenne, or from Bismarck or Fort Pierre or Sidney, Nebraska.

The coach had one driver and one messenger, warranteed gentlemanly, and carried eight passengers in the winter. In the summertime, when tempers were quicker, the limit was six. There were rules posted at the station forbidding the discussion of politics, religion, or shooting. The consumption of alcohol was also forbidden, unless the bottle was proffered to all passengers, and those that chewed were requested to spit leeward.

For every passenger the company lost to highwaymen, three of them killed each other. Or froze. It was not ordinary arguments that led to most of the gunplay, however, it was stomach problems. And in spite of Northwestern's rules, the casualties stayed constant.

The violence was built in. The huge Concord coaches were hung to their frames on leather braces to smooth the ride, and the motions that resulted were unfamiliar to anybody but children, who were used to swings, and trapeze artists. And there was something instinctive when a man threw up on your feet, even if you were on the edge of doing the same yourself, that made you want to shoot him. Especially if you were on the edge of doing the same yourself.

The stage stopped sixteen times between Cheyenne and Deadwood, for meals and fresh horses, and passengers were served hardtack, beans, and pork at each stop as part of the forty-four-dollar fare.

It was the pork that gave Agnes Lake summer complaint. It tasted tainted, but she'd eaten it anyway. She'd paid for it. She sat stone-complected now, between a peddler and a farm boy, staring across the aisle into the face of a man named Captain Jack Crawford, who said he was returning to Deadwood to settle accounts with the killer of Wild Bill Hickok.

The man on Crawford's right was smoking cigars. She judged that he did not mean it to be offensive. He had a silver flask in his hip pocket, which he somehow timed to finish just as the coach came into each new station. Each time he drank, he offered it around the coach. It was a rule of the Northwestern Express, Stage, and Transportation Company.

And each time he offered it to the man named Captain Jack Crawford, the captain retold a story of promising his mother on her deathbed never to allow liquor to pass his lips. Agnes Lake did not drink whiskey herself, but the captain was pushing her in that direction.

She did not complain out loud, though. Not when he told the story of his promise, not when he told the story of his friendship with Bill Hickok. "If only I had been present when it happened," he said. And she noticed the awkward places he fit that into his story, and knew him for a liar.

He looked at her now and saw her discomfort. "It's nothing to be ashamed of, ma'am," he said, "to have a regurgitation. I have seen the hardest men in this country caused to do the same until they got their sea legs."

She stared at him, unblinking. Agnes Lake had cold eyes, but the captain was immune. "If you want, I could signal the driver to stop," he said. "He'd do it, on account of you being a lady." Everyone except Agnes Lake and the captain had already been sick, and the inside of the coach was sour enough now so the senses did not need Captain Jack Crawford's further suggestion.

The other passengers moved in their seats, trying to put it out of mind.

"I am quite comfortable," she said, looking into his eyes. She cramped, low in her stomach, and broke into a sweat. Her eyes were steady and calm. She had fallen once from the trapeze, thirty feet to the ground, and seen herself on the way down. She had seen other things too; some of them were comical. You never knew exactly when you would hit the ground, but that hadn't made her afraid to look.

And she stared into his eyes. The things that made Agnes Lake afraid—the things that had always made her afraid—were things that she couldn't see. She crossed her legs now, relieving the cramps, and looked out the window.

Captain Crawford watched the outline of her big legs under the skirts and then looked out the same window. "This is the richest country in the world," he said. "I've been from one end of the map to the other, ma'am, and this right here is the richest and the wildest and the best."

Agnes Lake stared at pine trees and wondered how the place had looked to Bill. Some of his letters—there were eight, and she carried all of them in her handbag—sounded like Captain Crawford, and some of them, when she thought back over them later, were telling her that he was dying. She knew she should never have let him out of her sight.

Agnes Lake was forty-two years old when she married Bill. She had been to Europe and Africa and Egypt, and to every city in America of sufficient population to attract a circus. She walked the tightrope and performed on the flying trapeze, and did tricks on horses that no one else did—man or woman. She could stand on a saddle horse at full gallop. With her own horses at canter, she could do flips on their backs, forwards and backwards. She was born with balance everywhere in her body, and had known it since she was three.

She was as strong as most men, but it was unnoticeable except in her legs, where she was stronger than any man. Bill had liked the muscles of her calves and told her not to be ashamed. He would find her like that out of nowhere, and touch her heart. No one else had ever seen that she was ashamed.

And he could say that one moment, and the next he would be staring at the sky, expounding on the nature of the problems it caused to be famous, like there was some secret to it that only the two of them knew. And that was as far from her interests as the moon.

"Are you able to continue?" the captain said. She brought her gaze back inside the coach and saw he was pale. She smiled now, but the smile seemed to bring back her cramps. "It wouldn't be any inconvenience whatsoever to notify the driver to pull over," he said. "It's been a long time between stops."

When she didn't answer, the captain leaned across the man with the flask and put his head out the window. He shouted twice, and she heard the driver shout back. She could not decipher the words, if it was words they were shouting.

As she watched, the trees on the side of the coach where Captain Crawford was conducting his conversation with the driver got closer. Then there was a sudden drop, as a wheel went off the road, and then the back end of the coach was going sideways and the driver was shouting at his horses. She heard the panic in his voice, she heard it as the horses themselves would hear it. Something fell past the window—she glimpsed it in her side vision—and then the farm boy next to her fell into her lap.

The coach lost a wheel and dropped again, farther this time, and she watched the faces across the aisle. She was not afraid. Captain Crawford rolled into the aisle and covered his head, and the boy in her lap began pushing against her legs, trying to right himself. His hands touched her thighs, but in the confusion and noise he did not notice their structure. The man with the flask and cigar fell into the aisle on top of Captain Crawford, and the boy rolled off her lap and joined them.

The coach hit a fallen tree and stopped. She saw it all; the others lay in their seats and on the floor, waiting for another concussion, until the driver opened the low-side door. Then they began to un-tangle themselves and open their eyes. Captain Crawford was first out of the coach. He stepped past the driver without a word and headed into the bushes.

Agnes Lake was last out, and as she stepped into the fresh air she was pleased to hear the captain vomiting. The driver took her hand as she came through the door. "Careful, miss," he said. "It's a tricky balance."

She smiled politely and disengaged her hand. Agnes Lake did not enjoy the touch of skin. She walked behind the coach, and then to the front. The horses were lathered and excited, and one had been blowing blood from his nostrils, probably for miles. None of them seemed hurt, although the larger of the lead horses was cut on both legs.

The messenger had fallen off fifty yards up the road, and when she looked he was limping toward them, cradling a muddy shot-gun. She studied his face and saw it was fortunate that he was warranteed gentlemanly.

"When I looked, you was gone," the driver said to him.

The messenger saw Agnes Lake watching them and smiled when he spoke. "When you looked at what?" he said. "You sure as hell wasn't looking at the road." He nodded to her then, and touched his hat, which was muddy and squashed. " 'Secuse my language, ma'am," he said, showing teeth.

"You was asleep," the driver said.

The messenger nodded to Agnes Lake and touched his hat again. "Perhaps we ought to walk into the woods a little ways and discuss it," he said.

"Perhaps you goddamn right we ought to," the driver said. He was not warranteed, and under no obligations to watch his language. They went into the trees, and Agnes Lake walked back up the road toward the place where the accident began. The wheel had come off where the messenger did—the tracks left the road back there and a trench began a few yards beyond. The loose wheel had rolled to a rest against the slope in the ground.

The axle had dragged through the mud for twenty yards or so, and then hit the tree that stopped it. She noticed the thickness of the pine, thinking one of the horses could have broken a leg. The axle had torn the bark off the tree trunk and wedged itself between the trunk and the biggest branch; you could not lift the axle without lifting the tree.

She felt the cramps again and walked back to the coach, keeping the hurry out of her steps. She found a toilet kit in one of her traveling bags. She crossed the road—the opposite side from Captain Crawford and the driver and messenger—and found a place to take care of herself.

When she returned, the other passengers, including Captain Crawford, were standing together beside the coach, talking about Indians. The messenger and the driver were still in the trees fighting. The man with the flask took a drink but, removed from the coach's regulations, did not offer it around. In the woods, the driver screamed once. The farm boy who had fallen across Agnes Lake's lap jumped at the sound of the yell. The captain noticed it and laughed.

"That's not Indians," he said. "That was a bite. I'd say a finger, most likely." And he winked at her. Agnes Lake felt a crawling come over her, and made herself move to keep it from settling.

The peddler and the man with the flask sat on the ground against one of the coach's remaining wheels. They each lit cigars. The noises from the trees were slower now. Agnes Lake noticed the captain watching her again. His eyes went down her body to her feet. His gaze was not the rudest she had come across, but it was plain enough in its intention, and she felt the crawling come over her again. She moved away.

Those gazes always made her move. Not the men themselves, but the intentions.

Agnes Lake was forty-three years old, and could have passed for twenty years younger anywhere there were farm women for comparison. She had always eaten fruits and stayed out of the sun. It was the sun and absence of citrus that aged women. She saw them everywhere in their hats on their way to church, baked and washed out, sitting in wagons with their farmer husbands and four or five barefoot children. The work had turned them old too. It seemed to Agnes Lake that, more than the work, they shrank under the weight of knowing it was always there to do. She saw these women and pitied them, turning old in the fields, still bearing their husbands' children. It seemed to her that at the least, the husbands could notice what they had done to their wives' looks and leave them alone at night.

She knew, though, that there were things between farmers and their wives that she didn't understand, and never judged them openly.

The captain's gaze found her face, and he smiled. The feeling ran fresh over her body, and she moved again to keep it from settling. She did not want to wake up in the night feeling that look on her skin. She walked past him and climbed onto the driver's seat of the coach. The horses stirred and she calmed them with soft words. "Here, now," she said.

She found the toolbox under the messenger's seat. The lock was broken. There were two hammers inside it and a mallet, a bottle of Huron City mineral spirits and a bottle of Hood's Sarsaparilla, a blond wig, and a small axe. Under the wig were a dozen modern cartridges loose on the floor of the box. There was no saw.

She took the axe and the mallet and jumped to the ground, landing as softly as if she had been dropped there by the wind. The others noticed the jump and regarded her in a new way. None of them moved. She put the tools on the trunk of the tree next to the axle of the coach and walked back up the road for the wheel.

She set the wheel on its rim and rolled it back toward the coach. It was not dissimiliar to setting Bill on the vertical and walking him to bed. The trick was all in the balance. The captain took off his hat and moved to help her, and doing that, he stepped in front of the wheel. It bounced into his legs and then dropped onto the ground.

"Let me help you with that, miss," he said. He retrieved the wheel and winked at the others. "Now," he said when he had it up, "where were you taking it to, anyway?"

"This will do nicely," she said. "If you would just hold it." The captain smiled and held the wheel. She turned her back on him and picked up the axe, and went to work on the fallen tree.

She started at the base of the branch where the axle was caught, cutting down twice, then once across. The limb was a foot thick and the wood was still fresh. The sap streaked the axe blade, and the air filled with its smell.

Agnes Lake cut with short, accurate strokes. She guided the axe into the base of the limb, but did not try to do its work. The power came from the top of her swing, and seemed connected in some way not only to her arms and shoulders, but to her back and legs. Captain Jack Crawford stood behind her, holding the wheel, holding his smile. The man with the flask seemed to toast her before he drank.

There was a rhythm to her work. There was the sound of the axe hitting the tree—two down and one to the side—and a little gasp just before, as she sent it down again and again. The wood caught the axe on the deeper cuts, and she pried it out, and then returned the blade to the same spot, as if to punish it. The wood came out in wedges and flew up over her head.

The others watched, and in a quarter of an hour the sound of the axe against the tree changed, and a few strokes afterwards the limb holding the axle broke loose from the trunk, and she pushed it away.

"A woman that can wield an axe is a gift from God to her husband," the captain said, smiling again.

She was perspiring now and damp-backed. It was a good feeling, after all the hours cramped inside the coach. "If you would be kind enough to bring the wheel to the other side of this tree," she said, "I believe we can repair the coach."

Captain Jack Crawford looked at the axle and shook his head. "It's too low to the ground," he said. "Half a foot at least."

The peddler got up off the ground and looked too. "I'm afraid he's right, miss," he said to her. "When the driver and the messenger come back, we'll have to rig a pulley to lift it up." She did not answer them. The cramps returned, and she walked across the road and found another place in the woods.

The summer complaint gave her chills, and she began to shake, feeling her skin against the damp dress. She stayed in the woods a long time, until the sensations eased. When she came back to the coach, the driver and the messenger had finished their business. She noticed the way they regarded each other and knew it was not over for good. From their looks the messenger had gotten the best of it—the driver's left eye was closed and he'd taken a fearful bite on the cheek, while the messenger was only dabbing at a bloody nose—but she had been hurt herself, and knew that the worst injuries did not always reveal themselves to others.

The men had rolled the wheel next to the empty axle and were measuring the distance they needed to lift the axle—and the coach—to slide the wheel back on. "It's half a foot, at least," the captain said.

The messenger gave him a long look but kept his thoughts to himself. He was warranteed polite, in emergencies as well as when events ran normal. "If all the men lifted, we might get it up, boys," the captain said.

The messenger closed his eyes. The new Concord coaches were built as heavy as banks. The driver spit blood. "We ought put the horses in there and lift them too," he said. "Or just wait for a train, and we could pick up that."

"We're seven able men," the captain said. He went to the axle and gave it a meaningless tug. The driver wasn't watching. He looked into the woods and finally spotted a narrow, smooth-skinned tree with gray bark, and he went for that with the axe.

It took him about as long to drop the tree as it had taken Agnes Lake to remove the branch. His work was not as pretty as hers, though, and he missed the spot often. Once he missed the whole tree. Agnes Lake stood away from the men, studying the axle and the wheel and the ground.

Presently, the driver cussed and the tree fell. He took the branches off the trunk, and then cut the last ten feet off the top. "What we got to do," he said when he was back, "is to wedge this here under the axle and lift the coach up whilst one of us fits the wheel back on."

Before there was time for objections, he moved behind the coach to find a spot to place the tree. There was no boulder or tree stump there to use as a fulcrum for the lever, so the driver placed the thick end of the tree under the coach, and everyone but the messenger and Agnes Lake found a spot on the tapered end and pushed up.

The wagon moved forward a foot or two, and then rocked back to the spot it had been. "We got to have more back in it than that," the driver said. "It's a long walk in if we don't."

"All right, boys," the captain said, "on the count of three. Wild Bill and I once pulled a full-grown moose up a hundred-foot gully, just the two of us, on the count of three. This problem here is child's play, compared to that."

They blocked the front wheels and pushed again, and the back end of the coach rose an inch or two, and then dropped. "Son of a bitch," the driver said.

They tried again. The coach came up, the same inch, and then dropped. "We got to build a goddamn pulley," the driver said. All the passengers except Captain Jack Crawford let go of the tree. "One more time," the captain said. "We can get it, boys."

The driver looked at the messenger for the first time since Agnes Lake came out of the woods. "I hate the ones that enjoy an accident," he said. The messenger held on to his ribs.

"Pardon me," Agnes Lake said, "but there's a spot twenty yards up the road—"

"'Secuse me for sayin' so, ma'am," the driver said, "but we got a situation here, and need quiet to think it out." It was quiet for a minute or two, and then the driver cussed and they all lined up again on the tree and pushed until the peddler fell on the ground and the driver's nose bled. "Son of a bitch," he said.

Agnes Lake said, "I do not mean to interrupt—"

The driver had thrown his head back and was holding his nose with the fingers of both hands, his feet spread apart as if to hold the weight. "'Secuse me for sayin' so, ma'am," he said, "but can't you see ever' damn thing in creation's gone to hell?"

Agnes Lake put her hands on her hips and looked around her. Only the messenger met her eyes. He was hurt inside, she saw it clearly now.

She walked to the coach, kicked the blocks from under the front wheels, and climbed onto the driver's seat. "I ain't responsible," the driver said behind her. "She's determined to get her neck broke, and I ain't responsible, and neither is the Northwestern Express, Stage, and Transportation Company, unless she gets off there right now."

She untied the reins and calmed the horses. "Here, now," she said. The horses moved slowly, in a straight line, until the coach was clear of the fallen tree. The empty axle rode a foot lower than the center of the wheels, and a strong wind would have blown the whole thing over. " 'Secuse me, ma'am," the driver said behind her. "Ma'am?"

She kept the horses slow and steady, headed on a diagonal back up onto the road, bringing the one remaining inside wheel within a few inches of the drop in the shoulder. Then she stopped the coach next to the drop, calming the horses again, set the brake, and climbed down. She blocked the front wheels and walked past the driver, who was following her now, trying to talk.

She picked the wheel up and set it on the road.

The driver followed her down and followed her back up. " 'Secuse me," he said. "Ma'am?"

She rolled the wheel down the road to the coach, and then off the road until it rested a foot beneath the empty axle. She wiped her hands, and then fit them underneath the wheel and lifted. The weight of it shook her arms as she fit it over the axle.

No one moved to help. When the lip of the wheel casing slipped over the axle, though, the messenger produced the mallet she had taken from the toolbox. He did not try to hammer the wheel on himself. That was the easy part, and he left it for her to finish.

She liked him for that.

When she had finished with the mallet, he turned to the driver and said, "You think you could find the lady a lock pin so's she could finish saving us, or you going to stand there with your thumb up your sitter and wait for the Indians?"

The driver looked at what she had done. He said, "Son of a bitch," and climbed up into his seat and found a pin in the toolbox to replace the one that had broken. Without another word, he hammered the pin into the axle and then climbed back into his seat and waited for the others to load.

They took the same seats they'd had before, with Agnes Lake between the farm boy and the peddler, staring across the aisle at Captain Jack Crawford. She smoothed her skirt over her legs, and he smiled at her in a secret way.

"There's some women, they can do as much as a man," he said after a while. She put her eyes on him, flat and hard. He didn't care. "I noticed you weren't wearing a wedding ring."

She looked down at her fingers, which were short and thick and strong. There had been a ring, a family ring, but it was too small.

She wore it on a chain beneath her blouse. Bill had hung it there himself, a few minutes after the ceremony. He'd said, "It fits fine." She touched her chest now, pressing the ring into her skin.

"It's a hard country for a woman alone," the captain said.

"I have been alone before," she said.

THE NEWS OF WILD BILL'S ASSASSINATION REACHED JANE CANNARY at the first bar she entered after her escape from Sister of Mercy Hospital. It was early September. She was walking with a crutch, and had not bathed since she broke her leg.

The doctor at the hospital was a young woman, who had told her that she had been thrown and then kicked by a bull on Main Street. "I expected as much," Jane said, looking at her leg. It was wrapped and heavy, and tied to the ceiling. She had just come to.

The doctor said it was a double fracture. "We thought it was a skull fracture too," she said.

Jane said that was a hoot. "I got double-thickness," she said, and rapped herself on the crown of her head. "They ain't invented the bull yet that could penetrate this."

She was in the hospital five weeks, waiting for the woman doctor to cut her leg off the ceiling. In the end she did it herself, with a letter opener, and hobbled two blocks back toward Main Street until she found a bar. She expected that was how the hospital business ran—when you were well enough to wean, you'd figure a way out. She had taken an interest in the hospital business, watching the doctor for her own use later, but after two weeks it began to repeat itself, and she saw that she had learned all she was going to. The rest was a matter of waiting to leave. That and mending. The break was just above the knee, and sometimes at night it seemed to her that she felt a tiny hammering in there as it was repaired.

And that was one of the first things she explained when she walked into the bar on Main Street. "The human body," she said to the bartender, "is the only true doctor there is. Mine has been working an extra shift, and now desires a drink."

She drank four shots of whiskey in about half an hour, and then her leg started to hurt. "Get the hammer, boys," she said. "I may need to be hit over the head."

The bartender was not interested in healing, though, and the men in the place gave her a wide berth. She got tired of waiting to be recognized and when the bartender had poured her another, she grabbed his wrist and held on until he met her eyes. "I hereby charge you with the duty to keep me away from them bulls," she said.

The bartender squinted and looked closer. "Calamity?"

She nodded and released his wrist. "I'd heard you was in town, riding bulls agin," he said. He started to smile now. "But there wasn't no picture in the paper."

"I didn't give notice," she said. "Sometimes it just comes over me to ride a bull before they can collect the reporters."

The bartender called down to the other customers. "Come over here and meet Calamity Jane," he said. The others looked at each other and stayed where they were. Every third drunk whore in Rapid City claimed to be Calamity Jane. "It's the real goods," the bartender said. "I seen her picture in the paper from last time. Broke her leg riding bulls on Main Street, come look if she ain't lame."

And the others picked up their drinks and came to the front end of the bar for a closer look. She pulled her hat brim down even with her eyes and turned to face them. She rested her elbows on the bar and let her fingers hang loose, an inch above her pistols.

There were half a dozen men, and they moved closer a step at a time. The bartender stood behind, smiling like he'd invented her. "See?" he said. "What'd I tell you?"

She picked her glass up off the bar and drank what was inside it. Without looking back, she held it over her shoulder to be refilled. "All I asked for was a hammer, boys," she said. "I didn't intend to stand parade inspection for you sheep-lovers."

"It's her," one of them said. And they began to smile, the same way the bartender did, and before long, against her wishes, she was smiling too. "I heard you was with Custer the night before Little Big Horn," one of them said.

She scratched her head. "I can't say," she said. "It could of been then, it could of been the night after." She threw down the new drink and began to feel comfortable, everywhere but her leg. She moved from the bar to a chair, and had the men situate her foot on another chair. When the relief came, she noticed she was sweating. She wondered if maybe she'd left the hospital before she was ready.

"I heard you was with Wild Bill too," one of them said. They had all followed her to the table, like there was something they wanted.

"Me and Bill is as close as a shell in its casing," she said.

One of the customers said he had heard different stories about what had happened.

She felt it coming then. "What stories?"

"I heard Bill had shot the man's family back in Kansas," the man said, "and then I heard the man had no reason at all. Just snuck up out of meanness and did his work."

"What are you saying?" she said.

"Just what I heard of how it happened."

She sat up and narrowed her eyes. She felt dizzy from too long in a bed.

"How he got kilt," he said. "You knew he got kilt, didn't you? Being close, I thought you'd of known . . ."

Jane's hat had fallen back on her head, and she tightened it now, down over her eyes the way she liked it.

"Close," she said, "shit, Wild Bill Hickok was my husband." And saying those words, she heard her voice break.

She meant to find her horse and ride directly to Deadwood that afternoon. She did not care about the Indians. She walked on her crutch to a livery off Dakota Street and asked there about the animal. "His name is Warpaint," she said. "A handsome gray stallion, got a peeder on him, he could join the circus . . ."

The man at the livery knew the horse. "The animal-lovers brought him in here about a month ago," he said. "He died."

"Died?" she said. "Warpaint died too?" She grabbed the livery man by the front of the shirt and pulled him close. "What'd he die of?" she said. "He was perfect, the last I saw him."

The livery man let himself be grabbed. "Old age," he said.

"That's a damn lie," she said. "That pretty old gray wasn't but eleven years old."

The livery man did not mind being called a liar, it went with the horse business. "He wasn't gray but in the face," he said. "Didn't have a tooth left in his mouth."

She let go of him and sat down on some hay. Her leg ached and she needed morphine. "The truth is," she said after a while, "I can't do much riding with this broke leg anyway."

The livery man scratched his head. "I'm a widow now," she said, "and I got to travel to Deadwood and make sure they done right by burying my husband."

He stood over her, looking at her crutch. She thought he looked sympathetic. "Perhaps you heard of him," she said. "Wild Bill Hickok."

He looked at her in the same way. He touched the crutch. "You heard of Calamity Jane Cannary?" she said.

"Yes, I did," he said.

"Then you know I'm good to my word. My money's in Deadwood, but if you rent me a horse and buggy, I'll pay when I return, the day after tomorrow."

He shook his head. "It ain't what I heard, that you were good to your word," he said. "I heard you ride bulls on Main Street."

"I got to get to Deadwood," she said. "My husband's been murdered."

He scratched under his hat. "You probably got a swamp fungus on your head," she said. "Let it alone and stay out of the rain."

He picked up her crutch. "This here," he said. "I'll rent the buggy, four dollars a day, and you can pick this up when you return, the day after tomorrow."

"I can't walk five steps," she said. "What am I supposed to do without my crutch?"

"It's to remind you," he said. "When you take a step, you'll remember you got somebody's horse and buggy."

She left the crutch with the livery man and took the road to Sturgis, where she spent the night with a doctor in trade for morphine, and then approached Deadwood from the northeast the next day. She had not eaten since she left the hospital and felt weak from the toes up. The doctor had given her an extra needle in the morning, for a promise never to mention his name to any living person, and the thought of food turned her stomach queasy.

She drove the buggy without urgency, without the idea of time at all. Her thoughts of Bill were slow and sweet. She pictured his gratitude if she had been at the bar to save him. He would have married her afterwards. She pictured them in front of the church, standing together for the photographers, each of them holding a buffalo gun.

The buggy hit rocks and holes, hurting her leg, but the hurt seemed unconnected in some way she couldn't get a fix on. And it didn't seem like anything she needed to get a fix on. She stopped twice to drink from streams, parking the buggy a yard or two from the water and crawling to the edge. Coming back, she would pull herself up with the wheels.

The second time she stopped, she looked into the water before she drank, and she stayed there, frozen, on her hands and knees a quarter of an hour, staring at her reflection. She was twenty-nine years old, and never had looked at herself and seen pretty before.

The sun moved in the sky and the buggy followed the sun, and Jane sat watching, until it came to her that she was in the middle of circling events and places. She thought if she got enough time on earth, it would all come by again. "The next time," she said out loud, "I won't leave you a minute, Bill. I will be there in the bar when this skunk-lover comes in, and we will see him answer for this cowardice . . ."

The trail flattened and then began to climb. Time hung in the air with the sun, and somehow it moved. Presently, she came around a formation of rocks and realized she was looking at the city. She smelled a trick—it didn't feel like more than an hour since she left Sturgis—but she saw the sun had moved again, and she saw the Gem Theater, and decided not to concern herself further with time.

She sat taller and straightened her leg across the floor of the buggy; she pulled her hat brim even with her eyes, and drove through town. The horse did not like the mud, and she used the whip to encourage him. She did not curse him, though, the way she would have cursed bulls, because horses were more complicated and sensitive. You could say the wrong thing to a horse and he wouldn't move at all.

She drove past the Gem and the Green Front, noticing three new bars in the badlands, waiting to be recognized. It wasn't until she got into town proper, though, that she saw someone she knew. It was Sheriff Bullock, who tipped his hat. She pulled the horses up and tipped her hat back. "Morning," she said. The word seemed to come out slower than it was supposed to.

"Miss Cannary," he said.

"I have been injured and laid up in Rapid City," she said, "and have just now returned to visit the grave of my husband." The sheriff stared up into the buggy, wordless. "My leg was injured, or I'd of been here for the burial," she said.

"I didn't know you had married," he said. "Not that you wouldn't make someone a wife . . ."

She laughed and felt the sun lying across the horse's back. "You knowed about me and Bill," she said. "Everybody knowed about us."

The sheriff was wordless again, and she didn't trust the time to pass at regular speed, or she would have waited him out. "I intend to mourn him now," she said, "and then track the assassin, so's I can sleep again at night, knowing Bill's avenged."

"Too late, miss," he said. "Jack McCall's been arrested in Cheyenne and taken to Yankton for trial and hanging."

The news hit Jane as hard as the assassination itself. "That ain't right," she said. "He's mine, I got privleges in this." The sheriff looked up and down the street, as if he was embarrassed to be seen talking to her. She didn't move. "A widder's got privleges," she said.

"Jack McCall would never of got caught, except for his own self," the sheriff said. "He went into Cheyenne pulling that old rusty gun out of his pants every twenty minutes, anybody that didn't believe he'd done Wild Bill, Jack McCall put his gun under their nose. What I heard, the deputy arrested him twice for it, and then got the U.S. marshal. It was the marshal who said a miner's court wasn't a legal trial and took him back to Yankton."

"It ain't fair," she said.

"It's his own doing," the sheriff said. "A man puts his own head in the noose, you can't feel tender for his neck." The sheriff looked up into the buggy and saw Jane was crying. "Here now, miss," he said, "the law is the law . . ."

She wiped at her cheeks with the back of her hand. "Where is my husband?" she said.

He studied her a moment, deciding if this was any of his business. "The far end of the cemetery," he said.

"By hisself?" she said. "You didn't put him in next to Chinese or soft-brains, did you? Or miners."

"He's got his own place," the sheriff said. He saw Jane's face change. Like a different person. She opened her mouth then, slowly, and made her eagle scream. Then she whipped the horse and headed south on Main Street, and then turned east on Pine, in the direction of the cemetery.

The sheriff wondered whose horse and buggy she'd stolen. He hoped it was somebody a long way off, who would not think to look in the Black Hills.

CHARLEY UTTER CUT DOWN THE STUMP MARKING BILL'S GRAVE AND replaced it with a marker of his own.

Wild Bill—J. B. Hickok. Killed by the assassin Jack McCall in Deadwood Black Hills August 2nd 1876.

Pard we will meet again in the Happy Hunting ground to part no more. Good bye—Colorado Charley, C. H. Utter

He burned the letters into a piece of good oak and nailed that to a fence post. He was pounding the post into the ground when he heard the buggy. He stopped his work and reached for his shirt, not to offend widows or children visiting the deceased.

Before he got to the first button, though, he heard Jane's voice. "Git up, now," she said to the horse, "git, git, git . . ." He buttoned himself faster and turned around in time to see the horse skid in the mud. Jane whipped him until he straightened. Then she pulled back hard against his bit. He wondered where she'd stolen him.

She said, "Whoa, there, damnit, whoa . . ."

The horse stopped and Charley stood still. "Colorado Charley," she said over the sounds of the horse. "I didn't expect to find you."

Charley didn't answer. "I been hurt," she said, "or I would of been here sooner." He nodded. "It's my leg," she said. "I broke it two places, so they tied it to the ceiling in Rapid City."

Charley noticed the creases in her neck had a green hue. He surmised it was mold. She saw him staring and pulled the brim of her hat down even with her eyes, but there was more wrong than shadows could cover.

"You got bad legs yourself, as I remember," she said.

"Not too bad," he said. The work had started them aching, though, and he knew it would be three or four days before they gave him any peace.

"They tie yours to the ceiling?" she said.

Charley shook his head. He didn't like to talk about his leg injuries with just anybody. There was something in the nature of bad legs that people felt free to bring up their condition as polite conversation, like the weather. It was like they all had an equal stake in it.

"Well, they tied mine," she said, "and left me more than a month, whilst poor Bill got shot with nobody there to watch his back."

Charley felt the bite in that, but let it pass. Bill was like bad legs—common property. "I heard the coward's been arrested and took to Yankton," she said.

"I heard that."

"A pity," she said, "that Bill's friends couldn't of caught up with him first, and done it, tit for tat." She slid over the seat of the buggy and looked at him closer. It was mold, all right, and she smelled like a dead cat.

"I thought you would of done it yourself," she said.

He shook his head. "You don't know a thing about it."

She pulled back away from him and fixed him a stare. "Ain't no call to talk like that," she said. "I got as much stake in this as anybody, I expect."

"You don't have any such thing," he said.

"The hell I don't. That man was my husband."

Charley stood dead still and looked up into the buggy. She pulled her hat down farther on her head and said it again. "We was married," she said.

He stared at her, she stared back. "I'm not going to allow this," he said.

"I ain't after no inheritance," she said.

"I know what you're after," he said, "and you can't have it."

She moved again and began to lower herself out of the buggy. She put her weight on her arms and he saw that she was going to fall. Against his will, he grabbed her sides and saved her.

She stood on one leg when he let her go, looking at the new grave marker. "That ain't bad for now," she said, "but Bill ought to have a statue."

He looked at what he'd done and thought she was probably right. "It's temporary," he said. "They put one up before this, it said Bill was forty-eight years old."

She laughed out loud. "He wasn't but twenty-seven when we got married," she said. He picked the sledgehammer back up and finished pounding the post into the ground. He felt her behind him, watching.

"The man at the livery took my crutch," she said. "To remind me whose buggy it was. I never heard of anywhere but Rapid City that they'd take a widder's crutch."

"You're no widow," he said, "unless you married an Indian and he committed suicide."

"I ain't going to set here arguing it in front of Bill's grave," she said. "I got more respect for the dead than that." She hobbled from the buggy to the head of the grave, and rested her weight on the marker. The move exhausted her, and she hung on to the marker like it was Bill himself.

"I hurt right down to my toes," she said after a while. "You never felt the way I do right now."

Charley looked her over and said, "Probably not."

She cried out then, and lowered herself onto the ground. He saw her leg bent a couple of inches below the knee. "It's a damn bobcat in there," she said, and he began to feel sorry.

"That's the healing," he said. "The more it hurts, the faster it mends." He made that up, and she believed it. Jane let go of the leg and lay on her back, holding her face in her hands.

"Is there a sawbones in this city would part with some morphine for a widder?" she said. "Or do they all want cash?"

"You never married Bill," he said. He would give her anything else, but not that.

"You wasn't with him every minute of his life," she said. "You wasn't even there when he got kilt, so how do you know what he done?"

"The same way I know a horse never climbed a tree," he said. She closed her fingers in front of her eyes and he saw he had hurt her feelings.

"It's true," she said. "Him and me loved each other."

"No," he said. Anything else, but not that.

"I can prove it," she said. "We was married in Lincoln, Nebraska, and I got the legal papers, except they took them at the hospital whilst my leg was tied to the ceiling."

Charley shook his head. "Bill never went to Lincoln except once by accident, from Chicago on the Union Pacific. He said the place was full of card cheats."

"It don't have to be Lincoln," she said, "but it was Nebraska. I remember that." And she began to cry again, in earnest. "That man and me was married," she said.

And he pitied her and let it go.

"Dr. O. E. Sick's got morphine," he said after a while, and that seemed to take her mind off Bill.

"Is he tight with a dollar? Would he trust me for it?"

"He doesn't care much about payment, now that you mention it."

She said, "That don't sound like a doctor."

Charley said, "I saw his work up close, and he can scowl as well as the next one."

She dried her cheeks with the back of her wrist and sat up. She touched her leg below the knee and made a painful face. Charley's own legs were pounding, and he wondered how long she meant to stay there on the ground.

"You might catch the doctor in his office, if you went now," he said. "He hates it to be summoned after office hours."

She shook her head. "I come out of a hospital bed to pay my respects, and I mean to do it before I deliver myself back into the hands of doctors." Charley waited. "You just going to stand there," she said after a while, "or you got enough manners to help a widder to her feet?" He got behind her and put his hands under her arms. She felt soft and unhealthy. He got her up, and she stood on one foot, looking down at the fresh grave. He started into the trees, to give her some privacy. "Where the hell are you going?" she said.

"I'll be back," he said. He walked fifty yards uphill and found her a straight piece of birch five feet long, almost no taper at all. A limb had been broken off about halfway up. He sat on the ground and put the wood between his legs and planed off the knots with his knife. He took the bark off the limb and rounded the end. It took less than ten minutes, and when he was finished he stood up and put one end against his shoulder and saw that the limb was a good height for a handle, and that the crutch was light enough so Jane would be able to use it.

He went back to the cemetery and found her still on one foot, leaning against the marker again. He stepped into dried branches, so she would hear him coming.

"You finished?"

She looked at him without answering, and he saw she needed something for the pain. "We can find the doctor now," he said. He handed her the piece of birch.

"I got to ast you something," she said. "Betwixt you and me, on threat of death if it gets out."

Charley shook his head. His own legs hurt, and he didn't like talking to Jane Cannary in a cemetery. "How come it's always got to be on threat of death?" he said. "How come you can't just ask me what you want to ask? How come you can't just feel bad for Bill like anybody else, instead of marrying him after he's gone?"

"We was married before," she said. He closed his eyes. "I can prove it."

"The doc will be closed soon," he said.

"He can wait a minute more." She bit her lip and framed her

question. "What I want to know is what you're s'posed to do at graveside."

He'd wondered the same thing.

"I come out of a hospital bed, compounded-fractured, to pay my respects, but I'm damned to hell if I can figure out what I'm doin' here, or what I'm s'posed to say."

"There isn't any rule," he said. "It's better not to say anything, though, than to lie. It's just you and the dead, so there's no reason to make anything up. It's sacrilegious."

Jane took it serious.

He walked back into the trees again, thinking that underneath all her habits and affectations, Jane was true. He heard her voice then, which got louder as he got farther away. "Bill," she said, "I'm sorry you got kilt from behind like that, and I'm sorry I wasn't there to help you when it happened." There was a pause while she drew breath.

"And it makes a girl feel horrible," she said, "to be away from her husband at a time such as that."

THE FUNERAL SERVICE FOR PREACHER SMITH WAS CONDUCTED BY Sheriff Seth Bullock, who read from the Episcopal Book of Common Prayer. It was the first Episcopal service ever held in Deadwood, and followed by one day the celebration of the China Doll's passing into the next world.

Among those attending both services was Malcolm Nash, who felt no preference, one over the other. He went from each service back to Preacher Smith's cabin, where he sat on the cot and waited. The preacher had taught him to wait. "You are lost, so shall you be found," he said. The preacher was writing a new Bible—the Bible of the Black Hills—and after he said that, he wrote it down in the book.

The book had red covers and sat on the table near the preacher's cot. It was still the preacher's cot; Malcolm slept on the floor. The book had three inches of pages—the biggest, heaviest diary you could buy at Farnum's—but only the first ten were written on. That's how far he had gotten. Preacher Smith said it was a life work, and then he'd looked at Malcolm and smiled. "Perhaps two lives," he said. And five days later was dead on the trail to Crook City.

A delegation of Methodists came to the cabin to look for an address for the preacher's wife. "At least the Indians didn't mutilate him," they said. "At least that."

There was no address in the cabin, nothing written down at all except the first ten pages of the Bible of the Black Hills, and Malcolm hid that. Preacher Smith had said it wasn't for everyday Christians. "This Bible is for those that seen too much," he said. "You will recognize them, because you have seen too much also." The boy accepted that, without remembering what it was that he had seen.

The preacher worked at the book in the evening, after he came back from the sawmill. He bent over his writing, his left hand curled around his pen. The boy could see from the look on his face that it hurt to write.

He was afraid to be hurt.

Preacher Smith believed God spoke through his hand, and he told the boy that God might speak through his hand too, when it was his turn. And when the preacher was buried and quiet, with a dozen tears in his chest where the arrows and knives had been, the boy looked at the new Bible and hoped it wasn't his turn yet.

He walked to the table near the cot and let his fingers touch the letters that Preacher Smith had pressed into the cover. BIBLE OF THE BLACK HILLS. Beneath that, he had drawn a sketch of the Hills. An angel with a serpent's head and a halo hung over the mountain peaks.

It was a perfect serpent—detailed right down to the indentations below the eyes—and an imperfect angel. The angel-serpent was the first thing Preacher Smith drew, and the boy commented on the exactness of the snake's head.

"That's because I seen a snake," the preacher said. And the boy stared at him a long time that night, after the preacher had gone to sleep, because he had thought all ministers had seen angels.

He traced the serpent head with his finger now; the preacher had pressed it deep into the Bible. Then the boy opened the book, before he had time to consider the consequences, and stared at the first page.

THE BOOK OF HIRAM

In the beginning, there was the Hills and God, who is of two sides. In these regions, His evil side roamed, whilst His good occupied Itself in places where it was flatter and easier to see. Like Kansas.

And whilst He created light and dark, and the seas and land, and

man and woman; His evil side created the Indians and put gold in the
earth.

   And God did not know that was what His evil side did, but
dreamed it at night, in dreams He could not remember when He woke.
And God was afraid, because he knew of His evil side, but did not
know how powerful it was.

The boy closed the book and put it back on the table. He stared
at the serpent's head, and saw Preacher Smith's body laid out naked
and torn and white in the back room of the barber shop. And he
saw that the preacher was right, and saw what the evil side of the
Lord had done.

He was suddenly fearful, and sat down on the cot. He knew,
even before the thought shaped in his head, that it had been given
to him to finish the preacher's work. Not to finish the Bible of the
Black Hills—the boy could barely write—but to find the evil side
of the Lord, the one that had spoke to Preacher Smith in his
dreams.

He did not know where the battleground would be, it did not
concern him, now that he saw his purpose. He lay back on the
preacher's cot and found it accommodated his size. He closed his
eyes and waited. It was a time of change in the forces of good and
evil, and the boy had been picked. He waited to see what for.

He saw the preacher again, laid out on a table in back of the
barber shop. One of his long, thin arms hung almost all the way to
the floor. The boy moved on the cot, clearing his head of the picture, and in a little while another came.

And this picture was the evil side of the Lord. It had a beard and
a hard peeder, and it came after him while others held him helpless.
When he opened his eyes the room was dark. He was afraid again,
and a sweat had broken out over his chest and stomach and head.
Afraid right down to his fingers and toes.

He lay on the cot, listening for noises in the night. He remembered the preacher had seen things in his sleep too, and had been
fearful of them.

The boy tried to remember what the evil side of the Lord had
looked like, but it would not come back. He couldn't remember
what it had done, but he still shook in its consequences. He lay
the rest of the night with his eyes open, afraid to return to his
dreams.

And the next night he went back to his spot on the floor, and the
dreams did not follow him there.

He stayed out of the preacher's cot.

In the mornings he got up as soon as the sky turned rose in the north and made a fire. He ate the preacher's food and then straightened his house. Then he walked down the steep hill into Deadwood, dressed in the preacher's black coat, and wandered the streets, waiting to confront the evil side of the Lord. Knowing he wasn't ready. He covered the town from south to north, and then entered Chinatown.

Sometimes the whores in the badlands threw firecrackers at him from their windows, sometimes Johnny the Oyster—the Trickster of the Badlands—would induce him to sit on a tack. But the boy kept to his purpose, at least as long as the sun was up. At dusk he returned to the cabin and lay in the corner, trembling at the thought that the thing he looked for during the day was looking for him at night.

He kept no track of days or weeks, and did not know how long he had been at his work when he finally saw what he was after.

He had walked to the far north end of Deadwood and was coming back, stalled at the fork in the road where Main Street and Sherman Street divided, when he saw Al Swearingen. The boy did not recognize him in the ordinary meaning of the word—he did not remember him from the wagon train or the afternoon Swearingen and the others had come to his camp by the Whitewood—he only looked at him and felt afraid clear through, and knew as clear as the moon in the afternoon sky, he was looking at the evil side of the Lord.

Swearingen was crossing Sherman Street when the boy saw him. He turned a corner and headed east on Wall Street, about two hundred yards south of the fork. The boy began to run. By the time he came to Wall Street, Al Swearingen was just reaching Main, and turned north, back toward the Gem Theater.

The boy ran, throwing mud up over his shoulders, his feet making sucking noises in the street. And there was a different kind of sucking as the air came into his lungs. He reached Main Street in time to see Swearingen turn into the theater, and the boy stopped running.

When he caught his breath, he walked to a bench in front of the Bella Union, across the street from the Gem, and sat down to think. In a few minutes he realized he couldn't remember the man's features, except his beard.

The evil side of the Lord had took a man's body, and looked out through his eyes. The boy stayed the rest of the day, watching the doors, but the man never came out. He considered the chance that the evil side of the Lord might have disguised his looks, but it was not his features that the boy had recognized.

The boy did not leave the bench until the sun had moved behind the hills and the air had turned cool. He did not keep track of time, but he noticed the season was changing. He stood up, still watching the Gem Theater, and began to walk back up Main Street to the south.

And that night, lying on the floor in the dark, the thought suddenly came to him that he occupied the preacher's cabin the same way the evil side of the Lord occupied the bearded man's body.

The air in the cabin was cold and the boy curled into himself, and he wondered if it was cold where the evil side of the Lord was too.

THE NEWS THAT BILL HICKOK'S WIFE HAD MOVED INTO A ROOM AT THE Grand Union reached Mrs. Langrishe at home, a few minutes after she returned from a reception for General George Crook and his officers.

The general had led his men into Deadwood the day before and spoken from the steps of the hotel. He described the destruction of a small Indian village at Slim Buttes, and spoke his hopes that the U.S. Army would be brought into the Hills permanently to protect the good people of Deadwood from the dusky foe and all those who would befriend them.

He was then greeted from one end of town to the other; women and men both kissed his hand. He lost more than a score of men in the badlands, that many being pulled from their horses by the whores and taken into the dark corners of the Gem and the Green Front and the Bella Union.

The next morning, the general and his officers went to Jack Langrishe's theater, where they shook hands with all comers. Mrs. Langrishe dressed herself in lavender and enjoyed the way the officers looked at her chest. She overheard Mayor Farnum telling the general that his men were always welcome at the bathhouse. Which was a study in good manners, because the pony soldiers stunk worse than Chinatown. She sometimes wished the rest of the town was more like Mayor Farnum.

And two hours later her husband came into her bedroom, before she even took off her party dress, and said, "The widow of Wild Bill Hickok has arrived at the Grand Union." Jack's announcements always came out of his mouth sounding like offstage voices.

It seemed to her an occasion for another reception. "Any woman married to Mr. Hickok has the social graces," she said. "I am certain of that."

"Whatever you want, blossom," he said.

She sat at her desk to make an invitation list. She decided to hold the reception at home. The theater was too big, and she wanted the affair to feel warm. She decided on Sunday afternoon, coffee and rolls and sweet butter. "Do you think we should serve liquor, Jack?"

"If you want, blossom."

"I don't think so," she said. "It might still be too close to the assassination." She made her list, beginning with Mayor Farnum, Sheriff Seth Bullock, and Solomon Star. Then she added all the businessmen in town, except tavern owners, owners of theaters of ill repute, Jews, and coloreds. Then she added the most amusing bachelors she knew in Deadwood and finally, Charley Utter.

She did not consider Charley Utter amusing—although she did remember the way his member rose up under her touch as they sat in the theater, and again in her living room before his imbecile friend had fallen through her window. She had no use for softbrains, or those that encouraged them, but she overlooked that now. Charley was Bill's true friend, and she wanted the widow to feel herself among friends.

"Perhaps we could serve wine. That might warm the event without reflecting disrespect."

Jack was looking at himself in the dressing mirror, pulling his moustache up to see his teeth. She saw that he was on his toes; he always stood on his toes in front of the mirror.

"Whatever you want," he said.

When he had left her room she counted the names on the list. There were thirty-three. She pictured herself and the widow of Bill Hickok, entertaining thirty-three men.

She changed clothes and put a shawl around her shoulders—it was September, and the afternoons could turn unexpectedly cold—and went out of the house.

"Perhaps you could invite Mrs. Hickok to the theater," he said as she walked out the door.

She kissed the top of his head. "Jack," she said, "the woman has just lost her husband . . ."

Elizabeth Langrishe found Agnes Lake Hickok sitting at a window table in the dining room of the Grand Union Hotel, looking out over the street, eating asparagus and eggs. Her first thought was that the woman was too old. Her presumption was that Bill's wife would be beautiful and young and helpless. Mrs. Langrishe had looked forward to offering her the advice of a mature woman.

But the lady sitting next to the window was at least thirty—Mrs. Langrishe's age—and not pretty in an ordinary way. There was something self-assured about her, though. Yes, it was Bill's wife. Mrs. Langrishe watched her half a minute and changed some of her thoughts about Bill Hickok.

Agnes Lake suddenly looked up and met her stare. Bill's wife had eyes like Bill himself—like there was nothing playful in this world—and the thought blew through Mrs. Langrishe's mind that this woman might shoot her.

She walked across the room, hearing her feet on the floor, conscious of her clothes and what another woman of her own age and experience might make of them. She stopped over the table and Mrs. Hickok looked up with flat eyes and no interest.

"Mrs. Hickok?" Agnes Lake nodded. Elizabeth Langrishe smiled a believable smile—she could smile at her own hanging—and offered her hand. Mrs. Hickok took it, and Mrs. Langrishe sensed its uncommon strength. She had never encountered a woman with hands like these. They had the same thickness as Jack's, but Mrs. Hickok's were rougher to the touch, and harder. They were too clean to have done field work.

"I am Elizabeth Langrishe," she said. "My husband operates the legitimate theater . . ." Mrs. Hickok stared at her, waiting. "We were friends of your husband's," she said. "Not close, but Bill often enjoyed an evening at the theater."

Elizabeth Langrishe let go and Agnes Lake put her hand in her lap. "He had an appreciation of the fine arts," Mrs. Langrishe said.

"I didn't know that."

Elizabeth Langrishe sat down, feeling vaguely poleaxed. "He was a man of a multitude of interests," Mrs. Langrishe said. Then she blushed and put a hand against her cheek. "Here I sit," she said, "telling you about your own husband . . ."

"I am grateful to know anything you might tell me," she said, and Mrs. Langrishe saw her a different way. "Bill and I weren't together long."

"No woman understands her husband all the way through," Mrs. Langrishe said. "I have been with my Jack nine years . . ." She had begun to say she didn't understand him at all, but she stopped, suddenly not wanting to lie. She shook her head. "Jack isn't like your Bill," she said.

Agnes wiped at the corner of her mouth with a napkin. She felt ashamed for what she'd said about herself and Bill. "No," she said, "I don't expect many are."

She thought of him then, when she met him, coming into her tent behind the circus, dignified and reeking of whiskey. He'd taken off his hat and bowed, and introduced himself as James Butler Hickok. It took her five minutes to realize who it was. She had been sitting in her circus tights, and pulled a blanket over her legs, pretending to be cold. It was peculiar. She never worried how they appeared from the trapeze or the tightrope.

Mrs. Langrishe was smiling in a kind way that didn't fit her. "He was highly esteemed," she said.

Agnes Lake was suddenly impatient; she didn't know with what. "What did he do?" she said.

"Do?" Mrs. Langrishe smiled at the question. "He was Bill Hickok."

"What did he do?" she said again. "He wrote once that he and Charley Utter were mining gold, he wrote another time that they were into business." She looked at her plate like something on it had moved. "I knew him better than that."

Mrs. Langrishe tried to remember what Bill did, but she'd never heard it discussed.

"Where did he stay?" Agnes Lake said. "Where did he take his meals?" She looked out the window, as if it wasn't possible this was the right place. When she looked back into the dining room of the Grand Union Hotel, she was blinking tears. She didn't try to brush them off, and there was no other sign in her face of what she felt.

Mrs. Langrishe covered Mrs. Hickok's hand again. "He stayed with Charley," she said. "They had a little camp on the creek."

Agnes waited.

"I don't know where he went for his meals," she said, "but he kept healthy, you could see that. He carried himself well . . ."

The tears came down Agnes Lake's cheeks, but her voice stayed dry. "I don't mean to question you," she said, "but I never met a human being that struck me as helpless as Bill, and I never understood how he got by. Before we married, or after."

"He was esteemed. People took care of him."

Agnes Lake shook her head. "People don't take care of anybody," she said. "Not all their lives."

The two ladies fell into a silence that was no more uncomfortable than their conversation. Elizabeth Langrishe moved her hand off Agnes Lake's, and then it came to her. "Charley took care of him," she said.

Agnes Lake thought it over. She said, "He wrote me a letter of comfort when Bill was killed."

Mrs. Langrishe said, "There's some out here that need others to take care of." And they sat quietly, both of them forgiving Charley Utter for things he never did.

"I had planned to invite several of Bill's friends into my home this Sunday," Mrs. Langrishe said. "I'm sure Charley will be among them."

Agnes Lake said, "That was very considerate of you."

And it occurred to Mrs. Langrishe that perhaps it was. "I'm pleased to offer my home. Bill's friends have wanted to make your acquaintance."

And they went quiet again, Elizabeth Langrishe feeling as if something had already been done. To Agnes Lake, it felt like the beginning of a fall.

IN THE AFTERNOON CHARLEY TOOK JANE TO VISIT BILL AGAIN. SHE insisted. They stayed ten minutes, and then he drove her back down the hill to his camp beside the Whitewood. He stayed at the Grand Union now; she had no place else.

He unhitched the horse and tied him to one of the wheels. He drew the animal a bucket of creek water, and fed him oats in a bucket.

"Where you headed?" she asked when he'd finished.

"I have business to attend," he said.

"What if I need somethin'?"

He looked at her a minute, and then crossed the street and bought her a bottle of whiskey. "That's all I can do," he said.

She took the cork out of the bottle and smelled what was inside.

"I'm going to need more morphine," she said. She took a drink from the bottle but her lips barely opened. She wanted to look thirstier than she was.

"I'll try to find the doc," he said. He'd bought her morphine before in Chinatown.

"You'll forgit all about me," she said.

"No, I'll send the doc."

She said, "You can't wait to get away from here."

"That's true," he said.

Doc O. E. Sick was not in, but he'd left a pencil and a pad of paper beside his door for messages. Charley wrote,

> *I regret to report I got another victim, although this one was none of my doing. Her name is Jane Cannary, and she is staying in my camp and in need of morphine. I will settle accounts at your convenience.*
>
> Charley "Colorado Charley" Utter

He went back to the Grand Union for fresh clothes on the way to the bathhouse. Alphonso the Polite himself was behind the desk, wearing his bartender's uniform. Alphonso bowed, Charley bowed back. Alphonso always bowed when he saw Charley, it was not impossible that he was part Chinese.

"There was a lady by, sir," he said.

Charley stopped dead in his tracks. His first thought was that it was Jane, which was a sight more pleasant than his second thought, which was Matilda. "Was she limping?" he said.

Alphonso shook his head. "She carried herself with strength and bearing," he said.

"How old?"

"I couldn't say," he said. Alphonso the Polite never commented on a lady's age. He handed Charley an envelope with his name written in careful script on the side opposite the seal. "She asked me to deliver this personally," he said.

Charley gave Alphonso a dollar and stared at the envelope. It wasn't Matilda's writing, hers was smaller. And she pressed harder into the paper. He put it in his pocket and walked down the hallway to his room.

Dear Mr. Utter,
> *I received your letter concerning Bill's death on the 27th of August, and came as soon as my obligations in St. Louis were fulfilled. I am*

staying in room 19 of this Hotel, and am Anxious to meet with you to discuss the circumstances frankly.

Thank you for your Prompt attention.

It was signed *Agnes Lake Hickok*.

Charley refolded the note and put it back in the envelope. It slid in easily, as if the matter itself wanted to be put away. He thought of Jane then, drinking whiskey, shooting morphine into her veins, and sitting out in front of his camp claiming that she was Bill's widow.

The first thing Charley determined was to keep Agnes Lake away from the camp. The second thing was to keep Jane drunk. Not wild drunk—he didn't want her shooting off guns to announce herself—but to find the place that bordered on wild, where she turned morose, and to keep her there until Agnes Lake left the Black Hills.

He put the envelope on the table next to his bed and found a clean shirt and fresh socks in the drawer. He liked having a drawer, it was a neatness you could see just sliding it open. In the weeks since Bill's death Charley's orderliness had slipped away from him, and left him open to every kind of trouble the wind picked up and blew his direction. It was unsettling, not choosing your own trouble, and Charley's instincts pulled him in small ways back to his natural protections. He closed the drawer and centered the envelope on the table and headed for the bathhouse. There was a bath at the end of the hall, but Charley was accustomed to the Bottle Fiend's company, and did not like to bathe alone.

The Bottle Fiend was napping in the chair beside the door when Charley came in. His arms were crossed and his chin rested against his chest. He looked ordinary as boiled potatoes. The thought came to Charley that the Bottle Fiend only gave himself away when he talked, or fell through glass windows, or walked up and down Main Street with his gunnysack collecting bottles. It seemed to Charley those things could be avoided.

He stepped up onto the porch and his shadow crossed the Bottle Fiend's face, and he opened his eyes. He looked tired and old. Charley never thought of him that way—young or old—and it surprised him to see the age so clear. "You look wilted," he said.

The Bottle Fiend checked the gunnysack next to his chair; the bottles shifted and made flat, musical sounds. "It's the general's pony soldiers," he said.

The general had ordered all his officers and men to bathe, and more than one hundred of them had lined up outside the bathhouse. "They left all these bottles," the soft-brain said, and touched the sack.

Charley said, "Did you remember to charge?"

"American soldiers don't pay for nothing," he said.

"Who told you that?"

"Them."

Charley took off his shirt and pants and sat down in his regular tub. The Bottle Fiend heated water and poured it over his shoulders. "Did the biter die?" he said after a while.

Soft-brain or not, the man had the knack of sliding into a conversation.

Charley said no. He hadn't seen Lurline in three weeks, and then she was sitting with Handsome Banjo Dick Brown at the Eatephone on Main Street, cutting beefsteak into bite-size pieces for him.

As long as Charley could remember, it was always too much peeder business or none at all. Mostly none at all. "I shook hands with the general," the soft-brain said, "and the lady was there that had us to the theater. She could bite you . . ."

Charley shook his head. "That one's likely to bite something off," he said. He turned in the tub and looked over his shoulder. "What's all this talk of lady biters anyway? I don't remember that you took an interest."

"I heard some things," the soft-brain said. "That you shot Handsome Dick over an upstairs girl."

"I shot him because he was about to shoot me."

"I heard it was an upstairs girl. You bested him in a gunfight, and then give him his life."

"I shot him from under a bed," Charley said.

"Whose bed?"

Charley dropped himself deeper into the tub, until the water covered his shoulders. The soft-brain said, "I heard you was the best gunfighter the Hills has left."

Charley saw where it was going then. He said, "Oh shit."

"They said you was as good as Bill." And a little later, "Bill got shot."

Charley said, "There isn't anybody knows that better than me."

"Gunfighters get shot."

Charley heard the worry in that, and thought worrying must be unnatural to the soft-brain, and regretted bringing it into his life.

"I wasn't intended for that," he said. "It was an accident."

"Because you wanted to get bit."

"Because there isn't anybody that can't be shot." The Bottle Fiend sat still, waiting. Charley's thoughts turned to Lurline; he had ideas to hire her to run a house for him in Lead, where things were quieter.

He had considered it from every business angle, and couldn't see that it was worse than the other things he'd done for money. It wasn't being a whore man itself that he was against, it was the way whore men treated their girls. His would come and go as they pleased, quit if they wanted. The only rule he'd settled on was daily baths, and some of the upstairs girls had inclinations that way on their own.

The soft-brain said, "Did Bill know that he could get shot too?"

"Don't worry about Bill," he said. "He met God by now, and he was ready. He didn't keep secrets from himself, what he was, and in the end he was ready."

"I'm ready to meet God," the soft-brain said.

"Not yet," Charley said. "There's plenty of time, when things take their natural course."

"Not too much," he said. And Charley wondered at the things that the Bottle Fiend's heart told him, and that they never scared him. "I'm ready," he said, "I got a present."

The Bottle Fiend touched the sack of bottles.

"You going to give all those to God?" Charley said.

"I'm going to turn over my secrets," he said.

And, reflecting on it there in the bath, it seemed like they were talking about the same thing.

THE PRESENCE OF BILL'S WIFE IN DEADWOOD AFFECTED CHARLEY'S sleep, which was fitful even before her arrival. He lay in bed all night, trying to concentrate on old arguments he'd had with himself over the whorehouse in Lead. Her note lay on the table next to his bed; he could not keep her out of his thoughts. It felt like Bill himself had come back to ask where he'd been the last days of his life.

He left his bed before sunrise and collected his gelding at the livery. He rode uphill into the mountains toward Lead, and the sun broke behind him before he reached town. In the sudden warmth he thought for a moment he had gleaned something about night and day and what happened to Bill, that things came to relieve each other. He tried to put that into words but it wouldn't fit.

It was one of the mysteries of his life, the thoughts he had that existed without words. Bill had once said the same thing.

The house he meant to buy was on the north side of Lead, at the lowest elevation in town. There were five bars within a hundred feet, and that was as close to a badlands as Lead had. The house itself had been built for L. D. Kellogg, who was sent out from California by the mining speculator George Hearst to buy the Homestake Mine and every property adjacent. Kellogg had arrived with his wife, and moved out of the house within one week. His wife was intolerant of drinking. The house had stayed empty since—anyone with the two-thousand-dollar asking price preferring to settle in Deadwood.

The structure had eleven rooms and a balcony off the second floor. There were brass door handles and locks, and little hooks in the walls where Mrs. Kellogg had hung pictures. Standing in the living room, you could hear Mr. Hearst's men digging the first mining tunnel in the Black Hills. It was a distant sound, you had to hold still to notice.

Charley stood in the front room now and listened. The house had a peaceful feeling, and while the feeling lasted he walked uphill two hundred yards to the bank, woke the manager, and signed over a draft from the Bank of Colorado for two thousand dollars. It took fifteen minutes to settle the sale—George Hearst owned the bank too.

Charley walked back to the house then, and stood in the front room again, but the place had turned restless. He thought of Bill's wife, waiting in room 19 of the Grand Union Hotel with eyes as cold as frost. He went cold himself, remembering her eyes.

He left the house, crossed the street, and bought himself a bottle. He got on his horse and began to drink—he hadn't drunk so early since the day he shot Handsome Dick Brown.

He had to force the whiskey.

Twice he regurgitated. His nose stung and his eyes watered, but he replaced what he'd lost. He rode in and out of the shadows of trees until he approached Deadwood, where the trees stopped. His balance was impaired, and the third time he leaned over in the saddle to regurgitate, he fell off the horse. He lay still on the ground, holding on to the bottle. The horse put his nose in Charley's stomach and blew. Charley had landed on his back, and it was a while before his breathing pains eased enough to slap the animal's head away.

He shaded his eyes and looked at the horse upside down. He sat up to take another drink, he lay back down. He talked to the horse. He said, "Man was not intended to fear woman until they were married."

The horse blew again, and dropped a thick line of spit onto the ground next to Charley's head. "If you'd hit me with that," he said, "I'd of had to shoot you." As a rule, Charley did not talk to a horse, believing, as he did, that the animal was nothing but a cow with bad nerves. But the gelding was smarter than most, and had seen some things, and Charley felt more comfortable about lying on the ground talking to him then than he did about getting up and trying to ride him.

"It's nothing personal," he said. "Now that I shot Handsome Dick in the leg, I have a reputation to keep, and I can't allow some old bastard who's had his balls cut off to come spitting in my gun-fighter face." He brought the bottle to his lips again, spilling alcohol down his chin. The horse blew. And then there was a voice. Charley was drunk, but he knew it wasn't four-legged.

"Charley?"

He leaned farther back, his eyes moving down the horse's head to his neck. At shoulder height, he found the face of Agnes Lake. He recognized the eyes.

"Charley?"

He sat up in the dirt, not trying to get up, not trying to hide the bottle. He noticed it was only dented, and wondered how, only three weeks before, he'd been able to finish one this same size in a single night. "I was just coming to see you," he said, "and this animal threw me off and tried to spit on my head."

She knelt in back of him and he smelled her perfume and the soap she had used to bathe. She was still humid from the bath, he knew there were still wet spots in her ears. She looked younger than he remembered, and softer. Her hair was tied this way and that, it made him dizzy trying to follow it around her head.

"You caught me at the disadvantage," he said. "I have been tangling with this horse." The horse moved a step to the side. Charley said, "Watch him, he spits." She stared into Charley's face, upside down, and it felt to him like they knew each other longer than they did. "Well," he said, because she was still watching him, "how was your trip?"

"I came as soon as I could," she said.

"There was no hurry," he said. "I took care of things as they came up." She was still looking into his face and Charley started to get up. He felt her hands under his arms, and then he was on his feet. Bill had said she was strong.

"Charley," she said. She looked him up and down, he brushed the dirt off his pants and shirt, thinking it was luck he'd fallen where he did because if he'd waited another hundred feet, it would have been mud. Of course, if he'd waited another hundred feet, the landing would have been softer.

"I was gone when Bill got shot," he said, "but I did what I could when I got back." He tried a few slow steps, testing his legs, and then took the horse's reins in his hand and began to walk in the direction of town. She fell in next to him, slipping sideways looks. It felt like she was waiting for him to tell her something, he didn't know what. He considered explaining the whorehouse in Lead, he considered explaining his drinking.

When he finally spoke, though, it wasn't considered at all. He just said, "Sometimes, you know, it feels like Bill's come back from the dead. Or like he isn't dead all the way, that it was some kind of misunderstanding."

She looked at him, the horse tugged at the reins. He couldn't read what was in her heart; there wasn't time to compose something to comfort her. He thought she might be stronger than he was, and he knew it was useless making anything up.

"I felt him watching me," he said, "more than once. I felt him asking me, '*Charley?*,' the same way you did. Only he doesn't mean why am I lying on the ground talking to horses."

She smiled at him, not frosty. He began to feel an attraction. "I went to Cheyenne," he said. "I was on the way back . . ."

There was something about the woman, though, that he couldn't let half a fact sit between them. He felt like he had to explain every other fact, and every other direction it took him, right down to what happened at the river and how his brother Steve went and shot somebody's pig after Charley gave him the pony express.

He began it again. "I was the same as Bill, and I was different. I never killed anybody, on purpose or accidental, and I never had to be hard about my feelings. Bill was more practical, he had to be or he couldn't of lived . . ."

She was holding on to every word. It made him cautious. "I don't intend to say he didn't have feelings," he said. "He spoke of you with tender affection."

"What did he say?"

"He said you were two of a kind."

She smiled and shook her head. "He told me that about the two of you."

"Well, we were and we weren't. I couldn't walk away from my feelings."

"Was that all he said? He and I were two of a kind?"

He thought about it, trying to remember the words. "He said you were as famous as he was, and understood the nature of celebrity."

She laughed out loud, startling him. "I never knew what he meant about that," she said. "He knew the inklings inside me as well as I know them myself, but he'd toss that aside to talk about being famous."

"It weighed on him," Charley said. "He never met a human being that didn't already have an opinion on him, and it was his nature to feel an obligation to fill their expectations. Myself, I can lie in the dirt talking to horses if I feel like it."

"You don't do that."

"I got an eyewitness."

She smiled again, and Charley noticed it was more comfortable between them. He stopped walking to look at her, and the horse bumped into his back. When they were walking again, he noticed that she moved her feet in and out of even the deepest mud without effort. She never lost balance. He brought the bottle halfway to his lips, and reconsidered.

"Why don't you quit that bottle?" she said.

"I got a friend who collects them," he said. But he dropped it in the mud. It landed mouth-up, with a sound as final as a body hitting the end of the rope. He made a note of where it was, in case things turned dry later.

They took the gelding back to the livery. She waited outside while he settled his account, and then they walked to the Grand Union. He noticed again how easily she moved through the mud, and was attracted to it. She ordered coffee at the front desk, and led him to number 19. The room had two chairs and a table and a view of the hills. General George Crook's officers had most of the hotel, and they wandered the halls with whores Charley knew from the Gem Theater. It reminded him he had to talk to Lurline.

Agnes Lake smoothed her dress over her legs and sat on the bed. Charley took a chair next to the table. The pot of coffee was between them and the steam rose into his face. Charley did not like coffee or its humidity. Especially after he'd gotten drunk and fallen off a horse.

"I've got a lock of Bill's hair for you," he said. "Doc Pierce cut it before he buried him." He pointed out the window. "He's up on the hill there," he said.

"I was coming from the grave when I saw your accident," she said.

"From a distance, it probably didn't look like much reason it happened . . ."

"It looked like gravity," she said.

He said, "That horse is tricky. Tricky and subtle." She was smiling, softer now, and he saw why Bill loved her. "I'm relieved you aren't a crier," he said.

He thought for a moment she hadn't understood. He was about to repeat himself when she said, "You were coming back from Cheyenne . . ."

He nodded. "He was buried by the time I got to Deadwood. Nobody stole anything off the body except Doc Pierce, who took about five locks of hair. I've been meaning to collect them . . ."

She looked at her lap. "Was he sick?" she said. "His letters seemed to hold secret warnings."

Charley thought of the day Bill asked him how blood disease affected a woman. "No," he said. "His eyes had lost their sharpness, but he was strong." He wished he knew her better, to tell her this lie.

She stared at him, weighing what he'd said.

"It wasn't like him to talk of dying," she said, "but from the day he got into the Hills, his letters took that turn."

"He wasn't unhappy," Charley said. "You were on his mind all the while."

She shook her head.

"The place lends itself to the dark aspects," he said. "There's nothing ordinary here, not even weather. You never saw lightning like here. The day we arrived there were two men in the street carrying human heads . . ."

He saw he had confused her. "Heads," he said, holding his in both hands. "A Mex with an Indian, and a bug-eye miscreant named Boone May carrying the outlaw Frank Towles. Any intelligent man would turn his thinking to mortal matters . . ."

She sat back on the bed and closed her eyes. "He told me once the bullet was never made with his name on it." Charley closed his eyes too and lost his balance. He caught himself before he fell off the chair, and when he looked up she was watching him again.

"It's a trick chair," he said. She smiled at him, but he saw the joke was wearing thin.

"He told me the bullet was never made with his name on it," she said again.

He looked out the window. "They manufacture new bullets all the time."

"Did he know that?"

"It's the place," he said. "There's nobody immune here."

Even looking out the window he felt the attraction, he didn't know what it was. His ideas of women went a different way.

"This is uncomfortable," Agnes said.

"Just this trick chair," he said, wearing it all the way out. She looked at him and he looked at his hands. "I can't talk about Bill except to soft-brains and horses," he said.

When she spoke again it was so low Charley had to lean forward to hear. "The letter came in the afternoon," she said. "It felt like falling. I fell twice in my life from the tightrope, it isn't what you'd think."

"I fell off a horse," he said. "Once."

She looked at him like she knew him. "I know why Bill liked you," she said. "You kept him human."

"I know why he liked you." And that was the truth, he could feel it.

"When you fall," she said, "the thing that presses to you is the newness. It's a new world, and nothing from the other world can save you. You're helpless again, like a baby, scared of loud noises, and you don't know what's serious and what isn't, because you don't know what it means."

They stared at each other across the coffee pot, and he understood her. "That's what it felt like, to read your letter," she said. "I only had a few months with him, I didn't know him like you did."

"A few months could be worth fifteen years," he said.

"No," she said, "it couldn't. It never got past the newness. I married Bill and loved him . . ." She thought for a minute. "If I didn't, it was as close as I ever got, but I never understood him. I know you better. He saw things about me I never even saw myself, but I didn't know his heart at all." Charley was suddenly uncomfortable again, and sorry he'd left his bottle in the mud. She said, "That's why I ask you things. I don't know how else to find out what I lost."

She said that and stopped, and Charley saw she was through talking now. He ran his hands through his hair—it was Bill's gesture. He thought of the things he'd lost when Bill died, there weren't words to explain them. But she needed him to explain something.

"Things end out of balance," he said after a while. "There isn't any other way they can end, because that's the way they happen. At the end, you want things equal, but it doesn't happen." He saw her eyes begin to fill, he never expected it.

And he stood up and crossed the room, dizzy, and sat down next to her on the bed. He smelled soap again, fresh-scrubbed skin. He noticed age marks around the bottom of her neck. He put his arms around her and held her a long time.

And he loved her for all the lost parts of his life.

AL SWEARINGEN WAS COMING OUT OF THE GEM THEATER AT EIGHT o'clock Sunday morning when he saw the boy. He looked bigger than Swearingen remembered him, and older. Years and years.

The boy was sitting on the bench in front of the Bella Union, holding a book, wearing a black coat that was half a foot too short for his arms. It had just begun to rain.

The boy saw him too, and began to cross the street. Swearingen went back into the Gem and locked the door. His wife was standing in the door to his office, holding a handkerchief against her nose. He'd barely hit her and she'd bled all over the floor. It seemed to him that she was bleeding easier all the time.

"Get away, Al," she said, and took a step backwards. "I'll get even . . ."

He came back into the saloon and pulled the goose gun out from behind the bar. It was top-heavy and as tall as a man. He sat down at a poker table and laid the gun across his lap.

His wife blew her nose, knowing it would make the bleeding worse. She liked evidence. "Go ahead and shoot me," she said.

He kept his eyes on the door. "I ain't going to shoot you," he said. "Not yet."

"I ain't scared of you," she said, and stepped back into the main room. "They'll hang you, that's why you're afraid to shoot, you don't want to hang."

There were footsteps outside, stepping onto the porch, stopping at the door. Swearingen lifted the gun and his wife disappeared into his office and slammed the door. He heard her scream, "Murder! Murder!"

The boy tried the door; Swearingen began to shake. There were three knocks. Swearingen didn't move, and there was more knocking. "We're closed," he shouted.

Then he heard the boy's voice, stranger than he remembered it. It was dry and hollow, like it was coming from a long time ago. "I am here," it said, "in the name of the Bible of the Black Hills."

Swearingen moved the gun, slowly, until he looked down the long barrel and saw the door. He brought the hammer back and heard it cock. The boy knocked again. "I have found the evil side of the Lord, and I am here to meet it," he said. And when he knocked again, Swearingen pulled the trigger. He had never fired the goose gun before; it went off almost by itself.

Swearingen had been sitting low in his chair, resting the gun barrel between his feet on the table. He was unprepared for the noise or the recoil. The air seemed to shatter around his ears, and then he smelled the smoke, falling backwards onto the floor. He felt sparkles of pain in his shoulder, little points of light in a sudden dark.

He was lying face-up on the floor. The air had exploded, and little pieces of it still were falling around his ears, and the points of light in his shoulder gathered on themselves until they seemed to take it over.

He sat up carefully, moving his body and shoulder as one piece, and looked at the door. The goose gun had blown a hole in it half a foot across, dead center. The smoke hung over the table where Swearingen had been sitting, and as he looked through it now the boy's face appeared at the hole in the door.

He had eyes like a horse in a barn fire, and his voice cracked. "The Bible of the Black Hills is here," he said. The boy's head disappeared, and his arm came through the hole, feeling for the bolt. The arm looked a yard long.

Swearingen got to his feet and saw his wife, still holding a bloody handkerchief to her nose, looking out a crack in the door to his office. "I need a shotgun," he said.

She smiled—he saw her smile—and then she closed the door and locked it. He ran upstairs, one arm dead at his side, and then to the far end of the hallway. He waited, listening, until the boy found the bolt. He heard the door open.

Then he heard the boy's voice again. "It's time to settle," he said.

And then he heard something else, that he would hear again and again in his head, every day for as long as he lived. It was his wife. "He went upstairs," she said.

The boy came slowly. Swearingen waited until he heard him start up the stairs, and then he slipped down the back way and out the side door. He crossed Main Street and ran west, behind the Bella Union, until he came to the one-room shack where Boone May slept. The place had belonged to Edmond Colwell, the first Negro in the Black Hills, until Boone took it away. Swearingen found him now, lying on a brass bed in the corner. The bed was worth more than the shack. Boone had taken it out of the Gem.

Boone May didn't look good. His nose was red and swollen and his voice seemed to come from his nostrils. There was a bottle of Tutt's Pills on the floor next to him, and next to that was a spoon with some kind of medicine collected in the bottom.

"Get up," Swearingen said.

Boone May pulled the blanket around his neck and looked at him with both eyes, that's how serious he was. "Close that door or I'll shoot you where you stand," he said.

Swearingen closed the door. Boone coughed, cleared his throat, and spit. Swearingen watched the spit drop. There were a dozen wet spots on the floor. "Get up," Swearingen said.

Boone closed his eyes and dropped his head back onto the mattress. "Get me a pillow," he said. "I got torpid fever, I need a pillow to rest my head."

Swearingen looked at Boone's face, which was pasty and white. "You ain't the color for torpid fever," he said. "You're supposed to be yellow . . ."

"In a pig's ass," he said.

Swearingen cracked the door and looked outside. The boy wasn't there. "I need fluids," Boone said.

Swearingen picked up the bottle of Tutt's Pills and read the symptoms of torpid fever out loud off the label. "Loss of appetite, bowels constive, pain in the head with a dull sensation in the back part, pain under the shoulder blade, fullness after eating . . ." Boone groaned and held his stomach. ". . . A disinclination to exertion of body or mind, irritability of temper, low spirits with a feeling of having neglected some duty, weariness, dizziness, fluttering at the heart, dots before the eyes, yellow skin, headache, and constipation." He put the bottle back on the floor. "See there?" he said. "It said yellow skin. You're the wrong color."

Boone glistened with sweat. "I got it," he said, "or I got something worse. Get me fluids."

"I got something better," Swearingen said. He took all the money out of his pocket—it was close to four hundred dollars—and laid it on the bed next to Boone. "All you got to do is get up," he said. "Put your pants on and shoot one pilgrim, then you can go right back to bed."

Boone lifted his head far enough to see the money. "I can't shoot nothin' now," he said. "I got spots in front of my eyes."

Swearingen had a vision of the boy's face, it appeared through the hole in the Gem's door. He heard his wife again. *He went upstairs.* He decided to strangle her after Boone shot the boy.

"I should of killed him when I had the chance," Swearingen said. He thought of how the boy had looked with the knife in his mouth and his britches pulled down. He'd felt generous after it was over, and now the boy was back to revenge himself.

Boone was still looking at the money. "That's a rule to live by," he said, "always kill them when you got the chance, or it's a law of nature that they'll come back to kill you."

Swearingen suddenly couldn't draw enough air into his lungs to breathe. The room seemed cold, and he had to piss. "I'll give you five hundred," he said.

Boone groaned. "Five hundred dollars don't do any good if I'm dead from torpid fever," he said. He put two fingers on his left wrist and felt his pulse. He moved the hand from there to his forehead. He said, "I never felt like this in my life."

Swearingen cracked the door again; the boy hadn't found him yet. "Let me stay a while," he said. "If you start to die, I'll go find the doc."

Boone's good eye narrowed. "How long?" he said. It struck Swearingen as a peculiar question from a man planning to die.

"A day," he said.

Boone picked up the money and held it in front of his face, like a relative he was trying to recognize from his deathbed. "One day," he said, "but don't mess nothin' up." He put the money on the mattress and lay flat on his back, on top of it, and closed his eyes.

There was one window in the cabin. Swearingen stood beside it and looked outside. From that angle the Hills appeared steep and dangerous. The window frame had warped in the fall rains, and stuck when he tried to pull it open. He tried again, resetting his feet, and it came up two inches and stopped.

Swearingen checked the bed, but Boone hadn't moved. He unbuttoned his pants. The crack in the window was a foot lower than his peeder, and he stood there a minute deciding how to get it done. If he was alone, he would have just taken a step back and pissed. There was something about Boone May, though, that you didn't want to piss any distance across his floor, and so Swearingen moved closer to the window and bent his knees—as much as he could, standing against a wall—until his peeder was even with the opening.

He looked behind himself once more—Boone's eyes were still closed—and let it go. And when he looked back out the window— it couldn't have been two seconds—the boy was standing six feet tall on the other side, holding the book under his arm, watching him. "You can't hide," he said.

Swearingen began to run, but couldn't stop himself pissing. He yelled, no words, just the sound. Urine hit the window, the walls, his shoes. Swearingen hated to have piss on his shoes. The boy held the book up in front of him, and Swearingen saw a picture on the cover of a snake with wings. He yelled again, and heard Boone moving on the bed.

The boy stood still, staring at him over the book.

Swearingen got his peeder back in his pants and backed away from the window. Boone was sitting on the bed in his long underwear, his feet on the floor. He had the money he'd taken from Swearingen in his hand.

"Five hundred dollars," Swearingen said, pointing out the window. "I'll get it for you as soon as he's dead."

"I need fluids," he said.

"The chance is now," Swearingen said. "All you got to do is shoot him, I'll go get five hundred dollars, more if you want."

Boone stood up and walked to the window. He looked out, the boy looked in. Boone cleared his throat. "Could you get me some tea?" he said. "I got torpid fever."

Swearingen looked around the room for something to shoot, but couldn't find even a squirrel gun.

"I am here for the Lord," the boy said.

Boone said, "The Lord don't want me to die," and then he coughed. He said, "That's why he brung you here, to save me." Swearingen stood by the bed, watching the boy over Boone May's shoulder.

"I come to confront the evil side," he said.

Boone May started to laugh, but it broke into a cough. He said, "What kind of evil are you hunting, son?" The boy didn't answer. Boone turned around and looked at Swearingen. "He's the evil side of something," he said. "But a missionary's first obligations is to minister to the sick."

The boy stood quiet. Then he said, "What kind of tea?"

"Hot tea with honey." The boy tried to look around Boone for Swearingen. "There's time for that later," Boone said, moving into his view. "When winter comes and everything's froze, there ain't nothing else to do but hunt evil. Right now, though, you could save a man's got torpid fever . . ." He coughed again, deep, and spit on the floor.

"I'll be back," the boy said. "Evil cannot hide from good, for they are of the same Lord."

Boone said, "Make sure they give you honey, it runs right through you without the honey."

The boy left the window and Boone went back to his bed. He pulled the blanket back, and as he got in Swearingen saw the flash of a shotgun. "You got your gun in there with you?" he said. "In bed?" Boone closed his eyes. "How come you didn't just shoot him, you had your gun right there?"

"I'm sick," he said, without opening his eyes. "How come you didn't shoot him yourself?"

The panicky feeling returned then, the same feeling he got when the boy stood up and started across the street to the Gem. "I want my money back," Swearingen said. "That money was to kill somebody."

As sick as he was, Boone smiled.

Swearingen opened the door and looked outside. He saw the boy had probably gone to the hotel, if he meant to bring tea. He considered running the other way. "I put a goose gun right on him," he said, as much to himself as Boone May. "But when I fired, he wasn't there. It's something spooky about that boy . . ."

"I don't see the peril," Boone said.

"You heard what he said, he come to do battle with evil."

Boone sighed. "Did you think he meant to beat you to death with his book?" he said. And then he began to cough from deep in his lungs, and Swearingen sat down in the corner and listened to it until he believed Boone May was dying. And he knew, in some way he couldn't explain, that he was dying too.

It was eleven o'clock Sunday morning.

CHARLEY WAS COMING OUT OF THE GRAND UNION HOTEL ON THE WAY to Mrs. Langrishe's house and the party for Agnes Lake, wearing a necktie and a brand-new hat, when he saw the boy.

"Malcolm?" The boy was walking through the front doors, carrying a tray of hot tea. He had pressed a heavy-looking book between his arm and his side, and was in danger of dropping it all. Charley had last seen him lying in the back of the wagon, when Bill was alive. "Malcolm?"

The boy stopped and looked at him, blinking. His face was thinner and older and glazed, but it was Malcolm, although he might not of known it himself. He stood still, holding the tray and the book, and stared into Charley's face. "I thought you'd gone back to Colorado," Charley said.

The boy didn't answer. Charley had the sudden thought that he'd lost his tongue to infection. "Can you talk?" Charley said. The boy nodded. Things were moving in his eyes now. "Where you going with all that?" Charley said. He wanted to hear words from the boy's mouth.

"To save a man from torpid fever," he said.

Charley was washed with gratitude. "That's good," he said, and touched the boy's shoulder. The teapot rattled. "I'll report to your sister that you've recovered from your accident as good as new." Charley watched the boy to see if he knew he had a sister.

"Report that I have become a disciple of the Preacher Henry Hiram Weston Smith and the Bible of the Black Hills," he said.

"Preacher Smith's dead," Charley said. The boy nodded, as if that were the whole point. "What kind of religion is that—the Bible of the Black Hills?"

"It is the Bible of the two sides of the Lord," the boy said. "I have found the evil now, and it cannot hide."

Charley looked around him, at Deadwood. "It isn't the evil side of things that's hard to find," he said.

The boy nodded again. "First," he said, "I have to minister to the sick." He started off in the direction of the badlands. Charley watched him a minute, making up his mind, and then started out after him.

He fell in beside Malcolm and walked fifty feet trying to think of something else to say. "Where is this dying man?" he asked.

"In his cabin," the boy said.

"How do you know it's torpid fever? It could be something else . . ."

The boy walked past Nuttall and Mann's and turned left before he got to the Bella Union. The ground was firmer off the street, slippery and wet, and had a thin coat of pine dust. Charley saw the cabin then, and put a hand on the boy's shoulder to stop him.

"How did you find this patient?" he said.

The boy stopped walking and looked at him. "I followed the evil side of the Lord," he said.

Charley scratched his ear, fought off a vision of Matilda. "The Lord doesn't get sick," he said gently. "He doesn't live in any jerry-built cabin in back of the badlands . . ."

The boy agreed with that. "He lives in the Gem Theater," he said. "It's the other one that's sick."

Charley looked at the shack again. He took his hand off Malcolm's shoulder, and the boy moved two steps before Charley could stop him again. "Let me do it," he said.

The boy looked at the tray in his hands. Charley said, "I'll take it in, in case you're not immune. I already had torpid fever . . ."

The boy let Charley have the tray, and moved the book to his hands. Charley heard him walking a step behind, all the way to the cabin. Just before he got there, though, he turned around and held out his hand. "You wait," he said.

The boy stopped and Charley moved his hand back, underneath his coat, and lifted and dropped the knife in its sheath, making sure it wasn't stuck. Then he knocked on the door, and a voice came from just the other side. "Who is it?"

"Charles Utter," he said.

The door opened an inch; Charley saw one eye and a beard. It was the whore man. The door closed, and Charley heard conversation. When it opened again, the whore man was standing in front of him, legs spread; it smelled like he'd wet his pants.

"Where's the boy?" Swearingen said.

Charley looked past him to the bed and saw Boone May's face, flattened against the mattress. There was a blanket pulled all the way up to his chin, hiding something, and he looked worse than most of the dead men Charley had seen.

"Where's the boy?" Swearingen said again.

Charley stepped into the room and Boone moved under the covers. Charley thought it was probably a shotgun, and stopped with Swearingen between himself and the bed. He was still holding the tray in his left hand.

"I heard you shot it out with Handsome Dick, pretty," Boone said. He sounded frail as fall leaves.

"I heard you were dying," Charley said. Swearingen moved one step, and Charley moved with him. He handed him the tray, watching Boone. "You'd best drink that while it's still warm," he said.

Boone brought his hands out from under the covers and sat halfway up, resting his head against the wall. Charley saw the outline of the scattergun under the blanket. Swearingen put the tray in Boone's lap and stepped away from the bed. He looked out the window for the boy.

Boone lifted the pot to his lips and drank everything in it. Then he picked up one of the cups.

"You'd best keep the boy away from here," Swearingen said.

Boone started to laugh, but it broke in his throat, and he spilled the tea from the cup down the front of his underwear while he coughed. When he stopped, he wiped himself off and looked at Charley. "Mr. Swearingen's got the idea that the boy is a messenger from the Lord, come to beat him to death with a book for the way he's lived."

"That boy's gone soft-brained," Swearingen said. "Keep him away from me." He was still looking out the window.

"He doesn't carry a thing but that book, whore man," Charley said, not knowing if that was true or false. "Anything happens to him, you got more than the Lord to settle with."

Swearingen looked at Boone. Boone shrugged. "The man shot it out with Handsome Dick," he said, "and then spared his life. It was me, I'd let the boy alone."

It was in Swearingen's eyes what he was going to do, and Charley saw it even before he reached inside his coat. And before Swearingen's knife came out, Charley cut him, elbow to wrist. His coat sleeve split in a clean curve down the front, and beneath that the shirt, and beneath that the flesh split too.

The knife spilled out of the coat and broke when it hit the floor. Boone laughed. Swearingen bent over the split arm, little surprised noises coming out of him, and a moment later drops of blood began to pattern the floor in front of his feet.

Boone stayed where he was. He made no move to put his hands back under the covers, he gave no appearance of any such thought.

The knife felt warm in Charley's hand. Boone coughed; the only other noise was Swearingen breathing through his teeth as he rocked, up and down from the waist. It didn't feel like there was an idea in the room.

"That boy never threatened anything but himself," Charley said, talking to Swearingen now. His voice was quiet, but it filled the air. Swearingen didn't answer. Charley turned his back on the whore man and moved toward the door, watching Boone. Boone was looking sicker again, and put his head back on the mattress to rest. Charley wondered what it felt like, to carry a head that size around on your shoulders.

He stopped at the door and considered Swearingen again, knowing he ought to kill him. Boone looked the same direction, holding the same thought. "You forgived more trespassers than Jesus Christ," he said.

Charley stepped outside and closed the door. He heard Boone cough, and then spit. He looked down at the knife in his hand and wiped the blade with his fingers. There was already blood on them. It had settled into the joints and begun to dry.

He put the knife in the sheath, lifting it once to see that it wasn't stuck. Malcolm was standing on the spot where he'd left him, holding the book against his chest. "Did you see him?" he said.

"I saw them both, and I delivered the tea."

"Did you see the evil one?"

Charley started to walk back toward Main Street, the boy stayed where he was. Charley backed up and took him by the arm. "Don't come here again," he said.

The boy followed him back into the badlands, thinking thoughts Charley did not like. Without knowing what they were, he didn't like them. They walked south, up Main Street, the boy half a step behind. Every now and then he looked behind him.

Charley knew the boy would go back; turning evangelist hadn't changed how he was.

They passed Wall Street, Gold Street, Lee Street, and Shine. At the far south end of town Charley stopped and looked the boy over. "Where do you sleep?"

Malcolm pointed up into the hills, in the same general direction as the Bottle Fiend's cabin, but in a politer district of the hill. "Preacher Smith's house," he said. "But not on his bed. I sleep where he told me."

"Do you read the Bible?" His thought was to send him home to read, that had a safe feel to it.

The boy shook his head. He patted the book in his hands, though. "I carry the Bible," he said.

Charley saw the snake-head angel on the cover.

"It ain't meant to read," the boy said. "Preacher Smith's dreams is in here of the evil side of the Lord."

Charley looked at the book, and at the boy. He wondered what kind of dreams the preacher had, and if they were anything like what happened to him. "I got something to do," Charley said. "Bill's widow is here and I'm invited to attend her reception." The boy blinked, nothing else moved. "You remember Bill?"

Malcolm nodded. "I didn't forget things," he said, "I only forgot how I fit into them." He said that like he was reading it out of his book.

"Something happened to you," Charley said, and the boy froze. "It doesn't matter," Charley said, watching his face. "You didn't die . . ." Charley saw the boy had rung the alarm bells, and stopped what he was saying. "There's no hurry to sort things out," he said. "For now, why don't you go back to the preacher's digs and rest?"

"There is no time to rest now," he said.

Charley grabbed him before he could move away. "Malcolm," he said, calmer than he felt, "stay away from that whore man."

The boy shook his head. "It's no man," he said.

"That's the second time you said that," Charley said. "And I will tell you what I said before. That kind does things when they turn bad that nobody else would think up."

The boy blinked. Charley turned him slowly in the direction he had pointed before. "Go back to the preacher's now," he said.

Charley watched him start up the hill. He went into a small stand of pines, then came out the other side. He walked east, across the hill, and then disappeared into more trees. He was higher already than any of the other shacks or tents, and Charley shuddered to think of the climb in the winter. He wondered that a preacher would choose such a place to live.

Charley waited another ten minutes, satisfying himself that the boy wasn't coming back down, and then returned to town, turned left on Wall Street, and climbed the hill to Mrs. Langrishe's house. He was preoccupied with the boy and did not remember the blood on his fingers until he was in her living room, shaking hands with a man named Solomon Star.

Solomon Star had soft, tiny hands and a flat sadness in his eyes. Charley had seen that sadness before, and knew it was not a temporary condition. There were some things that happened you could never get away from.

"I don't recall your business," Charley said, to be polite.

Solomon Star said, "I've got the brickworks," being polite too. There were half a hundred people in Mrs. Langrishe's living room, and more spilled out into the hallway and kitchen. The room was twenty degrees hotter than the afternoon, and filled with the smells of every kind of perfume and soap available in the Hills. It was a complaint among the town ladies that they were forced to buy the same perfumes and colognes as the whores.

Charley did not see Agnes. Solomon Star let go of his hand and walked away, into a corner, and stared out the window. Charley noted the heaviness in his moves, and wondered at the unlikely people chosen in this place to carry extra weight.

The thought was still in his mind when he felt Mrs. Langrishe's hand slip through his arm. Without looking he knew who it was. His peeder knew too.

"Mr. Utter," she said. "I was afraid you couldn't attend."

"I was occupied with unexpected business," he said, closing his hand to hide the blood.

She smiled at him and pressed herself into his arm until her breasts rose up to him, almost out of her dress. He was romanced by her freckles all over again. "What kind of business does a Christian man do on Sundays?" He felt a playfulness in her, but it didn't seem mean.

He thought of Malcolm, wondering if he'd stayed in the cabin. "Church business," he said. She smiled, bringing color into her chest. A Negro passed, carrying red wine. The glasses looked like they'd break if you sneezed.

She stopped the Negro, addressing him as "uncle," and took two of the drinks. She put one in Charley's hand and then sipped at the other while she looked into his eyes. He felt her playing with him; he wasn't sure now that it was playing.

She moved her hand off his sleeve and slid it into the middle of his back. His peeder jumped at the fresh touch. "I'm afraid I was unkind to you," she said. "I hope you'll forgive me."

"Oh, I'm used to it," he said. "I've been married."

Her hand pressed into his back, and he looked around to see if anyone was watching. The room had no focus, though, no one paid attention to anyone else. It was like a grazing. She said, "I'm afraid I was disappointed with the town's civilities and took it out on you." He smiled at her and she smiled back. "I hope you'll give me a chance to make it up."

"I get disappointed with the civilities myself," he said.

He felt himself sweating under her hand and took a drink of the wine. It had a vinegar taste that did not agree with him. He swallowed, but the taste stuck in his mouth like it was painted on.

She moved her hand then, and took his. "Would you care to see the rest of the house?" She pulled him out of the living room, into the hallway. He caught a glimpse of Agnes Lake as Mrs. Langrishe led him up the stairs. She was standing in a corner in a long dress that went from her neck to her feet. There was something in the dress, or in Agnes, that suggested its use was not decoration but to cover as much of her as it could. She was listening to the sheriff. Charley couldn't see his face, but the only other man in Deadwood of that size was Boone May, who was giving his own party.

She pulled at Charley's hand now, and he followed her off the stairs, watching Agnes until she was eclipsed by the angle of the ceiling. He wondered what the sheriff could be saying about Bill.

Mrs. Langrishe squeezed his hand.

There were four doors on the second floor, all of them closed. She walked him to the far end, opening doors as they went. The rooms had different colors and different smells. All of them were female except the first, which was white and smelled of cigar smoke. The next room was blue, the one after that was yellow.

The last one was purple, and Charley looked at the bedspread and imagined how his place in Lead would look with purple bed-spreads. He imagined purple walls. The noise downstairs seemed a long ways off, and he stood in the door, thinking purple thoughts, noticing that he still had Mrs. Langrishe's hand.

"This is my room," she said, turning to face him in the door. He smiled at that. She said, "You're amused?"

"No."

She said, "You don't smile for no reason, Mr. Utter. You're not frivolous."

"I never thought of a man and wife with separate rooms." Separate parts of the country, yes; rooms, no.

She stared at him a long time, until the smile on his face was dead weight. "My husband has no interest in women," she said finally.

She was still looking into his eyes, and he felt himself getting wormy, waiting for something to come into his mind. "What is his interest?" he said. It came out of his mouth, he heard it, but something in him denied he said it.

She kept her eyes on his but let go of his hand. "Would you care to see the third floor?" she said.

She shut the door to the purple room and walked ahead of him up the stairs. The stairway here was narrow and dark, and the air turned dustier and warmer the further up they went. She stopped at the top and he bumped into her from behind, his nose touching her back just at the spot where the dress quit.

He felt satin with his lips and skin with his nose.

He heard her finding the lock with a key, and then a cut of light appeared overhead and grew, and she stepped into it, disappearing for a minute, and then he stepped into it too. The room was smaller than any of the bedrooms, and the ceiling dropped on one side all the way to the floor. The light came from a window, as big as the one the Bottle Fiend had come through on the way into Mrs. Langrishe's living room. The only piece of furniture was a davenport against the opposite wall. "This is my secret place," she said. She walked past him, brushing his arm, and closed the door. The sound was reminiscent of cocking a gun.

"What's a lady with a purple bedroom need with secret places?" he said.

She did not answer that question.

She walked to the window and looked out, holding herself as if she were cold. With the door closed, the noise from downstairs was like something past, that you heard in your head remembering it. Little specks of dust floated in the air around her shoulders. The room was full of motion, and nothing moved at all.

"It looks like a place you might keep a soft-brain that was the family secret," Charley said.

She smiled and he was relieved to see she wasn't going to cry. The room seemed ripe for that, he couldn't say why. "What is it you're doing with that man?" she said, meaning the Bottle Fiend.

Charley shrugged. "We're amigos," he said.

She laughed out loud. "You watch over him like your own child," she said.

He caught something hard in her face and suddenly thought she had probably had a child of her own once. "No," he said, " he isn't my child. He sleeps in his own house and runs his own business . . ."

There was a yard between them and she closed that while he spoke. The room was warm, and her cheek felt damp when it touched him. She put her arms around his head and pushed herself into his peeder, which was still daydreaming purple. "You take care of people," she said. She kissed him and then pulled back, looking at him like it was a question.

He thought of Bill, and denied it. "It's not that," he said. "Amigos take care of each other."

And she kissed him again. Her hands slid down off his head, over his back, and came to rest on his bottom. She pushed him into herself, and he helped her. He felt her chest and her stomach and her damp cheeks. Her perfume was all over him, and underneath she was as clean as ironed clothes.

Her mouth slid over his, trailing tongue. It went from one of his ears to the other, pushing itself as deep into his head as it could get. It was sloppier than Charley liked, he guessed she had let go of something and he was still holding on. She said, "Will you take care of me too?"

And he looked at her for a minute, holding her face in his hands, but he couldn't tell if she was real or acting. His peeder had no such reservations—he wondered sometimes if they were run by the same motor.

As he held her face, her hands moved from behind to the front and unfastened his buttons. Starting at the collar of his shirt and finishing at the fork in his pants. He couldn't help noticing how practiced she was at it. "That must of been twenty buttons," he said.

She had found his peeder, though, and held it in her fingers. Other fingers ran across his stomach and then down one of his legs. His pants fell in a pile around his feet, and he stepped out of them to follow her to the davenport. She sat down first and pulled him after her. Her fingers let go of his peeder and loosened her own clothes. Her buttons were on the side and in back, but they opened almost before she touched them. "You're a button-sharp woman, Mrs. Langrishe," he said.

She leaned closer and touched his lips with her finger. "Practice," she said. "Costume changes." Then she moved her finger and re-placed it with one of her breasts, so fast Charley couldn't have said which one. He was sitting on the middle pillow of the davenport—it was a cool, smooth fabric on his bottom—and she moved herself up onto his lap, her legs folded underneath, one on each side, and reached again for his peeder.

"Will you take care of me too?" she said. Her weight seemed to rest on the spot where Steve had shot him.

And there was an entanglement at work that he hadn't consid-ered. "I don't know," he said.

Mrs. Langrishe moved on his lap and he felt the smooth lining of her dress where it draped over his legs. Her hair fell over his neck and some of it lay on his shoulder. The sun came around her head, and as he stared up at her she seemed to glow.

She reached between their legs and found his peeder, and then slid herself forward until it was inside her. Then she threw her head back, away from him toward the ceiling, and pushed herself against him, up and back, and it came to him before long that she had probably forgotten who she was with. She spent herself in two minutes, crying out at the end, and then she sat still, his peeder still inside her, and smiled into his face and touched his cheeks with the tips of her fingers, as if he had pleased her. She asked it again, but in a different way. "Will you take care of me, Charley?"

And he told her the same thing. He didn't know.

IT TOOK MRS. LANGRISHE LESS TIME TO DRESS THAN CHARLEY. OF course, her clothes were still on her. She buttoned her buttons and patted her hair, and then watched from the davenport with a peculiar smile while he climbed into his pants. Charley was slow with his buttons, and smoothed the front of his shirt as he dressed. He did not like a shirt to look like it had been found rolled up in a ditch with himself inside it.

"You're an unusual man," she said.

He tucked his shirt in as deep as it would go, all the way around. His peeder felt wet against his pants. It was still enlarged; he was unsure if it had culminated or not. There had been no friction to speak of inside Mrs. Langrishe. The movement had all been outside, she'd rubbed herself against him, holding him inside her in one place. All in all, he felt more milked than loved.

He wondered what new style of fornication it was, or if it was somehow the old style, except Mrs. Langrishe and himself had reversed parts. She was an actress.

"What are you thinking?" she said.

He tightened his belt and checked his shirt. She stood up and walked to the door. "This might be how it feels to be the woman," he said.

She laughed at that without looking back and started down the stairs. Charley closed the door behind him and was suddenly blind. It was cooler, though, and he could hear Mrs. Langrishe on the stairs below him, walking steady and sure, as if she could see in the dark. They might have been upstairs ten minutes.

He heard the party again when they were back on the second floor. She stopped at the bottom of the stairwell and waited for him, taking his arm to walk him down the hall to the first flight of stairs.

She seemed new all over again, and as they walked back down to the party there was something in her pose that established a distance between them, and by the time she let go of his arm at the bottom of the stairs, looking for guests to flatter, it was like they'd never been upstairs at all.

The first person Charley saw after Mrs. Langrishe let go of him was her husband. He was standing between the staircase and the front room with a woman Charley didn't know. He was holding a long-necked glass of wine in one hand and a cigar in the other, talking about the deplorable state of the arts in the Black Hills.

He met Charley's eye without interrupting himself. Charley returned the look, not as uncomfortable as he would have expected, still wet with Mrs. Langrishe's fluids. It changed the way he felt, knowing that Jack Langrishe had no interest in women. Whatever agreement he and his wife had, Charley hadn't broken any of it.

Langrishe took a long pull on his cigar and blew smoke around the woman's head. Then he stepped around her and offered Charley his hand. Charley allowed Langrishe to crush his fingers. "I trust you're enjoying yourself," Langrishe said. Charley couldn't read if that had meaning or not.

Behind Langrishe, the woman was smiling at him. Jack Langrishe's cigar smoke hung to her head like a swarm of summer bugs. "It's a kind thought," Charley said, "having a party for Mrs. Hickok."

"A charming lady," Langrishe said. He still had Charley's hand, pressing the knuckles into each other. From then on, for as long as he lived, Charley would wonder about any man who squeezed other men's hands.

"She's something of a performer herself," Langrishe said. "I was hoping to convince her to stay on long enough to appear in one of our productions."

"I don't think she favors acting," Charley said. He thought of her shyness. "Her talent runs a different way."

Langrishe let go of Charley's hand. "A performance is a performance, am I right?"

"I don't know," Charley said. The words sounded queerly familiar, and as he said them Mrs. Langrishe appeared, holding on to Solomon Star's arm, reminding him that he'd just said them to her.

She looked at him in a way that might have been friendly, but spoke only for Solomon Star. "I'm afraid I have to watch you every minute, Mr. Star," she said, "or you'll leave us. Here, have you met Mr. Tan? I saw him right over here . . . Some of our Chinese are very keen businessmen . . ."

Charley walked into the front room and took a long-necked glass of wine from the Negro. It tasted more familiar than the first glass, and he sat on a chair near the window and sipped it. When the Negro came past again, Charley stood up and traded glasses— empty for full—and caught a glimpse of himself in the mirror between two of the front windows. It looked like it fit him, to have a wineglass in his hand. With the next glass, the wine got easier to swallow and his mouth accustomed itself to the taste.

He tried to remember what it had felt like, being with Mrs. Langrishe, and if he wanted to be with her again. He didn't know. He had another glass of wine and looked around the room to see where she was. He couldn't see her, or Agnes, or anyone else he recognized. He caught his reflection in the mirror again, and for a second he didn't recognize it either. He looked into his wineglass, and his reflection was there too.

He sat down on the davenport and closed his eyes against his reflections. And being in that posture, he did not see Solomon Star attempt to assassinate the Chinaman.

There was a voice—the sheriff's, when he considered it later— and then a shot. When Charley opened his eyes, the Chinaman was running through the front room toward the door, holding his elbow. Sheriff Bullock was standing at the other end of the room, holding Solomon Star.

Solomon did not need to be held, though. He stood quietly, as agreeable as good weather, and watched the Chinaman run out the door. He did not object when the sheriff took the gun out of his hand.

The gun was a derringer with a barrel wide enough to accommodate a middle finger. It had gone off in a crowd and now, a minute later, there were already different stories about what had happened. Charley heard this from the couch: "The Chinese drew first."

Charley looked at the floor and saw spots of blood. When he

looked back at Solomon Star, the sheriff had changed his hold. He had his arm around his shoulder now, and he was smiling, squeezing Solomon against himself over and over, explaining that it was an accident.

Solomon did not argue, or pull himself away. There was a look on his face that wasn't far from a smile itself, as if he knew good news that nobody else had heard. Charley noticed the sheriff had put the derringer out of sight. He had not let go of Solomon's shoulders.

Mrs. Langrishe came into the front room then, looking for the source of the trouble. Her head moved from one place to another in a way that suggested a bat in the attic.

The sheriff stepped into her path, bringing Solomon with him. "I am afraid we have had a small accident in your absence," he said.

She smiled in a forgiving way, not knowing yet what she was forgiving.

Bullock said, "Mr. Star was showing the Chinese gentleman his pocket gun, and somehow it went off."

"Mr. Tan?"

The sheriff nodded. "It wasn't a serious wound," he said, "but Mr. Tan decided to have it attended to right away." Then he stared at his partner, who stood quietly, with no inclination to speak for himself.

"Mr. Star is mortified," the sheriff said, "that a firearm would go off in your home. And deeply upset."

Solomon nodded at that, and Mrs. Langrishe's gaze dropped to the floor and followed the spots of blood from there to the davenport. At the end of the blood she found Charley. "Mr. Tan was injured?" she said.

"Entirely superficial," the sheriff said. "Nothing much more than powder burns . . ." The smell of powder was still in the air, sweet and sour at the same time. The guests, who had frozen at the sound of the shot, edged back into their conversations, and their wine. The place had gone still all at once, and little by little life returned.

The sheriff kept his arm around Solomon, smiling at Mrs. Langrishe. He said, "I think Mr. Star and I are going to take our leave early, and satisfy ourselves on Mr. Tan's condition."

It looked to Charley like Solomon was already satisfied.

A moment after they left, Mrs. Langrishe sat down next to him on the davenport. The Negro walked by with more wine. "Well,

well," Charley said, feeling what he'd already drunk, "keeping the sabbath."

She closed her eyes. "A kindness," she said. "I tried to do a simple kindness, and it turned out morbid. I should never have come to this place."

Charley patted her hand, wondering if what she had done upstairs was included in the kindness or the morbidity. "It could of been worse," he said. He finished the wine in his glass and looked past Mrs. Langrishe for the Negro.

"I hope the shot didn't distress Mrs. Hickok," she said.

Charley wet his finger and ran it around the edge of the glass, but failed to produce music. "I expect she's hard to startle," he said. He looked toward the far end of the room, wanting to see her or the Negro.

"She has beautiful manners," Mrs. Langrishe said. "She appears so reserved, yet so determined . . ."

"There is an uncommon directness to her," Charley said.

Mrs. Langrishe turned on the cushion to look at him. "Do you find directness an attractive quality in women, Mr. Utter?"

"I find it a relief," he said. He saw from her face it wasn't the answer. He spotted the Negro and stood to wave him down. Glasses were exchanged, two for one. It was unpleasant stuff, but it grew on you, and he drank one before he resumed the conversation.

"This drink is closer to love than love itself," he said. He was looking at the glasses together—one full, one empty—when he said that.

She smiled at him and cocked her head, waiting for him to finish. He noticed the freckles on her chest again—where had the freckles been when they were upstairs?—and the tendons in her neck where it met her shoulders. He was hypnotized by her tendons. "Was that a toast?" she said. "'This drink is closer to love than love itself'?"

He felt himself changing ten ways a second. "Just that it grows on you until you need it," he said.

She smiled at him from the davenport, complimented, and he smiled back. It seemed to him that they were suddenly getting along better.

"Perhaps you would care to see the rest of the house," she said.

"That's a thought," he said. She took his arm and they went back up the stairs to the little room on the third floor. This time, though, he stopped her hands before he was halfway unbuttoned and stared into her face.

"What?" she whispered.

He shook his head, trying to remember what. "It's these tendons," he said, touching her neck. "And these freckles into your dress." He touched the freckles with the tip of his finger, moving from one to another. "I need time to count these freckles."

She put her hands on her hips and turned once in front of him, stopping halfway around to look over her shoulder. He touched the back of her neck and kept his fingers motionless while she turned under them.

He unfastened her dress from the top, one button at a time. She stood very still, and little bumps came up all over her chest. He kissed the bumps where he saw them, and then sat on the davenport, feeling dizzy.

She stepped out of her dress and all the silk and ruffles beneath it. She turned around again, slowly, and as she faced the window he reached out and touched her bottom. She stood still and he moved his hands over her cheeks, trying to think of something to say about them that she would like. They were soft and cool, and he saw the little bumps again, above his hands on her back.

"Do you like what you see, Mr. Utter?" she said.

He kissed the small of her back, and she moaned. Then he answered her, and she moaned again. "They're just damn near identical," he said.

He put one of his hands on her leg then, just above the knee, and slid it up until his thumb touched her bottom. He heard her breathing change, he felt a wetness in her hairs. He separated her lips and then pushed a finger inside, surprised at how small the opening was. It was nothing compared to Lurline's. Of course, Mrs. Langrishe didn't associate with the notorious. "I've got to ask Lurline sometime if bad men have naturally bigger peeders," he said out loud.

Mrs. Langrishe had been moving into him in a subtle way, but she stopped. "I beg your pardon?"

He said, "I was wondering if bad men had bigger peeders than normal citizens." She pulled away from him and turned around with an expression Charley didn't remember seeing before. It didn't look like anything you learned being an actress.

"It seems like it would go the other way," he said. "I mean, if it was a thing to make you one way or the other, it seems like a little peeder would make you mean."

She was just beginning to smile at him—he knew now that he could make her smile—when they heard the shots. There were four of them, from two different guns. He watched it change her face, and saw she was afraid, and then hateful. The civilities would not leave her alone.

The shots came from outside, and he went to the window. "It's probably a drunk," he said. "A miner or a tourist, of no consequence except to themself."

He got to the window, though, and saw that he was wrong.

NOT THAT SHE WASN'T DRUNK.

Jane was sitting in the flower garden. He knew it was Jane from her hat and her crutch, which was resting on the ground next to her. She had a pistol in each hand, and was holding them at different angles, one pointed more or less at the window. She cocked the other gun and pulled the trigger, and disappeared in smoke. A pinecone fell out of a nearby tree.

At the sound of the shot, Mrs. Langrishe covered herself with her dress and climbed into a corner of the davenport. "It's nothing to upset yourself," Charley said, watching Jane. She moved her head then, looking skyward, until he saw her chin under the brim of her hat, and then her nose, and then the bottle between her legs. Before he could see her eyes, she cocked the other gun and shot a board off the house. Charley pulled away from the window, and Mrs. Langrishe jumped at his movement, as if he were there to hurt her. "It's nothing to worry yourself," he said.

"Don't look at me," she said, and pulled the dress tighter against her body.

Charley looked back out the window in time to see Jane getting to her feet. She used one of her pistols, pressing the nose of it into the ground and pushing herself up, and the crutch. She stood up, swaying, and collected the other pistol and her bottle off the ground. Then she looked at the house in a vengeful way and started for the front door. "What is it?" Mrs. Langrishe said.

He turned around. She was still pressed into the corner of the davenport, but she was in her clothes. Elizabeth Langrishe's dressing habits defied the laws of time. "It's Jane Cannary," he said.

"It's a woman?"

"In a manner of speaking."

She stood up and walked to the window. Jane was gone. "Why would a woman be shooting a gun in my yard?" Mrs. Langrishe said, "Unless she was attacked . . ."

Charley shook his head. "There's nothing in the Black Hills to attack her," he said.

"Where did she go, then?"

Charley smiled an uncomfortable smile. "She may of invited herself to the party."

This time Mrs. Langrishe did not wait for him at the bottom of the stairs. By the time Charley got to the second floor, she was at the other end of the hallway, holding her skirts away from her feet, heading down into the party.

Charley felt an obligation to stop her, but he didn't know how. Mrs. Langrishe was a woman of sudden passions. The thought crossed his mind that Jack Langrishe might have lost his interest in womanhood and taken up crushing hands after he married her. A woman like Mrs. Langrishe, you might need a diversion.

The voice of Jane Cannary carried up the stairs and into his thoughts. Drunk and hoarse, she could not hide her apprehensions that she didn't fit. "I am here to see this woman claims to be married to my Bill," she shouted. "I aim to clear this up so I can get on to my career."

Charley moved to the top of the stairs. From there he could see her, standing in the doorway, squinting under the brim of her hat, holding a gun in one of her hands, leaning on the crutch with the other. The bottle was stuck into her coat pocket. Jane reeled, pointing the pistol at everything she saw. There was a weed stuck to the mud in the barrel.

Mrs. Langrishe was standing close to her, in a circle of guests. The resolve in her face was gone now, and Charley was struck again by how deep her fears went. He started down the stairs for Jane.

She sensed the movement and turned, falling back into the door, pointing the gun at the ceiling over his head. Her crutch bounced on Mrs. Langrishe's pine floors. She said, "Don't move, fancy, I'll shoot your peeder out your ass."

Charley came down the stairs. "It's only me," he said. "Nobody fancy."

"I seen who it is, Mr. Necktie," she said. Losing the crutch freed her left hand, and she reached into her pocket and found the bottle. She spit the cork on the floor next to her crutch.

She took a drink and her eyes watered. Charley took a step down the stairs. "This isn't any way to act," he said. She aimed the gun in the direction of his head and he stopped. Women were known for pulling the trigger when their eyes watered. The circle of guests opened between them, not to interfere with her trajectory.

"I don't need some damn fool tellin' me how to act at fancy parties," she said. She looked around the hallway then, at the guests and then at the ceiling. "I might just shoot this place up."

One of the women screamed, and that seemed to please her. A smile came across her face, and some of it came into her eyes too. "Now, where is this claim-jumper says she was married to my Bill?" she said. "Give her up or I'll make a scene . . ."

Charley was three stairs from the bottom, watching the gun, wondering how deep the mud went up into the barrel. He pictured the cylinder exploding and blowing apart all the glass in Mrs. Langrishe's house. He wondered how it got to be his concern. "Jane," he said, "you got a barrelful of mud in there."

"Then you wouldn't mind," she said, squinting down the barrel at his head, "if I was to squeeze off one in your direction." He stood still and waited to see if she would do it. She held him there a minute and then smiled and lowered the gun. "I couldn't shoot a friend of Bill's," she said. "It was a promise I made him before he died."

There was movement in the circle of guests then. Jane started, pointing the weapon at a dozen different people, and then Agnes Lake stepped out of the circle. She stood half a head taller than Jane, twice as strong, wise as the Bible. Her dress was a red color and her face was smooth and calm. "Well, well," Jane said. She lowered the pistol halfway to her side and stared at Agnes. Charley saw the chance to take it away, but he stood where he was.

"I heard you claimed you was the wife of Bill Hickok," Jane said. Agnes didn't move or answer. She looked as if she were trying to decide what this was in front of her.

Jane looked around the room, as if she had just noticed where she was. "I'd better get some answers," she said to the guests—not to Agnes—"Bill never told me about nobody else." Jane straightened herself as she spoke, trying to match Agnes Lake's height. She put her bottle back in her pocket and pulled the brim of her hat down until it bent the tops of her ears. She brushed at some of the weeds sticking to her coat. Then she considered Agnes Lake again, who still hadn't moved. Jane took a step backward and someone laughed out loud. She pointed her gun in the direction of the sound, but without an intention to shoot.

"I am Agnes Lake," Agnes said then. Her voice was slow and even. Charley noted the change that came over her in the presence of violence, it was the opposite of Mrs. Langrishe's change. "I married Bill Hickok in Cheyenne, Wyoming, in the spring of this year," she said, "and he took me back to my home in St. Louis until he could locate a proper position."

Jane shook her head. "Bill would of mentioned it," she said. "He never said a word."

The guests began to notice Jane's smell, and edged away, smiling at each other. Charley said, "Let me take you somewhere else, Jane."

She looked at him, as sorry as she had ever been in her life. "Where?"

"Somewhere else," he said.

She looked at him a long minute, and then turned back to Agnes Lake. "Bill loved me," she said. "Me and him were partners."

Then she said, "He was my husband as much as yours." She had dropped back to normal height and was leaning against the door frame, her crutch and the cork to her bottle on the floor at Agnes's feet. One of the guests laughed; this time Jane didn't bother to point her gun.

"Somebody give me my damn crutch," she said. "This ain't my kind of party." Charley stepped toward the crutch, but Agnes Lake bent first. She handed Jane the crutch and then patted her shoulder. Jane jumped at the touch.

"A man like Bill, there must have been a lot of us that loved him," Agnes said. Jane shook at the words. "And he loved us back," Agnes said, "in his own way, each of us different."

Jane blinked and wiped at her eye. Charley thought she would cry. "You ain't too bad for a fancy," Jane said. "I'm surprised Bill didn't mention you." And then, still holding a gun, and in front of forty witnesses, Calamity Jane Cannary bowed her head and did as much of a curtsy as her bad leg would allow.

Then she pulled the brim of her hat down over her eyes and walked out the door. Once it had closed, Mrs. Langrishe excused herself and could be heard a few minutes later, in the back, emptying her stomach. The guests exchanged small smiles, and added Mrs. Langrishe's discomfort to the stories of the afternoon. Charley found the Negro in the kitchen and sat down next to him in front of the west window, intending to drink what was left of the wine.

"That Miss Calamity," the Negro said, "she surely do know how to light up the room."

Charley nodded. "It was getting dull, with only the Chinese shot," he said. The sun was moving toward the hills, long shadows lay in the yard. He thought of Bill in the ground; he wondered if Jane would find someplace and go to sleep. The guests had begun to leave and Mrs. Langrishe stood at the door, looking pale, thanking them for coming. There was dried blood on her floors and the smell of gunpowder hung dead in the air.

"Thank you for joining us," she said.

He did not see Agnes Lake until she sat down in the chair next to him and poured herself a glass of the wine. She looked at the Negro, who excused himself to a different part of the house. "I got to help the missus clean up," he said.

They sat still and looked out the window. "I am leaving here tomorrow," she said. He thought she might be asking him to come along. She put her hand over his and left it there, and it was more private than anything that had gone on with Mrs. Langrishe upstairs.

In the yard the shadows had moved and grown. He felt the shadows coming for him before he was ready.

"Bill had his own life," she said a little later. "And he left it unfinished. This place is unfinished too."

He said, "This place feeds off its dead." He poured from a fresh bottle of wine. He said, "It feels like there's something more to do."

She smiled at him and shook her head. She spoke so deep in her throat Charley could barely hear it. "He had his own life, and he lived it unfinished. There's some like that, people and places . . . It isn't what's left to do at the end, it's the things left unfinished along the way." He thought she might be asking him again.

"That was a kind thing you did," he said, meaning her meeting with Jane.

She looked at their hands on the table. "He had his own life," she said again, "there's nothing to blame or forgive in that, it was just his life. The way he lived it leaves an ache in your heart, but that's my heart and yours, not Bill's."

"There's no hurry to leave," Charley said.

She squeezed his hand and finished what was left in her glass.

She nodded toward the door, where Mrs. Langrishe and her guests were thanking each other for being there. "I'll leave Bill to them," she said. "They'll keep him alive."

"They don't know the first thing."

She smiled at him and filled their glasses. "That wasn't accidental," she said. She held her glass between them and he touched it with his. He wasn't sure what they were toasting, it wasn't Bill.

"Mending hearts," she said, sounding like Bill now. Sounding like Bill forgiving him.

"Things ought to of happened another way," he said.

And she touched him a different way—maybe the way she'd touched Jane—and drank her wine. It left the tips of a tiny wet moustache on her lip. "Things don't care how they happen," she said, "that's left for us, to care." And he thought she was asking him again, and he would have gone with her then, if he had been sure.

In the door, Mrs. Langrishe had thanked the last of her guests and turned to the kitchen, watching him and Agnes holding hands across the table. He picked up something ungracious in her expression.

"I'll picture what you did for Jane," he said. "That will stick with me." Agnes smiled at him—a smile like Bill's—and leaned across the table to kiss his cheek. He felt the wine on her lip. Then she stood up, straightened herself, and started for the door. The sight of Mrs. Langrishe stopped her cold.

"There's no need to hurry off," he said.

And then she was crying. Not sobs and wails—that didn't fit her—just crying. He stood up and put his arms around her again, the second and last time in their lives. He whispered in her ear. "Mending hearts," he said. "We got mending hearts."

And in two minutes Agnes Lake had composed herself and wiped the wine and tears off her face, and Charley stood, nose to nose with her, wanting to go with her wherever she went, from then on, for all the lost places of his life. He said, "You don't have to hurry off."

And she smiled at him again—he swore he could see Bill in it—and she said good-bye.

He tried to walk her back to the hotel, but she shook her head—it didn't look like much more than a sudden chill—and left him there in the kitchen, with Mrs. Langrishe watching him from the front door.

He sat down and finished what was left in the bottle. In a few minutes Mrs. Langrishe touched the back of his neck, moving his hair apart in back and smoothing the muscles there with her fingers.

"Would you care to see the rest of the house, Mr. Utter?" she said.

He shook his head, trying to clear himself of the feeling he'd just lost his last chance. The feeling would not shake loose, so he tried something else.

"Why not?" he said.

SOLOMON STAR SAT ON THE BED IN HIS ROOM, WATCHING SETH BULLOCK search his personal property for weapons. First the closet, then the trunk, then the drawers. "I only possess the one side arm, Mr. Bullock," he said, "and the derringer."

Seth Bullock didn't answer. He finished in the drawer and then he moved Solomon off the bed and looked under the mattress. When he put the mattress back, Solomon sat back down.

Bullock stood in the middle of the room, studying the ceiling. "There has never been a false word between us," Solomon said.

Bullock stared at him then, angry and afraid. He didn't know where to start. "I thought you were quits with this damn business," he said after a minute. "You said you were through with it." He walked from the center of the room to the closet and looked inside again. Everything in there was spaced and neat and exact, his suits hung in the order of the week he wore them, his shoes reflected the lamp on the table. For some reason, Solomon's shoes were never muddy. There was nothing in his closet to suggest a streak of violence. In Bullock's experience—which was not as wide as was claimed—the violent were messy. "The time's come," he said, "to explain yourself and the Chinese."

Solomon sat on the bed with his hands in his lap. He was still wearing the suit he'd worn to Mrs. Langrishe's party, still wearing his hat. He shook his head no.

"I saved you twice," Bullock said. Solomon seemed to go into a trance. He began to rock back and forth on the bed, he didn't seem to hear the words. Bullock said, "If that was anything but a Chinese, I couldn't of got you out of it."

Solomon looked at his hands and rocked. Bullock raised his voice, which he had never done in Mrs. Tubb's rooming house. It was one of her rules. No hats at the table, no dynamite in the rooms, no raised voices. "Is it all the Chinese or just the one? You know how many slant-eyes there are?" he said. "There's more of them than us. They got a whole country of them . . ." Solomon rocked on the bed. "What happened to that Chinese girl?" Bullock said quietly. Solomon looked at his soft, small hands. Bullock tried to picture them holding the instruments of death, but it wouldn't come.

Of course, he couldn't picture Solomon pulling a derringer out of his pants pocket and shooting a two-hundred-pound Chinese in Elizabeth Langrishe's living room either. The lack of harmony in that scene had froze him, with the rest of the room, until it was too late to stop it. The Chinese had believed it earlier, and he'd turned and begun to run. The bullet caught him just above the elbow and spun him halfway around. Bullock had grabbed Solomon a second later. Solomon hadn't fought him at all, it was a violence without passion.

"You got to promise me something," Bullock said after a while.

"No, I don't." His voice sounded flat and queer.

Bullock slapped him. It knocked Solomon off the bed, his hat rolled into a corner. Bullock stood still; Solomon got to his hands and knees, and then used the bed to pull himself back up. A drop of blood rolled out of one side of his nose into the gully of his lip.

Bullock wondered if he'd gone crazy himself.

Solomon took a handkerchief out of his pants pocket and blotted his nose. The side of his face where the blow landed was puffed and red, and the eye was watering. He was as calm as Bullock had ever seen him.

"Are you hurt?" Bullock said. He sat down next to him on the bed and examined his nose. "I never intended to put a hand on your person," he said. "Not in this life."

Solomon seemed uninterested. He studied the blot in his handkerchief, then held it against his nose again. Bullock said, "You see where this has led? Partner against partner."

"It doesn't matter," Solomon said.

"We got a business to run." Bullock touched the side of Solomon's nose with the pad of his finger. Solomon didn't move. It was beginning to swell; Bullock thought it was probably broken. "What doesn't matter?"

Solomon stood up and began to take off his clothes. The blood in his nose was thick and slow, and had begun from the other nostril too.

Solomon hung his coat and pants in the closet. He folded his shirt and put it in one of the drawers Bullock had searched. He stood in the middle of the room, bare-chested in long underwear, and waited.

"What?" Bullock said.

"Nothing."

"Nothing what?" Bullock stood up and followed Solomon around the room asking him questions he wouldn't answer.

With Bullock off the bed, Solomon lay down. He didn't wash his face or scrub his teeth, he didn't clean the blood off his lips. He pulled the blanket up around his chin and stared at the ceiling, and Bullock thought he saw a secret smile.

"In what manner did the Chinese offend you?" Bullock said.

Solomon didn't answer. Bullock stood in the middle of the room, feeling awkward and strange. "Did I hurt you?"

There was no answer.

"Let me get a rag and wash off that blood." He didn't want to leave it like this. He poured a little water from the pitcher into the washbowl and wet a cloth. He sat down on the bed and began to wipe at Solomon's lip and chin. The side of his nose was turning dark and Bullock was careful not to touch it with the cloth.

"Say something, Solomon."

Solomon shook his head. Bullock stood up to leave. He put the damp cloth over the top of the lamp and waited until the flame died. He opened the door and looked back into the room.

"It doesn't matter, Mr. Bullock," Solomon said.

Bullock stepped back into the room, suddenly wanting to slap him again. "Tell me the damn words."

He shook his head. "There are none."

"There's always words. If something happens, there's names for it."

"Not in this." He spoke slowly. "Nothing matters less than the words. The heart of things is the event, and nothing spoken changes it, Mr. Bullock. You might as well blow back at the wind."

There was a lamp in the hallway, and the light from it came through the open door and lay across the blanket. Solomon's face lay in the half-dark beside it. It might have been the shadows, but it looked like he was smiling. He closed his eyes and lay as still as the dead.

"Solomon?"

He didn't open his eyes, or move in any way.

And Bullock waited by the door another minute, staring at him through the dark. It took a minute, and then he saw it. He knew he saw it, a secret smile.

"I got to watch you the rest of my life, don't I?" he said.

PART FOUR

JANE

1878

On the spring of 1877, a woman named Nell McCleod was found half naked, wandering in Spearfish Canyon west of Deadwood. Her face had been laid open by Indians, top to bottom, blinding her in one eye. She was discovered by the horse-trader Brick Pomeroy and his brother Mike, who returned her to her farm outside Deadwood, and there recovered the bodies of four children—all girls—dead several days.

Charley was sitting on the porch of Lurline's House of Distinction when he saw the story in the *Black Hills Pioneer*. The services were a week past, and Mrs. McCleod, according to the newspaper, had been taken to the state asylum at Yankton to prevent her from furthering her injuries. He knew right away Nell McCleod was the widow woman he had gone to for milk when Malcolm was hurt, and that her babies were the ones who held on to his fingers and pants legs, as if they knew what was coming.

He had moved into Lead that year, two miles south of Deadwood, to oversee the operation of the house. He owned ninety percent, Lurline owned ten, for the use of her name. She claimed to have stolen the cream of Deadwood's upstairs girls for him. They did not look like stolen cream to Charley, but ever since Agnes had left he'd lost interest in those matters, and wasn't inclined to make judgments.

Once a week he visited the third floor of Mrs. Langrishe's home, once in a while Lurline would come to his room at night and bite his legs, but his heart wasn't in any of it. He thought it was the years catching up to him.

Lurline had eight girls in all; one of them was sitting on the railing at the other end of the porch. Her name was Lu-Lu, and she claimed to be seventeen years old. Lurline liked to keep her outside because she was the prettiest, except for Lurline herself, and made an impression on the miners.

Charley read the story in the newspaper again, slower, not to miss any facts. "That poor woman," Lu-Lu said. Charley looked up, wondering how the girl knew what he was reading. "I heard it was in the paper," she said, "how the Indians raped and murdered her daughters."

Charley looked across the porch, thinking the girl was probably closer to fourteen. The way she said the words, it didn't sound like she knew what *murdered* and *raped* meant. Then she said, "They ought to cut the peeders off every buck in the Hills, to get even."

Charley thought of the woman, the day he saw her at the cemetery. She seemed strong enough then, she didn't ask him for help. The babies had asked, though. He could still feel the little one wrapped around his leg, how hard it was to pry her loose.

The ground shook, and rattled the insides of the house. The Hearst Company was under the town now, following the gold. The hard-rock miners bore into the quartz with drills and sledgehammers, drilling holes a few yards apart and filling them with giant powder. They cut their fuses different lengths, allowing for the time it took them to burn.

When it went right, the charges all exploded together. The ground shook and the houses rattled. When it went wrong—when the charges didn't all fire—the miners could either stay where they were, trying to light half-burned fuses by hand, or they could return the next day and hope they didn't drill into a pocket of powder.

Any man with missing parts was assumed to have been a miner, and the one-handed were always welcome at the eateries and bars in Lead, even without money. The town had turned rich off the Hearst Company and the hard-rock miners, while the placer claims in Deadwood had ebbed. And the towns were as different as their finances.

A man who owned Lurline's House of Distinction featuring the cream of the Hills' upstairs girls would be close to respectable in Deadwood, but it was a different circumstance in Lead. Lurline had told him there were already petitions to remove the business from city limits.

If there was one thing Charley hated, it was petitions.

The ground shook again; there was yelling inside the house. He thought of the widow, trying to remember everything she'd said. You couldn't always tell when somebody was asking for help. He wondered why she'd stayed in the Hills after her husband died, he wondered what the choices were. He would not let himself think of the babies, and their choices.

"They ought to cut the peeders off all the bucks," Lu-Lu said again, "and then they ought to cut the balls off Captain Jack Crawford and every one of them Minutemen, not that they got any to remove."

"What do you want with Jack Crawford's balls?" he said.

She sat forward on the rail, showing the front of her chest. "Them cowards was out there," she said. "Watched the whole thing happen."

"Nobody's like that," he said.

"They did," she said. "I heard it twice last night alone, that they stood and watched it, some of them laughed."

Charley said, "People get things wrong, child. It feeds on itself."

"It's what I heard," she said. "That they made a secret pact not to tell, but they all went out and got drunk that night and every one of them cowards blubbered it out."

"Don't believe anything you hear in a whorehouse," Charley said.

"I believe everything."

"You're still a baby."

"Well, then," she said, "what does that make you?"

Charley chewed on that while Lu-Lu smiled at passing miners. The ground shook and Lurline came to the door, red-faced and out of breath. She said two of the girls were rolling on the floor upstairs, biting until it bled. Nothing took away an upstairs girl's attraction faster than infected bites, and Charley stood up to follow her inside.

As he went through the door Lu-Lu said, "It's true, what I said."

He stopped for a moment and looked at her again. "Whatever you heard, it was different from the way you heard it. You can count on that."

She bunched her mouth into a little pout. "I believe what I believe," she said. He couldn't fathom why it mattered what this girl thought.

Lurline called to him from inside the house. She said the girls were ruining each other's looks, and had torn down the purple curtains. He heard them crying but stayed a minute longer in the doorway, trying to think of something else to say to Lu-Lu. Nothing came, though, and he headed upstairs to release the whores from each other's jaws.

That night he walked to Deadwood. He could have taken the gelding, but the sky was clear and the air smelled like rain, and he craved the quiet. He didn't realize he was going to the cemetery until he arrived at the south end of town and had to choose a direction to walk. His legs were beginning to ache by then, and he was thinking of getting out of the whore business.

He turned right and crossed the little bridge over the Whitewood Creek, and began to climb. Once, halfway up, he stumbled in the dark, and stood motionless until the pain passed. In the pause he considered evening walks, and was against them for anybody who'd ever been shot in the legs. Or bitten by whores. His middle finger, where one of them had gotten him that afternoon, felt like it was the size of a potato.

He heard a noise above him. He listened, concentrating, but it didn't repeat. He reached behind his coat and loosened the knife in his belt. He was careful up the hill, feeling the ground with his moccasins before he committed his weight. He walked in that way unconsciously, and the pain was gone from his legs and hips. Then he came to the cemetery and stopped and listened again. Something was there, off to the right, hiding.

He stepped a few feet into the treeline and passed the graves earliest dug, getting closer to the source. He saw Bill's marker in the dark, and beyond that four little piles of dirt in a line, pointed to the north star. It stopped him, those piles of dirt, and for a moment he forgot he was not alone. He turned away.

It was a moonless night, but in the light from the stars he could see the inscription he'd left on Bill's grave. His eyes blurred and he wiped at them with the sleeve of his coat.

When he looked up, there was Captain Jack Crawford. He was sitting on a stump a few feet into the trees, behind the last of the four piles of dirt. He was holding his hat in his hands, staring inside it. From the look of the pose, the Poet of the Prairie had been sitting there waiting for him. One thing was certain, all the actors in the Hills weren't in the employ of the Langrishe Theater.

Charley stepped toward Captain Jack, letting himself kick pine needles and break twigs. Captain Jack looked up slowly, showing

Charley his face. "You ought to announce yourself," he said. "I could of mistook you for an Indian."

Charley didn't answer. He looked at the fresh graves, and saw that they were dug slightly different sizes. At the far end was the baby. Something caught in his throat, and he couldn't have spoken then, even if there had been something he wanted to say. Captain Jack's eyes hung on him like wet clothes.

"I just came to pay my respects," Captain Jack said. "There wasn't a thing could of saved them."

Charley looked at the graves. "You don't have to say a thing to me," he said. "I didn't ask any questions."

"You heard the stories."

"A whore told me a story, I don't believe whorehouse gossip."

"It's not just whores."

The pain crawled back into Charley's legs, starting in the hips and moving down. Captain Jack said, "There's stories all over town, what happened at the McCleod farm."

The pain had little voices, the voices were the babies'.

"It isn't right," Captain Jack said, "to circulate stories without giving a man a chance to defend himself. It's got me half ashamed, and there's nothing I could of done . . ."

Charley's eyes filled again and he pitched his head back and looked at the stars.

"It's not right."

Charley took a deep breath, and his eyes came back to the graves. He couldn't keep himself from looking. "It's not right to be babies in the ground either," he said.

"I'm no coward," Captain Jack said.

Charley looked at the graves.

"I got to explain myself in this."

"Not to me," he said.

Captain Jack didn't seem to hear him. "I can't tell it in town, every pilgrim and rough in the Hills already got their own version. Rumors and lies . . ."

Charley was quiet. There were dead babies' voices in his legs and he felt Bill there, watching.

"By the time we came onto the property," Captain Jack said, "all of them were already dead but the widow and one of the girls. There were thirty Indians that I counted in the yard, we were only eight. The widow was holding the little girl. The Indians were scared of the widow—she was crazy—but they wanted the little one."

Charley began to walk away.

"Wait."

"I can't hear stories of Indians killing babies," Charley said.

"I'll leave that end of it out."

Charley waited.

"It was over fast, anyway. The widow faced them in the yard, them on their ponies, her holding one of her hands like a claw, baring her teeth. They were scared of her, but they kept at it, poking and teasing, until she dropped what she had on the ground. It was that fast."

It was quiet in the cemetery and Charley heard the voices clearer. There were little round mouths in there making them. Bill had settled into his place over the brim of Charley's hat and watched, as if it was Charley's idea to accommodate this poser in the first place.

"It was thirty Indians," he said again, "and we were eight. That's death's odds when none of your men are trained in battle. It was all I could do to keep them from breaking ranks and running . . ."

Charley smelled fresh dirt and the pines. He wanted to leave the hill now, and Captain Jack Crawford, and the dead babies and Bill. He wanted to find a bottle of brown whiskey. He thought he might visit Mrs. Langrishe and have her show him the third floor.

On reconsideration, he thought he might find Pink Buford's bull-dog and feed him boiled eggs instead. The dog was better company afterwards, even with that egg gas.

On reconsideration, he didn't know what he might do. He needed to do something, though, to hold off the voices.

He left Captain Jack without another word and walked down the road into town, mindless of where his feet fell, tripping again and again on rocks. He felt Bill, just out of sight over his shoulder. "Don't you ever sleep?" he said out loud. He didn't mean it in a serious way, more to lighten the mood of the night, but as soon as he heard it, he pictured Bill trying to sleep with the four murdered babies planted into the ground next to him.

He held that picture and crossed the Whitewood back into town. He stood for a minute at the head of Main Street, deciding where to go for a bottle. There was no place in Deadwood he hadn't used up. Standing still, though, the babies' voices came clearer, and so he moved.

A wood plank sidewalk had been constructed on the east side of Main Street from the south end of town all the way to the badlands, and Charley walked from one end to the other without muddying his pants. He considered civilization and progress, and wasn't against it as long as it wasn't planned more than two weeks in advance.

He walked into the badlands and into the mud, and went straight to Nuttall and Mann's Number 10. Harry Sam Young poured him a drink and refused payment.

"I heard you were running a house up the hill," the bartender said. Charley put his finger in the whiskey and stirred until the specks floating on top disappeared into the funnel. Then he drank it, all, before it could settle, and Harry Sam Young filled it again.

"It's onerous work," he said, feeling the whiskey right away. "I got bit today." He showed him the finger. "It's a worse business than bartending," Charley said, "at least you can bite back."

Harry Sam Young touched the finger, admiring the swelling. "That's likely broke," he said. "Can you move it?"

"Didn't try yet."

"It won't move, it's broke."

Charley shrugged and looked at one side of the finger, then the other, noticing the spots where she had broken the skin.

"I expect it's infected," the bartender said. "I'd as soon be bit by a snake as a whore, they don't pay no attention whatsoever to where they put their mouth."

Charley stuck the finger in the glass of whiskey and it stung him clear to the elbow. "Stings, don't it?" Harry Sam Young said.

Charley looked at him. "If it stings," Harry said, "it's infected. That's what the sting is, whiskey fighting germs."

"You ever splashed whiskey in your eye?" Charley said.

Harry Sam Young thought it over. "You don't need infected eyes for whiskey to sting," he admitted after a while. "But if they was infected, you don't think they'd sting worse?"

Harry Sam Young spent half his life in bars, and could argue logic with anybody. A loser at the card table abused him then, calling for a gin and bitters, and the bartender moved off to serve him. Charley saw a platform had been erected over the door to display Bill's death chair. There was a sign that said, IN THIS CHAIR THE FEARLESS GUNFIGHTER JAMES BUTLER (WILD BILL) HICKOK MET HIS MAKER ON AUGUST 2, 1876. SHOT IN THE BACK BY JACK MCCALL WHILST HOLDING ACES AND EIGHTS.

Looking closer, Charley saw there were cards propped against the legs of the chair, spotted with dried blood.

Harry Sam Young finished with the gambler and returned. "They put it up for the tourists," he said. "It draws people, the death chair of the famous."

"Is it Bill's blood?"

Harry Sam Young shook his head. "It ain't even his chair, for sure," he said. "The cleaning boy come in that morning and had the place spotless by the time anybody else got out of bed."

Charley stared at the platform, unable to decide if that made it better or worse. "Whose blood is it?"

Harry Sam Young scratched his head. "Originally?"

Charley stared at him.

"I believe it belonged to Pink Buford's bulldog. Pink fought him with another bulldog—it was a reprobate come in from Chicago with this animal in a cage. Like it was wild. Pink, he don't care. He's run out of local dogs to fight."

"I'd hoped he'd retired him." Thinking of Bill.

Harry Sam Young shook his head. "Pink don't retire nothing that can still make money. He fought him with a pig last month, the noisiest event in the history of the badlands. Sheriff Bullock himself showed up to stop it, said it was waking up respectable people. By then, though—"

"A *pig*?"

"They been known to kill farmers."

"So has lightning." Charley drank what was in the glass and Harry Sam Young poured him another. Charley took five dollars out of his shirt pocket and put it on the bar. Harry Sam Young ignored it. "Farmers stay alone too much," Charley said, "they get strange. They get so strange pigs kill them."

The bartender said, "Well, as fighters pigs are loud, but not much else."

Charley felt the whiskey in his ears, meaning it had soaked through his brain to get there. "A *pig*?"

"Pink's dog killed the pig, he's killed a wolf, there was rumors of a Colorado man had a bobcat that fought. Pink don't care, bring your contestant and your money. He says he'll fight a bear, so another dog don't scare him, even a dog that looks like Pink's and they kept him in a cage."

"I don't like to see anything in a cage."

"Pink's dog got his leg chewed half off before he killed him. He'd ripped out his stomach and the animal from Chicago still wouldn't let go of his leg. Afterwards, Pink brought him in here to clean his cuts. Mr. Nuttall seen the blood, and got it in his head to drip some on a poker hand and put it up there with the chair."

Charley looked at the platform again. "There's worse blood," he said. "Bill had an affection for the dog's spirit."

An hour later Captain Jack Crawford walked through the doorway. Half of the talk that evening still concerned the McCleod woman and her babies—it would until there was something bloody to replace it—and when Crawford came in, that half of the talk stopped.

He took an empty seat at one of the tables and looked toward the bar. The men sitting there turned away. He called to Harry Sam Young for a glass of milk. Harry refused him. "It spoilt," he said.

The room went quieter. Captain Jack smiled and looked around him, found nobody who would meet his eye. "That's how it is, is it?"

"All I said was the milk's spoilt," Harry Sam Young said. "The lady we got it from's left town." He stared at Captain Jack and Captain Jack stared back.

"I'll have something else."

Harry Sam Young poured him a glass of the same whiskey Charley was drinking. He put it on the bar and said, "One dollar."

Captain Jack stood to collect his drink. Somebody said, "Momma ain't going to like this." A whore laughed and then it was quiet. He drank the whiskey where he found it and put another dollar on the bar. Harry Sam Young refilled the glass, and Captain Jack took it to the table.

There had been two men there before, but both of them moved while he was at the bar. He sat down, alone now, and looked at the glass in his hand. Charley drank what was left in his and stood up to leave.

Captain Jack called to him from across the room. "Charley Utter, I'm no worse than you, or nobody else." His voice was already a little slower than his lips. Men that didn't drink shouldn't drink.

"I got no appetite for this tonight," Charley said to the bartender. Captain Jack made his lips into a circle and put them against the lip of the glass. He poured half of what was in it into his mouth, and held it there a minute trying to get it down.

"Let me fill that once more," Harry Sam Young said to Charley. "It's been a long time, and you ain't told me nothing about the whore business yet."

Charley considered it, and Harry filled the glass. That's all the edge a bartender needed, for a man to consider. Captain Jack got up again, holding his glass, and Harry Sam Young filled it too. "There ain't a man here," he said in his poetry-reciting voice, "would have done any different from me."

It was not the first time Charley had heard a man lose his English usage when he drank, it was a sign of forced schooling.

"I fought with Custer, I been wounded in battle," he said. He was pushing his voice now. "And a battle's one thing, death's odds is another. There wasn't nothing the Minutemen could of done but got killed ourselves. There was forty Indians that I counted in the yard, that many again in the trees, waiting."

One of the men who had moved from Crawford's table said, "You couldn't get forty Indians one place if you was giving away puppies."

Captain Jack's face turned red and he drank his whiskey. A gambler shouted, "I'm sorry, Momma," and killed his drink too, and in the time it took to say those words, they became famous. And a long time after Captain Jack Crawford and the McCleod woman and the Minutemen were gone and forgotten, the gamblers and miners and whores who drank in the badlands shouted "I'm sorry, Momma" before they drank. Tourists took the expression to other parts of the country, and at least one of them named a bar that. The I'M SORRY MOMMA. He was from California.

Captain Jack got himself another drink. And another. "Being around them girls all day long," Harry Sam Young said to Charley, "do you ever dally with more than one at once?"

Charley scratched his chin. "I've heard of it, but I never tried it."

"I heard whore men try every girl they hire."

Charley closed one eye to look at it from a business angle. "My advice on that," he said, "would be to visit somebody else's house, if you were inclined that way."

"Whilst you got it free right there?"

"None of it's free. The cheapest kind is what you only paid for once." He had received a letter from a lawyer in Empire, Colorado, earlier in the week, addressed to him in care of Lurline's House of Distinction, notifying him that Matilda had filed for dissolution of their marriage. He reflected at the time that her letters had been cool lately.

And he wondered at the cost, and he wondered what kind of ties were left after a marriage was dissolved. More to the point, he wondered if Malcolm was still his relation, and what obligations he had to keep him out of trouble.

The boy had set up ministries in every mining camp for twenty miles, and spent the week on horseback, traveling from one to the other in Preacher Smith's old clothes, preaching the Bible of the Black Hills. Whenever he was in Deadwood he stalked Al Swearingen, waiting for his confrontation with the evil side of the Lord.

"I might like to try two at once," Harry Sam Young said. "I begun to think about it last week, one of the whores in here mentioned it in passing to a tourist."

Charley said, "You're always welcome at Lurline's, Harry. You're a gentleman."

"You don't have no rules against two at once?" He filled Charley's glass, which was already full, and offered him a cigar. Charley bit off the end and allowed Harry Sam Young to light it.

"The only rule is no hurting the girls, and not to shoot in the rooms. It's the tourists that seem to want to hurt them, I don't know why."

Harry Sam Young said, "I never wanted to hurt a girl. I just want to try two at once. Ever since I heard about it I don't want one at a time."

"Peeder's a contrary thing," Charley said. "Given a choice, anything else in the body prefers what it's used to."

It was quiet while they both fit their cigars this way and that in their mouths and thought about the nature of peeders. After a while the bartender said, "I expect that's what keeps a whorehouse in business."

Charley said, "What keeps it in business is those that would otherwise go without. There's miners come in every week, don't even take off their pants."

"I heard of that, they just talk."

"It's to have somebody know they're here."

Sometime later Handsome Banjo Dick Brown came in on crutches. They had amputated him just above the knee, and he'd cut off his pants leg on that side and sewn the ends together so it looked like that was the way pants came from the store. Even so, nobody called him Handsome Dick anymore. He never sang in public, he'd quit womanizing, although there were plenty still interested.

Charley kept track of Handsome from Lurline, first one thing and then another. She'd said Handsome didn't hold it against him that he was the one that crippled him. He came further into the saloon, awkward on his crutches, and hopped the last few feet into the only empty chair in the room, next to Captain Jack.

Charley stared at his cigar. There was no pleasure in seeing what he'd done.

"Nobody forgot who shot Handsome Dick," the bartender said. He meant it as a compliment. Ever since Charley invited him to visit Lurline's, Harry hadn't left him more than thirty seconds without a compliment.

Charley looked again at the seam where Handsome Dick had sewn his pants leg together. Lurline had told him that Handsome's leg hurt him after it was cut off. He could still feel it there after it was two weeks buried in the ground.

She said sometimes he still felt it.

Charley tried another sip of whiskey; it tasted like somebody had poured tree sap in it. "My last remark on the subject," he said, leaning closer to the bartender. "The only pure thing is a thought. When you first think something, it's pure. Shooting or business or peeders. But everywhere betwixt the thought and the deed are impurities and distractions, until in the end if the deed resembles the thought at all, you can count yourself luckier than most."

Harry Sam Young poured himself a drink and looked troubled. "That could be true for some and not for others."

"We're all the same flesh and blood."

The bartender looked at the chair on the platform over the door.

"He had his distractions," Charley said.

"Not with a gun in his hand."

"No," he said, "there was a purity in him that way."

The bartender moved to fill Charley's glass. Charley pulled it away. He heard Captain Jack and Handsome at the table. "There was fifty Indians in that widow's yard. It wasn't a thing we could of done but give them eight extra scalps."

"I don't hold no grudges," Handsome Dick said.

"It ain't fair to be accused by rumor."

"I don't want no revenge, Indians or nobody else. I killed my share of men, I don't need to get even with nobody over this."

"I been shot myself," Captain Jack said. "Wounded twice at the Battle of Spottsylvania, the Forty-seventh Regiment of Pennsylvania Volunteers, 1864."

"Don't hold grudges," Handsome Dick said. "Don't ever hold grudges."

"I forgave the South when Lincoln did. And though my body bears the scars of conflict, there is no such in my heart." He raised his voice. "And I do not judge other men, else I have walked in their footsteps."

"Or their footstep," Handsome said. He laughed, too loud, and false. He hadn't shaved in days, his shirt was dirty. He'd lost his leg and his shine; he wasn't even handsome anymore, when you looked close.

"It's one thing to meet the red devil in fair combat," Captain Jack said after a while, "but fifty Indians—Custer had as much chance."

"I heard Custer died with a smile on his face, that he had forgiven his enemies and overcome the evil side of the Lord."

Captain Jack squinted at his drink. "I didn't hear nothing like that. I heard he killed with his last breath."

"Father Malcolm told me," Handsome said.

Charley decided he'd have the drink after all.

"I never heard of an evil side to the Lord," Captain Jack said. "It sounds Indian."

"It's as white as you or me, a blue-eyed white boy in a black coat. The disciple of Preacher Smith, who died with a smile on his face."

"I believe in forgiveness," Captain Jack said.

A gambler shouted, "I'm sorry, Momma," and killed a shot of whiskey. Captain Jack did not acknowledge the insult.

Charley could not get his eyes away from the table and the seam where Handsome Dick's leg had been. He pictured Malcolm and a whole ministry of the lame. He pictured Matilda.

"What is your experience with the aftermaths of the dissolution of marriage?" he said.

Harry Sam Young looked startled. "All this talk of the evil side of the Lord, it's a passing fancy, like pink gin. No reason to get morose."

"Dissolution of a marriage," Charley said. "There must be somebody comes in here's had a marriage dissolved."

"Brick Pomeroy shot his wife," the bartender said. "He said it was accidental, and it might of been."

Over at the table, Handsome Dick and Captain Jack Crawford

were leaning into each other, getting farther away. "I promised my mother, liquor would never pass my lips."

"She'll forgive you," Handsome said. "You got to sin to be forgiven. It's two sides to everything."

"There wasn't a thing could of saved that woman's babies . . ."

"I don't want revenge on nobody, I told you that."

Even the tourists had turned their backs on the table now, and Captain Jack and Handsome were left to each other.

Charley walked back to Lead, talking to Bill to keep the voices in his legs quiet. He was worn down, and he did not think he could stand to hear the babies' voices again.

IN OCTOBER OF 1877, BOONE MAY WAS APPOINTED SHERIFF OF THE town of Lead. He was too sick to hunt highwaymen for Sheriff Bullock anymore, and his credit had become an off-and-on thing, even in the Gem Theater.

He asked for and received two hundred dollars a month, payable in advance, and in exchange agreed to remove Charley Utter and his whorehouse from Lead city limits. There were petitions nailed to walls all over town, some of them signed by regular customers at Lurline's House of Distinction, saying the proper place for a whorehouse in the northern Hills was Deadwood. No one said a word to Charley except Lurline, who was unworried. "They're all scairt of you," she said, "on account of you shot off Handsome Dick's leg."

It turned out, of course, that the Hearst Company's supervisors were also scared of their wives, who objected to looking at the business on their way to and from the bakery or church. And in the end, the supervisors induced the mayor to hire Boone May to remove the nuisance.

Boone had been sick more than a year, long enough to know he would never get well. There was the first spell, which resembled torpid fever, and that had changed into something else, something quieter, that took his strength a little every day.

He drank at night, lying in bed, and sometimes he thought he felt his body dying bit by bit under his long underwear. He never took his underwear off, for fear of what he would see. In the mornings he was sick, sometimes too weak to dress. He was a size, though—head and body—that no one noticed. On the occasions he walked into the bars of the badlands, the sight still frightened the tourists.

And so it happened that on the first Friday in October Charley looked up from his newspaper and found Boone May sitting on a horse in front of Lurline's House of Distinction. Lu-Lu was perched on the railing, smiling at Boone in a business-related way. Charley saw the star pinned to Boone's shirt as he climbed off the horse. There was a yellow cast to his skin and something unsure in his movements, as if he didn't trust his hands and feet. His clothes hung on him like there was nothing under them at all.

"I ain't takin' that one," Lu-Lu said. Being the best looking, Lu-Lu had turned temperamental, refusing the roughs and common miners and anybody ugly or missing as much as one finger.

Lurline had tried to get Charley to slap her. He wouldn't do it. He said, "You just have to talk to her yourself." He was tired of the whore business, Lurline was stealing from him, the girls took advantage because they knew he wouldn't hit them.

Lu-Lu looked over at Charley now from her spot on the railing and made a face that Boone couldn't see. It was a horrible, rubber face—children could do that—but it was prettier than Boone's.

Boone took the two steps up the porch slowly, holding on to the hand rail, and Charley sensed the sickness in him and measured the distance between them, willing him to stop before he got communicable.

Boone wore one gun; it hung three or four inches off his hip and moved when he moved. He seemed to feel the weight of it as he climbed the steps. He stopped at the top and leaned against the railing.

He stared at Charley with one eye. "I heard you had a whorehouse, pretty," he said.

"I ain't going nowhere with this one," Lu-Lu said.

Charley said, "Why don't you run inside the house, child?"

She shook her head. "I want to see this."

Boone turned his head and put his eye on her. She got off the railing and went inside. "We might have a position for you," Charley said, "the girls aren't scared of me."

Boone said, "I got a job already."

"So I see."

He dropped his hand close to his gun, heavy and slow. "I'm the sheriff."

"I didn't remember that there was one."

"They give me two hundret dollars, and now they got one." He patted his shirt pocket, where the money was. His fingers were dark and he smelled like he'd been all month in a buffalo skin.

"This isn't the place to spend it," Charley said. "Deadwood's the spot for you."

"They told me that same thing about yourself," Boone said.

"I've been to Deadwood, and I moved here." The ground shook and rattled the insides of the house. It seemed closer today, Charley guessed they were right under the street. "I like the quiet," he said.

Boone didn't move. "The town fathers would insist to see you move your place down the hill," he said, meaning Deadwood.

"It's going to make most of them a longer walk."

"Well," Boone said, "the point here is, they made me sheriff on account of you."

"There's no law broken here."

Boone yawned.

"I obey the law," Charley said.

"That's what they given me the two hundret dollars for, to come tell you the law don't want a house in Lead."

"Where's the papers?"

Boone fixed that single, dark eye on him. Charley saw the fire start and then die, for lack of fuel. "No papers," he said, "just you and me."

"The law is papers now," Charley said. "You can't shoot a bad dog without the papers."

Boone stepped back and rested his hand on the butt of his gun. Charley didn't move. He was not anxious to shoot Boone May, not after the stories that followed his duel with Handsome Dick. He did not have the nature for taking human life, and one episode led to another.

"I ought to of spanked you like a baby," Boone said. "You and the gunfighter both."

"I obey the law," Charley said. Boone looked around him, smiling at a few spectators who had stopped in the street to watch.

Charley heard Lu-Lu inside the house, shouting, "Charley's going to shoot the sheriff." And Boone smiled at that too, but he was sick and he was weak, and he saw he'd misjudged the pretty. Charley sat still.

"I ought to throw you in the mud and drown you," Boone said. "It's no point in being polite."

Charley thought of drowning and stood up, straightening his legs one at a time, and walked across the porch. Boone smiled, dropping his gaze as Charley came closer, until his chin was right on his chest. "I hope you aren't contagious," Charley said, and he picked Boone up, grabbing a leg and his ribs, and threw him off the porch.

Both places Charley touched him, he felt bones. Boone landed on his shoulder and lay still a moment, stunned. Charley walked after him, hearing the girls in the house. "Charley's kilt the sheriff!"

"Don't ever say *drown* to me," he said.

Boone got to his feet, slow and weak, and then dove at Charley's legs. He got one of them, and Charley hit him behind the ear. Boone held on with one hand, reaching for Charley's privates with the other. Charley hit him again, and his head dropped an inch down the leg. Boone bit him, a long, deep bite. Worse than being shot.

Charley brought both fists down on the back of Boone's neck, glimpsing Lurline standing in the doorway now, her hands on her hips, watching. He wondered if she was jealous, seeing him bit by somebody else. He hit Boone again, feeling something tear in his leg, and then Boone was lying in the mud.

Charley's pants were torn and the blood ran down his leg into his moccasins. He sat down on the steps to examine the damages. A piece of flesh the shape of a tongue was torn from his thigh, connected only by skin, and Charley pushed it back into the crater, and pressed it there until the bleeding slowed.

He looked over his shoulder at Lurline, who was still in the door. "I need gauze," he said.

"I don't think we got any," she said. Her voice was soft and scared.

"We got to have bandages," he said, "it's a whorehouse." Boone lay face-down in the street.

Lurline left and then reappeared with bandages and a bottle of clear local whiskey. Charley looked at the bottle, he looked at her. "I could get the good whiskey," she said. "I didn't know you want the good . . ."

He had never seen her timid before, he guessed it was the blood. He took the knife out of his belt and cut his pants leg from the knee up, regretting to further ruin good clothes. He took the bottle out of Lurline's hand and poured half of it right into the bite. The sting was a second behind the cold, and Charley closed his eyes until it passed.

When he opened them again, Boone May was on his hands and knees, clearing his head. It was like trying to smash a wasp. Charley took the bandage from Lurline and wound it slowly, four times around his leg, so tight he could feel his pulse underneath.

Boone stood up, holding the back of his head. The assembly of citizens moved back and Boone swayed in the mud. There was blood on his chin and his bug-eyes were pushing out of his head. Charley stood up, beginning to feel pure.

Boone pointed a finger at him as dark and wide as a gun barrel. "Death is on the way," he said. "Ain't nothing can help you, pretty, because there's more ways to kill a man than to stay alive."

He felt something then that Bill must have felt. There wasn't hate or love or remorse or misgivings in it, it was someplace he was going. He dropped his left foot behind his right, offering less of himself to shoot at, and took the right-hand gun out of its holster.

There was no hurry, Boone was still talking. He cocked the hammer and Boone's eyes retreated back into his head. He held up a hand. "Whoa, pretty. Death is coming, but not today. This ain't our day yet."

And then Boone lost his footing, backing up, and fell, and Charley lost his killing feeling. Shooting was too good for Boone May anyway.

The hurt in Charley's leg gathered itself and came back at him, and he limped to the bench in front of the bakery and sat down. Boone got up and followed him over, smiling and sick, and then sat down in the street.

"How you going to take care of all them girls and watch for me too, pretty?" he said.

Charley looked at the way he was sitting and saw he was hurt, and saw he was right. And what to do about it. He made up his mind in two seconds. "I'm not," he said. "Right here, on whatever date this is, I hereby publicly and legally turn over fifty percent of the operation to you, and the rest to Lurline Monti Verdi."

Boone watched him to see if he was serious, and then he began to smile. "You're a strange one, pretty," he said.

Charley went inside to get his things, passing Lurline in the doorway. She was smiling too, blinking tears. "Nobody ever went fifty-fifty with me in my life before," she said.

And it almost made him feel bad, to hear her grateful.

IN THE SUMMER OF 1878, SMALLPOX CAME TO THE NORTHERN HILLS. There had been a mild strain two years earlier, a month before Bill and Charley had arrived, which had claimed three lives. A pesthouse had been built then, first near a brewery on Spring Creek in Elizabethtown, a mile from Deadwood, then on Spearfish Road, and finally in South Deadwood, where the Deadwood and Whitewood creeks met. The last site was agreed to in the belief there was nothing that could come out of a pesthouse that wasn't already in the Whitewood Creek.

The pesthouse was used by roughs and miners and whores, and avoided by anyone with a roof of his own to be sick under. For the two years between outbreaks of smallpox, the building sat empty.

The epidemic of 1878 brought a different strain of the disease. There had been one hundred cases in Sidney, Nebraska, in the spring, killing thirty-four people. Jane had nursed the sick there, and returned to Deadwood in early July on the stagecoach.

The stay in Nebraska had renewed her spirit—which the bartenders of the badlands had spent two years discouraging—and her commitment to the medical profession. She was still lame in the leg she had broken in Rapid City.

Charley had left Lead the day he gave away his whorehouse and was living in the Grand Union Hotel again. He saw Jane get off the stage—she took off her hat and kissed the ground and then screamed her eagle scream and headed for the Gem Theater.

Deadwood was changing in small ways, and there was something in Jane's manner that reminded him of the way things had been before. Before what, he couldn't say. There was talk of telephones and streetlights now, but those were not the changes that tugged at him.

And he was glad to see Jane, but avoided the Gem Theater all week just the same.

He heard from her, though. Her eagle scream would carry the length of Main Street in a hailstorm, and he got reports on her behavior from the Bottle Fiend. She claimed to have doctored the population of Sidney, killed most of the Indians in Nebraska, visited the widow of General George Armstrong Custer, and had sexual congress with a rooster.

The Bottle Fiend repeated what he heard and asked Charley what was true. Charley would sit in the tub nearest the door, where he could catch the light to read the paper. "She would have nursed the sick," he said. "Jane has a nursing instinct." Sometimes he thought it was Deadwood changing, sometimes he thought it was himself. Things seemed to be shaded darker. His eyes saw what they always saw, but in some subtle way the light fell tangent now, never right on what he wanted to see. Sometimes he thought of Agnes Lake as just out of sight, sometimes he thought he might have seen too much. It hadn't entered his thoughts yet that he was going blind.

"The rooster," he said, "don't believe that. If Jane took a rooster, it was just to show off. It wasn't anything she meant."

"It's what I heard," the Bottle Fiend said. He had grayed and aged that winter, beyond anything normal. It seemed to Charley there were two kinds of constitutions, and one took to the Hills and one didn't. And it seemed to him that a man who looked in the mirror and saw himself getting a year older every week would find a new climate. Even a soft-brain.

The history of the northern Hills was a history of its claims, though—even the Bottle Fiend's—broken hearts and broken backs. There was something undiscovered that nobody would leave. It held Charley too.

He thought sometimes of leaving to look for Agnes Lake, but his thoughts of her were like dreams, and in his dreams Deadwood was where she was, and he was afraid he would lose her if he left.

THE FIRST CASE OF SMALLPOX BROKE OUT ON A FRIDAY, TWO WEEKS to the day after Jane's return. It was one of the upstairs girls at the Gem Theater. She was found in her bed by Al Swearingen, sweating, blistered skin, running a fever that Jane—who had been pulled from her sleep under a table downstairs—put at 106 degrees.

"Get her out," Swearingen said, when Jane told him what it was. "I don't want none of that in here."

Swearingen never left the theater now, an adjustment he'd made to the boy in the preacher's clothes sitting across the street waiting for him. He had even quit going to the windows. It was useless, because he worried one way when the boy was gone and another way when he was there.

Swearingen had given up on having the boy killed—there were roughs who would shoot off their own toes for a hundred dollars that had refused to put a bullet in a preacher—and found his safety inside. He stayed upstairs, where he'd taken a corner room. Several times he had begun to read the Bible, for protection, but he couldn't read enough of the words to fight the boy.

The discovery of smallpox in his place—two doors from his own room—was a sign to Swearingen that the boy and his Bible were beginning to force him out into the open. And he stood at the door while Jane worried over the girl, wondering how things had gone so wrong. Jane soaked rags in a fixer she had mixed in secret and pressed them against the girl's forehead, holding them there with one hand, drinking from the fixer with the other.

"It's smallpox, all right," she said, sounding proud. "Just like in Sidney, and Elk Point before. It's a lucky thing I got here, the regular sawbones is scairt to treat it."

"Get her out," he said.

Jane shook her head. "No such thing. I ain't takin' this poor child to no pesthouse." She wiped at the girl's forehead and patted her cheek. The girl's eyes were shiny and inattentive.

"It's God's will," Jane said, "that he puts me to a place in time to nurse the pox."

"This is my place," he said.

She didn't even look back when she answered. "I am a screamin' eagle from Bitter Creek, the further you go the bitterer it gets, and I'm from the head end. Now git before I shoot the toes off your feet."

Jane had been saying that, every time she got happy, ever since her return from Nebraska.

A line of sweat broke out across Swearingen's forehead and a trembling occurred in his hands. He stepped out of the room and watched Jane tend the whore from the hall. He felt it coming after him now—a judgment before he was ready. He touched his cheek, testing for fever. Jane had begun to hum. The upstairs girl pulled at her nightclothes and a bubble of spit hung on her chin. He took the handkerchief out of his back pocket and held it against his face. Through it, he felt the trembling in his hands.

Jane poured fresh fixer into the rag, took another drink for herself.

"This is my place," he said again.

She laughed at him. "Move her yourself, then," she said. "You touch this child, and you'll be dead in three weeks."

The upstairs girl's eyes came back into focus for a moment, and her breathing turned faster and shallow. "Don't be scairt," Jane said, and put the rag against her forehead. "I been through this about six hundred times and you ain't got a killing case." She considered the sores on the girl's face and shook her head. "There is going to be some disfigurations, though . . ."

"You got one hour," Swearingen said.

Jane unholstered one of her pistols, cocked it, and set it on the bed next to the girl. "Ain't nobody takin' this child to the pesthouse," she said. "Nobody that wants to live."

He stared at the girl on the bed. One minute she twisted with the fever, the next she lay still as the dead. He tried to see if the boy was behind it, but the image of the girl on the bed was strong and clear, and wouldn't move aside for him to look for the cause.

"I'm going to need about six helpers," Jane said. "Git me plain girls without no medical education. I don't need arguments. They can take turns to sit here and empty pans."

He closed the door and walked downstairs, into the bar. The whores had seen the girl's affliction, and they crowded around him to ask what it was. One of them said if it was poison, she knew who did it.

Swearingen pushed through them and walked behind the bar. He found himself a bottle of clear whiskey and a glass. "Is she dead?" one of the girls asked.

He walked back through them, up the stairs and into his room. He locked the door and pulled back the window curtain, and sat on his bed, watching the street.

The boy was gone, but he would be back.

THE SECOND AND THIRD CASES OF SMALLPOX WERE REPORTED THE next day at the Bella Union, across the street from the Gem. It was another upstairs girl and a gambler, both of them broke. Dr. H. Wedelstaedt was called to the bar early in the afternoon, and he ordered them quarantined in the pesthouse.

He never put his hands on either of them, a fact reported to Jane that night when she stopped in the bar on her way home. She had found a lean-to on the north end of town, built by children, and claimed it for her own. She knew it was children because it was built on a hill with the open end facing up—an evening shower could drown you—and because she'd found a broken top inside. The place wasn't badly built, but she thought parents ought to teach their children to face a lean-to downhill.

She stood with one elbow on the bar, taking the weight off her bad leg, and listened while a whore told her that Doc Wedelstaedt wouldn't touch either victim. "The doctors is all afraid to mix with smallpox," Jane said.

The girl was plain-looking and fat. She said, "Doc Wedelstaedt is the only one that tends the Chinese, that's how come they called him for this."

Jane sighed. She looked at her hands, black-nailed and soft. "For some reason I don't know, God give me the touch to cure and heal, and I best be about my business."

She was tired and drunk, but she headed out the door and followed the Whitewood all the way to the pesthouse. It was a small, windowless shack in the mud beside the creeks. The door was shut, and there was a sign nailed to it that said, QUARANTINED BY ORDER OF DR. H. WEDELSTAEDT. STAY THE HELL OUT.

Jane read the sign slowly, drinking from a bottle of fixer. She laughed out loud and threw her head back and let go of an eagle scream Bill himself could of heard, up in the cemetery. "I am a screamin' eagle from Bitter Creek, the further you go the bitterer it gets," she said, "and I'm from the head end. Now git before I shoot the toes off your feet." She pulled the sign off the door and tore it in half and walked in.

The only light inside was what came from the door, and it took her a moment to locate her charges. They had been laid on narrow cots in opposite ends of the room. The gambler lifted his head to see who it was, the girl lay still. She went to him first. He had damped his clothes and the sheets with his sweat, and he was blistered everywhere she looked.

He asked for water.

There were sixteen cots in the pesthouse, and she pulled an empty one close to his and sat down to administer her healing. "That ain't what you need," she said. She hadn't brought rags, so she tore some out of the sheet she was sitting on. She used the teeth on her right side, the only place where her uppers touched her lowers, and when she had finished there was a taste of blood in her mouth. She reached in with her fingers and found two teeth that moved when she touched them.

"Don't ever eat fruit," she said. The gambler smiled, but she saw he didn't understand. "I had the prettiest teeth in the West," she said, "but fruit rotted my gums." She poured fixer over one of the rags and wiped the gambler's head. She felt the heat an inch off his forehead.

On the other side of the room, the girl turned in her sleep and began to cry. Jane soaked another rag and pressed it against the gambler's chest. "I got to tend that poor girl," she said.

She crossed the room, the floor giving under her feet all the way across. The air was hot, and Jane broke a sweat on her neck and under her arms. She wiped it away and drank from the bottle of fixer. It was how she stayed immune, cleaning her insides with the fixer. It was the secret of the cure, too. The trick was knowing when. Administered at the crossroads of the disease, it never failed.

In her fever, the girl had pulled most of the clothes off herself, and was lying uncovered on the cot, naked except for her petticoat, moving her head back and forth on the pillow, making a wheezing noise in her throat.

Jane sat on a cot and studied the girl's condition. She was worse than the gambler, close to the crossroads already, if not beyond. She had a pretty, round face and puffy lips. There were bruises on her legs and arms, Jane guessed she had a regular man. Jane washed her forehead with fixer and the girl jumped under her touch.

"There, there," Jane said, "God sent me here to cure you, child." The girl opened her eyes at the sound of the voice, studied Jane's face, and then resumed her death wheeze.

Jane put her hand against the girl's cheek. "You got a fever, all right," she said. "About a hundret and ten degrees." The girl didn't seem to hear. Jane said, "It's time, child."

She looked behind her to make sure the gambler wasn't watching, then she cradled the girl's head in her elbow and lifted her up off the pillow. The girl's head fell back and her mouth opened. Jane fastened down her grip and brought the bottle of fixer slowly to the girl's lips. "You got to drink about half of this now," she said.

The girl opened her eyes again and Jane stuck the neck of the bottle two inches into her mouth, hinged it there, and brought the bottom straight up. The girl choked and spit, and the fixer ran out both sides of her mouth. She fought it, trying to get her head loose, but Jane held on. "There, now," she said, "God sent me . . ."

The girl began to choke deep in her chest, a sign that the fixer was down where it would do its work. Some of it came out her nose. The girl's nails dug into Jane's arms, but Jane held tight until the bottle was half empty.

The girl ceased to struggle.

Jane laid her gently back on her pillow, wiped at some blood where her lip had been cut. "That treatment's the only thing that could save you, child," she said. The girl didn't appear to be breathing, and Jane leaned closer, listening at the girl's mouth, and waited a long time.

Finally it came, a little warm air in Jane's ear, it sounded like a tiny sigh. The girl began to breathe. Jane wiped at her head and then moved away a few feet, not to be hit by the regurgitate.

The convulsions lasted most of an hour. Jane sat on the cot, watching. If the fixer failed to purge a victim, it was time to meet God. She wiped the girl's blood off the lip of the bottle and drank from it herself.

She heard the gambler snoring in the half-dark, across the room. It was a peaceful, even sound, but she knew he was dreaming horrible deaths. It was an early symptom of the disease. She put her hand on the girl's forehead again, and it was cooler now.

Jane took another swallow of the mix, and smiled. "When they're coolin' and breathin'," she said out loud, "they're healin'."

She sat and drank another hour, until the girl began to chill. Jane moved into her cot and lay down next to her. She put her arms around her narrow shoulders and pulled her close, smelling perfume and vomit and the disease. It was sweet to Jane, and she pulled the girl's head into the soft junction of her neck and shoulder.

She felt herself nodding, and drank the fixer to hold off her sleep. The girl shook and Jane held her tight, and after a while she began to hum.

"The Battle Hymn of the Republic."

AL SWEARINGEN SAW JANE EARLY THE NEXT MORNING, IN THE HALL-way outside his room. He was on the way to the bar for another bottle of local; she had just climbed the stairs. Swearingen's nerves were shot and he screamed.

He had been awake all night, watching the street, thinking of the diseases in the air, in his room. Even the local couldn't calm him down. And an hour after daybreak he stepped out into the hallway, the only noises in the place his own feet on the pine floor, and ran into Calamity Jane Cannary.

He heard his own scream, and then saw who it was. Jane's eyes were blood-red and her skin had sagged and paled in the night.

There was blood caked in one corner of her mouth, and her hair was like snakes.

She stopped when he screamed, and squinted at him. "That is the most cowardly thing I seen yet," she said. "A whore man scairt in his own whorehouse. If you've woke my patient, your peeder's as good as shot off."

He stood in the hallway, trying to find his breath. He smelled it then, there was death all over her. "I told you to remove that girl out of here," he said.

She spit on the floor. "There ain't nobody movin' that child until I say so," she said. "She ain't reached the crossroads yet." She stared into Swearingen as she spoke, and gradually her expression changed. Her hand crossed the distance between them and lay against his forehead.

He swayed and closed his eyes. "You might of got it yourself," she said. "What is your dreams like?"

He turned in the hall and went back into his room. It was an act of will not to run. He heard her calling after him, warning him. "Don't trifle with this," she said. He shut the door and locked it. He put a chair under the doorknob and then pushed towels against the crack at the bottom. He stood in the middle of the room, trying to find his breath, and noticed he was sweating. He felt his forehead, and it was damp and hot.

Jane knocked at the door. "Heed me, whore man," she said. "There ain't nobody immune except me. If you want to live, you best put yourself in my hands." He moved to the far end of the room and stood near the window. Her voice stopped, but there were no footsteps moving away. "You hear me in there?"

He stood still, feeling his pulse in his hand and his head. Then he saw the boy, on the bench across the street. He wore the preacher's coat and the preacher's hat and sat with both his hands folded across the Bible in his lap. Waiting.

It reminded Swearingen of cats, or Indians. He pulled the curtains shut and began to pack. He pushed a handful of clothes and a Bible into an old valise he kept under his bed and then stood still again, looking around him, wondering what else he would need.

She banged on the door. "I ain't through talkin' to you," Jane said. "You'd best change your attitude, whilst I'm still in a forgiving mood."

He moved close to the door, not to be overheard, and pressed his cheek against the wood. "Get my wife," he said.

"What?"

"Get my wife."

"She can't help you now," Jane said. "I'm the only one . . ."

"Get my wife," he said again.

There was a long silence, and then she said, "I might just turn this whole damn floor into a hospital. Ain't no reason nursin' has got to go on four miles from the nearest bar."

"All right, but get my wife."

"All right what?"

"Whatever you want."

There was another silence. "I want a signed paper," she said.

He hugged the door.

"A deed," she said. "Your word ain't worth nothing. Don't never trust a whore man, that's the first thing I learned."

He opened the new bottle of local and sat down on the bed. He took a long drink, leaving her at the door. In a better world he could have opened the door and shot her, but everything he did—everything since the day he'd left the boy alive by the creek—turned back on him now, moving him someplace unprotected. He found a glass on the floor and filled it. He drank in one motion, watching the room reveal itself through the bottom of the glass as the liquor disappeared, until it was all gone and he could see the window, waiting for him.

He realized then he'd forgotten how to breathe. Not himself, exactly—he could do it as long as he thought about it—but his body. He lay back and watched his chest move up and down, and every time he stopped concentrating, his chest stopped too.

Swearingen was suddenly too tired to get up. Too tired to roll this way or that in bed, or to take off his boots. He was warm and then he was cool. He was tired of looking at the world and he lay on the bed with his eyes closed, afraid to sleep for fear of forgetting to breathe.

Sometime later it came to him that he was alone. That Jane was gone from the other side of the door. He thought about what she had said. *If you want to live, you'd best put yourself in my hands . . .*

He pictured her snake hair and her red eyes. It was clear, almost like a real picture, and as he watched, her hair turned golden and her eyes turned kind, and he saw it was true. She was the only one that could save him.

He called for her.

There was no answer. "Jane . . ." He opened his eyes and sat up.

Time had passed, he knew his chances had passed too. There was business on the street, the noises sounded a hundred miles away. Someone knocked at the door—not Jane, it didn't shake the walls. He got up slowly and stood on the other side.

"What do you want?"

"I don't want nothin'. What do you want?" It was his wife. She lived alone in the apartment in back of the Gem, and kept a gun in every room. She'd swore to kill him if he ever put a hand on her again. He saw now that his problem with her was connected to the rest of what had happened, that it was another way to get him alone and unprotected. "You there?" she said.

He moved the chair that was wedged under the doorknob and opened the door. She was standing with her hands on her hips, and when she saw him it startled her. He hadn't seen her startled in a long time. "What is it?" he said.

He knew he was someway marked, he didn't know how.

He stepped to the side to let her in, but she stood where she was. She had a hand in the pocket of her skirt; he saw the outline of a gun. "You aged twenty years," she said. Her eyes fixed on his, as if that was where it showed.

He almost reached for her then, to pull her inside, but he remembered what was in her skirt. "There's disease in the hallway," he said.

She said, "You gone soft-brained too."

He stepped farther away. She put her head into the room and looked left and right. She took a step in, then another, and when he could, he closed the door and locked it.

"I never seen you like this," she said. There was no worry in it at all.

"I got to leave."

She looked around the room as if she hadn't heard him. "There's contamination in this place," he said.

She smiled at him.

He said, "I got some of it inside me already."

"You look sick," she said, matter-of-fact. "But mostly you look old."

He wanted to hit her; he waited until it passed to speak. "I put my money in the bank," he said.

Her mouth fell open. "You? You trusted somebody else to hold the money?"

"It's fireproof," he said.

She laughed and he saw the happiness in her eyes. "There ain't no such thing," she said.

"It is," he said. He felt it rise up again. There was something about Swearingen, or his wife, that he always wanted to hit her when she got happy. He waited until it passed. "I need you to get my money," he said.

She sat down on the chair he had used to secure the door and picked up the bottle of local. "They ain't going to give your money to me," she said. She smelled the lip of the bottle and made a face. "They gave money away to wives, it wouldn't be anybody would put their money in banks."

"I'll write a note," he said.

She smelled the bottle again. "This is what made you old," she said.

He took the bottle out of her hand and put it back on the floor. "It don't matter what made you how you are," he said. "What matters is what you do now."

She thought that over, and he was grateful to have her listening again. There was a time she listened to everything he said. Of course, there was a time when she didn't carry a pistol in the pocket of her skirt, too.

He checked the window and the boy was gone. "I'll give you a note for Jim Miller," he said, "don't give it to any other party."

"I don't know Jim Miller."

"Miller and McPherson," he said. "Tell him I want a bank draft for all of it but five hundred dollars."

"They ain't going to let me in Miller and McPherson's," she said.

"He'll charge a tenth, but I can't argue," he said. "Let him have what he asks."

"I think you ought to go yourself. It's too much confusion in this . . ."

He saw that she was afraid of the bank, and it made him want to slap her. "There's no confusion," he said. "I'll write it down. All you do is put it in Jim Miller's hand."

"I don't know him."

"Ask for him. Say who you are and you'd like to see Mr. Miller."

She looked at her skirt. "I don't have nothin' to wear to Miller and McPherson's. They'll ask me to get out."

Swearingen sat down on his bed again and covered his eyes with his fingers. "I got a hundret and seventy-two thousand dollars in that bank," he said, sightless. "They ain't going to notice what you're wearing."

The number stopped her. Al Swearingen never told anybody how much he had, he just said when something was his. She looked at her clothes again, and the little room where he lived since they had quit each other.

"You had that and lived like this?"

"I live the fashion I want," he said.

"Holed up on the second floor of a whorehouse, scairt to go outside to collect your own money?"

"Events have moved against me," he said.

"You got old overnight."

He removed his fingers and stared at her. "You ain't exactly covered with morning dew yourself."

"You never wanted me pretty," she said, and he saw some of her pleasure had gone out of his circumstance. "You never wanted me to be nothing."

He found a pencil and a piece of paper on the desk and wrote the note. When he'd finished, she was crying. "Don't be long," he said. "I don't want the boy to see you coming out the bank."

She looked at herself again. "I got to get cleaned up, to go see Jim Miller."

He started to argue, but saw it was useless. He put the note in her hand and closed her fingers around it. "What happens later?" she said.

"Later don't matter," he said. "What matters is now."

She put the note in her skirt pocket, with the gun. He checked the window again and returned himself to bed. When she had gone he stood up and pushed the chair under the doorknob. He noticed that his breathing was coming of its own accord again. The boy was still gone from the bench across the street, and the smell of disease was gone from the room.

He waited for his wife to return from the bank. It seemed like an hour passed, but time moved strange speeds when you laid in bed during the day. He slept, picturing her changing clothes before she went out of the badlands. He woke wanting to hit her.

More time went by. He saw that she had taken a bath first, maybe washed her hair. The sun moved into the afternoon sky and lay in a casket shape across the floor. He wondered if the woman could have gone to Goldberg's first and bought herself a hat.

He picked up the bottle of local and watched the sun spread across the floor. It was not until he'd filled the glass twice that he saw the casket was growing to a size to fit him. Shortly after that, he again forgot how to breathe.

The sun moved across the floor, and he moved to avoid it. He sat in a chair at the side of the window and watched the street for her.

The sun dropped behind the mountains and the bottle lay on its side, empty, before he realized she wasn't coming back.

IN TWO WEEKS THE NUMBER OF SMALLPOX CASES WAS TWENTY-TWO. All the cots in the pesthouse were occupied; the three latest victims lay in blankets on the floor. Still, no one had died.

Every morning Jane began at the Gem Theater—there were two cases there—and then went to the pesthouse. Her first three patients—the two upstairs girls and the gambler—had reached the crossroads and recovered. The girls were badly scarred, which she said was probably in their best interests. She fought disease, she fought turpitude.

The gambler, in fact, had gone delirious and reached under her skirts, and she'd hit the back of his wrist with the butt of her pistol. "I don't consort whilst I'm curing the sick," she said. "I stay pure so I can heal. I give you your life, now don't make me take it back."

She knew every patient by name, and what stages of the disease they were in. She could predict when they would come to the crossroads a day in advance, and she was always there with fixer. She loved them best in that moment when she forced the bottle into their mouths, and made them live.

All day she went from bed to bed, cooling foreheads, mothering the girls. She mopped the floor and emptied pails and fed those who could eat. She hung a pulley from the ceiling and put the gambler's wrist in traction. He had tried to leave when his fever broke, but she lay him back down, saying the germs from the cured helped the stricken fight the disease.

She couldn't stand to lose even one.

At night she went to the bars in the badlands, collecting for the sick. She took off her hat and walked among the gamblers and tourists and upstairs girls, moving in close to them until they gave up their money.

And she drank as she made her rounds, sometimes from the

fixer, sometimes local whiskey. Glass-washing became common in the badlands.

"God give me the touch to cure," she said, and some believed her, and some didn't, but nobody wanted her breathing too long in their face. Once Jane took over smallpox, charity and fear went arm in arm.

Her eyes were rubbed red, night and day, and whole evenings passed in the bars without her eagle scream. She was seen to yawn in public. There were rumors she had the African sleeping sickness.

She spoke less to the tourists—only to ask them for money—and sometimes sat alone, drinking from her fixer and talking endearments to herself. "You are the only one that can cure it," she would say. "God sent you."

Nobody interrupted her. It was better her talking to herself than issuing eagle screams, or toe threats, or mourning Bill, and as the days went by there was a sentiment she was right. "The Lord works in strange ways" was heard in unlikely places.

There were places in the badlands, in fact, where men gave up their seats when they saw her walk in the door. There were places where she was bought drinks without begging them. And she took the chairs and the drinks as her due, and never thanked a soul.

The news of the first deaths came five weeks after the first case was discovered in the Gem Theater. Two men and two women died the same morning in the pesthouse. Swearingen heard it from the upstairs girl who brought his meals. Her name was Lu-Lu, and she had once worked for Charley Utter in Lead, before he'd turned the business over to Boone May and Lurline, who killed it and almost each other in less than a month. Lu-Lu kept herself cleaner than most, and he paid her two dollars a day to come to his room with food and water and empty his bucket. Al Swearingen hadn't been out of the room since his wife left Deadwood with all his money.

He sat at the window, day after day, watching the boy come and go from the bench across the street, worrying that his bartenders and dealers were stealing from him downstairs. He had detailed visions of revenging himself on his wife.

The girl came in with his lunch and told him there were four dead at the pesthouse. "And I knowed one of them," she said.

He lost his knack for breathing again, and thought of his wife to restore it. He'd noticed early on it restored his functions to think of bringing her to justice. He sat down on the bed and put his face in his hands to concentrate. Lu-Lu put the food on the table by the window and sat beside him. She didn't believe his wife had gotten away with all the money.

"Poor Mr. Swearingen," she said. "Did you knowed one of them too?" She patted his leg, and he sat still. She had seen men in grieving before, and rested her hand on his thigh. "Which one was it?" He didn't answer, and she floated her hand farther up his leg. "You know what makes a body feel better?" she said.

She leaned into him then, pushing her chest into his arm, and felt him shake. His breathing was deep and passionate. She stuck her tongue in his ear—it tasted bitter and old—and he hit her flush on the jaw. She rolled off the bed onto the floor, trying to get to her tongue with her fingers, watching the blood spill all over her dress. It was a new dress, shipped all the way from Chicago.

She cried out, but the pain it caused stopped her, and she covered her mouth with both hands, and her nose ran and her eyes watered and the blood streaked over her cheeks and neck. He came after her, dropping to his knees on the floor, reaching for her neck. She held tight to her mouth, and it kept him off.

He pulled her hair, bringing her closer, and hit her again. She had been hit before, but never serious, not in the face. Lurline said it again and again, "The man that hurts my looks should never sleep with both eyes closed again," and she'd thought that protected her too.

Swearingen's fist caught her on top of the forehead and rolled her into the wall. The blow knocked her hands away from her mouth, and the blood followed her, wherever she went. She tried to say she was sorry, but her tongue had swollen and the words caught behind it in her mouth. He was coming after her again, eyes like the Fourth of July, smiling. She tried to smile back, but the blood ran into her lap.

He bent over her and reached for her neck. She let his hands settle there, trying to please him, and the pressure forced her chin back. She felt him take over her weight. She saw the ceiling, then the far wall, the door. Her head glowed and shook, and her eyes played tricks. The ceiling opened up and became the sky, the walls moved farther away. The door opened, and a preacher in black clothes stood there to take her to heaven.

She tried to smile, but the muscles in her face had froze. The preacher held up the Good Book, and suddenly the pressure in her head changed, a deep hammering replaced the glow, and the preacher spoke, it sounded like a hundred miles away.

"I have come for you now," he said.

Swearingen screamed. That sounded closer. The pressure changed again, and she felt cooler. She felt herself dropping, a long way to the floor. "The path to good is through evil," the preacher said.

She felt the footsteps as Swearingen ran across the room, she heard the glass break as he went through the window. The preacher walked past her and looked down at the street. He didn't seem to notice she was there.

She sat halfway up and moved her hands. Her fingers stuck to each other, her chin stuck to her shoulder. The front of her new dress was soaked and heavy and it clung to her chest. She wasn't dead.

She started to cry.

The preacher turned away from the street with a satisfied look on his face. She got off the floor and he watched her. The bleeding slowed and she wiped at herself with the sheet on Al Swearingen's bed. "I have driven the evil side of the Lord from this place," he said.

And she looked at herself and saw what he meant. God had taken his revenge, and she was forgiven. She crossed the room and kissed the back of the preacher's hand, leaving a little spot of red blood between his knuckles.

She tried to thank him, but the words died in the back of her mouth, behind her tongue. He looked into her eyes a long time, and she knew he understood her. And loved her, and forgave her.

And she knew she was saved.

THE DEATHS IN THE PESTHOUSE CONTINUED FOR TWO WEEKS, AND then stopped. There were nine in all. Jane took them all personal, and refused to attend the funerals. She pulled a gun on Doc Pierce and his nephews when they came for one of them, a ten-year-old child. She said the baby wasn't dead until she agreed to it. Doc Pierce had to send for the child's mother—an upstairs girl at the Green Front—to talk Jane out of the body.

In the bars at night, Jane turned sullen. She sat alone, sometimes staring at her hands, sometimes staring at tourists. She drank harder than she had when there was more work. The disease's course was run. Since the first victims died, there had been no new episodes. She talked about moving on. "I got the gift to cure," she said, "but my work's about done here."

Now that the new cases had stopped, the bartenders agreed with her, and one of them invented a story that there was sickness in Cheyenne.

She considered that, and him. "What symptoms?" she said. "Burnin' brow? Sweats? Is there disfigurements?"

The bartender shook his head. "That's all I heard, that there was sickness."

Later that night Jane shot a roach off the bar. She said they were carriers of disease, worse than flies. "If it wasn't they liked to sit in dog shit," she said, "flies never would of got a bad reputation."

The next night, every bartender in the badlands had heard of the disease in Cheyenne. They knew the symptoms, which were identical to the pox that had come through Deadwood, and the numbers of victims. They said there were over two hundred.

The news lifted Jane's spirits. She went spot to spot, confirming the numbers. "A city like Cheyenne, it could be five hundret victims before I get there," she said.

The bartender she was talking to at the time said, "The sooner the better." And a little later he said, "Your work here's good as done, Jane. They ain't nobody caught the pox in three weeks."

She sighed at the misfortune in Cheyenne. "The pox takes the good along with the bad," she said. "That's the trouble with it. The only one it won't take is me, I'm immuned by the Lord to cure."

Later she shot her guns into the floor and screamed her eagle scream, and prepared herself for the trip. "All right," she said, "I'm going to need about two hundred and ten dollars to buy fixer for them poor victims in Cheyenne." She passed her hat up and down the bars in the badlands all that night and the next. She only collected thirty dollars, but nobody stole the hat.

And so the last time Charley ever saw Calamity Jane, he gave her a dollar. It didn't seem like much, but it was what she wanted. He put it in her hat at the Gem Theater, where he sometimes stopped at night, now that Al Swearingen had flown out of the second floor window in a rain of glass, got on his horse, and galloped off into the Hills.

The hat was passed up the bar and then around the tables where Charley was sitting. Charley put his dollar in without touching the insides—there was fresh life growing out of the stains in there. Jane was standing at the end of the bar, her hands wrapped around two glasses of local whiskey, watching the hat to make sure nobody stole money from the sick. She looked worse to Charley than the last time he'd seen her, but Jane always looked worse than the time before. It could of just been there was always something you hadn't noticed before.

Her skin had yellowed and her stomach hung like a boulder in the moment before it goes over the side. Charley knew stomachs, and this kind resulted from local whiskey. It wouldn't be long before she was throwing up blood, if she wasn't already.

Her eyes followed the hat, and when Charley dropped the dollar inside she looked at him, and for half a minute forgot the hat as it went past and around the table. Her eyes were narrow and black; he saw she couldn't remember who he was.

She put one of the drinks on the bar and crossed the room, pushing an upstairs girl and a tourist out of the way. Charley nodded, Jane nodded back. "I been through a lot," she said finally, "and I don't recollect your name."

"Charley Utter."

She nodded. "I thought it was you." She didn't remember.

"Charley Utter," he said again. "Bill's friend."

She nodded again; it wasn't there. Him or Bill. "I am a screamin' eagle from Bitter Creek," she said, "the further you go the bitterer it gets, and I'm from the head end."

Charley said, "I know where you're from."

She looked confused. "You come here from my hometown?"

"No," he said.

"'Cause I ain't from there anymore. This right here is my hometown now, where my husband is buried."

He said, "I heard you nursed the sick."

"Some of them died, but it wasn't my fault. The Lord picks who He wants and leaves us the rest."

She staggered, and nearly fell. There were miners around her, a few tourists, all of them moved at once, not to be touched.

"It's tired you out," he said.

She brought a glass to her lips and drank everything inside it. "That's true," she said.

And then, because his kindness embarrassed her, she screamed her eagle scream and left him there at the table, without another word. At the bar she took the money out of her hat and stuck it down the front of her britches, and then patted herself there to make sure it was secure.

"I ain't never been robbed," she said, to no one in particular. She put the hat on her head and picked up the drink on the bar and walked to the door. Before she went through it, she stopped and fired her gun once into the floor, and screamed an eagle scream.

"I leave tomorrow," she said, "at sunrise."

And she did.

The next night at eight o'clock the bartender at the Gem Theater looked at the door and smiled. Jane had been reported mounted and headed south, into the Hills, at six o'clock that morning. "Just now is when she always come in," he said.

"I expect she'll find something to do when it gets dark," Charley said. "If there's a bar in the Hills, she's headed there right now."

The bartender smiled. "Headed the other way," he said.

"She had a good heart," Charley said. "All that was wrong with Jane, she needed an epidemic to bring it out."

"You wasn't in here enough," the bartender said. "That scream was the bane of the badlands. Stole drinks, scared tourists, the woman never told the truth yet."

Charley looked around the room. "Like the rest of these war heroes."

"Jane was the worst," the bartender said. "Ain't nobody told the lies she did."

Charley shrugged. "She didn't mean anything by it," he said. "She nursed the sick . . ."

"She mentioned that," the bartender said. "Here and there and everyplace betwix. The less disease there was, the more miraculous the cures."

Charley pulled his hat down over his eyes, the way Jane liked hers, and looked at his drink. The bartender crossed his arms. "You think it was wrong, what we did," he said after a while.

Charley looked up.

"Tellin' her there was pox in Cheyenne," the bartender said. "You wouldn't of done that, if you was us."

"You invented it?"

"Not me, but I went along."

Charley shook his head.

"You wasn't here listening to that eagle scream every night," the bartender said. "Tellin' people she was married to Wild Bill."

"She didn't mean anything by it," Charley said. "She was just lonely without an epidemic."

The bartender said, "Well, she's gone now. She's on the road to Cheyenne. Live by the lie, die by the lie. She got what she deserved, although I don't know what Cheyenne done to deserve her."

Charley thought of her, drunk and probably lost by now in the Hills, maybe asleep on her feet with the horse. And he saw that in some way it was what she wanted.

"What we did," the bartender said, "was strictly self-protection. We didn't mean nothing by it either." Then he poured himself a drink, and touched his glass to Charley's before he drank. "You got to admit this," he said, "whoever named her Calamity knew what they was doing."

"She named herself," Charley said.

JANE RODE STRAIGHT THROUGH THE NIGHT, AND DID NOT REST UNTIL the sun had gone down the next. She woke before daybreak, drank her coffee unsweetened by liquor, and started out again.

If her horse hadn't died, she would have made Cheyenne in five days. As events happened, it was eight. She arrived in town with a supply train, sharing the back of a wagon with half a dozen cats and a load of cheese. Her healing fever was such, she didn't mind the indignity.

She never drew her pistols once on the trip from Deadwood, she offered no eagle screams into the night air, for fear of waking the driver. Once in Cheyenne, she jumped from the wagon on lower Main Street, and walked into the first bar she saw. "I am here to heal," she said. "Where's the victims?"

She went from place to place, bars to sporting houses; there was no pox. She stopped a preacher on the street and explained what she had come for, and Who had sent her. "Could you direct me to the pesthouse?" she said.

He looked at her, up and down. He was tall and handsome and gray-haired. "If we had such," he said, "you may be assured I would direct you."

The woman with him tittered at that; Jane saw they wasn't married. She walked past him into another bar, and then another, until she satisfied herself they were hiding the truth.

She slept at the west end of town, under the stars. She found a half-built store there, and curled herself into a corner. She spent her nights in the store, her days returning to the saloons, waiting to overhear news of the disease. It was there in Cheyenne, she felt it.

And fourteen days after she arrived, she walked into one of the sporting bars and heard what she had come for. She stood where she was, listening, and then found her eyes had puddled and wet her cheeks.

Two of their girls had caught the pox.

IN JUNE OF 1879, A DEAD CHINESE WAS FOUND FLOATING FACE-DOWN in the shallows of the Whitewood Creek, caught there in a tangle of wood. There was construction all over town that spring, new houses were built all the way up into the Hills. There was a new store every week. All of it was made from the same pine, and all of it looked the same.

The Chinese was removed from the creek and taken to Doc Pierce, who accepted the body but then reported to Sheriff Bullock that he had buried the same Chinese before. "I never forget a body," he said, "and I already put this one in the ground."

Seth Bullock said, "Then put him in the ground again."

On the next day, the decomposed body of a child was found in the same place as the Chinese. Pierce recognized this one as one of widow McCleod's. The second-oldest, from the size.

Bullock saw the problem was political. "It isn't a popular thing, to move a cemetery," he told the barber. "You move bodies, it stirs up memories of the dead."

Doc Pierce was standing in Bullock's office. There was mud from the little girl's body still stuck to his hands. "I'll get blamed," he said. "Every time it happens, people's going to say it was because I buried them wrong. They don't care nothing about underground water, Sheriff. Things like this lead to violence."

Bullock saw the undertaker was right. He saw that as sheriff, he might be held to account too. "Then we got to move it up the hill," he said.

And the cemetery was renamed, and moved to the top of the hill, a coffin and a marker at a time. They called it Mount Moriah. The city hired miners and roughs to dig new graves for the dead who had no relatives. They had to pay more to get them to dig up the old.

The move began in early July, as soon as a new road was cut, and all that month, day and night, the wagons moved up and down the hill, the sounds of wheels carrying over the miners and roughs, who had never worked around the dead before, and barely spoke. Sometimes there were small services over the deceased, more often there weren't. It was the first anyone had heard of moving a cemetery, and it was anybody's guess what was right to do.

Charley put off moving Bill until he had time to think. He wrote Agnes in St. Louis, but there was no reply. Something had told him she wasn't there anymore. He put it off, though, waiting for her letter, until the city began to unearth the graves behind Bill's, and the footprints and wheel tracks from the day's work lay every evening all over Bill's bed.

He saw that on a Saturday afternoon, and moved him the following morning. He took the Bottle Fiend with him, and two men to use the shovels. Their names were John McLintock and Lewis Schoenfield, and both of them stunk of alcohol. They came along free, for the honor of burying Wild Bill.

Charley put them in back of the wagon and allowed the soft-brain to sit in front with him on the way up. The soft-brain did not believe Bill would be in his grave. "He ain't there," he said. "He's in heaven."

Charley looked straight ahead and kept a tight rein. "Part of him's still here," he said. "The other part's in heaven."

The Bottle Fiend did not believe it. "You don't go part by part," he said. "Angels carry you, all at once."

They stopped under a tree and Charley sat with the Bottle Fiend and watched the two men dig. This part of the cemetery had been emptied now, except for Bill. There were piles of dirt every ten feet, and he could hear the men's breathing as they dug. The Bottle Fiend was wearing a clean shirt, and sat straight in the seat.

Charley stared at the trees, he stared at the town. He watched a wagon leave the other side of the cemetery and begin the climb toward Mount Moriah. He looked everywhere but into the hole.

The ground had been packed hard by the tourists, and the digging was slow. The men soaked through their shirts, but they never stopped. And even when John McLintock clipped Lewis Schoenfield over the eye with his shovel, there were no words. Charley saw the look on Lewis Schoenfield's face, though, and surmised they would discuss it later.

The hole went deeper, the color of the earth changed. It was the blackest dirt Charley had seen in the Hills. The men were chest-deep into the hole when they hit the top of the box. Lewis Schoenfield touched it first; a little cry came out of him.

Charley climbed out of the wagon, the Bottle Fiend stayed where he was. "He ain't here," he said. "He's in heaven."

Charley was sorry he'd brought him; he hated to realign the soft-brain's thinking, it made him brood. People that thought a soft-brain only had one mood had never paid attention. The Bottle Fiend liked things the way he understood them, and felt tricked when they turned out different. That's because he knew he was soft-brained.

Charley walked to the edge of the hole and looked down. The men scraped dirt off the lid of the box, it didn't seem nearly big enough for what it held. Behind him the Bottle Fiend said, "He's flew off with angels."

Charley didn't answer. You couldn't protect anybody from the world. McLintock got two ropes out of the wagon and put one under each end of the box. "Angels got wings, they fly where they want," the Bottle Fiend said, and Charley suddenly thought of him, lying on the floor in Mrs. Langrishe's living room, trailing glass that looked like broken wings. He thought of the blood.

"Come help with the ropes," he said.

He thought the Bottle Fiend might balk—there was a streak of that in him—but he left the wagon seat backwards and took the rope Charley held, standing on the other side of the open hole. McLintock and Schoenfield took a similar pose at the foot end of the casket, and together they began to pull the box up.

The Bottle Fiend was not as strong as the other men, and Charley could feel his strainings through the rope, he didn't know how. They were connected, but between them lay the weight of the dead. The box rose toward them, a few inches at a time, out of the blackest dirt Charley had ever seen in the Hills. The Bottle Fiend stumbled two steps toward the hole, but caught himself before he went in.

"Hold on, Bottle Man," Charley said. The soft-brain liked being called "Bottle Man."

The weight was unnatural, Charley expected the box was half full of water. The Bottle Fiend's face turned red and the veins showed in his neck. And the box came toward them out of the dark, a few inches at a time. The soft-brain stumbled again. Charley said, "Just hold on. Let me do the pulling."

The Bottle Fiend didn't seem to hear. The box was halfway out, and Charley saw he was afraid of what was in it.

The box seemed to get heavier as it came to the lip of the grave. "Hold on," Charley said. The Bottle Fiend's hands were bleeding, Charley couldn't protect him at all. There wasn't any such thing.

Charley pulled, and the end of the box came out of the hole. And in that moment, McLintock or Schoenfield slipped, pulled each other off balance, and dropped the bottom end of the casket back into the grave. Schoenfield fell in with it.

The casket landed on end and broke open.

There was no water. The back end of the box had swung back into the hole, hitting about where the head had been. The end Charley and the Bottle Fiend held sprung forward and rested against the far wall of the grave. McLintock looked into the hole while Schoenfield climbed out.

"What happened?" McLintock said.

Schoenfield bit his lip and brushed fresh dirt off his pants and shirt.

"One minute we had it out, the next minute you was in the hole with Bill," McLintock said.

Schoenfield stared at him through a puffy eye in a way that made Charley glad they'd left their guns in the wagon to dig. "It's no consequence," Charley said, but murder was on Schoenfield's mind, anybody could see that.

"The matter at hand is the box," Charley said, and Schoenfield unlocked his eyes from McLintock's throat and they all looked into the grave. McLintock said, "That one end's dug itself into the ground. I don't see how a rope could be got under it." He moved to the other side of the hole, shaking his head. "They ain't no way to get in there and set it back down flat to start over either."

"Shut up," Schoenfield said, looking at Charley. "Let the man think."

"I was only remarking on what I seen. They ain't no reason to tell me to shut up."

Schoenfield fingered the swelling over his eye, but neither of them went further. Charley studied the box and scratched his head. "Another foot and we'd of had him," he said.

McLintock looked at Schoenfield. "You think that's so smart? 'Another foot and we'd of had him'? I didn't even bother to say that."

"Shut up," Schoenfield said. "He ain't thinking yet, he's getting ready to think."

Charley squatted on his heels. One of his legs cracked going down, and he knew there was a moment coming, as he got back up, when it would feel like his leg might break. He looked into the grave from this angle, and saw the box had been split, bottom to top. Something inside was pushing out the crack.

If they tried to lift the casket out face-down, Bill would spill out into the hole.

"Is he thinkin' yet?" McLintock said. Charley stared at them all, one at a time.

It was the soft-brain who spoke. "Why not put a rope around the top?"

For half a minute they all stood still, looking at it. "Shit," McLintock said, "the soft-brain's got better sense than either one of you."

"I didn't see you coming up with no ideas," Schoenfield said.

"You told me to shut up."

"I'm telling you again."

Charley tied the rope around the top of the box, about a foot from the end, and laid the rest in a straight line leading away from the other graves, trying to prevent a fall and a broken leg. The day had that accidental feel.

He stood at the end of the rope, separated Schoenfield and McLintock with the Bottle Fiend, and they all pulled together, on Charley's count. The box came out, but too easy. Bill stayed inside. Only the Bottle Fiend looked into the hole.

"The wood must of rotted," Schoenfield said.

It was a situation that somehow obligated an explanation. Charley stood with the rope limp in his hand, staring at the box. Nobody moved.

It was the soft-brain who spoke. "It's a statue," he said. "The angels took Bill to heaven and left us a statue for a souvenir."

"It isn't a statue," Charley said. "It's earthly remains. The other part's in heaven."

"It's a statue," the soft-brain said. "Look for yourself." Charley dropped the rope and walked to the edge. He put a hand on the Bottle Fiend's shoulder to pull him away; he was sorry he'd brought him along. The soft-brain wouldn't move, though. He had a streak of that in him.

Charley looked then and Bill was almost vertical in the corner, leaning against the wall of dirt. His clothes were decomposed, scarcely clothes at all. His color was bad, and the cross in his cheek where Jack McCall's ball exited had opened and the skin had rolled back on itself.

Even so, Charley had seen him looking worse. He lowered himself into the hole to carry Bill out. When he tried to lift him, though, the body had an unnatural weight. The legs were as hard as wood.

"Give a hand," he said, and a moment later the Bottle Fiend's head showed at the lip of the grave. "Get the rope."

He tied the rope under Bill's arms, and guided the body while the other three hauled him up. He heard McLintock complain it felt like three hundred pounds. Charley kept the body face-up as they pulled it out; he held Bill's shoulders, then his waist. The legs passed through his hands, and finally the feet. He recognized the shape of Bill's legs from their rassling. Nothing had changed, and he wondered at the secrets that lay underground.

When he climbed out of the hole, McLintock and Schoenfield were standing over the body. The Bottle Fiend was back by the wagon, afraid. Bill was face-up, still full in the chest and shoulders, straight and dignified. Charley thought of Agnes, and the day he had held her in her room at the Grand Union Hotel. He felt her in his heart now, her spirit was as familiar in him as Bill's.

McLintock found a stick and poked, gently, into Bill's arm. Charley did not move to stop him. Then he poked the shoulder, his legs, his stomach. He looked up, half afraid. "He's pertrified," he said. "He's pertrified hard as a rock."

Schoenfield took the stick—McLintock was not reluctant to give it up—and he poked the body too. Harder, until the stick bent and then broke. Charley and the soft-brain watched from the wagon, thinking their own thoughts.

"Touch it," Schoenfield said.

"I ain't touching nothin'," McLintock said.

"It's a statue," the soft-brain said, to Charley.

Charley thought of Agnes.

McLintock leaned close to the body and sniffed. "Ain't no smell at all," he said.

The soft-brain looked at Charley. "I told you," he said.

Charley didn't answer. He felt the pull of Agnes on him, and was somehow not surprised to unearth the cause of it, perfect and hard, hidden like a diamond three years in the dark.

"It ain't Bill," the soft-brain whispered, and it sounded like the voice inside Charley's own head. "It's a souvenir the angels left behind."

SOLOMON STAR SHOT TAN YOU-CHAU FOR THE SECOND TIME AT THE corner of Main and Wall streets, across from the newly built Bullock Hotel. It was September 24, 1879.

Seth Bullock was sitting in the dining room of his hotel at the time, and when he heard the shots he lifted a copy of the *Cheyenne Leader* over his face, not to be recognized. Although he'd given up official duties to John Manning, he had yet to wean the town of the notion he was the law. There was no emergency of any consequence, from mud fever among the mules to the miners refusing to work, that he was not called to relieve.

Once found, Seth Bullock never refused. His thoughts now were political. He was a famous man west of the river, and would not jeopardize it, refusing to help. He hoped not to jeopardize it getting shot.

And so, hearing the gun in the street, he lowered himself in his chair and covered his face with a newspaper. He had just finished a story about the telephone system that would be installed in Deadwood in November, the only one between Chicago and San Francisco.

It was the cook who found him. He'd hired Lucretia Marchbanks away from the Grand Union, and took all his meals at the hotel since. She walked into the dining room, heavy-footed and slow, and went directly to his table. She always knew where he was. "You best come look in the street," she said. "Mr. Star shot that Chinese again."

Bullock put the paper on the table in front of him and looked at her to make sure he understood. He always had trouble understanding Negroes. He treated them polite, though. "Pardon me?" he said.

"Mr. Star done shot the same Chinaman again," she said. "He don't have but two shots in that bitty gun or he'd shot him more."

Bullock found Solomon standing in the street, holding an empty derringer. There was blood on the porch of Ayers & Wardman's

Hardware, but the celestial was gone. Solomon stared north, in the direction of Chinatown. A woman was screaming inside the store, "Murder! Murder!" over and over.

Bullock took the gun out of Solomon's hand. "Where's the victim?" he said.

The cook had followed Bullock out of the hotel. "He run that way," she said, pointing north. "Talkin' that Chinese talk as fast as he can." Bullock took Solomon by the arm and led him the other direction, toward jail. Solomon could have been in Boston for all the attention he was paying.

Mrs. Ellsner came out of her bakery, a dozen ladies behind her. Bullock wondered, in the back of his head, what they did inside. There were always a dozen ladies in Mrs. Ellsner's bakery. One of them called to him.

"Is it safe, Sheriff? We heard the shots, but we thought it was only afternoon mischief in the badlands."

"It was an accident," Bullock said. "A Chinese gentleman was shot in the street."

She stood with her hands on her hips, the wife of one of the town's lawyers. He couldn't remember which one, there were half a hundred now, drawn by the legal disputes over ownership of claims. "Mr. Star's luck with the Chinese is very bad," she said.

Seth Bullock touched the brim of his hat. He walked Solomon into the new jail, a frame building next to the flouring mill, and shut the door. There were two chairs and a table inside. He sat Solomon down in one and took the other for himself. He stared across the table at his business partner for the better part of a minute.

Solomon was someplace else.

"You shot the same Chinese twice now," he said, sounding reasonable. Bullock always took a reasonable tone with those he arrested. Solomon nodded and looked at the ceiling. "I may not be able to call it an accident this time."

Solomon brought himself back to the here and now. "It wasn't an accident ever."

"This Chinese—"

"Tan You-chau," Solomon said.

Bullock was surprised that he knew the name. The names white men knew for the Chinese were the names they'd given them. Like Ding Dong and Hop Lee and Heap Wash. "One's like another," he said.

Solomon looked at the ceiling.

"I got to put you in jail," Bullock said. "The whole town's watching this now." Solomon was someplace else. Bullock made a fist and brought it down on the table.

Solomon never looked. "We trusted each other a long time," Bullock said, reasonable again. "If you told me what this grudge was, I could fix it. Did this Chinese put a curse on you?"

Solomon never looked.

Bullock took the keys out of the drawer in the table and stood up. "I got to put you in jail," he said again. "You see where this has led?" When Solomon didn't answer, Bullock unlocked the door and held it open.

"I'll locate the Chinese and see how bad he's hurt," he said. Solomon walked into the cell and sat on the cot against the wall. There was a faded yellow chamber pot in the cell, a dirt floor, iron grating across the window. Bullock shut the door and locked it. He looked at Solomon and thought of the business. "I should of done this the first time," he said. "For your own good, I should of locked you up."

Solomon never looked.

Bullock went back to his hotel. He found Lucretia in the kitchen and told her to make sure Solomon was fed. "Anything he wants," he said.

Bullock went into Chinatown, looking for the injured Chinese. The place stunk a hundred ways the rest of the town didn't. It was mostly the small animals strung from the windows, he thought, because the Chinese themselves, except for the whores, only smelled dusty.

He pounded on the door of Tan's theater, but there was no answer. He heard movements inside and went to the back. There were three girls there, lined up to use the bathroom. They opened their eyes wide when he asked for Tan, they shook their heads. He imitated a man being shot, they moved farther away. When he turned his back, he heard them giggle.

He crossed the street to the death house, but the old man there was blind, and stood in the doorway, looking over his head, saying, "No, no, no." Bullock imagined how big the old man thought white men were.

He noticed blood in the doorway.

He went back into town hopeful. If the Chinese refused to make a complaint or die, there was no case against Solomon.

He found Solomon on the cot and decided to leave him there for the night. "I found the Chinese," he said. Solomon looked out the window. "He's in their death house."

"He's not dead." Solomon sounded flat and strange.

"I never said he was dead. I said he was in the death house."

"When he's dead, I'll know."

"They'll probably hang you, is how."

Solomon went to the window he had been looking out. Bullock said, "John Manning's in Rapid City till tomorrow, but he comes back and finds the Chinese dead, he'll take it serious. He takes it all serious because sheriffing is all he does."

Solomon gazed out the window; there was no answer. And when Bullock checked back on him, after supper, Solomon was gone.

SOLOMON STAR TOOK THE KEROSENE FROM THE OFFICE—BULLOCK would find the jug they kept it in later, in the ashes of Chinatown—and splashed each side of the death house, feeling the coolness when it dripped onto his fingers.

He lit it with a match and then walked slowly to the Whitewood Creek, waded across it, and sat on the far bank to watch. The fire was slower than he had imagined—for several minutes there was only the blue kerosene flame, no smoke that he could see—but then it took, growing up one side of the death house, turning orange as it reached the roof.

It was in the roof before it was noticed, and Solomon sat still, listening to the screams in Chinatown, trying to pick out the one from inside the house.

Once it turned orange, the fire took the building in five minutes. Solomon watched a piece of the roof blow off and climb into the night sky; he realized he could not remember what her face looked like.

He stood up when he knew the Chinese was dead and wiped off the back of his pants. He wondered if he ought to return to the jail, or if he should sleep in his own bed. He thought of her again; the face was gone.

In a few minutes the first volunteers of the Deadwood Pioneer Hook and Ladder Company No. 1 appeared, wearing protective hats. But the fire laddies were helpless and soon left the street. There was a town ordinance requiring every building to keep a full barrel of water and two fire buckets, along with a ladder able to reach the roof. The Chinese never obeyed the white men's laws, though. They were afraid white men's laws led to white men's taxes.

Solomon watched another piece of the roof blow into the sky and carry across the street, then blow south, toward the town proper.

The gulch was naturally windy, and the heat from the death house created drafts of its own. The piece of roof dropped somewhere in the town and disappeared. More of the roof rose into the night as soon as the other was gone, and danced across the sky onto the roof of Tan's theater. In a few moments there was fire there too. It started at the top and spread slowly. The heat from the death house backed Solomon away from the creek. The fire grew, and he saw its reflection in the water.

Chinese ran out of the theater. Solomon recognized most of the girls, there wasn't the same turnover of upstairs girls here as in the badlands. It occurred to him there was no place else for the Chinese to go.

Tan's nephews came out of the door, then the old blind man who played the piano. He stood in the street, orange in the flames, and held his face up to the heat as if he could see it. He was crying Chinese words; the language lent itself to sorrow.

Solomon tried to remember how Ci-an's words had sounded, but they would not come back to him now either. He saw it was a kind of forgiveness. The fire spread to the building next to the theater. Children came from that house, some of them crying, and clung to one another in the street.

Solomon caught a flicker of light from the south, and presently there were shouts from there too. As he watched, the light grew and spread, and the wind grew with it, and carried the cries of the Chinese into the darkness of the Hills.

In a few minutes there was an explosion that shook the ground. It would be reported later that the fire had caught on the roof of Mrs. Ellsner's bakery and moved from there to Jensen and Bliss's Hardware, where it found eight kegs of black powder, which blew pieces of the fire and pieces of the store all over Deadwood.

Solomon moved farther away from the creek, back into the hills. Chinatown was empty now, the population running into town proper, and then beyond into the hills at the southeast end of town. The light from the fires lit faces in a different way from the sun, and showed truer feelings.

Solomon had never noticed a bleakness in the Chinese before, and it came to him gradually, as he stood alone on the hill, that he was the cause. He watched the houses disappear, clear to the southern limits of town; he heard cries in the wind.

It seemed to him that the wind gathered the cries, each in its place, and carried them to him, there on the hill, and then beyond, dropping them one by one, somewhere deep in the Hills, where they would never be claimed.

He knew then what he had done, and what he had lost; and one of the cries was his own.

THE WINDOW IN MRS. LANGRISHE'S ATTIC FACED WEST, AWAY FROM town. Charley did not see or sense the fire until the eight kegs of giant powder at Jensen and Bliss's went up, shaking every building in the gulch.

His peeder was knee-deep in Mrs. Langrishe at the time. Her eyes were closed under him, and her fingernails were fastened into his back. In a moment she would say, "Oh, Charley," and pull his mouth down to her breasts, and then she would smile at him, looking down somehow even though she was underneath, and watch until he spent himself.

Mrs. Langrishe had one way she liked to have intercourse and about two hundred ways she didn't. There wasn't an inch of bend in her. Charley was with her one night a week, always in this same dead room; and sometimes he thought of Matilda, who had divorced him and married a politician, and sometimes he thought of Lurline, who had married Handsome Banjo Dick Brown.

And he thought of Agnes, here and everywhere else.

Mrs. Langrishe said, "Oh, Charley," and a moment later the explosion shook the house. The davenport moved, the window rattled, and the trees in the hills suddenly showed in the light of the blast.

It was the most interesting thing that had ever happened to Charley in Mrs. Langrishe's attic, and he stood up and went to the window, ignoring the abandonment in her face. There was another explosion, softer than the first, and it turned the yard yellow and shadowy.

"What is it?" she said. The abandonment was in her voice. The yard went black and he heard her feet behind him on the floor.

"Fire," he said.

• 356 •

"They'll put it out," she said. "They always do."

He smiled in the dark. "When this fire quits," he said, "it's because it's finished burning." He found his pants on the floor, dressed, and then stood on the arm of the davenport and pushed open a small door to the roof.

The door was hinged on the outside, and swung back flat against the shingles. Charley put a hand on each side of the opening and pulled himself up until he was sitting on the roof, his legs hanging into the attic. The wind blew the hair off his neck and shoulders and he could feel the heat of the fire on his face.

There were two main fires, one in the town proper and one in Chinatown. Then there were smaller fires, all the way up into the hills. It would burn till it was finished burning. "What is it?" she said, beneath him.

"The end of Deadwood," he said.

He heard her getting dressed, and then her hands were on his legs. "Help me up."

He leaned back into the dark and put his hands under her arms, and then lifted her out onto the roof. She looked old in the yellow glow.

The fire moved up Main Street, taking everything in its way. There were flames thirty feet over the theater, and she watched the walls fold in on themselves and disappear. "Jack will be furious," she said, and when he looked she was smiling.

The wind blew the fires south and east, away from her house. They watched the shacks and jerry-built pine houses disappear, sometimes in only a few seconds. They listened to the cries.

She put her hand on his knee and rubbed her way up his pants leg. Charley paid no attention. The wind had changed—it belonged to the fire now—and blew west into the tents and shacks on the poor side of the hill south of town.

"They'll build it back," she said. One hand had found his peeder, the other was unbuttoning his pants. He shook his head, but didn't stop her undressing him. "It might be all to the best," she said, "to burn it down and start over."

The fire in Chinatown moved south, uphill, taking the badlands. The fire south of town moved uphill too. He tried to find the Bottle Fiend's house, remembering he had told him once, a long time ago, that this would happen.

"What are you looking for, off in the hills?" she said. "The sport's right in front of you." She popped his buttons and pulled his peeder out into the night air.

The Bottle Fiend's home was at the edge of civilization, the last place built before they gave up having the whole hill. Charley didn't think the fire had come to it yet, but he'd lost the road and the trees he'd always used to find it, and could only guess.

"They're building with bricks in Rapid City," she said. "Bullock and Star's got kilns, they'll fill the town with brick buildings and it will look like somebody lives here."

Charley stared at her, thinking of the soft-brain, that he'd told him a fire was coming. She held on to his peeder and the fire in the streets played in her eyes. "It always looked like people lived here to me," he said.

"Not like they intended to stay," she said. "You might get into the brick business yourself . . ."

"No," he said, "I've done all my business in Deadwood."

She put one hand on the shingle next to him and bent herself at the waist until her lips touched the end of his peeder. He saw the fire had excited her—it wasn't something she did on her own. She kissed him and spoke into his lap. "The place could use the permanence of brick," she said.

Her head moved in his lap and he laid a hand against her neck. He stared again at the fire in the hill, trying to locate the Bottle Fiend's place. "There's nothing to do about it now," she said.

And a little later, "What's wrong?"

"My friend sleeps like the dead," he said.

She pulled a few inches off his peeder. "There's nobody could sleep through this," she said. "You'd be smart to enjoy it."

"He isn't like other people."

"Oh," she said, "that friend."

Charley looked at the back of her head, and then at the south end of town. "He told me once he would burn up," he said.

She said, "There's some out here that aren't afraid to die."

Charley thought it over. "I don't know."

"He didn't seem afraid," she said.

"I can't find the road to get a fix where his house is," Charley said later. She put her mouth back over his peeder and her head began to ebb and flow, and he felt himself ebb and flow with her. And then he saw it, four hundred yards farther east than it should have been. He did not know how he'd gotten so turned around.

It was the road, and the fire was long since finished with the Bottle Fiend. "If he slept through," he said, "I hope it was all the way. Like one of his dreams."

"There's nothing to do about it now," she said again.

And then, later, she said, "You know, if you look at a fire in a certain way, it's pretty."

HE FOUND THE SOFT-BRAIN IN THE MORNING, IN THE ASHES OF HIS house. The clothes were burned off him, and the hair, and his fingers and toes were only stubs. By the time Charley got to the house the scavengers had come and gone, scattering the bottles all over the ground. They collided as he walked through them and made flat musical sounds. The soft-brain had thought there were secrets inside. Charley knelt beside the body and straightened the arms. The skin did not feel like skin, and he was afraid to pick the soft-brain up, that something would break inside him.

He could not stand to break his bones.

He eased himself onto the ground and looked out over the town. Everything from Chinatown to the jail was gone; the only way to tell the hotels from the shacks was the size of the piles of ashes. The wind came up out of the gulch and caught one of the bottles just right, and hung a long, low note in the air.

Below, the scavengers were going through the ashes, looking for gold and watches and tins of food. There were shots from the badlands; two men ran up the street.

At the south end of town the fire had spared Bullock and Star's brickworks, and the half block next to it. The houses on the west—Mrs. Langrishe and her neighbors—were spared too.

What had she said, *The place could use the permanence of brick?*

He stayed on the hill most of the morning, until the first soldiers arrived to protect against looters. Then he stood up, so stiff he could barely walk, and made his way back into town.

He found a fireman's shovel lying under a few inches of water in the Whitewood Creek, and took it back up the hill and buried the soft-brain. He dug the hole deep and wide, with enough room for some of the bottles.

The soft-brain had thought there were secrets inside, and planned to give them to God.

He picked some of the prettiest, and some of the ones with the signs of the fire, and then put them in the hole with him and replaced the dirt. He marked the grave with four smooth stones, stacked one on top of another at the head.

There was no wood for a marker, and it did not occur to him until he was halfway down the hill that he did not know the Bottle Fiend's name.

PART FIVE

CHARLEY, THE ISTHMUS OF PANAMA

1912

Malcolm Nash had given up his ministry in 1880 and come briefly under the tutelage of the writer Ambrose Bierce, who spent that year in Deadwood and then left for newer places, ending up in Mexico.

Charley was drawn south too, but he traveled slower and farther, and found Panama.

The boy stayed in the Hills, filing dispatches for the *Black Hills Pioneer*, and later the *Cheyenne Leader*. He saved his stories and sent them to Charley twice a year in envelopes that were yellowed in the months they spent traveling. Somehow it seemed to fit, that the boy had become a reporter.

Charley bought a drugstore, and when the Americans came, building their canal, he made a fortune. Everything in Panama was unhealthy for Americans, even the sun. Charley had never intended to make a fortune in Panama, but money was in the habit of falling his way; somehow he was always downhill. He'd only bought the drugstore for the location, and something to do.

The store sat on the eastern edge of a small fishing town called Pelican, on the eastern side of the isthmus, and overlooked a bay of the same name. The town was built on a rock plateau, a hundred feet above the water. From the porch you could close your eyes and feel the size of the ocean, and the world beyond it.

Charley had arrived in Panama in 1883, and by then he'd known he was going blind.

The first envelope came the next year, six months after he'd written to Merchant's National Bank in Deadwood to forward his funds. There was no letter from the boy then, there never was.

Just the stories, written in long narrow columns, and cut from the paper. *Malcolm Nash, correspondent* appeared over each one.

The first envelope included a dramatic account of the death of Al Swearingen, who died penniless in Denver, falling under the wheels of a train he was trying to hop. It was arranged first among the stories, although there were others—humorous incidents concerning the malfunctions of the local telephone system, for instance—that were written earlier.

Charley was never sure what the boy wanted him to know—that he had learned to write, or the news itself.

When the second envelope arrived, half a year later, he undertook to teach one of the village children to read English. He chose a small girl who hung on his fingers when he walked to the store for fish or beer.

She learned slowly, but he was patient. He was kind to her, and bought food for her family the year the fish disappeared from the ocean. He made presents for her on her birthdays and for Christmas, and told her stories of the Americanos and the places they lived.

In the beginning the stories were long and colored, but as he grew old and his eyes clouded, the stories were told in only a few words, and she came to understand that all the colors had fallen away from him, leaving only the moments. A woman who performed tricks in the air, an animal pulling a boat underwater, dead children who spoke in his bones. A man who loved bottles.

She knew he told true things.

She heard the stories a thousand times, but she always listened. He had fed her family the year the fish disappeared from the ocean.

She visited him in the mornings, on the porch of his store, sitting at a table he had built long after his sight was gone. Sometimes she read him old newspaper stories; she knew them all by heart.

Sometimes he told her his stories.

And as she grew into her middle years, she saw new meanings in them. She saw that even among the Americanos, he had been a foreigner.

In the afternoon she left him to his beer. Sometimes he sent for a whore. It was said he liked to be bitten. He kept himself clean, walking each evening down the steps to the ocean to bathe. It caused him great pain to climb back. There had been much leg-shooting in his life.

The last envelope arrived in the fall of 1912. The old man was dying, and used morphine to ease the way. There was a letter with the newspapers, the only one he ever got. She could not read it all—the hand was old and unsteady—but she did what she could.

He listened without a word, facing the morning sun and the ocean. It was from a woman named Agnes Lake, and much of it concerned her trip to Deadwood to find what had become of him. It said she loved him, it said they had mending hearts.

She saw the words moved the old man, and filled him, and she was sorry she could not read them all.

It pleased her to see him this way, though, and she thought it was fortunate the letter had come when it did, before he died. Not so fortunate it had to be God's will—he was a kind man and had been living unloved a long time, as foreigners always lived—and things had to happen sometime.

MAY 3, 1985
EARLEVILLE, MARYLAND

FOR THE BEST IN PAPERBACKS, LOOK FOR THE

In every corner of the world, on every subject under the sun, Penguin represents quality and variety—the very best in publishing today.

For complete information about books available from Penguin—including Pelicans, Puffins, Peregrines, and Penguin Classics—and how to order them, write to us at the appropriate address below. Please note that for copyright reasons the selection of books varies from country to country.

In the United Kingdom: For a complete list of books available from Penguin in the U.K., please write to *Dept E.P., Penguin Books Ltd, Harmondsworth, Middlesex, UB7 0DA.*

In the United States: For a complete list of books available from Penguin in the U.S., please write to *Dept BA, Penguin,* Box 120, Bergenfield, New Jersey 07621-0120.

In Canada: For a complete list of books available from Penguin in Canada, please write to *Penguin Books Canada Ltd, 10 Alcorn Avenue, Suite 300, Toronto, Ontario, Canada M4V 3B2.*

In Australia: For a complete list of books available from Penguin in Australia, please write to the *Marketing Department, Penguin Books Ltd, P.O. Box 257, Ringwood, Victoria 3134.*

In New Zealand: For a complete list of books available from Penguin in New Zealand, please write to the *Marketing Department, Penguin Books (NZ) Ltd, Private Bag, Takapuna, Auckland 9.*

In India: For a complete list of books available from Penguin, please write to *Penguin Overseas Ltd, 706 Eros Apartments, 56 Nehru Place, New Delhi, 110019.*

In Holland: For a complete list of books available from Penguin in Holland, please write to *Penguin Books Nederland B.V., Postbus 195, NL-1380AD Weesp, Netherlands.*

In Germany: For a complete list of books available from Penguin, please write to *Penguin Books Ltd, Friedrichstrasse 10-12, D-6000 Frankfurt Main 1, Federal Republic of Germany.*

In Spain: For a complete list of books available from Penguin in Spain, please write to *Longman, Penguin España, Calle San Nicolas 15, E-28013 Madrid, Spain.*

In Japan: For a complete list of books available from Penguin in Japan, please write to *Longman Penguin Japan Co Ltd, Yamaguchi Building, 2-12-9 Kanda Jimbocho, Chiyoda-Ku, Tokyo 101, Japan.*

☐ THE WOMEN OF BREWSTER PLACE
A Novel in Seven Stories
Gloria Naylor

Winner of the American Book Award, this is the story of seven survivors of an urban housing project — a blind alley feeding into a dead end. From a variety of backgrounds, they experience, fight against, and sometimes transcend the fate of black women in America today.

192 pages   *ISBN: 0-14-006690-X*

☐ STONES FOR IBARRA
Harriet Doerr

An American couple comes to the small Mexican village of Ibarra to reopen a copper mine, learning much about life and death from the deeply faithful villagers.

214 pages   *ISBN: 0-14-007562-3*

☐ WORLD'S END
T. Coraghessan Boyle

"Boyle has emerged as one of the most inventive and verbally exuberant writers of his generation," writes *The New York Times*. Here he tells the story of Walter Van Brunt, who collides with early American history while searching for his lost father.

456 pages   *ISBN: 0-14-009760-0*

☐ THE WHISPER OF THE RIVER
Ferrol Sams

The story of Porter Osborn, Jr., who, in 1938, leaves his rural Georgia home to face the world at Willingham University, *The Whisper of the River* is peppered with memorable characters and resonates with the details of place and time. Ferrol Sams's writing is regional fiction at its best.

528 pages   *ISBN: 0-14-008387-1*

☐ ENGLISH CREEK
Ivan Doig

Drawing on the same heritage he celebrated in *This House of Sky,* Ivan Doig creates a rich and varied tapestry of northern Montana and of our country in the late 1930s.

338 pages   *ISBN: 0-14-008442-8*

☐ THE YEAR OF SILENCE
Madison Smartt Bell

A penetrating look at the varied reactions to a young woman's suicide exactly one year later, *The Year of Silence* "captures vividly and poignantly the chancy dance of life." (*The New York Times Book Review*)

208 pages   *ISBN: 0-14-011533-1*